Tom Swift Omnibus #5

©2007 Wilder Publications

Wilder Publications, LLC.
PO Box 3005
Radford VA 24143-3005

ISBN 10: 1-60459-105-6
ISBN 13: 978-1-60459-105-7

First Edition

The Tom Swift Omnibus #5
by Victor Appleton

Tom Swift in Captivity
(Or a Daring Escape by Airship)

Tom Swift and His Wizard Camera
(Or Thrilling Adventures While Taking Moving Pictures)

Tom Swift and His Great Searchlight
(Or on the Border for Uncle Sam)

TOM SWIFT IN CAPTIVITY

Or A Daring Escape by Airship

TABLE OF CONTENTS:

A Strange Request

Tom Swift closed the book of adventures he had been reading, tossed it on the table, and got up. Then he yawned.

"What's the matter?" asked his chum, Ned Newton, who was deep in another volume.

"Oh, I thought this was going to be something exciting," replied Tom, motioning toward the book he had discarded. "But say! the make-believe adventures that fellow had, weren't anything compared to those we went through in the city of gold, or while rescuing the exiles of Siberia."

"Well," remarked Ned, "they would have to be pretty classy adventures to lay over those you and I have had lately. But where are you going?" he continued, for Tom had taken his cap and started for the door.

"I thought I'd go out and take a little run in the aeroplane. Want to come along? It's more fun than sitting in the house reading about exciting things that never have happened. Come on out and—"

"Yes, and have a tumble from the aeroplane, I suppose you were going to say," interrupted Ned with a laugh. "Not much! I'm going to stay here and finish this book."

"Say," demanded Tom indignantly. "Did you ever know me to have a tumble since I knew how to run an airship?"

"No, I can't say that I did. I was only joking."

"Then you carried the joke too far, as the policeman said to the man he found lugging off money from the bank. And to make up for it you've got to come along with me."

"Where are you going?"

"Oh, anywhere. Just to take a little run in the upper regions, and clear some of the cobwebs out of my head. I declare, I guess I've got the spring fever. I haven't done anything since we got back from Russia last fall, and I'm getting rusty."

"You haven't done *anything!*" exclaimed Ned, following his chum's example by tossing aside the book. "Do you call working on your new invention of a noiseless airship nothing?"

"Well, I haven't finished that yet. I'm tired of inventing things. I just want to go off, and have some good fun, like getting shipwrecked on a desert island, or being lost in the mountains, or something like that. I want action. I want to get off in the jungle, and fight wild beasts, and escape from the savages!"

"Say! you don't want much," commented Ned. "But I feel the same way, Tom."

"Then come on out and take a run, and maybe we'll get on the track of an adventure," urged the young inventor. "We won't go far, just twenty or thirty miles or so."

The two youths emerged from the house and started across the big lawn toward the aeroplane sheds, for Tom Swift owned several speedy aircrafts, from a big combined aeroplane and dirigible balloon, to a little monoplane not much larger than a big bird, but which was the most rapid flier that ever breathed the fumes of gasolene.

"Which one you going to take, Tom?" asked Ned, as his chum paused in front of the row of hangars.

"Oh, the little double-seated monoplane, I guess that's in good shape, and it's easy to manage. When I'm out for fun I hate to be tinkering with levers and warping wing tips all the while. The Lark practically flies herself, and we can sit back and take it easy. I'll have Eradicate fill up the gasolene tank, while I look at the magneto. It needs a little adjusting, though it works nearly to perfection since I put in some of that new platinum we got from the lost mine in Siberia."

"Yes, that was a trip that amounted to something. I wouldn't mind going on another like that, though we ran lots of risks."

"We sure did," agreed Tom, and then, raising his voice he called out: "Rad, I say Rad! Where are you? I want you!"

"Comin', massa Tom, comin'," answered an aged colored man, as he shuffled around the corner of the shed. "What do yo'-all want ob me?"

"Put some gasolene in the Lark, Rad. Ned and I are going to take a little flight. What were you doing?"

"Jest groomin' mah mule Boomerang, Massa Tom, dat's all. Po' Boomerang he's gittin' old jest same laik I be. He's gittin' old, an' he needs lots ob 'tention. He has t' hab mo' oats dan usual, Massa Tom, an' he doan't feel 'em laik he uster, dat's a fac', Massa Tom."

"Well, Rad, give him all he wants. Boomerang was a good mule in his day."

"An' he's good yet, Massa Tom, he's good yet!" said Eradicate Sampson eagerly. "Doan't yo' all forgit dat, Massa Tom." And the colored man proceeded to fill the gasolene tank, while Tom adjusted the electrical mechanism of his aeroplane, Ned assisting by handing him the tools needed. Eradicate, who said he was named that because he "eradicated" dirt, was a colored man of all work, who had been in the service of the Swift household for several years. He and his mule Boomerang were fixtures.

"There, I guess that will do," remarked Tom, after testing the magneto, and finding that it gave a fat, hot spark. "That ought to send us along in good shape. Got all the gas in, Rad?"

"Every drop, Massa Tom."

"Then catch hold and help wheel the Lark out. Ned, you steady her on that side. How are the tires? Do they need pumping up?"

"Hard as rocks," answered Tom's chum, as he tapped his toe against the rubber circlets of the small bicycle wheels on which the aeroplane rested.

"Then they'll do, I guess. Come on now, and we'll give her a test before we start off. I ought to get a few hundred more revolutions per minute out of the motor with the way I've adjusted the magneto. Rad, you and Ned hold back, while I turn the engine over."

The youth and the colored man grasped the rear supports of the long, tail-like part of the monoplane while Tom stepped to the front to twist the propeller blades. The first two times there was no explosion as he swung the delicate wooden blades about, but the third time the engine started off with a roar, and a succession of explosions that were deafening, until Tom switched in the muffler, thereby cutting down the noise. Faster and faster the propeller whirled about as the motor warmed up, until the young inventor exclaimed:

"That's the stuff! She's better than ever! Climb up Ned, and we'll start off. You can turn her over, Rad; can't you?"

"Suah, Massa Tom," was the reply, for Eradicate had been on so many trips with Tom, and had had so much to do with airships, that to merely start one was child's play for him.

The two youths had scarcely taken their seats, and the colored man was about to twist around the fan-like blades of the big propeller in front, when from behind there came a hail.

"Hold on there! Wait a minute, Tom Swift! Bless my admission ticket, don't go! I've got something important to tell you! Hold on!"

"Humph! I know who that is!" cried Tom, motioning to Eradicate to cease trying to start the motor.

"Mr. Damon, of course," agreed Ned. "I wonder what he wants?"

"A ride, maybe," went on Tom. "If he does we've got to take the Scooter instead of this one. That holds four. Well, we may as well see what he wants."

He jumped lightly from his seat in the monoplane and was followed by Ned. They saw coming toward them, from the direction of the house, a stout man, who seemed very much excited. He was walking so fast that he fairly waddled, and he was smiling at the lads, for he was one of their best friends.

"Glad I caught you, Tom." he panted, for his haste had almost deprived him of breath. "I've got something important to tell you. I hurried over as soon as I heard about it."

"Well, you're just in time," commented Ned with a laugh. "In another minute we'd have been up in the clouds."

"What is it, Mr. Damon?" asked Tom. "Have you got wind of a city of diamonds, or has some one sent you a map telling where we can go to pick up ten thousand dollar bills by the basket?"

"Neither one; Tom, neither one. It's something better than either of those, and if you don't jump at the chance I'm mistaken in you, that's all I've got to say. Come over here."

He turned a quick glance over his shoulder as he spoke and advanced toward the two lads on tiptoe as though he feared some one would see or hear him. Yet it was broad daylight, the place was the starting ground for Tom's aeroplanes and save Eradicate there was no one present except Mr. Damon, Ned and the young inventor himself.

"What's up?" asked Tom in wonderment.

"Hush!" cautioned the odd gentleman. "Bless my walking stick, Tom! but this is going to be a great chance for you—for us,—for I'm going along."

"Going where, Mr. Damon?"

"I'll tell you in a minute. Is there any one here?"

"No one but us?"

"You are sure that Andy Foger isn't around."

"Sure. He's out of town, you know."

"Yes, but you never can tell when he's going to appear on the scene. Come over here," and taking hold of the coat of each of the youths, Mr. Damon led them behind the big swinging door of the aeroplane shed.

"You haven't anything on hand; have you, Tom?" asked the odd gentleman, after peering through the crack to make sure they were unobserved.

"Nothing at all, if you mean in the line of going off on an adventure trip."

"That's what I mean. Bless my earlaps! but I'm glad of that. I've got just the thing for you. Tom, I want you to go to a strange land, and bring back one of the biggest men there—a giant! Tom Swift, you and I and Ned—if he wants to go—are going after a giant!"

Mr. Damon gleefully clapped Tom on the back, with such vigor that our hero coughed, and then the odd gentleman stepped back and gazed at the two lads, a look of triumph shining in his eyes.

For a moment there was a silence. Tom looked at Ned, and Ned gave his chum a quick glance. Then they both looked sharply at Mr. Damon.

"A—a giant," murmured Tom faintly.

"That's what I said," replied Mr. Damon. "I want you to help me capture a giant, Tom."

Once more the two youths exchanged significant glances, and then Tom, in a low and gentle voice said:

"Yes, Mr. Damon, that's all right. We'll get you a giant right away. Won't we, Ned? Now you'd better come in the house and lie down, I'll have Mrs. Baggert make you a cup of tea, and after you have had a sleep you'll feel better. Come on," and the young inventor gently tried to lead his friend out from behind the shed door.

"Look here, Tom Swift!" exclaimed the odd gentleman indignantly. "Do you think I'm crazy? Lie down? Rest myself? Go to sleep? Say, I'm not crazy! I'm not tired! I'm not sleepy! This is the greatest chance you ever had, and if we get one of those giants—"

"Yes, yes, we'll get one," put in Ned soothingly.

"Of course," added Tom. "Come on, now, Mr. Damon. You'll feel better after you've had a rest. Dr. Perkinby is coming over to see father and I'll have him—"

Mr. Damon gave one startled glance at the young inventor and his chum, and then burst into a peal of hearty laughter.

"Oh, my!" he exclaimed at intervals in his pyroxisms. "Oh, dear! He thinks I'm out of my head! He can't stand that talk about giants! Oh dear! Tom Swift, this is the greatest chance you ever had! Come on in the house and I'll tell you all I know about giant land, and then if you want to think I'm crazy you can, that's all I've got to say!"

THE CIRCUS MAN

Without a word Tom and Ned followed Mr. Damon toward the Swift house. Truth to tell the youths did not know what to say, or they would have been bubbling over with questions. But the talk of the odd man, and his strange request to Tom to go off and capture a giant had so startled the young inventor and his chum that they did not know whether to think that Mr. Damon was joking, or whether he had suddenly taken leave of his senses.

And while I have a few minutes that are occupied in the journey to the house I will introduce my new readers more formally to Tom Swift and his friends.

Tom though only a young man, was an inventor of note, as his father was before him. Father and son lived in a fine house in the town of Shopton, in New York state, and Mrs. Swift being dead, the two were well looked after by Mrs. Baggert their housekeeper. Eradicate Sampson, as I have said, was the man of all work about the place. Ned Newton who had a position in a Shopton bank, was Tom's particular chum, and Mr. Wakefeld Damon, of the neighboring town of Waterfield, was a friend to all who knew him. He had the odd habit of blessing anything and everything he could think of, interspersing it in his talk.

In the first volume of this series, called "Tom Swift and His Motor-Cycle," I related how Tom made the acquaintance of Mr. Damon, afterward purchasing a damaged motor-cycle from the odd gentleman. On this machine Tom had many adventures, incidentally saving some of his father's valuable patents from a gang of conspirators. Later Tom got a motor boat, and had many races with his rivals on Lake Carlopa, beating Andy Foger, the red-haired bully of the town, in signal fashion. After his adventures on the water Tom sighed for some in the air, and he had them in his airship the *Red Cloud*.

"Tom Swift and His Submarine Boat." is a story of a search after sunken treasure, and, returning from that quest Tom built an electric runabout, the speedest car on the road. By means of a wireless message, later, Tom was able to save himself and the castaways of Earthquake Island, and, as a direct outcome of that experience, he was able to go in search of the diamond makers, and solve the secret of Phantom Mountain, as told in the book dealing with that subject.

When he went to the caves of ice Tom had bad luck, for his airship was wrecked, and he endured many hardships in getting home with his companions, particularly as Andy Foger sought revenge on him.

But Tom pluckily overcame all obstacles and, later, he built a sky racer, in which he made the quickest trip on record. After that, with his electric rifle, he went after elephants in the interior of Africa and was successful in rescuing some missionaries from the terrible red pygmies.

One of the mission workers, later, sent Tom details about a buried city of gold in Mexico, and Tom and his chum together with Mr. Damon located this mysterious place after much trouble, as told in the book entitled, "Tom Swift in the City of Gold." The gold did not prove as valuable as they expected, as it was of low grade, but they got considerable money for it, and were then ready for more adventures.

The adventures soon came, as those of you who have read the book called, "Tom Swift and His Air Glider," can testify. In that I told how Tom went to Siberia, and after rescuing some Russian political exiles, found a valuable deposit of platinum, which today is a more valuable metal than gold. Tom needed some platinum for his electrical machines, and it proved very useful.

He had been back from Russia all winter and, now that Spring had come again, our hero sighed for more activity, and fresh adventures. And with the advent of Mr. Damon, and his mysterious talk about giants, Tom seemed likely to be gratified.

The two chums and the odd gentleman continued on to the house, no one speaking, until finally, when they were seated in the library, Mr. Damon said:

"Well, Tom, are you ready to listen to me now, and have me explain what I meant when I asked you to get a giant?"

"I—I suppose so," hesitated the young inventor. "But hadn't I better call dad? And are you sure you don't want to lie down and collect your thoughts? A nice hot cup of tea—"

"There, there, Tom Swift; If you tell me to lie down again, or propose any more tea I'll use you as a punching bag, bless my boxing gloves if I don't!" cried Mr. Damon and he laughed heartily. "I know what you think, Tom, and you, too, Ned," he went on, still chuckling. "You think I don't know what I'm saying, but I'll soon prove that I do. I'm fully in my senses, I'm not crazy, I'm not talking in my sleep, and I'm very much in earnest. Tom, this is the chance of your life to get a giant, and pay a visit to giant land. Will you take it?"

"Mr. Damon, I—er—that is I—"

Tom stammered and looked at Ned.

"Now look here, Tom Swift!" exclaimed the odd man. "When you got word about the buried city of gold in Mexico you didn't hesitate a minute about making up your mind to go there; did you?"

"No, I didn't."

"Well, that wasn't any more of a strain on your imagination than this giant business; was it?"

"Well, I don't know, as—"

"Bless my spectacles! Of course it wasn't! Now, look here. Tom, you just make up your mind that I know what I'm talking about, and we'll get along better. I don't blame you for being a bit puzzled at first, but just you listen. You believe there are such things as giants; don't you?"

"I saw a man in the circus once, seven feet high. They called him a giant," spoke Ned.

"A giant! He was a baby compared to the kind of giants I mean," said Mr. Damon quickly. "Tom, we are going after a race of giants, the smallest one of which is probably eight feet high, and from that they go on up to nearly ten feet, and they're not slim fellows either, but big in proportion. Now in giant land—"

"Here's Mrs. Baggert with a quieting cup of tea," interrupted Tom. "I spoke to her as we came in, and asked her to have some ready. If you'll drink this, Mr. Damon, I'm sure—"

"Bless my sugar bowl, Tom! You make a man nervous, with your cups of tea. I'm more quiet than you, but I'll drink it to please you. Now listen to me."

"All right, go ahead."

"A friend of mine has asked me if I knew any one who could undertake to go to giant land, and get him one or two specimens of the big men there. I at once thought of you, and I said I believed you would go. And I'll go with you, Tom! Think of that! I've got faith enough in the proposition to go myself!"

There was no mistaking Mr. Damon's manner. He was very much in earnest, and Tom and Ned looked at each other with a different light in their eyes.

"Who is your friend, and where in the world is giant land?" asked Tom. "I haven't heard of such a place since I read the accounts of the early travelers, before this continent was discovered. Who is your friend that wants a giant?"

"If you'll let me, I'll have him here in a minute, Tom."

"Of course I will. But good land! Have you got him concealed up your sleeve, or under some of the chairs? Is he a dwarf?" and Tom looked about the room as if he expected to see some one in hiding.

"I left him outside in the garden, Tom," replied the odd man. "I told him I'd come on ahead, and see how you took the proposition. Don't tell him you thought me insane at first. I'll have him here in a jiffy. I'll signal to him."

Not waiting for a word from either of the boys, Mr. Damon went to one of the low library windows, opened it, gave a shrill whistle and waved his handkerchief vigorously. In a moment there came an answering whistle.

"He's coming," announced the odd gentleman.

"But who is he?" insisted Tom. "Is he some professor who wants a giant to examine, or is he a millionaire who wants one for a body guard?"

"Neither one, Tom. He's the proprietor of a number of circuses, and a string of museums, and he wants a giant, or even two of them, for exhibition purposes. There's lots of money in giants. He's had some seven, and even eight feet tall, but he has lately heard of a land where the tallest man is nearly ten feet high, and very big, and he'll pay ten thousand dollars for a giant alive and in good condition, as the animal men say. I believe we can get one for him, and—Ah, here he is now," and Mr. Damon interrupted himself as a small, dark-complexioned man, with a very black mustache, black eyes, a watch chain as big around as his thumb, a red vest, a large white hat, and a suit of large-sized checked clothes appeared at the open library window.

"Is it all right?" this strange-appearing man asked of Mr. Damon.

"I believe so," replied the odd gentleman. "Come in, Sam."

With one bound, though the window was some distance from the ground, the little man leaped into the library. He landed lightly on his feet, quickly turned two hand springs in rapid succession, and then, without breathing in the least rapidly, as most men would have done after that exertion, he made a low bow to Tom and Ned.

"Boys, let me introduce you to my friend, Sam Preston, an old acrobat and now a circus proprietor," said Mr. Damon. "Mr. Preston, this is Tom Swift, of whom I told you, and his chum, Ned Newton."

"And will they get the giant for me?" asked the circus man quickly.

"I think they will," replied Mr. Damon. "I had a little difficulty in making the matter clear to them, and that's why I sent for you. You can explain everything."

"Have a chair," invited Tom politely. "This is a new one on me— going after giants. I've done almost everything else, though."

"So Mr. Damon said," spoke Mr. Preston gravely. He was much more sedate and composed than one would have supposed after his sensational entrance into the room. "I am very glad to meet you, Tom Swift, and I hope we can do business together. Now, if you have a few minutes to spare, I'll tell you all I know about giant land."

TOM WILL GO

"Jove! That sounds interesting!" exclaimed Ned, as he settled himself comfortably in his chair.

"It is interesting," replied the circus man. "At least I found it so when I first listened to one of my men tell it. But whether it is possible to get to giant land, and, what is more bring away some of the big men, is something I leave to you, Tom Swift. After you have heard my story, if you decide to go, I'll stand all the expenses of fitting out an expedition, and if you fail I won't have a word to say. If, on the other hand, you bring me back a giant or two, I'll pay you ten thousand dollars and all expenses. Is it a bargain?"

"Let me hear the story first," suggested our hero, who was a cautious lad when there was need for it. Yet he liked Mr. Preston, even at first sight, in spite of his "loud" attire, and the rather "circusy" manner in which he had entered the room. Then too, if he was a friend of Mr. Damon, that was a great deal in his favor.

"I am, as you know, in the circus business," began Mr. Preston. "I have a number of traveling shows, and several large museums in the big cities. I am always on the lookout for new attractions, for the public demands them. Once get in the rut of having nothing new, and your business will fall off. I know, for I've been in the business, man and boy, for nearly forty years. I began as a performer, and I can still do a double somersault over fifteen elephants in a row. I always keep in practice for there's nothing like showing a performer how to do a thing yourself."

"But about the giants, which is what I'm interested in most now. Of course I've had giants in my circuses and museums, from the beginning. The public wanted 'em and we had to have 'em. Some of 'em were fakes—men on stilts with long pants to cover up their legs, and others were the real, genuine, all-wool-and-a-yard-wide article. But none of them were very big. A shade under eight feet was the limit with me."

"I also have lots of wild animals, and it was when some of my men were out after some tapirs, jaguars and leopards that I got on the track of the giants. It was about a year ago, but up to this time I haven't seen my way clear to send after the big men. It was this way:"

Mr. Preston assumed a more comfortable position in his chair, nodded at Mr. Damon, who was listening attentively to all that was said, and resumed.

"As I said I had sent Jake Poddington, one of my best men, after tapirs and some other South American animals. He didn't have very good luck hunting along the Amazon. In the first place that region has been pretty well cleaned out of circus animals, and another thing it's getting too well populated. Another thing is that you can't get the native hunters and beaters to work for you as they did years ago."

"So Poddington wrote to me that he was going to take his assistants, make a big jump, and hike it for the Argentine Republic. He had a tip that along the Salado river there might be something doing, and I told him to go ahead."

"He shipped me what few animals he had, and lit out for a three thousand mile journey. I didn't hear from him for some time, and, when I did, I got the finest collection of animals I had ever laid eyes on. I got them about the same time I did a letter from Jake, for the mail service ain't what you could call rushing in that part of South America."

"But what about the giants?" interrupted Mr. Damon.

"I'm coming to them," replied the circus man calmly. "It was this way: At the tail of his letter which he sent with the shipment of animals Jake said this, and I remember it almost word for word:"

"'If all goes well,' he wrote, 'I'll have a big surprise for you soon. I've heard a story about a race of big natives that have their stamping ground in this section, and I'm going to try for a few specimens. I know how much you want a giant.'"

"Well?" asked Tom, after a pause, for the circus man had ceased talking and was staring out of the opened library window into the garden that was just becoming green.

"That was all I ever heard from poor Jake," said Mr. Preston softly.

"Bless my insurance policy!" gasped Mr. Damon. "You didn't tell me that! What happened to him."

"I never could find out," resumed Mr. Preston. "I never heard another word from him, and I've never seen him from the time I parted with him to go after the animals. The letter saying he was going after the giants was the last line of his I've seen."

"But didn't you try to locate him?" asked Tom. "Didn't he have some companions—some one who could tell what became of him?"

"Of course I tried!" exclaimed Mr. Preston. "Do you think I'd let a man like Jake disappear without making some effort to find him? But he was the only white man in his party, the rest were natives. That was Jake's way. Well, when some time past and I didn't hear from him, I got busy. I wrote to our consuls and even some South American merchants with whom I had done business. But it didn't amount to anything."

"Couldn't you get any news?" asked Ned softly.

"Oh, yes, some, but it didn't amount to much. After a long time, and no end of trouble, I had a man locate a native named Zacatas, who was the head beater of the black men under Jake."

"Zacatas said that he and Jake and the others got safely to the Salado river section, but I knew that before, for that was where the fine shipment of animals came from. Then Jake got that tip about the giants, and set off alone into the interior to locate them, for all the natives were afraid to go. That was the last seen of poor Jake."

"Bless my fire shovel!" cried Mr. Damon. "What did Zacatas say became of the poor fellow?"

"No one knew. Whether he reached giant land and was killed there, or whether he was struck down by some wild beast in the jungle, I never could find out. The natives under Zacatas waited in camp for him for some time, and then went back to the Amazon region where they belonged. That's all the news I could get."

"But I'm sure there are giants in the interior of South America, for Jake always knew what he was talking about. Now I want to do two things. I want to get on the trail of poor Jake Poddington if I can, and I want a giant—two or three of them if it can be managed."

"Ever since Jake disappeared I've been trying to arrange things to make a search for him, and for the giants, but up to now something has been in the way. I happened to mention the matter to my friend, Mr. Damon, and he at once spoke of you, Tom Swift."

"Now, what I want to know is this: Will you undertake to get a giant for me, rescue Jake Poddington if he is alive in the interior of South America, or, if he is dead, find out how it happened and give him decent burial? Will you do this, Tom Swift?"

There was a silence in the room following the dramatic and simple recital of the circus man. Tom was strangely moved, as was his chum Ned As for Mr. Damon, he was softly blessing every thing he could think of.

Tom looked out of the long, opened windows of the library. In fancy he could see the forest and jungles of South America. He saw a sluggish river flowing along between rank green banks, while, from the overhanging trees, long festoons of moss hung down, writhing now and then as the big water anacondas or boa constrictors looped their sinuous folds over the low limbs.

In fancy he saw dark-skinned natives slinking along with their deadly blow guns, and poisoned arrows. He thought he could hear the low growls and whines of the treacherous jaguars and see their lithe bodies slinking along. He saw the brilliant-hued flowers, saw the birds of gorgeous plumage, and listened in fancy to their discordant cries.

Then, too, he saw a lonely white man in a miserable native hut thousands of miles from civilization, waiting, waiting, waiting for he knew not what fate. Again he saw monstrous men stalking along— men who towered ten feet or more, and who were big and brawny. All this passed through the mind of Tom in an instant.

"Well?" asked Mr. Preston softly.

"I'll go!" suddenly cried the young inventor. "I don't know whether I can get you a giant or not, Mr. Preston, but if it's possible I'll get poor Jake Poddington, dead or alive!"

"Good!" cried the circus man, jumping up and clasping Tom's hand. "I thought you were that kind of a lad, after I heard Mr. Damon describe you. You've taken a big load off my heart, Tom Swift. Now to talk of ways and means! I'll have a giant yet, and maybe I'll get back the best man who ever shipped a consignment of wild animals, good Jake Poddington! Now to business!"

"Look out for My Rival!"

"You'll go in an airship of course; won't you, Tom?" asked Mr. Damon, when they had pulled their chairs up around a library table, and Mr. Preston had taken some papers from his pocket.

"An airship? No, I don't believe I shall," replied the young inventor. "In the first place, I'm a bit tired of scooting through the air so much, though it isn't to be denied that it's the quickest way of going. But in South America there are so many jungles that it will be hard to find a level starting ground for a take-off, after we land. Of course we could go up as a balloon, but this expedition is going to be different from any we were ever on before."

"How so?" asked Ned.

"Well, in the first place we've got to start at one end of a trail, and make careful inquiries all along the way. It isn't like when we went for the city of gold. There we had to look for a certain ruined temple, which was the landmark. When we went after the platinum in Siberia we had to look for the place of the high winds, so I could use my air glider. But now we're trying to locate a man who traveled on foot through the jungles, and if we went in an airship we might just miss the connecting link."

"So, I think the best way will be to do just as Mr. Poddington did—travel on foot or by horses and mules, and go slowly, making inquiries from time to time. Then we *may* get to giant land, we *may* find him."

"I don't hope for all that," said the circus man, "but if you can only get some news of him it will be a relief. If he died peaceably it would be better than to be a captive among some of those savage tribes. It's been a year now since I heard the last of him. But I agree with Tom that an airship won't be much good in the jungle. You might take along a small one, if you could pack it, to scare the natives with. In fact it might be a good thing to show to the giants, if you find them."

"That is my idea," declared Tom. "I'll take the Lark with me. That's a mighty powerful machine for its size, and it can be taken apart in sections. It will carry three on a pinch, and I have had five in her with two auxiliary seats. I'll take the Lark, and she may come in handy."

"When can you start?" asked Mr. Preston.

"As soon as we can fit out an expedition," answered Tom. "It oughtn't to take long. I don't have to build an air glider this time. It won't take long to take the Lark apart. I haven't finished work on my noiseless airship yet, but that can wait. Yes, we'll be ready as soon as you want us to start, Mr. Preston."

"It can't be too soon for me. I'll deposit a certain sum in the bank to your credit, Tom, and you can draw on it for expenses. I'll pay any amount to get word of poor Jake, to say nothing of having a giant for my circus. Now as to ways of getting there. Have you a large map of South America?"

Tom had one, and he and the others were pouring over it when Tom's father came into the room.

"Well, well!" he exclaimed. "What's this? What are you up to now, Tom, my boy? Mrs. Baggert said you took down the South American map. What's up?"

"Lots, dad? I'm going after giants this time!"

"Giants, Tom? Are you joking?"

"Not a bit of it, Mr. Swift," answered Mr. Damon. "Bless my check book! I believe if some one wanted the moon Tom Swift would try to get it for them."

Then Mr. Swift noticed the stranger present, and was introduced to the circus man.

"Is it really true, Tom," asked the aged inventor, when the story had been related, "are you going to have a try for giant land?"

"That's what I am, dad, and I wish you were going along."

"No, Tom, I'm getting too old for that. But I did hope you'd stay home for a while, and help me work on my gyroscope invention. It is almost completed."

"I will help you, dad, as soon as I get back with a giant or two. Who knows? maybe I'll get one myself."

"What would you do with one?" asked Ned with a laugh.

"Have him help Eradicate," answered the young inventor. "Rad is getting pretty old, and he needs an assistant."

"But are these giants black?" asked Mr. Swift.

"That's a point I don't know," answered the circus man frankly. "Jake didn't say in his letter. They may be black, white or midway between. That's what Tom has got to find out for us."

"And I'll do it!" exclaimed our hero. "Now let's see. I suppose the best plan would be to take a ship right to the Rio de la Plata, landing say at Buenos Ayres or Montevideo, and then organize an expedition to strike into the interior."

"Why don't you do just as Mr. Poddington did?" asked Ned, "start from the Amazon and work south?"

"It would take too long," declared Tom. "We know that the giants are somewhere in the northern part of Argentina, or in Paraguay or Uruguay. Or they may be on the other side of the Uruguay river in Brazil. It's quite a stretch of territory, and we've got to take our time exploring it. That's why I don't want to waste time working down from the Amazon. We'll go right to Buenos Ayres, I think."

"That's what I'd do," advised the old circus man. "Now I can give you some points on what to take, and how to act when you get there. The South Americans are a queer people—very nice when treated right, but very bad if not," and then he told some of his experiences as a circus man in South America, for he had traveled there.

"I'd go again, if my business didn't keep me here," he concluded, "for I'd ask nothing better than to hunt for giant land, or try to rescue poor Jake. But I can't. I'm depending on you, Tom Swift."

"What's that? Giant land?" exclaimed Mrs. Baggert, the motherly housekeeper, as she came in to announce that dinner was ready. "You don't mean to tell me, Tom, that you're going off again?"

"That's what I am, Mrs. Baggert. You'd better put me up a few sandwiches, for I don't know when I'll be back," and Tom winked at his chum.

"Oh, of all things I ever heard in all my born days!" cried the house-keeper, throwing up her hands. "Will you ever settle down, Tom Swift?"

"Maybe he will when Miss Mary Nestor is ready to settle down too," said Ned mischievously, referring to a girl of whom Tom was very fond.

"Say, I'll fix you for that!" cried our hero, as he made an unsuccessful grab for Ned. "But, Mrs. Baggert, can you put on a couple of extra plates? Mr. Damon and Mr. Preston will stay to lunch."

"Not if it's going to put you out, Tom," objected the circus man. "I can go to the hotel, and—"

"No, indeed!" exclaimed Mrs. Baggert graciously, for she prided herself on her housekeeping arrangements, and she used to say that unexpected company never "flustrated" her. Soon the little party was seated around the table, where the talk went from grave to gay, the subject of the giants being uppermost.

Mr. Preston told many funny stories of his circus days, and some of them had the spice of danger in them, for he had been all over the world, either as a performer or as the owner of amusement enterprises.

"Now, the next question to be settled," said the old circus man, when they were once more gathered in the library, "is how many are going?"

"I am, for one!" exclaimed Ned quickly. "I'm sure my folks will let me. Especially as we aren't going to use an airship, but will travel just as ordinary folks do."

"Except in case of emergency," explained Tom. "We'll have the Lark to use if we need her."

"Oh, of course," agreed Ned. "How about you, Mr. Damon? Will you go?"

The odd man looked around the room before replying, as though he feared someone might be listening on the sly.

"Go on, Andy Foger isn't here," invited Tom with a laugh.

"I'll go—if I can pursuade my wife to let me," said the odd man in a whisper, as if, even then, the good lady might overhear him. "I'm not going to say anything about giants. I'll tell her we are going to rescue a poor fellow from—er—well from the natives of South America, and I'm sure she'll consent. Of course I'll go."

"That's three," remarked Tom. "I think I can get Eradicate to go. He doesn't like airships, and when he knows we're not going in one it will please him. Then he likes it hot, and I guess South America is about as warm as they come. I am almost sure we can count on Rad."

"That will make a nice party," commented the circus man. "Now I'll make out a list of the supplies you'd better take, and tell you what to do about getting native helpers, and so on," and with that he plunged into the midst of details that took up most of the remainder of the day.

"Well, then I guess that settles most everything," remarked Tom, several hours later. "I'll begin at once to take the Lark apart for shipment, and begin ordering the things we need."

"Oh, there's one thing I almost forgot about," said Mr. Preston suddenly. "Queer, how I should overlook that, too. I don't suppose you mind a fight or two; do you?" he asked, looking sharply at Tom.

"Well, it all depends. We've had several fights on other expeditions, though I can't say that I like 'em," replied the young inventor. "Why do you ask?"

"Because you may have one—or several," was the answer of the circus man. "You'll have to beware of my rival."

"Your rival?"

"Yes, the bitterest foe I have is a rival circus man named Wayland Waydell. He, or some of his men, are always camping on my trail when I send out after a new consignment of wild animals, and I shouldn't be a bit surprised but what he'd try to get ahead of me on the giant game."

"But how does he know you want giants?" asked Tom.

"Because news of circus expeditions always leaks out somehow or other. I'm sure Waydell will learn that you are acting for me, and so I warn you in time. In fact, he tried to get ahead of me when I sent Jake Poddington out over a year ago, and I always had my suspicions that he had a hand in Jake's disappearance, but maybe I'm wrong. So that's what I mean when I say beware of Wayland Waydell, Tom."

"I will!" exclaimed Tom. "He'll have to get up early to get ahead of us." But Tom little knew the man against whom he was to pit himself in the search for giants.

ANDY FOGER LEARNS SOMETHING

Once Tom Swift made up his mind to do a thing, he did not waste time in setting about it. He had decided to go to giant land, and that was all there was to it. His father talked with him about the matter, pointed out the dangers, and suggested that, as the young inventor had had many adventures in the last few years, and had made considerable money from the discovery of the city of gold, and the platinum mines, the prize offered for a giant was not much of an inducement.

"But it isn't that so much, dad," explained Tom. "There's that poor circus man, maybe suffering in the centre of South America. I want to find him, if I can, or get some news that he died a natural death, and is decently buried."

"You never can do it, Tom."

"Well dad, I'm going to make a big try!" he returned; and that settled it as far as Tom was concerned.

For several days after the visit of Mr. Preston Tom was busy making plans for his trip to South America. He wanted to lay out a regular schedule before proceeding. Ned Newton had had hard work to persuade his folks to let him go, but they finally consented, and as for Mr. Damon, his plan was simple.

Without mentioning giants at all, he took Mr. Preston home with him, and the circus man's tale of his assistant lost in the wilds of South America was too much for Mrs. Damon.

"Go? Of course you'll go!" she said to her husband. "I demand that you go, and I want you to find that poor man and rescue him. If you could rescue the exiles from uncivilized Siberia I'm sure you can get a man out of a civilized country."

Mr. Damon did not stop to point out that South America was far less civilized, in some ways, than was Russia. He just kept still, and made his preparations to go. Mr. Preston was a distant relative of the odd man, and that was how he had happened to meet him and hear the story which was destined to play such an important part in the life of Tom Swift.

"Do you think we'll have much trouble after we get to South America, and strike into the interior?" asked Mr. Damon one afternoon, when he and Mr. Preston were helping Tom in the delicate work of packing the wing planes of the Lark.

"No, South America isn't a bad country to travel in," replied the circus man. "The natives are fairly friendly, and with a well-organized party, and plenty of money, which I shall see that you have, you ought to get along swimmingly. Only one thing bothers me."

"What's that?" asked Tom quickly.

"That's my rival, Waydell. He's sure to make trouble if he gets on your trail."

"Have you heard from him?"

"No, and that's what makes me all the more suspicious. If he'd come out and fight me in the open it wouldn't be so bad. But this underhand business gets on my nerves. I don't know what he's up to."

"Maybe he isn't up to anything," suggested Ned. "He may not even know you are going to make another try for the giants."

"Oh, yes, he does," replied the circus man. "He didn't succeed in beating me when poor Jake was after them, for the simple reason that it was a snap case, and even I didn't know that Poddington was trying for the giants until he had started. But Waydell was soon after him, and he knows that when I once set out for a freak or a certain kind of animal I keep on until I get it. So he has probably already figured out that I'm making new plans to get a giant."

"But how will he know that I am going?" inquired Tom.

"I don't know how he will know, but he will. We circus men have queer ways of finding out things. I shouldn't be a bit surprised but what he was already plotting and scheming to send an expedition on my trail, to take advantage of anything you may learn."

"Well, we'll try and fool him, the same as we did the Mexicans when we hunted for the city of gold," spoke Tom; and then putting aside that worry, he and the others labored hard to get matters in shape for a departure to South America.

"I suppose Eradicate is going," remarked Ned, in the intervals of packing the aeroplane.

"Well, I've hinted it to him," replied Tom, "but I haven't asked him outright. He said he wouldn't mind going to a hot country though. Here he comes now. Guess I'll see how he takes it."

The colored man shuffled up with a hammer and nails, for he had been putting covers on packing boxes.

"Then you are coming with us to South America; aren't you, Rad?" asked Tom, winking at Ned.

"Souf America? Am dat de hot country yo'-all was referencin' to?" asked Eradicate.

"That's it, Rad. It's nice and warm there. All you have to do is to lie under a tree and cocoanuts will drop off into your mouth."

"Cocoanuts in mah mouf, Massa Tom! 'Scuse me! I doan't want t' go to no sich country as dat. Cocoanuts in mah mouf! Why I ain't got but a few teef left, an' a cocoanut droppin' offen a tree would shorely knock dem teef out, shorely!"

"Oh, Rad, I didn't mean cocoanuts! I meant oranges and bananas—they're soft," and Tom glanced quickly at Ned, for he saw that he had made a mistake.

"Oh, well, den dat's diffunt, Massa Tom. I jes lubs oranges an' bananas, an' ef yo'-all is shore dat I'll find some, why, I'll come along."

"Find 'em? Of course you will!" cried Ned.

"And cocoanuts, too," added Tom. "Only, Rad, I meant to say that the monkeys would throw the cocoanuts down to you from the trees. That breaks the hard shells you see, and all you have to do is to take out the meat, and drink the milk. Then the monkeys throw you down a palm leaf fan to cool yourself off, while you're eating it. Oh, I tell you, Rad, South America is the place to go to have a good time."

"I believe you, Massa Tom. When do we-all start?"

"Pretty soon now."

"An' what all am yo' gwine arter, Massa Tom?"

The young inventor thought a moment. In times past he had not hesitated to confide in his colored helper, but of late years Eradicate had become somewhat childish, and he talked more than was necessary. Tom wondered whether it would be safe to trust the giant secret to him. After a moment's thought he realized that it would not be. But, at the same time, he knew that if he did not give some kind of an answer Eradicate would become suspicious, and that would be worse. The colored helper had been with Tom on too many trips not to know that his master never went without some object.

"Well, Rad, we're after big game this time," Tom said. "I don't know what it will be that we'll get, whether animals or plants, and—"

"Oh, I knows, Massa Tom. Yo'-all means dem orchard plants dat lib on air—dem big orchard plants." Eradicate meant orchids, of which many rare and beautiful kinds are found in South America.

"Yes, Rad, I guess we will get some big orchids," agreed Tom.

"An' I shorely will help climb de trees arter 'em. Or maybe we kin git de monkeys to frow em down, same as dey will de cocoanuts."

"Maybe, Rad. Well, now go ahead and nail up the rest of these boxes. We want to get started as soon as we can," and the colored man got busy, murmuring from time to time something about oranges and bananas and cocoanuts.

Everyone was occupied in getting matters in shape for the trip to South America, even Mr. Swift laying aside his work on his pet invention—a gyroscope—while he helped his son. And had Tom not been quite so engrossed with his preparations he might have gone about town more, in which case he would have learned something that might have saved him and the others considerable trouble and no little danger. And this fact was that Andy Foger had been in Shopton several times lately.

After the trouble which the red-haired bully and his father caused Tom and his friends on their trip to the city of gold, Mr. Foger moved away from Shopton. He had lost his fortune and had to begin all over again. The Foger homestead was closed up, and Andy ceased to be a fixture of the town, for which Tom and Ned were very glad.

But of late Andy had been seen in Shopton several times, and it was noticed that, on one or two occasions, he had a man with him—a man who seemed to have plenty of money—a man with an air about him not unlike that of Mr. Preston. A man with what newspaper men would have called a circus or theatrical "air."

This man had visited Shopton soon after Mr. Preston made the giant proposition to Tom, and before meeting Andy Foger had made special inquiries about Tom Swift.

"Who are the people who have a hard feeling against this young inventor in town?" the man had asked of several persons.

"Tom Swift has more friends than enemies," was the general reply.

"Oh, surely he must have some enemies," the man insisted. "He's been running his aeroplanes and autos around town a long time, and surely there must be some one who has a grudge against him. I suppose he has lots of friends, but who are his enemies?"

Then he learned about Andy Foger, and, hearing that Andy now lived in a nearby town, the man had at once gone there. It was not long before he reappeared—and the red-haired bully was with him.

"And you haven't learned anything yet, Andy?" asked this mysterious man one afternoon, when he met his tool in a quiet resort in Shopton.

"Nothing yet, Mr. Waydell. But give me a little more time."

"Time! You've had more time now than you need. When I agreed to pay you for finding out what part of South America Tom Swift would head for to get some sort of a freak or animal for Preston's circus I thought you'd make good quicker than this."

"So did I. But you see Tom is suspicious of me, and so is his chum, Ned Newton. I can't go to them, and if I'm seen sneaking around the house or shop, after what happened last, I'll be driven off."

"Well, it's up to you. I paid you to get the information and I expect you to do it. Why don't you tackle that old colored man whom, I understand, works for him? He ought to be simple enough to give the game away."

"Eradicate? I will! I never thought of that I'll get that information for you, Mr. Waydell, in a few days."

"You'd better, if you want to keep that money."

The two plotters parted, and that very afternoon gave Andy the chance he wanted. He met Eradicate on his way to the village where he was going after something Tom needed.

"Hello, Rad!" called Andy with a show of good feeling. "I haven't seen you in some time. I suppose you're getting too old to travel around with Tom any more?"

"Gittin' too old!" exclaimed the colored man indignantly, for that was his sore point. "What yo'-all mean, Andy Foger? I ain't gittin' old, an' neider am Boomerang."

"Oh, I thought you were, as you haven't been on any trips lately."

"I ain't, hey? Well I's gwine on one right soon, let me tell you dat, Andy Foger!"

"No! Is that so? Glad to hear it. Up to the North Pole I suppose?"

"No, sah; not much! No cold country for this coon! I's gwine where it's nice an 'warm, an' where de cocoanuts fall in yo' mouf—I mean where de bananas an' oranges fall in you mouf, an' de monkeys frow down cocoanuts an' palm leaf fans to yo'!"

"Where's that, Rad?" asked Andy, and he tried to make his voice sound indifferent, as though the matter did not interest him.

"South America, dat's where it am, an' I's gwine wif Massa Tom. We's gwine t' git a monstrous big orchard plant."

"Oh, yes; I've heard about them. Well, I hope you get all the oranges and bananas you want. South America, eh? I suppose along the Amazon river, where they have crocodiles forty feet long, that are always hungry."

"No, sah! No crockermiles fo' me! We ain't goin' neah de Amerzon riber at all. We's gwine away down in de middle part of South America. It's a place suffin laik Gomeonaway—or Goonaway, or suffin' laik dat."

"Oh, yes; I know where you mean!" and Andy could hardly conceal the note of triumph in his voice. He had the very information he wanted from the simple colored man. "Yes, I guess there are no crocodiles there, and plenty of monkeys and cocoanuts. Well, I hope you have a good time," and Andy hurried away to seek out the rival circus man.

ALARMING NEWS

"Hand me that hammer, Ned."

"There it is, right behind you, on the bench."

"Oh, so it is. Here are those nails you were asking for."

"Good. Now we'll make things hum," and Ned Newton's voice was drowned in the rapid driving of nails into boards.

"Bless my screw driver!" suddenly exclaimed Mr. Damon, who was sawing planks to make covers for boxes.

"What's the matter?" asked Tom, looking up from a bundle he was tying up. It contained the magneto of his aeroplane and he was putting waterproof paper about it. "Did you cut your finger?"

"No, but I just happened to think that I nailed my watch up in that last box."

"Nailed up your watch!" cried Mr. Preston, who, after a trip to New York to make arrangements for passages on a steamer, had come back to help Tom pack up.

"Yes, I took it out to see how long it took me to make a box cover, and then Tom asked me to nail up that box containing the motor parts, and I laid my watch right down on top, and put the boards over it."

"Well, the only thing to do is to take off the cover," remarked Tom grimly.

"Bless my chronometer! That will delay things," said the odd man with a sigh. "But I suppose there is no hope for it," and he proceeded to open the box, while Tom, Ned, the circus man and Eradicate busied themselves over the hundred and one things to be done before they would be ready for the trip to the interior of South America.

"Look out, Ned!" called Tom. "You're making those top boards too long. They'll stick out over the edge, and be ripped off if the box catches on anything."

"Yes, you can't be too careful," cautioned Mr. Preston. "Each box or package must be the right weight, or the porters and mule drivers won't carry them into the interior. You may have to cross rough trails, and even ford rivers. And as for bridges! well, the less said about them the better. You aren't going to have any picnic, and if you want to back out, Tom Swift, now is the time to say so."

"What! Back out?" cried our hero. "Never! I said I'd go and I'm going. Ned, pass that brace and bit over, will you. I've got to bore a hole for these screws."

And so the work went on in the big aeroplane shed, which they had made their packing headquarters.

The Lark, that small, but strong and speedy aeroplane, had been safely packed, and most of it had been sent on ahead to New York, where the travellers were to take the steamer. There remained to be transported their clothing, weapons and ammunition, and several bundles and cases of trinkets which would be of more value in bartering with the natives than money. Tom and Mr. Preston had selected the things with great care, and at the last moment the young inventor had packed a box of his own, and said nothing about it. Included in it were some of his own and his father's inventions, and had one been given a glance into that same box he would have wondered at the queer things.

"What in the world are you taking with you, anyhow?" asked Ned, of his chum, noticing the mysterious box.

"You'll see, if we ever get to giant land," replied Tom with a smile.

"How long before we can start?" asked Mr. Damon, late that day, when most of the hard work had been finished. He was as anxious and as eager as either of the youths to make a start.

"We ought to be ready at least a week from today," replied Tom, "and perhaps sooner."

"Sooner, if you can make it," suggested Mr. Preston. "The steamer sails a week from today, and if you miss that one you'll have to wait two weeks more."

"Then a week from today we'll sail," decided Tom, with emphasis. "We'll work nights getting things in shape."

Really, though, not much more remained to be done, and the next day Mr. Preston again went to New York, accompanying a shipment of boxes and cases that Tom sent on ahead.

The two chums were busy in the aeroplane hangar a few days after this, nailing up the last of some light cases containing medicines, personal effects and comforts that would accompany them on their trip.

"Well, I'm glad of one thing," remarked Tom thoughtfully, as he drove home the last nail in a box, "and that is that we won't be bothered with that Andy Foger on this trip. I haven't seen hide nor hair of him in some time. I guess he and his father are down and out."

"I guess so. I haven't seen him either."

"Massa Andy were in town a few days ago," ventured Eradicate.

"He was?" cried Tom. "Did you see him? What was he doing, Rad?"

"Nuffin, same as usual. He done say I were too old to go on any more hexpiditions wif yo' an' I proved dat I wasn't."

"Proved that you weren't, Rad? How?" And Tom looked anxiously at his colored helper.

"Why, I done say t' him dat I was gwine wif yo'-all dis time, t' dat Comeaway country after a big orchard plant. Dat's how I done prove it to dat Andy Foger."

"Rad, you didn't tell him we were going to South America?" asked Tom reproachfully.

"Suah I done so, Massa Tom. Dat were de only way t' prove t' him dat I wa'an't gittin' too old."

"Oh, Rad! I'm afraid—" and Tom hesitated.

"Oh, I don't believe it amounted to anything," interposed Ned. "Andy didn't have any one with him, did he, Rad?"

"No, Massa Ned. He were all alone by hisse'f."

"Then I guess it's all right, Tom. Andy was only rigging Eradicate, and he didn't pay any attention to what he said."

"Well, I hope so," and the young inventor wore a thoughtful air as he resumed the finish of the packing.

The colored man, blissfully unconscious that he had been the innocent cause of a grave danger that overhung Tom and his friends, whistled gaily as he gathered the boxes, bales and packages into a pile, ready for the expressman, who was to call in the morning.

Tom, together with Ned, Mr. Damon and Eradicate, were to leave the following afternoon, and stay in New York until the sailing of the steamer. They preferred to be a day or so ahead of time than half an hour late, and were taking no chances.

"Bless my timetable!" exclaimed Mr. Damon that night, as they sat in the library of the Swift home, checking over the lists to make sure that nothing had been forgotten, "bless my timetable, but it doesn't seem possible that we are going to start at last."

"Yes, we'll soon be on the way to giant land," spoke Tom in a low voice. Somehow the young inventor did not seem to be in his usually bright spirits.

"You don't seem very enthusiastic," remarked Ned. "What's the matter, Tom?"

"Oh, nothing much. Though I would feel better if I knew that Andy Foger didn't have any inkling of what our plans were," he added, for Eradicate was not present.

"Oh, nonsense!" exclaimed his chum. "Mr. Preston will be here in the morning, and he'll know whether his rival has any idea of camping on our trail. Cheer up!"

"Yes, I suppose I am foolish to worry," admitted Tom. "but, somehow I can't help it. I wish Mr. Preston was here now to tell us that Wayland Waydell had gone off to the centre of Africa for a dwarf. Then I'd know we had nothing to fear. But I guess—"

Tom did not finish his sentence for, at that moment, there came a peal at the door bell. Instinctively every one started, and Mr. Damon exclaimed:

"Bless my burglar alarm! What's that?"

"Someone at the door, Tom," replied Mr. Swift calmly. "That's nothing unusual. It's early yet."

But, in spite of his reassuring words, there was a feeling of vague alarm.

"I'll see who it is," volunteered Ned. "If it's Andy Foger—"

Mrs. Baggert entered the room at that moment. She had hurried to the door, and, as she entered she announced:

"Mr. Preston!"

"Yes, it is I!" added the circus man following her quickly into the room. "I came on to-night instead of waiting for the morning, Tom. I have bad news for you!"

"Bad news!" gasped the young inventor. "Has Waydell got hold of your plans."

"I'll wager it has something to do with Andy Foger!" exclaimed Ned.

"Neither one," spoke the circus man. "But I have just had a cable dispatch from one of my animal agents in Brazil, saying that war has broken out among the tribes in the central part of South America. A big native war is being waged all around giant land, as near as we can figure it out."

"War among the native tribes!" exclaimed Mr. Swift.

"Yes, and one of the worst in years. Of course, Tom, after such alarming news as this I won't hold you to your promise to go. It's all off. I'm sorry, but you'd better wait. It won't be safe to go there now. Better unpack, Tom."

For a moment there was a silence in the room. Then the young inventor leaped to his feet and faced the circus man.

"Unpack?" cried Tom in ringing tones. "Never! I'm going to giant land, fight or no fight! Ned, come with me and we'll put in some of my electric rifles. I wasn't going to take them along, but I will now. Unpack? I guess not! I'm going to get a giant for you, Mr. Preston, and save Jake Poddington if he's alive. Come on, Ned."

FIRE ON BOARD

"Your electric rifles!" exclaimed Ned Newton, as he followed his chum to the storeroom, where Tom kept a number of spare guns. "It's a good thing you thought of them, Tom."

"Yes, I didn't think we'd need them, for I believe peaceable means are the best to use on natives. But if there's a war, and we have to defend ourselves against the tribes, we'll take along something that will do more damage than an ordinary rifle, and yet I can regulate it so that it will only stun, and not kill."

"That's the stuff, Tom. No use in being needlessly cruel. How many will you take?"

"Two or three. We may need 'em all."

A little later the two lads returned to the library where Mr. Damon, Mr. Swift and the circus man were anxiously awaiting them. Mr. Preston looked curiously at several objects which Tom and Ned carried. The objects looked like guns but were different from any the giant-seeker had seen.

"What are they?" he asked Tom.

"Electric rifles. One of my inventions," and Tom showed how the weapon worked. Those of you who have read the volume entitled, "Tom Swift and His Electric Rifle" will remember this curious weapon. It was worked by a stored charge of magnetism of the wireless kind. By this a concentrated globule of electricity was projected from the muzzle, and it could be made strong or weak at the will of the marksman. It could be made so powerful that it would totally annihilate a whale, as Tom had once proved, or it could be made so mild that it would put an enemy, or several of them, to sleep almost as gently as some narcotic, and they would awaken after several hours, little the worse for their experience.

A charge of electricity as powerful as five thousand volts could be concentrated into a small wireless globule the size of a bullet, and this would fly through space, or even through solid objects until, reaching the limit of the range set, would strike the object aimed at. With his wonderful electric rifle Tom had not only killed elephants, and other big game, but fought off the red pygmies of Africa.

"And we may have a use for it in South America," he added as he explained the workings to Mr. Preston.

"Well, I'm glad you didn't back out," commented the circus man, "and this may come in mighty handy. I'll feel easier about you now, Tom, when I know you have some electric rifles with you."

The circus man was told of what Eradicate had said to Andy, but he was of the opinion that no harm would result from it.

"As far as I can learn," went on Mr. Preston, "my old rival Waydell has given up the giant idea. He is looking for a two-headed crocodile, said to be somewhere along the Nile river, and he's fitting out an expedition there I understand. I guess we won't be bothered with him. But the giant for mine! If I get that sort of an attraction his two-headed crocodile won't be in it. I hope you have luck, Tom Swift."

The last details of the expedition were considered. Nothing seemed to have been left undone, and though carrying the electric rifles would make a little more baggage, no one minded that.

"I kin carry dem," said Eradicate. "I ain't got much baggage of mah own."

So it was arranged, and early the next morning the little band of intrepid travelers, who were going in search of giant land, started for New York. They little knew what was ahead of them, nor what dire perils they were to pass through.

Of course Tom had said good-bye to Mary Nestor and half-jokingly, he had promised to bring back a giant of his own, that she might see one outside of a circus.

"But, Tom," Mary exclaimed with a laugh, "what will you do with one of the big creatures if you get one?"

"Have him help me on my newest invention—the noiseless airship," answered the young inventor. "I need some one to lift heavy weights. It will save putting up a derrick. Yes, I think I'll get a giant of my own."

The last good-byes were said, and the parting between Tom and his father was affecting.

"I'll soon be back, dad," he said in as cheerful a tone as he could assume, "and I'll help you finish your gyroscope."

"I hope you will, Tom," and then, with a pressure of his son's hand, Mr. Swift turned away and went into the house, closing the door after him.

The first part of the trip to New York was rather a silent one, no one caring to talk much. Eradicate was the only cheerful member of the party, which included the circus man, who was going as far as the steamer with Tom and his friends.

"Say," Ned exclaimed finally, "any one would think we were going to a funeral!"

"That's right," agreed Tom. "I guess something is on all our nerves. Let's do something to take it off. Here comes a boy with some funny papers. We'll buy some and read all the jokes."

This proved a diversion, and before the train had gone many miles more the giant-hunters were talking and laughing as though they were merely starting on a short pleasure trip, instead of an expedition to the dangerous jungles of South America.

They put up at a good hotel in New York, and as soon as they were established Tom and Mr. Preston went to the steamer Calaban which was to land them at Buenos Ayres. They found that there was some confusion about their luggage and boxes, and it took them the better part of a day to get the tangle straightened out, and their stuff stored together in one hold.

"It will be easier to get it out if it's all together," said Tom, at the conclusion of their labors, and then he and the circus man returned to the hotel. The ship was to sail two days later, and, several hours before the time set for the departure, Tom and his friends were on board.

"You don't see anything of your rival circus friend, do you?" asked Tom, of the man who wanted a giant.

"Not a sign," was the answer, as Mr. Preston glanced over the throng of on-coming passengers. "I guess we've either given him the slip, or he's given up the game. You won't have to worry about him. Just take it easy until you start for the interior, and from then on you'll have hard work enough."

The last of the cargo was being taken aboard, the late passengers had arrived and were anxiously watching to see that their baggage was not lost. As Mr. Preston stood talking with Tom near the gangplank, a clerical looking gentleman approached the circus man.

"I beg your pardon," he began in mild accents, "but could you tell me where my stateroom is?" and he showed his ticket. "I'm not used to traveling," he needlessly added for that fact was very evident. Mr. Preston informed him how to get to his berth, and the gentleman went on: "Are you going all the way to Buenos Ayres?"

"No, but my friend is," and the circus man nodded at Tom.

"Oh, I'm so glad!" the stranger exclaimed. "Then I shall have someone of whom I can ask questions. I am quite lost when I travel."

"I'll help you all I can," volunteered Tom, "and I'll show you to your stateroom now."

"Ah, thank you. Your name is—"

"Tom Swift," supplied the young inventor.

"Ah, yes, I believe I have read about your airships. I am the Reverend Josiah Blinderpool. I am taking a little vacation. I trust we shall become good friends."

"Humph, he's a regular infant, to be away from civilization," mused Tom, when he had showed the clergyman to the proper stateroom. "He'll get into trouble, he's so innocent." If he could have seen that same "clergyman" double up with mirth when he had closed his stateroom door after him, Tom would not have felt so sure about that same "innocence."

"To think that I was talking face to face with Sam Preston and he never tumbled to who I was!" exclaimed the newcomer softly. "That's rich! Now if I play my cards right I shouldn't be surprised but what they'd invite me to come along with them. That would just suit me. I wouldn't have any trouble then, getting on the track of those giants. The information Waydell got from that red-haired Foger chap wasn't any too definite," and once more the man wearing the garb of a minister chuckled.

"Well, I'll say good-bye," remarked Mr. Preston, a little later, when the warning bell had rung. "I guess you'll get along all right. I haven't seen a sign of Waydell, or any of his slick agents. You'll have no trouble I guess."

But if the circus man could have seen the "clergyman" at that same time looking over letters addressed to "Hank Delby," and signed "Wayland Waydell" he would not have been so confident.

Mr. Preston bade good-bye to his friends, the gangplank was hauled up, and a hoarse blast came from the whistle of the Calaban.

"Bless my pocketbook!" cried Mr. Damon. "We're off!"

"Yep, off t' git dat big, giant orchard plant," chimed in Eradicate.

"Hush!" exclaimed Tom, who did not like the use of the word "giant" even in that connection. "Don't tell everyone our business, Rad."

"Dat's right, Massa Tom. I clean done forgot dat it's a sort of secret. I'll keep mighty still 'bout it."

The Calaban swung out into the river and began steaming down the bay.

The first week of the voyage was uneventful. The weather was exceptionally fine, and hardly any one was seasick. The Reverend Mr. Blinderpool was often on deck, and he made it a point to cultivate the acquaintance of Tom and his friends. In spite of the fact that he said he had traveled very little, he seemed to know much about hidden corners of the world, but always, as on an occasion when he had accidentally let slip some remark that showed he had been in far-off China or Asia, he would suddenly change the conversation when it verged to travel.

"There's something queer about that minister," said Ned after one of these occasions, "but I can't decide what it is."

"Nonsense!" exclaimed Tom, who rather liked the man.

"No nonsense about it. Why should a minister take a trip like this when he isn't sick, and when he isn't going to establish a mission in South America? There's something queer about it, for, by his own words he just took this voyage as a whim."

"Oh, you're too fussy," declared Tom; and for the time the subject was dropped.

They ran into a storm when about ten days out, and for a while they had a rough time of it, and then the weather cleared again.

It was one evening, after the formal dinner, when Tom and Ned were strolling about on deck, before turning in, that, the quiet of the ship was broken by what is always an alarming cry at sea.

"Fire! Fire!" shouted a man, pointing to a thin wisp of smoke curling up from the deck amidships.

"Keep quiet!" yelled one of the stewards. "It is nothing!"

"It's a fire, I tell you!" insisted the man, and several others took up the cry.

A panic was imminent, and the captain came running from his quarters.

"What is it?" he asked.

An officer hurried to his side, and said something but in such a low voice that Tom, who was standing close beside the two, scarcely heard it. But he did hear this:

"There's a fire, sir, in hold number seventeen. We have turned the hose in there, and the pumps are working."

"Very good, Mr. Meld. Now try and quiet the passengers. Tell them it doesn't amount to much, and if it does we can flood that compartment."

Tom started at that.

"Come on, Ned!" he cried, grabbing his chum by the arm.

"Why, what's up? What's the matter?"

"Matter? Matter enough! The fire is in the hold where all our stuff is stored, and if the flames reach that box I packed last—well, I wouldn't give much for the ship!" and fairly dragging his chum along, Tom raced for the place where the smoke was now coming up in thicker clouds.

A Narrow Escape

"Here, come back! You can't go past here!"

"But I've got to go! I tell you I must go! It's important!"

The first speaker was one of the ship's officers, and the other was Tom Swift, who, accompanied by his chum, was trying to get past a rope that had been hastily stretched in front of the hold where the smoke was rolling up in ever-thickening clouds.

"It's important that you stay where you are," insisted the officer. "Look here young man, do you want to start a panic? You know what that is on board ship. Keep cool, we'll get the fire out all right."

"I am cool," responded Tom, and, though he did look a bit excited, he was calm enough to know what he was doing.

"Then keep back!" insisted the officer.

A crowd was gathering and there were ominous whispers sent back and forth. Some hysterical women were beginning to scream, and there were anxious looks on all faces.

"I tell you it's important that I go down there," insisted Tom. "I want to get a box—"

"We'll look after the baggage of the passengers," declared the officer. "You don't need to worry, young man."

"But I tell you I do!" and Tom's voice was loud now. "It isn't so much on my account, as—" and then, stepping quickly to the side of the officer he whispered something.

"What!" cried the officer. "You don't tell me? That was a risk! I guess I'll have to help you get it out. Here, Mr. Simm," he called to one of the mates, "stand guard here. I'm going down into the hold with this young man."

"Shall I come?" cried Ned.

"No, you go stay with Mr. Damon and Eradicate," answered Tom. "Tell them everything is all right. And for cats' sake keep Rad cool. Don't let him get excited and start a panic. I'll be back in a minute."

With that Tom and the officer disappeared from view, and Ned, after wondering what it was all about, hastened to reassure Mr. Damon and the colored man that there was no danger, though from the manner in which Tom had acted his chum was convinced that something was wrong.

Meanwhile our hero, accompanied by the officer, was groping his way through the thick smoke in the compartment. The officer had switched on the electric lights, and they shone with a yellow haze through the clouds of choking vapor.

"Can you see it?" asked the officer anxiously.

"I had it put where I could easily get at it," answered Tom with a cough, for some of the smoke had got down his throat. "I had an idea I might need it in a hurry. Here it is!" and he pointed to a large box, marked with his initials in red paint. "Give me a hand and we'll get it out."

"Yes, and send it on deck. See, there's the fire!" and the officer pointed to where a glow could be seen amid some bales of cotton. "It will be slow burning, that's one good thing, and by turning steam into this compartment we can soon put it out."

"It's pretty close to my box," commented Tom, "but there isn't as much danger as I thought."

It did not take him and the officer long to move the box away from its proximity to the fire, for the case was not heavy, though it was of good size, and then the officer having called up an order to some of his fellow seamen on deck, a rope was let down, and the box hoisted up.

"Whew! That was a narrow escape!" exclaimed Tom as he saw his case go up on deck. "I suppose I shouldn't have had that stored here. But there were so many things to think of that I forgot."

"Yes, it was a risk," commented the officer. "But what are you going to do with that sort of stuff, anyhow?"

"I may need it when we get among the wild tribes of South American Indians," answered Tom non-committally. "I'm much obliged for your help."

"Oh, that's nothing. Anything to save the ship."

At that moment there were confused cries, and a series of shouts and commands up on deck.

"We'd better hurry out of here," said the officer.

"Why?"

"The captain has just ordered steam turned in here. I hope there isn't anything of yours that will be damaged by it."

"No, everything else is in waterproof coverings. Come on, we'll climb out."

They hurried from the compartment and, a little later clouds of quenching steam were poured in from a hose run from the boiler room. The hatch was battened down, and then the smoke ceased to come up.

"The danger is practically over," the captain assured the frightened passengers. "The fire will be all out by morning. You may go to your staterooms in perfect safety."

Some did, and others, disbelieving, hung around the hatch-cover, sniffing and peering to discover traces of smoke. But the sailors had done their work well, and a stranger would not have known that a fire was in the hold.

The captain had spoken truly, and in the morning the fire was completely out, a few charred bales of cotton being the only things damaged. They were hauled up and dumped into the sea, while Tom, making a hasty inspection of his other goods placed in that compartment saw, to his relief, that beyond one case of trinkets, designed for barter with the natives, nothing had been damaged, and even the trinkets could be used on a pinch.

"But what was in that box?" asked Ned, that night as they got ready to retire, the excitement having calmed down.

"Hush! Not so loud," cautioned Tom, for Mr. Damon was in the next stateroom, while Eradicate had one across the corridor. "I'll tell you, Ned, but don't breathe a word of it to Rad or Mr. Damon. They might not intend to give it away, but I'm afraid they would, if they knew, and I depend on the things in that box to give the native giants the surprise of their lives in case we—well, in case we come to close quarters."

"Close quarters?"

"Yes, have a fight, you know, or in case they get so fond of us that they won't hear of letting us go—in other words if they make us captives."

"Great Scott, Tom! You don't think they'll do that, do you?"

"No telling, but if they do, Ned, I've got some things in that box that will make them wish they hadn't. It's got—" and Tom leaned forward and whispered, as though he feared even the walls would hear.

"Good!" cried his chum! "That's the stuff! No wonder you thought the ship might be damaged if the fire got to that!"

It seemed that the slight fire was about all the excitement destined to take place aboard the Calaban, for, after the blaze was so effectually quenched, the ship slipped along through the calm seas, and it was actually an effort to kill time on the part of the passengers. As they progressed further south the weather became more and more warm, until, as they approached the equator, every one put on the lightest garments obtainable.

"Crossing the line," was the signal for the usual "stunts" among the sailors. "Neptune" came aboard, with his usual sea-green whiskers made from long rope ends, and with his trident much in evidence; and there was plenty of horseplay which the passengers very much enjoyed.

Then, as the tropical region was left behind, the weather became more bearable. There were one or two storms, but they were of no consequence and the steamer weathered them easily.

Torn and his friends had several talks with the "Reverend Josiah Blinderpool," as the pretended clergyman still called himself. But he did not obtrude his company on them, and though he asked many questions as to where Tom and his party were going, the young inventor, with his usual caution in talking to strangers, rather evaded them.

"Hang it all! He's as close-mouthed as a clam," complained "Mr. Blinderpool" to himself one day, after an attempt to worm something from Tom, "I'll just have to stick close to him and his chum to get a line on where they're heading for. And I must find out, or Waydell will think I'm throwing the game."

As for Tom and the others, they gave the seeming clergyman little thought—that is until one day when something happened. Ned had been down in the engine room, having had permission to inspect the wonderful machinery, and, on his way back he passed the smoking cabin. He was rather surprised to see Mr. Blinderpool in there, puffing on a big black cigar, and with him were some men whom Ned recognized as personages who had vainly endeavored to get a number of passengers into a card game with them. And, unless Ned's eyes deceived him, the seeming clergyman was about to indulge in a game himself.

"That's mighty queer," mused Ned. "Guess I'll tell Tom about this. I never saw a minister play cards in public before, and this Mr. Blinderpool has been trying to get thick with Tom, of late. Maybe he's a gambler in disguise."

Filled with this thought Ned hastened off to warn his chum.

"Forward March!"

"You don't say so!" exclaimed the young inventor, when Ned had told him the queer news. "Well, do you know I've been suspicious of that fellow ever since he tried to make friends with us."

"Suspicious? How so? You don't think—"

"Oh, I mean I think he's some kind of a confidence man who has adopted the respectable clothes of a minister to fool people. He may be a card sharper himself. Well, we won't have anything more to do with him. It won't be long before we arrive at Buenos Ayres, and then we won't be bothered with card sharpers or anybody else but—"

"Giants and fighting natives," finished Ned, with a laugh. "You forget, Tom, that there's a war going on near the very place we're headed for."

"That's so, Ned. But with what we have with us I guess we can make out all right. I'm going to have the electric rifles handy the minute we start for the interior."

The voyage continued, and was fast drawing to a close. "Mr. Blinderpool" made several more attempts to strike up a friendship with Tom, or his chum, but they were on their guard now, and, failing to get into much of a conversation with the two young men, the pretended clergyman turned his attentions to Mr. Damon.

That eccentric gentleman welcomed him at first, until a quiet hint from Tom brought that to an end.

"Bless my fire shovel!" cried Mr. Damon. "You don't say so! Not a clergyman at all? Dear me!"

And then, getting desperate, and needing very much to learn how long a journey his rivals were to undertake, so that he, too, might prepare for it, Mr. Hank Delby, alias Blinderpool, began to "pump" Eradicate.

But the latter was too sharp for him. Well knowing that a white man would not get suddenly friendly with one of the black race unless for some selfish object, Eradicate fairly snubbed the seeming minister, until that worthy had to go off by himself, saying bitter things and casting black looks at our friends.

"But I'll get ahead of them yet!" he muttered, "and I'll get their giants away from them, if they capture any."

The box on which Tom set such an importance, and which had so nearly been the cause of a disaster, had been stored in one of the fire-proof compartments of the ship, and now, as a few days more would see the vessel entering the harbor of the Rio de la Plata, thence to steam up to the ancient city of Buenos Ayres, Tom and the others began to think of what lay before them.

"How do you propose to head into the interior?" asked Mr. Damon one afternoon, when the captain announced that the following morning would see them nearly opposite Montevideo.

"I'm going to hire a lot of burrows, donkeys or whatever they have down here that answers the purpose," replied Tom. "We have a lot of things to transport, and I guess pack mules would be the best, if we can get them. Then I've got to hire some drivers and some porters, camp-makers and the like. In fact we'll have quite a party. I guess I'll need ten natives, and a head man and with ourselves we'll be fifteen. So we'll need plenty of food. But then we can get that as we go along, except when we get away into the interior, and then we'll have to hunt it ourselves."

"That's the stuff!" cried Ned. "We haven't had a good hunting expedition since we went to elephant land, Tom. The electric rifles will come in handy here."

"Yes, I expect they will. Now come on, Ned, and help me get a list ready of the things we've got to take with us, and how they can best be divided up."

Thick weather delayed the ship somewhat, so it was not until evening of the next day that they made Montevideo, where part of the cargo was to be discharged. As they would lay over there a day, the boys decided to go ashore, which they did, wondering at the strange sights in the old city.

Tom watched to see if the pretended minister would land, and endeavor to force his acquaintance, but Mr. Hank Delby, to give him his right name, was not in evidence. In fact he was turning over scheme after scheme in his mind in order to hit on one that would enable him to take advantage of the preparations which had been made by his rival in the circus business.

"I've just got to get a line on where those giants are to be found," mused Mr. Delby, in the seclusion of his stateroom, "even if I have to take some other disguise and follow that Swift crowd. That's what I'll do. I'll put on some other disguise! I wonder what it had better be?"

Tom and Ned, to say nothing of Mr. Damon and Eradicate, found much to interest them in the capital of Uruguay, and they were rather sorry, in a way, when it was time for them to leave.

"But we'll see plenty more strange sights," remarked Tom, as the steamer started off for Buenos Ayres. "In fact our trip hasn't really begun yet."

In due time they dropped anchor at the ancient city, and then began a series of confused and busy times. In fact there was so much to do, seeing to the unloading of their stuff, arranging for hotel accommodations, seeing to hiring natives for the expedition into the interior, and other details, that Tom and his friends had no time to think anything about the pretended clergyman who had caused them a little worry.

Eventually their belongings were stored in a safe place, and our friends sat down to a good dinner in a hotel that, while it was in far-off South

America, yet was as good as many in New York, and, in some respects the boys, and Mr. Damon, liked it better.

They found that the Spanish and Portuguese languages were the principal ones spoken, together with a mixture of the native tongues, and as both Ned and Tom, as well as Mr. Damon, had a working knowledge of Spanish they got along fairly well. Some of the hotel people could speak English.

Tom made inquiries and found that the best plan would be to transport all his stuff by the regular route to Rosario, on the Parana river in Argentina, and there he could make up his pack train, hire native carriers, and start for the interior.

"Then we'll do that," he decided, "and take it easy until we get to Rosario."

It took them the better part of a week to do this, but at last they were on the ground, and felt for the first time that they were really going into a wild and little explored country.

"Are you going to stick to the Parana river?" asked Ned.

"No," replied Tom, in the seclusion of their room, "if there are any giants they will be found in some undiscovered, or at least little traveled, part of the country. I don't believe they are in the vicinity of the big rivers, or other travelers would have heard about them, and, as far as we know, Mr. Preston's animal agent is the only one who ever got a trace of them. We'll have to go into the jungle on either side of the river."

"Bless my walking stick!" cried Mr. Damon. "Have we really to go into the jungle, Tom?"

"I'm afraid we have, if we want to get any giants, and get a trace of Mr. Poddington."

"All right, I'm game, but I do hope we won't run into a band of fighting natives."

In Rosario it was learned that while the "war" was not regarded seriously from the fact that the fighting tribes were far inland, still it was going on with vigor, and large bands of natives were roaming about, stealing each others' cattle and horses, burning villages, and taking captives.

"I guess we're in for it," remarked Tom grimly. "But I'm not going to back out now."

Unexpected complications, difficulties in the way of getting the right kind of help, and a competent man to take charge of the native drivers, so delayed our friends that it was nearly two weeks after their arrival in Rosario before they could start for the interior.

Of course the object of the expedition was kept a secret, and Tom let it be known that he and his friends were merely exploring, and wanted rare plants, orchids, or anything in that line. The natives were not very curious.

At last the day for the start came. The mules, which had been hired as beasts of burdens, were loaded with boxes or bales on either side, the natives were marshaled into line. Tom, Ned, and Mr. Damon, each equipped with a rifle had a saddle animal to ride, and Eradicate was similarly equipped, though for a weapon he depended on a shotgun, which he said he understood better than the electric rifles.

The aeroplane, divided into many small packages, the goods for barter, their supplies, stores, ammunition, and the box of which Tom took such care—all these were on the backs of the beasts of burden. Some food was taken along, but for a time, at least, they could depend on scattered towns or villages, or the forest game, for their eating.

"Are we all ready?" called Tom, looking at the rather imposing cavalcade of which he was the head.

"I guess so," replied Ned. "Let her go!"

"Bless my liver pad!" gasped Mr. Damon. "If we've got to start do it, and let's get it over with Tom."

"All ready, Rad?" asked the colored man's young master.

"All ready, Massa Tom. But I mus' say dat I'd radder hab Boomerang dan dish yeah animal what I'm ridin'."

"Oh, you'll do all right, Rad. Then, if we're all ready, forward march!" cried Tom, and with calls to their animals, the drivers started them off.

Hardly had they begun the advance than Ned, who had been narrowly watching one of the natives, hurried up to Tom, and rapidly whispered something to his chum.

"What?" cried Tom. "Armed with a six-shooter, is he? Well, we'll see about that! Halt!" he cried in Spanish, and then he called San Pedro the head mule driver, to him.

A WILD HORSE STAMPEDE

"Who is that man?" demanded Tom pointing to the one Ned had indicated. Tom's chum had had a glimpse of a shining revolver in the hip pocket of one of the mule drivers, and knowing that the simple natives were not in the habit of carrying such weapons, the lad had communicated his suspicions to Tom.

"What man, senor?" asked the head mule driver.

"That one!" and the young inventor again pointed toward him. And, now that Tom looked a second time he saw that the man was not as black as the other drivers—not an honest, dark-skinned black but more of a sickly yellow, like a treacherous half-breed. "Who is he?" asked Tom, for the man in question was just then tightening a girth and could not hear him.

"I know not, senor. He come to me when I am hiring the others, and he say he is a good driver. And so he is, I test him before I engage him," went in San Pedro in Spanish. "He is one good driver."

"Why does he carry a revolver?"

"A revolver, senor? Santa Maria, I know not! I—"

"I'll find out," declared Tom determinedly. "Here," he called to the offending one, who straightened up quickly. "Come here!"

The man came, with all the cringing servility of a born native, and bowed low.

"Why have you a weapon?" asked the young inventor. "I gave orders that none of the drivers were to carry them."

"A revolver, senor? I have none! I—"

"Rad, reach in his pocket!" cried Tom, and the colored man did so with a promptness that the other could not frustrate. Eradicate held aloft a large calibre, automatic weapon.

"What's that for?" asked Tom, virtuously angry.

"I—er—I—" and then, with a hopeless shrug of his shoulders the man turned away.

"Give him his gun, and get another driver, San Pedro," directed our hero, and with another shrug of his shoulders the man accepted the revolver, and walked slowly off. Another driver was not hard to engage, as several had been hanging about, hoping for employment at the last minute, and one was quickly chosen.

"It's lucky you saw that gun, Ned," remarked Tom, when they were actually under way again.

"Yes, I saw the sun shining on it as his coat flapped up. What was his game, do you suppose?"

"Oh, he might be what they call a 'bad half-breed' down here. I guess maybe he thought he could lord it over the other drivers when we got out in the jungle, and maybe take some of their wages away from them, or have things easier for himself."

"Bless my wishbone!" exclaimed Mr. Damon. "You don't think he meant to use it on us, Tom?"

"Why no? What makes you ask that?"

"Oh, I'm just nervous, I guess," replied the odd man.

But if Mr. Damon could have seen that same half-breed a little later, as he slipped into a Rosario resort, with the yellow stain washed from his face, the nervousness of the eccentric gentleman would have increased. For the man who had been detected with the revolver muttered to himself:

"Caught! Well, I'll fool 'em next time all right! I thought I could get away with the pack train, and then it would have been easy to turn the natives any way I wished, after I had found what I'm looking for. But I had to go and carry that gun! I never thought they'd spot it. Well, it's all up now, and if Waydell heard of it he'd want to fire me. But I'll make good yet. I'll have to adopt some other disguise, and see if I can't tag along behind."

All unconscious of the plotter they had left back of them, Tom and his companions pushed on, rapidly leaving such signs of civilization as were represented by small native towns and villages, and coming nearer to the jungles and forests that lay between them and the place where Tom was destined to be made a captive.

They were far enough away from the tropics to escape the intolerable heat, and yet it was quite warm. In fact the weather was not at all unpleasant, and, once they were started, all enjoyed the novelty of the trip.

Tom planned to keep along the eastern shore of the Parana river, until they reached the junction where the Salado joins it. Then he decided that they would do better to cross the Parana and strike into the big triangle made by that stream and its principal tributary, heading north toward Bolivia.

"For it is in that little-explored part of South America that I think the giants will be found." said Tom, as he talked it over with Ned and Mr. Damon in the privacy of their tent, which had been set up.

"But why should there be giants there any more than anywhere else?" asked Ned.

"No particular reason," answered his chum. "But, according to the last word Mr. Preston had from his agent, that was where he was heading for, and that's where Zacatas, his native helper, said he lost track of his master. I have a theory that the giants, if we find any, will turn out to be a branch of a Patagonian tribe."

"Patagonians!" exclaimed Ned.

"Yes. You know the natives of the Southern part of Argentina grow to a considerable size. Now Patagonia is a comparatively bleak and cold country. What would prevent some of that big tribe centuries ago, from having migrated to a warmer country, where life was more favorable? After several generations they may have grown to be giants."

"Bravo!" exclaimed Mr. Damon. "It's a good theory, at any rate, Tom. Though whether you can ever prove it is a question."

"Yes, and a big one," agreed the young inventor with a laugh.

For some days they traveled along over a comparatively flat country, bordering the river. At times they would pass through small native villages, where they would be able to get fresh meat, poultry and other things that varied their bill of fare. Again there would be long, lonely stretches of forest or jungle, through which it was difficult to make their way. And, occasionally they would come to fair-sized towns where their stay was made pleasant.

"I doan't see any ob dem oranges an' bananas droppin' inter mah mouf, Massa Tom," complained Eradicate one day, after they had been on the march for over a week.

"Have patience, Rad," advised Tom. "We'll come to them when we get a little farther into the interior. First we'll come to the monkeys, and the cocoanut trees."

"Hones' Massa Tom?"

"Surely."

And though it was pretty far south for the nimble simians, the next day they did come upon a drove of them skipping about in the tall palm trees.

"There they are, Rad! There they are!" cried Ned, as the chattering of the monkeys filled the forest.

"By golly! So dey be! Heah's where I get some cocoanuts!"

Before anyone could stop him, Eradicate caught up a dead branch, and threw it at a monkey. The chattering increased, and almost instantly a shower of cocoanuts came crashing down, narrowly missing some of our friends.

"Hold on, Rad! Hold on!" cried Tom. "Some of us will be hurt!"

Crack! came a cocoanut down on the skull of the colored man.

"Bless my court plaster! Someone's hurt now!" cried Mr. Damon.

"Hurt? Bless yo' heart, Massa Damon, it takes mo' dan dat t' hurt dish yeah chile!" cried Eradicate with a grin. "Ah got a hard head, Ah has, mighty hard head, an' de cocoanut ain't growed dat kin bust it. Thanks, Mistah Monkey, thanks!" and with a laugh Eradicate jumped off his mule, and began gathering up the nuts, while the monkeys fled into the forest.

"Very much good to drink milk," said San Pedro, as he picked up a half-ripe nut, and showed how to chop off the top with a big knife and drain the slightly acid juice inside. "Very much good for thirst."

"Let's try it," proposed Tom, and they all drank their fill, for there were many cocoanuts, though it was rather an isolated grove of them.

The monkeys became more numerous as they proceeded farther north toward the equator, for it must be remembered that they had landed south of it, and at times the little animals became a positive nuisance.

Several days passed, and they crossed the Parana river and struck into the almost unpenetrated tract of land where Tom hoped to find the giants. As yet none of their escort dreamed of the object of the expedition, and though Tom had caused scouts to be sent back over their trail to learn if they were being followed there was no trace of any one.

One day, after a night camp on the edge of a rather high table land, they started across a fertile plain that was covered with a rich growth of grass.

"Good grazing ground here," commented Ned.

"Yes," put in San Pedro. "Plenty much horse here pretty soon."

"Do the natives graze their herds of horses here?" asked Tom.

"No natives—wild horses," explained Pedro. "Plenty much, sometimes too many they come. You see, maybe."

It was nearly noon, and Tom was considering stopping for dinner if they could come to a good watering place, when Ned, who had ridden slightly in advance, came galloping back as fast as his steed would carry him.

"Look out! Look out!" he cried. "There's a stampede of 'em, and they're headed right this way!"

"Stampede of what? Who's headed this way?" cried Tom. "A lot of monkeys?"

"No, wild horses! Thousands of 'em! Hear 'em coming?"

In the silence that followed Ned's warning there could be heard a dull, roaring, thundering sound, and the earth seemed to tremble.

"The young senor speaks truth! Wild horses are coming!" cried San Pedro. "Get ready, senors! Have your weapons at hand, and perchance we can turn the stampede aside."

"The rifles! The electric rifles, Ned—Mr. Damon! We've got to stop them, or they'll trample us to death!" cried Tom.

As he spoke the thundering became louder, and then, looking across the grassy plain, all saw a large troop of wild horses, with flying manes and tails, headed directly toward them!

CAUGHT IN A LIVING ROPE

"Quick! Peg out the mules!" cried San Pedro, after one look at the onrushing horses. "Drive the stakes well down! Tie them fast and then get behind those rocks! Lively!"

He cried his orders to the natives in Spanish, at the same time motioning to Tom and Ned.

"Get off your mules!" he went on. "Peg them out. Peg out the others, and then run for it!"

"Run for it?" repeated Tom, "Do you think I'm going to leave my outfit in the midst of that stampede?" and he waved his hand toward the thundering, galloping wild horses which were coming nearer every moment. "Get out the electric rifles, and we'll turn that stampede. I'm not going to run."

"Bless my saddle!" cried Mr. Damon. "This is awful! There must be a thousand of them."

"Nearer two!" cried Ned, who was struggling to loosen the straps that bound his electric rifle to the side of his mule. Already the pack animals as well as those ridden by the members of the giant-hunting party were showing signs of excitement. They seemed to want to join the stampeding horses.

"Peg our animals out! Peg them out! Make them so they can't join the others!" yelled San Pedro. "It's our only chance!"

"I believe he's right!" cried Mr. Damon. "Tom, if we wait until those maddened brutes are up to us they'll fairly sweep ours along with them, and there's no telling where we'll end up. I think we'd better follow his advice and tie our mules as strongly as we can. Then we can go over there by the rocks, and fire at the wild horses. We may be able to turn them aside."

"Guess that's right," agreed the young inventor after a moment's thought. "Come on, Ned. Peg out!"

"Peg out! Peg out!" yelled the natives, and then began a lively scene. Pegging stakes were in readiness, and, attached to the bridle of each mule was a strong, rawhide rope for tying to the stake. The pegs were driven deeply into the ground and in a trice the animals were made fast to them, though they snorted, and tried to pull away as they heard the neighing of the stampeding animals and saw them coming on with an irresistible rush.

"Hurry!" begged San Pedro, and hurry Tom, Ned and the others did. Animal after animal was made fast—that is all but one and that bore on its back two rather large but light boxes—the contents of the case which Tom had rescued from the fire in the hold.

"What are you going to do with mule?" asked Ned, as he saw Tom begin to lead the animal away, the others having been pegged out.

"I'm going to take him over to the rocks with me. I'm not going to take any chances on this mule getting away with those things in the boxes. Give me a hand here, and then we'll see what the electric rifles will do against those horses."

But the one mule which Tom had elected to take with him seemed to resent being separated from his companions. Bracing his feet well apart, the animal stubbornly refused to move.

"Come on!" yelled Tom, pulling on the leading rope.

"Bless my porous plaster!" cried Mr. Damon. "You'd better hurry, Tom! Those wild horses are almost on us!"

"I'm trying to hurry!" replied the young inventor, "but this mule won't come. Ned, get behind and shove, will you?"

"Not much! I don't want to be kicked."

"Beat him! Strike him! Wait until I get a club!" yelled San Pedro. "Come, Antonia, Selka, Balaka!" he cried, to several of the natives who had already started for the sheltering rocks a short distance away. "Beat the mule for Senor Swift!"

Ned joined Tom at the leading rope, and the two lads tried to pull the animal along. Mr. Damon rushed over to lend his aid, and San Pedro, catching up a long stick, was about to bring it down on the mule's back. Meanwhile the stampeding animals were rushing nearer.

"Hold on dere, Massa Tom!" suddenly called Eradicate. "Yo'-all done flustered dat mule, dat's what yo' done. Yo'-all am too much excited 'bout him. Be calm! Be calm!"

"Calm! With that bunch of wild animals bearing down on us?" shouted Tom. "Let's see you be calm, Rad. Come on here, you obstinate brute!" he cried, straining on the rope.

"Let me do it, Massa Tom. Let me do it," suggested the colored man hurrying to the balky beast.

Then, as gently as if he was talking to a nervous child, and totally oblivious to the danger of the approaching horses, Eradicate went up to the mule's head, rubbed its ears until they pointed naturally once more, murmured something to it, and then, taking the rope from Ned and Tom, Eradicate led the mule along toward the rocks as easily as if there had never been any question about going there.

"For the love of tripe! How did you do it?" asked Tom.

"Bless my peck of oats!" gasped Mr. Damon. "It's a good thing we had Rad along!"

"All mules am alike," said the colored man with a grin. "An dish yeah one ain't much different from mah Boomerang. I guess he's a sorter cousin."

"Come on!" yelled San Pedro. "No time to lose. Make for the rocks!"

Tom, Ned and Mr. Damon sprinted then, and there was need to, for the foremost of the galloping horses was not a hundred feet away. Then came Eradicate, leading the mule that had at last consented to hurry. The natives, with San Pedro, were already at the rocks, waiting for the white hunters with the deadly electric rifles.

"If they stampede our mules we'll be in a pickle!" murmured Ned.

"I guess those ropes will hold unless they bite them through," remarked Tom.

"Yes, they sure hold," cried San Pedro, and indeed one had to shout now to be heard above the thundering of the horses. Now the tethered mules were lost to sight in the multitude of the other steeds all about them.

"Come on, Ned!" yelled Tom, as he sighted his rifle. "Pump it into them! We must turn them, or they may come over this way, and if they do it will be all up with us."

"Shoot to kill?" asked Ned, as he drew back the firing lever of his electric rifle.

"No, only a stunning charge. Those horses are valuable, and there's no use killing them. All we want to do is to turn them aside."

"That's right," agreed Mr. Damon, forgetting in the excitement of the moment to bless himself or anything. "We'll only stun them."

The rifles were quickly adjusted to send out a comparatively weak charge of electricity, and then they were trained on the dense mass of horses, while the three marksmen began working the firing levers.

At first, though horse after horse fell to the ground, stunned, there was no appreciable effect on the thousands in the drove. The poor mules were hidden from sight, though by reason of divisions in the living stream of animals it could still be told where they were tethered, and where the horses separated to go past them. Fortunately the ropes and pegs held.

"Fire faster!" cried Tom. "Shoot across the front of them, and try to turn them to one side."

From the rocks, behind which the natives and our friends crouched, there came a steady stream of electric fire. Horse after horse went down, stunned but not badly hurt, and in a few hours the beasts would feel no ill effects. The firing was redoubled, and then there came a break in the steady stream of horseflesh.

Some hesitated and sought to turn back. Others, behind, pressed them on, and then, as if in fear at the unknown and unseen power that was laying low animal after animal, the great body, of horses, suddenly turned at right angles to their course and broke away. There were now two bodies of the wild runaways, those that had passed the tethered mules, and those that had swung off. The stampede had been broken.

"That's the stuff!" cried Tom, jumping up from behind the rocks, and swinging his hat. "We've turned them."

"And just in time, too," added Ned, as he joined his chum. Then all the others leaped up, and the sight of the human beings completed the scare.

The stampeding animals swung off more than before, so that they were nearly doubling back on their own trail. The others thundered off, and the ground was strewn with unconscious though unharmed animals.

"One mule gone!" cried San Pedro, hastily counting the still tethered animals which were wildly tugging at their ropes.

"Never mind," spoke Tom, "it's the one with some of that damaged bartering stuff I intended for trading. We can afford to lose that. Rad, is your animal all right?"

"He suah am, Massa Tom. Dish yeah mule am almost as sensible as Boomerang, ain't yo'?" and Eradicate patted the big animal he was leading.

"I'll send a man down the trail, and maybe he can pick up the missing one," said San Pedro, and while the other natives were quieting the restless mules, one tall black man hastened in the wake of the retreating horses.

He came back in an hour with the missing animal, that had broken its tether rope and then, after running along with the wild horses had evidently dropped out of the drove. Aside from the loss of a small box, there had been no damage done, and the cavalcade was soon under way once more, leaving the motionless horses to recover from the effects of the electricity.

"Bless my saddle pad!" cried Mr. Damon. "I don't think I want to go through anything like that again."

"Neither do I," agreed Tom. "We are well out of it."

"How much you take for one of them rifles?" asked San Pedro admiringly.

"Not for sale," answered Tom with a laugh.

They camped in a fertile valley that night, and had a much-needed rest. As yet Tom had made no inquiries as to the location of giant land from any of the natives of the villages or towns through which they passed. He knew as soon as he did begin asking questions, his own men would hear of it, and they might be frightened if they knew they were in an expedition the object of which was to capture some of the tall men.

"We'll just go along for a few days more," said Tom, to Ned, "and then, when I do spring my surprise, they'll be so far from home that they won't dare turn back. In a few days I'll begin making inquiries."

They traveled on for three days more, ever heading north, and coming more into the warmer climate. The vegetation began to take on a more tropical look, and finally they reached a region infested with many wild beasts and monkeys, and with patches of dense jungle on either side of the narrow trail. Fruits, tropical flowers and birds abounded.

"I think we're getting there," remarked Tom, on the evening of the third day after his talk with Ned. "San Pedro says there's quite a village about half a day's march ahead, and I may learn something there. I'll know by to-morrow whether we are on the right trail or not."

The natives were getting supper, and Eradicate was busy with a meal for the three white hunters. Mr. Damon had strolled down to the bank of a little stream, and was looking at some small animals like foxes that had come for their evening drink. They seemed quite fearless.

Suddenly something long, round and thick seemed to drop down out of a tree close to the odd gentleman. So swift and noiseless was it that Mr. Damon never noticed it. Then, like a flash something went around him, and he let out a scream of terror.

San Pedro, who was nearest to him, saw and heard. The next instant the black muleteer came rushing toward the camp, crying:

"He is caught in a rope! Mr. Damon is caught in a rope!"

"A rope!" repeated Ned. not understanding.

"Yes, a rope in a tree. Come quickly!"

Tom caught up one of the electric rifles and rushed forward. No sooner had he set eyes on his friend, who was writhing about in the folds of what looked like a big ship cable, then the young inventor cried:

"A rope! Yes, a living rope! That's a big boa constrictor that has Mr. Damon! Get a gun, Ned, and follow me! We must save him before he is crushed to death!"

And the two lads rushed forward while the living rope drew its folds tighter and tighter about the unfortunate man.

A NATIVE BATTLE

"Bless my—!" but that was as far as poor Mr. Damon could get. The breath was fairly squeezed out of him by the folds of the great serpent that had dropped down out of the tree to crush him to death. His head fell forward on his breast, and his arms were pinioned to his sides.

"Quick, Ned!" cried Tom. "We must fire together! Be careful not to hit Mr. Damon!"

"That's right. I'll take the snake on one side, Tom, and you on the other!"

"No! Then we might hit each other. Come on my side. Aim for the head, and throw in the highest charge. We want to kill, not stun!"

"Right!" gasped Ned, as he ran forward at his chum's side.

San Pedro, and the other natives, could do nothing. In the gathering twilight, broken by the light of several campfires, they stood helpless watching the two plucky youths advance to do battle with the serpent. Eradicate had caught up a club, and had dashed forward to do what he could, but Tom motioned him back.

"We can manage," spoke the young inventor.

Then he and Ned crept on with ready rifles. The snake raised its ugly head and hissed, ceasing for a moment to constrict its coils about the unfortunate man.

"Now's our chance—fire!" hoarsely whispered Ned.

It seemed as if the big snake heard, for, raising its head still higher, it fairly glared at Ned and Tom. It was the very chance they wanted, for they could now fire without the danger of hitting Mr. Damon.

"Ready?" asked Tom of his chum in a low voice.

"Ready!" was the equally low answer.

It was necessary to kill the serpent at one shot, as to merely wound it might mean that in its agony it would thresh about, and seriously injure, if not kill, Mr. Damon.

"Fire!" called Tom in a whisper, and he and Ned pressed the triggers of the electric rifles on the same instant.

There was a streak of bluish flame that cut like a sliver through the gathering darkness, and then, as though a blight had fallen upon it, the folds of the great snake relaxed, and Mr. Damon slipped to the ground unconscious. The electric charges had gone fairly through the head of the serpent and it had died instantly.

"Quick! Mr. Damon! We must get him away!" cried Tom. "He may be dead!"

Together the chums sprang forward. The folds of the serpent had scarcely ceased moving before the two youths snatched their friend away.

Dropping their rifles, they lifted him up to bear him to the sleeping tent which had been erected.

"Liver pin!" suddenly ejaculated Mr. Damon. It was what he started to say when the serpent had squeezed the breath out of him, and, on regaining consciousness from his momentary faint, his brain carried out the suggestion it had originally received.

"How are you?" cried Tom, nearly dropping Mr. Damon's legs in his excitement, for he had hold of his feet, while Ned was at the head.

"Are you all right?" gasped Ned.

"Yes—I—I guess so. I—I feel as though I had been put through a clothes wringer though. What happened?"

"A big snake dropped down out of a tree and grabbed you," answered Tom.

"And then what? Put me down, boys, I guess I can walk."

"We shot it," said Ned modestly.

"Bless my insurance policy!" exclaimed the odd gentleman. "I—I hardly know what to say. I'll say it later. You saved my life. Let me see if any bones are broken."

None was, fortunately, and after staggering about a bit Mr. Damon found that he could limp along. But he was very sore and bruised, for, though the snake had squeezed him but for part of a minute, that was long enough. A few seconds more and nearly every bone in his body would have been crushed, for that is the manner in which a constrictor snake kills its prey before devouring it.

"Santa Maria! The dear gentleman is not dead then?" cried San Pedro, as the three approached the tents.

"Bless my name plate, no!" exclaimed Mr. Damon.

"Praise to all the saints! The brave young senors with their wonderful guns saved him. Now you must rest and sleep."

"I feel as if that was all I wanted to do for a month," commented Mr. Damon. His soreness and stiffness increased each minute, and he was glad to get to bed, while the boys and Eradicate rubbed his limbs with liniment. San Pedro knew of a leaf that grew in the jungle which, when bruised, and made into poultices, had the property of drawing out soreness. The next day he found some, and Mr. Damon was wrapped up in bandages until he declared that he looked like an Egyptian mummy.

But the leaf poultices did him good, and in a few days he was able to be about, though he was still a trifle stiff. Of course the cavalcade had to halt in the woods, but they did not mind this as they had traveled well up to this time, and the enforced rest was appreciated.

"Well, do you feel able to move along?" asked Tom of Mr. Damon one morning, about a week later, for they were still in the "snake camp," as they called it in memory of the big serpent.

"Oh, yes, I think so, Tom. Where are you going?"

"I want to push on to the next village. There I hope to get some line on giant land, and really I ought to begin making inquiries soon. San Pedro and the others are wondering what our object is, for we haven't collected any specimens of either flowers or animals, or the snake skin, and he thinks we are a sort of scientific expedition."

"Well, let's travel then. I'm able."

So they started off once more along the jungle and forest trail. As San Pedro had predicted, they came upon evidences of a native village. Scattered huts, made of plastered mud and grass, with thatched roofs of palm leaves, were met with, as they advanced, but none of the places seemed to be inhabited, though rude gardens around them showed that they had been the homes of natives up to recently.

"No one seems to be at home," remarked Tom, when they had gone past perhaps half a dozen of these lonely huts.

"I wonder what can be the matter?" asked Ned. "It looks as if they had gone off in a hurry, too. Maybe there's been some sort of epidemic."

"No, no sickness," said San Pedro. "Natives no sick."

"Bless my liver pill!" cried Mr. Damon, who was almost himself again. "Then what is it?"

"Much fight, maybe."

"Much fight?" repeated Tom.

"Yes, tribes at war. Maybe natives go away so as not be killed."

"By Jove!" exclaimed the young inventor. "That's so. I forgot about what Mr. Preston said. There's a native war going on around here. Well, when we get to the town we can find out more about it, and steer clear of the two armies, if we have to."

But as they went farther on, the evidences of a native war became more pronounced. They passed several huts that had been burned, and the native mule drivers began showing signs of fear.

"I don't like this," murmured Tom to his chum. "It looks bad."

"What can you do?"

"Nothing, I guess. We've got to keep on. No use turning back now. Maybe the two rival forces have annihilated each other, and there aren't any fighters left."

At that moment there arose a cry from some of the natives who, with the mules and their burdens, had pressed on ahead.

"What's that?" exclaimed Tom.

"Something's happened!" gasped Ned.

"Bless my cartridge box!" cried Mr. Damon.

The three went forward and came to a little hill. They looked down into a valley—a valley that had sheltered a native village, but the village was no more. It was but a heap of blackened and fire-scarred ruins, and there were still clouds of smoke arising from the grass huts, showing that the enemy had but recently made their assault on the place.

"Bless my heart!" cried Mr. Damon. "The whole place has been wiped out."

"Not one hut left," added Ned.

"Hark!" cried Tom.

An instant later there arose, off in the woods, a chorus of wild yells. It was followed by the weird sound of tom-toms and the gourd and skin drums of the natives. The shouting noise increased, and the sound of the war drums also.

"Look!" cried Mr. Damon, pointing to a distant hill, and there the boys saw two large bodies of natives rushing toward one another, brandishing spears, clubs and the deadly blow guns.

They were not more than half a mile away, and in plain view of Tom and his party, though the two forces had not yet seen our friends.

"They're going to fight!" cried Tom.

And the next moment the two bodies of natives came together in a mass, the enemies hurling themselves at each other with the eagerness and ferocity of wild beasts. It was a deadly battle.

THE DESERTION

"Say, look at those fellows pitch into one another!" gasped Ned.

"It's fighting at close range all right," commented Mr. Damon.

"If they had rifles they wouldn't be at it hand to hand," spoke Tom. "Maybe it's just as well they haven't, for there won't be so many killed. But say, we'd better be thinking of ourselves. They may make up their quarrel and turn against us any minute."

"No—never—no danger of them being friends—they are rival tribes," said San Pedro. "But either one may attack us—the one that is the victor. It is better that we keep away."

"I guess you're right," agreed Tom. "Lead the way, San Pedro, and we'll get out of sight."

But there was a fascination in watching the distant battle that was hard to resist. It was like looking at a moving picture, for at that distance none of the horrors of war were visible. True, natives went down by scores, and it was not to be doubted but what they were killed or injured, but it seemed more like a big football scrimmage than a fight.

"This is great!" cried Tom. "I like to watch it, but I'm sorry for the poor chaps that get hurt or killed. I hope they're only stunned as we stunned the wild horses."

"I'm afraid it is more serious than that," spoke San Pedro. "These natives are very bloodthirsty. It would not be well for us to incur their anger."

"We won't run any chances," decided Tom. "We'll just travel on. Come on, Ned—Mr. Damon."

As he spoke there was a sudden victorious shout from the scene of the battle. One body of natives was seen to turn and flee, while the others pursued them.

"Now's our time to make tracks!" called Tom. "We'll have to push on to the next village before we can ask where the gi—" he caught himself just in time, for San Pedro was looking curiously at him.

"The senor wishes to find something?" asked the head mule driver with an insinuating smile.

"Yes," broke in Eradicate. "We all is lookin' fo' some monstrous giant orchards flowers."

"Ah, yes, orchids," spoke San Pedro. "Well, there may be some in the jungle ahead of us, but the senors have come the wrong trail for flowers," and he looked curiously at Tom, while, from afar, come the sound of the native battle though the combatants could no longer be seen.

"Never mind," said our hero quickly. "I guess I'll find what I want. Now come on."

They started off, skirting the burned village to get on the trail beyond it. But hardly had they made a detour of the burned huts than one of the native drivers, who was in the rear, came riding up with a shout.

"Now what's the matter?" cried Tom, looking back.

There was a voluble chattering in Spanish between the driver and San Pedro.

"He says the natives that lived in this village have driven their enemies away, and are coming back—after us," translated the head mule driver.

"After us!" gasped Ned.

"Yes," replied San Pedro simply. "They are coming even now. They will fight too, for all their wild nature is aroused."

It needed but a moment's listening to prove this. From the rear came wild yells and the beating of drums and tom-toms.

"Bless my fountain pen!" cried Mr. Damon. "What are we going to do?"

"Stop them if we can," answered Tom coolly. "Ned, you and I and Mr. Damon will form a rear guard. San Pedro, take the mules and the men, and make as good time as you can in advance. We'll take three of the fastest mules, and hold these fellows back with the electric rifles, and when we've done that we'll ride on and catch up to you."

"Very good," said San Pedro, who seemed relieved to know that he did not have to do any of the fighting.

Three of the lighter weight mules, who carried small burdens, were quickly relieved of them, and mounting these steeds in preference to the ones they had been riding since they took the trail, Tom, Ned and Mr. Damon dropped back to try and hold off the enemy.

They had not far to ride nor long to wait. They could hear the fierce yells of the victorious tribesmen as they came back to their ruined village, and though there were doubtless sad hearts among them, they rejoiced that they had defeated their enemies. They knew they could soon rebuild the simple grass huts.

"Small charges, just to stun them!" ordered Tom, and the electric rifles were so adjusted.

"Here's a good place to meet them," suggested Ned, as they came to a narrow turn in the trail. "They can't come against us but a few at a time, and we can pump them full of electricity from here."

"The very thing!" cried Tom, as he dismounted, an example followed by the others. Then, in another moment, they saw the blacks rushing toward them. They were clad in nondescript garments, evidently of their own make, and they carried clubs, spears, bows and arrows and blow guns. There was not a firearm among them, as they passed on after the party of our friends whom they had seen from the battle-hill. They gave wild yells as they saw the young inventor's friends.

"Let 'em have it!" called Tom in a low voice, and the electric rifles sent out their stunning charges. Several natives in the front rank dropped, and there was a cry of fear and wonder from the others. Then, after a moment's hesitation they pressed on again.

"Once more!" cried Tom.

Again the electric rifles spoke, and half a score went down unconscious, but not seriously hurt. In a few hours they would be as well as ever, such was the merciful charge that Tom Swift and the others used in the rifles.

The third time they fired, and this was too much for the natives. They could not battle against an unseen and silent enemy who mowed them down like a field of grain. With wild yells they fled back along the trail they had come.

"I guess that does it!" cried Tom. "We'd better join the others now."

Mounting their mules, they galloped back to where San Pedro and his natives were pressing forward.

"Did you have the honor of defeating them," the head mule driver asked.

"I had the *honor*," answered Tom, with a grim smile.

Then they pressed on, but there was no more danger. That night they camped in a peaceful valley and were not disturbed, and the following day they put a good many miles behind them. On the advice of San Pedro, they avoided the next two villages as they realized that they were in the war zone, and then they headed for a large town where Tom was sure he would hear some news of the giants.

They had to camp twice at night before reaching this town, and when they did get to it they were warmly welcomed, for white explorers had been there years before, and had treated the natives well. Tom distributed many trinkets among the head men and won their good will so that the party was given comfortable huts in which to sleep, and a plentiful supply of provisions.

"Can you arrange for a talk with the chief?" asked Tom of San Pedro that night. "I want to ask him about certain things."

"About where you can find giant flowers?" asked the mule driver with a quick look.

"Yes—er—and other giant things," replied Tom. "I fix," answered San Pedro shortly, but there was a queer look on his face.

A few hours later Tom was summoned to the hut of the chief of the town, and thither he went with Ned, Mr. Damon and San Pedro as interpreter, for the natives spoke a jargon of their own that Tom could not understand.

There were some simple ceremonies to observe, and then Tom found himself facing the chief, with San Pedro by his side. After the greetings, and an exchange of presents, Tom giving him a cheap phonograph with which the chief was wildly delighted, there came the time to talk.

"Ask him where the giant men live?" our hero directed San Pedro, believing that the time had now come to disclose the object of his expedition.

"Giant men, Senor Swift? I thought it was giant plants—orchids—you were after," exclaimed San Pedro.

"Well, I'll take a few giant men if I can find them. Tell him I understand there is a tribe of giants in this country. Ask him if he ever heard of them."

San Pedro hesitated. He looked at Tom, and the young inventor fancied that there was a tinge of white on the swarthy face of the chief mule driver. But San Pedro translated the question.

Its effect on the chief was strange. He half leaped from his seat, and stared at Tom. Then he uttered a cry—a cry of fear—and spoke rapidly.

"What does he say?" asked Tom of San Pedro eagerly, when the chief had ceased speaking.

"He say—he say," began the mule driver and the words seemed to stick in his throat—" he say there ARE giants—many miles to the north. Terrible big men—very cruel—and they are fearful. Once they came here and took some of his people away. He is afraid of them. We are ALL afraid of them," and San Pedro looked around apprehensively, as though he might see one of the giants stalking into the chief's hut at any moment.

"Ask him how many miles north?" asked Tom, hardly able to conceal his delight. The giants had no terrors for him.

"Two weeks journey," translated San Pedro.

"Good!" cried the young inventor. "Then we'll keep right on. Hurrah! I'm on the right track at last, and I'll have a giant for the circus and we may be able to rescue Mr. Poddington!"

"Is the senor in earnest?" asked San Pedro, looking at Tom curiously. "Is he really going among these terrible giants?"

"Yes, but I don't believe they'll be so terrible. They may be very gentle. I'm sure they'll be glad to come with me and join a circus— some of them—and earn a hundred dollars a week. Of course we're going on to giant land!"

"Very good," said San Pedro quietly, and then he followed Tom out of the chief's hut.

"It's all right, Ned old sport, we'll get to giant land after all!" cried Tom to his chum as they reached the hut where they were quartered.

The next morning when Tom got up, and looked for San Pedro and his men, to give orders about the march that day, the mule drivers were nowhere to be seen. Nor were the mules in the places where they had been tethered. Their packs lay in a well ordered heap, but the animals and their drivers were gone.

"This is queer," said Tom, rubbing his eyes to make sure that he saw aright. "I wonder where they are? Rad, look around for them."

The colored man did so, and came back soon, to report that San Pedro and his men had gone in the night. Some of the native villagers told him so by signs, Eradicate said. They had stolen away.

"Gone!" gasped Tom. "Gone where?"

"Bless my railroad ticket!" cried Mr. Damon.

"We're deserted," exclaimed Ned. "They've taken the mules, and left us."

"I guess that's it," admitted Tom ruefully, after a minute's thought. "San Pedro couldn't stand for the giants. He's had a frightful flunk. Well, we're all alone, but we'll go on to giant land anyhow! We can get more mules. A little thing like this can't phase me. Are you with me, Ned—Mr. Damon—Eradicate?"

"Of course we are!" they cried without a moment's hesitation.

"Then we'll go to giant land alone!" exclaimed Tom. "Come on, now, and we'll see if we can arrange for some pack animals."

IN GIANT LAND

When it first became sure that San Pedro and the other natives had deserted—fled in the night, for fear of the giants—there was a reactionary feeling of despondency and gloom among Tom and his three friends. But the boldness and energy of the young inventor, his vigorous words, his determination to proceed at any cost to the unknown land that lay before them—these served as a tonic, and after a few moments, Ned, Mr. Damon, and even Eradicate looked at things with brighter spirits.

"Do you really mean it, Tom?" asked Ned. "Will you go on to giant land?"

"I surely will, if we can find it. Why, we found the city of gold all alone, you and Mr. Damon and I, and I don't see why we can't find this land, especially when all we have to do is to march forward."

"But look at the lot of stuff we have to carry!" went on Ned, waving his hand toward the heap of packs that the mule drivers had left behind.

"Bless my baggage check, yes!" added Mr. Damon. "We can never do it. Tom. We had better leave it here, and try to get back to civilization."

"Never!" cried Tom. "I started off after a giant, and I'm going to get one, if I can induce one of the big men to come back with me. I'm not going to give up when we're so close. We can get more pack animals, I'm sure. I'm going to have a try for it. If I can't speak the language of these natives I can make signs. Come on, Ned, we'll pay a morning visit to the chief."

"I'll come along," added Mr. Damon.

"That's right," replied the young inventor. "Rad, you go stand guard over our stuff. Some of the natives might not be able to withstand temptation. Don't let them touch anything."

"Dat's what I won't, Massa Tom. Good land a massy! ef I sees any ob 'em lay a finger on a pack I'll shoot off my shotgun close to der ears, so I will. Oh, ef I only had Boomerang here, he could carry mos' all ob dis stuff his own se'f."

"You've got a great idea of Boomerang's strength," remarked Tom with a laugh, as he and Ned and Mr. Damon started for the big hut where the chief lived.

"Do you really think San Pedro and the others left because they were afraid of the giants we might meet?" asked Ned.

"I think so," answered his chum.

"Bless my toothpick!" gasped Mr. Damon. "In that case maybe we'd better be on the lookout ourselves."

"Time enough to worry when we get there," answered the young inventor. "From what the circus man said the giants are not particularly cruel. Of course Mr. Preston didn't have much information to go on, but—well, we'll have to wait—that's all. But I'm sure San Pedro and the others were in a blue funk and vamoosed on that account."

"Hey, Massa Tom!" suddenly called Eradicate. "Heah am a letter I found on de baggage," and he ran forward with a missive, rudely scrawled on a scrap of paper.

"It's from San Pedro," remarked Tom after a glance at it, "and it bears out what I said. He writes that he and his men never suspected that we were going after the giants, or they would never have come with us. He says they are very sorry to leave us, as we treated them well, but are afraid to go on. He adds that they have taken enough of our bartering goods to make up their wages, and enough food to carry them to the next village."

"Well," finished Tom. as he folded the paper, "I suppose we can't kick, and, maybe after all, it will be for the best. Now to see if the chief can let us have some mules."

It took some time, by means of signs, to make the chief understand what had happened, but, when Tom had presented him with a little toy that ran by a spring, and opened up a pack of trading goods, which he indicated would be exchanged for mules, or other beasts of burden, the chief grinned in a friendly fashion, and issued certain orders.

Several of his men hurried from the big hut, and a little later, when Tom was showing the chief how to run the toy, there was a sound of confusion outside.

"Bless my battle axe!" cried Mr. Damon. "I hope that's not another war going on."

"It's our new mules!" cried Ned, taking a look. "And some cows and a bony horse or two, Tom. We've drawn a rich lot of pack animals!"

Indeed there was a nondescript collection of beasts of burden. There were one or two good mules, several sorry looking horses, and a number of sleepy-eyed steers. But there were enough of them to carry all the boxes and bales that contained the outfit of our friends.

"It might be worse," commented Tom. "Now if they'll help us pack up we'll travel on."

More sign language was resorted to, and the chief, after another present had been made to him, sent some of his men to help put the packs on the animals. The steers, which Tom did not regard with much favor, proved to be better than the mules, and by noon our friends were all packed up again, and ready to take the trail. The chief gave them a good dinner,—as native dinners go,—and then, after telling them that, though he had never seen the giants it had long been known that they inhabited the country to the north, he waved a friendly good-bye.

"Well, we'll see what luck we'll have by ourselves," remarked Tom, as he mounted a bony mule, an example followed by Ned, Mr. Damon and Eradicate, They had left behind some of their goods, and so did not have so much to carry. Food they had in condensed form and they were getting into the more tropical part of the country where game abounded.

It was not as easy as they had imagined it would be for, with only four to drive so many animals, several of the beasts were continually straying from the trail, and once a big steer, with part of the aeroplane on its back, wandered into a morass and they had to labor hard to get the animal out.

"Well, this is fierce!" exclaimed Tom, at the end of the first day when, tired and weary, bitten by insects, and torn by jungle briars, they made camp that night.

"Going to give up?" asked Ned.

"Not much!"

They felt better after supper, and, tethering the animals securely, they stretched out in their tents, with mosquito canopies over them to keep away the pestering insects.

"I've got a new scheme," announced Tom next morning at breakfast.

"What is it? Going on the rest of the way in the aeroplane?" asked Ned hopefully.

"No, though I believe if I had brought the big airship along I could have used it. But I mean about driving the animals. I'm going to make a long line of them, tying one to the other like the elephants in the circus when they march around, holding each other's tails. Then one of us will ride in front, another in the rear, and one on each side. In that way we'll keep them going and they won't stray off."

"Bless my button hook!" cried Mr. Damon. "That's a good idea, Tom!" It was carried out with much success, and thereafter they traveled better.

But even at the best it was not easy work, and more than once Tom's friends urged him to turn back. But he would not, ever pressing on, with the strange land for his goal. They had long since passed the last of the native villages, and they had to depend on their own efforts for food. Fortunately they did not have any lack of game, and they fared well with what they had with them in the packs.

Occasionally they met little bands of native hunters, and, though usually these men fled at the sight of our friends, yet once they managed to make signs to one, who, informed them as best he could, that giant land was still far ahead of them.

Twice they heard distant sounds of native battles and the weird noise of the wooden drums and the tom-toms. Once, as they climbed up a big hill, they looked down into a valley and saw a great conflict in which there must have been several thousand natives on either side. It was a fierce battle, seen even from afar, and Tom and the others shuddered as they slipped down over the other side of the rise, and out of sight.

"We'd better steer clear of them," was Tom's opinion; and the others agreed with him.

For another week they kept on, the way becoming more and more difficult, and the country more and more wild. They had fairly to cut their way through the jungle at times, and the only paths were animal trails, but they were better than nothing. For the last five days they had not seen a human being, and the loneliness was telling on them.

"I'd be glad to see even a two-headed giant," remarked Tom whimsically one night as they made their camp.

"Yes, and I'd be glad to hear someone talk, even in the sign language," added Ned, with a grin.

They slept well, for they were very tired, and Tom, who shared his tent with Ned, was awakened rather early the next morning by hearing someone moving outside the canvas shelter.

"Is that you, Mr. Damon?" he asked, the odd gentleman having a tent adjoining that of the boys.

There was no answer.

"Rad, are you getting breakfast?" asked the young inventor. "What time is it?"

Still no answer.

"What's the matter?" asked Ned, who had been awakened by Tom's inquiries.

Before our hero had a chance to reply the flap of his tent was pulled back, and a head was thrust in. But such a head! It was enormous! A head covered with a thick growth of tawny hair, and a face almost hidden in a big tawny, bushy beard. Then an arm was thrust in—an arm that terminated in a brawny fist that clasped a great club. There was no mistaking the, object that gazed in on the two youths. It was a gigantic man—a man almost twice the size of any Tom had ever seen. And then our hero knew that he had reached the end of his quest.

"A giant!" gasped Tom. "Ned! Ned, we're in the big men's country, and we didn't know it!"

"I—I guess you're right, Tom!"

The giant started at the sounds of their voices, and then his face breaking into a broad grin, that showed a great mouth filled with white teeth, he called to them in an unknown tongue and in a voice that seemed to fairly shake the frail tent.

IN THE "PALACE" OF THE KING

For a few moments after their first ejaculations neither Tom nor Ned knew what to do. The giant continued to gaze at them, with the same good-natured grin on his face. Possibly he was amused at the small size of the persons in the tent. Then Tom spoke.

"He doesn't look as if he would bite, Ned."

"No, he seems harmless enough. Let's get up, and see what happens. I wonder if there are any more of them? They must have come out on an early hunt, and stumbled upon our camp."

At this moment there arose a cry from Mr. Damon's tent.

"Bless my burglar alarm!" shouted the odd gentleman. "Tom—Ned—am I dreaming? There's a man here as big as a mountain. Tom! Ned!"

"It's all right, Mr. Damon!" called Tom. "We're among the giants all right. They won't hurt you."

"Fo' de good land ob massy!" screamed Eradicate, a second later, and then they knew that he, too, had seen one of the big men. "Fo' de lub ob pork chops! Am dis de Angel Gabriel? Listen to de blowin' ob de trump! Oh, please good Massa Angel Gabriel, I ain't nebber done nuffin! I's jest po' ol' Eradicate Sampson, an' I got a mule Boomerang, and' dat's all I got. Please good Mr. Angel—"

"Dry up, Rad!" yelled Tom. "It's only one of the giants. Come on out of your tent and get breakfast. We're on the borders of giant land, evidently, and they seem as harmless as ordinary men. Get up, everybody."

As Tom spoke he rose from the rubber blanket on which he slept. Ned did the same, and the giant slowly pulled his head out from the tent. Then the two youths went outside. A strange sight met their gaze.

There were about ten natives standing in the camp—veritable giants, big men in every way. The young inventor had once seen a giant in a circus, and, allowing for shoes with very thick soles which the big man wore, his height was a little over seven feet. But these South American giants seemed more than a foot higher than that, none of those who had stumbled upon the camp being less than eight feet.

"And I believe there must be bigger ones in their land, wherever that is," said Tom. Nor were these giants tall and thin, as was the one Tom had seen, but stout, and well proportioned. They were savages, that was evident, but the curious part of it was that they were almost white, and looked much like the pictures of the old Norsemen.

But, best of all, they seemed good-natured, for they were continually laughing or smiling, and though they looked with wonder on the pile of boxes and bales, and on the four travelers, they seemed more bewildered and amused, than vindictive that their country should have been invaded.

Evidently the fears of the natives who had told Tom about the giants had been unfounded.

By this time Mr. Damon and Eradicate had come from their tents, and were gazing with startled eyes at the giants who surrounded them.

"Bless my walking stick!" exclaimed Mr. Damon. "Is it possible?"

"Yes, we've arrived!" cried Tom. "Now to see what happens. I wonder if they'll take us to their village, and I wonder if I can get one of these giants for Mr. Preston's circus?"

"You certainly can't unless he wants to come," declared Ned. "You'd have a hard tussle trying to carry one of these fellows away against his will, Tom."

"I sure would. I'll have to make inducements. Well, I wonder what is best to do?"

The giant who had looked in the tent of Ned and Tom, and who appeared to be the leader of the party, now spoke in his big, booming voice. He seemed to be asking Tom a question, but the young inventor could not understand the language. Tom replied in Spanish, giving a short account of why he and his companions had come to the country, but the giant shook his head. Then Mr. Damon, who knew several languages, tried all of them—but it was of no use.

"We've got to go back to signs," declared Tom, and then, as best he could, he indicated that he and the others had come from afar to seek the giants. He doubted whether he was understood, and he decided to wait until later to try and make them acquainted with the fact that he wanted one of them to come back with him.

The head giant nodded, showing that at least he understood something, and then spoke to his companions. They conversed in their loud voices for some time, and then motioned to the pack animals.

"I guess they want us to come along," said Torn, "but let's have breakfast first. Rad, get things going. Maybe the giants will have some coffee and condensed milk, though they'll have to take about ten cupsful to make them think they've had anything. Make a lot of coffee, Rad."

"But good land a massy, dey'll eat up eberyt'ing we got, Massa Tom," objected the colored man.

"Can't help it, Rad. They're our guests and we've got to be polite," replied the youth. "It isn't every day that we have giants to breakfast."

The big men watched curiously while Rad built a fire, and when the colored man was trying to break a tough stick of wood with the axe, one of the giants picked up the fagot and snapped it in his fingers as easily as though it were a twig, though the stick was as thick as Tom's arm.

"Some strength there," murmured Ned to his chum admiringly.

"Yes, if they took a notion to go on a rampage we'd have trouble. But they seem kind and gentle."

Indeed the giants did, and they liked the coffee which they tasted rather gingerly at first. After their first sip they wanted more, made as sweet as possible, and they laughed and talked among themselves while Eradicate boiled pot after pot.

"Dey suah will eat us out of house an' home, Massa Tom," he wailed.

"Never mind, Rad. They will feed us well when we get to their town."

Then the pack animals were laden with their burdens. This was always a task, but for the giants it was child's play. With one hand they would lift a box or bale that used to tax the combined strength of the four travelers, and soon the steers, horses and mules were ready to proceed. The giants went on ahead, to show the way, the first one, who seemed to be called "Oom," for that was the way his companions addressed him, walked beside Tom, who rode on a mule. In fact the giant had to walk slowly, so as not to get ahead of the animal. Oom tried to talk to Tom, but it was hard work to pick out the signs that meant something, and so neither gained much information.

Tom did gather, however, that the giants were out on an early hunt when they had discovered our friends, and their chief town lay about half a day's journey off in the jungle. The path along which they proceeded, was better than the forest trails, and showed signs of being frequently used.

"It doesn't seem possible that we are really among giants, Tom," spoke Ned, as they rode along. "I hardly believed there were giants."

"There always have been giants," declared the young inventor. "I read about them in an encyclopedia before I started on this trip. Of course there's lots of wild stories about giants, but there have really been some very big men. Take the skeleton in the museum of Trinity College, Dublin. It is eight feet and a half in height, and the living man must have even taller. There was a giant named O'Brien, and his skeleton is in the College of Physicians and Surgeons of England—that one is eight feet two inches high, while there are reliable records to show that, when living, O'Brien was two inches taller than that. In fact, according to the books, there have been a number of giants nine feet high."

"Then these chaps aren't so wonderful," replied Ned.

"Oh, we haven't seen them all yet. We may find some bigger than these fellows, though any one of these would be a prize for a museum. Not a one is less than eight feet, and if we could get one say ten feet—that *would* be a find."

"Rather an awkward one," commented Ned.

It did not seem possible that they were really in giant land, yet such was the fact. Of course the country itself was no different from any other part of the jungle, for merely because big men lived in it did not make the trees or plants any larger.

"I tell you how I account for it," said Tom, as they traveled on. "These men originally belonged to a race of people noted for their great size. Then they must have lived under favorable conditions, had plenty of flesh and bone-forming food, and after several generations they gradually grew larger. You know that by feeding the right kind of food to animals you can make them bigger, while if they get the wrong kind they are runts, or dwarfs."

"Oh, yes; that's a well-known fact," chimed in Mr. Damon.

"Then why not with human beings?" went on Tom. "There's nothing wonderful in this."

"No, but it will be wonderful if we get away with one of these giants," spoke Ned grimly.

Further talk was interrupted by a sudden shouting on the part of the big men. Oom made some rapid motions to Tom, and a little later they emerged from the woods upon a large, grassy plain, on the other side of which could be seen a cluster of big grass and mud huts.

"There is the city of the giants!" cried Tom, and so it proved, a little later, when they got to it.

Now there was nothing remarkable about this city or native town. It was just like any other in the wilder parts of South America or Africa. There was a central place, where, doubtless, the natives gathered on market days, and from this the huts of the inhabitants stretched out in irregular lines, like streets. Off to one side of the "market square," as Tom called it, was a large hut, surrounded by several smaller ones, and from the manner in which it was laid out, and decorated, it was evident that this was the "palace" of the king, or chief ruler.

"Say, look at that fellow!" cried Ned, pointing to a giant who was just entering the "palace" as Tom dubbed the big hut. "He *looks* eleven feet if he's an inch."

"I believe you!" cried Tom. "Say, I wonder how big the king is?"

"I don't know, but he must be a top-notcher. I wonder what will happen to us?"

Oom, who had Tom and his party in charge, led them to the "palace" and it was evident that they were going to be presented to the chief or native king. Back of our friends stretched out their pack train, the beasts carrying the boxes and bales. Surrounding them were nearly all the inhabitants of the giants' town, and when the cavalcade had come to a halt in front of the "palace," Oom raised his voice in a mighty shout. It was taken up by the populace, and then every one of them knelt down.

"I guess His Royal Highness is about to appear," said Tom grimly.

"Yes, maybe we'd better kneel, too," spoke Ned.

"Not much! We're citizens of the United States, and we don't kneel to anybody. I'm going to stand up."

"So am I!" said Mr. Damon.

An instant later the grass mat that formed the front door of the "palace" was drawn aside, and there stood confronting our hero and his friends, the King of Giant Land. And a mighty king was he in size, for he must have been a shade over ten feet tall, while on either side of him was a man nearly as big as himself.

Once more Oom boomed out a mighty shout and, kneeling as the giants were, they took it up, repeating it three times. The king raised his hand as though in blessing upon his people, and then, eyeing Tom and his three friends he beckoned them to approach.

"He wants to see us at close range," whispered the young inventor. "Come on, Ned and Mr. Damon. Trail along, Eradicate."

"Good—good land ob massy!" stammered the colored man. And then the little party advanced into the "palace" of the giant king.

THE RIVAL CIRCUS MAN

Tom Swift gazed fearlessly into the face of the giant ruler who confronted him. The young inventor said later that he had made up his mind that to show no fear was the only way of impressing the big king, for surely no show of strength could have done it. With one hand the giant could have crushed the life from our hero. But evidently he had no such intentions, for after gazing curiously at the four travelers who stood before him, and looking for some time at the honest, black face of Eradicate, the king made a motion for them to sit down. They did, upon grass mats in the big hut that formed the palace of the ruler.

It was not a very elaborate place, but then the king's wants were few and easily satisfied. The place was clean, Tom was glad to note.

The king, who was addressed by his subjects as Kosk, as nearly as Tom could get it, asked some questions of Oom, who seemed to be the chief of the hunters. Thereupon the man who had looked into Tom's and Ned's tent that morning, and who had followed them into the palace, began a recital of how he had found the little travelers. Though Tom and his friends could not understand a word of the language, it was comparatively easy to follow the narrative by the gestures used.

Then the king asked several questions, others of the hunting party were sent for and quizzed, and finally the ruler seemed satisfied, for he rattled off a string of talk in his deep, booming voice.

Truly he was a magnificent specimen of manhood, being as I have said, about ten feet tall, and built in proportion. On either side of him, upon rude benches covered with soft jaguar skins, sat two men, evidently his brothers, for they looked much like the king. One was called Tola and the other Koku, for the ruler addressed them from time to time, and seemed to be asking their advice.

"They're making up their minds what to do with us," murmured Tom. "I only hope they let us stay long enough to learn the language, and then I can make an offer to take one back to the United States with me."

"Jove! Wouldn't it be great if you could get the king!" exclaimed Ned.

"Oh, that's too much, but I'd like one of his brothers. They're each a good nine feet tall, and they must be as strong as horses."

In contrast to some giants of history, whose only claim to notoriety lay in their height, these giants were very powerful. Many giants have flabby muscles, but these of South America were like athletes. Tom realized this when there suddenly entered the audience chamber a youth of about our hero's age, but fully seven feet tall, and very big. He was evidently the king's son, for he wore a jaguar skin, which seemed to be a badge of royalty. He had seemingly entered without permission, to see the curious strangers, for the king spoke quickly to him, and then to Tola, who with a friendly grin on his big face lifted the lad with one hand and deposited him in a room that opened out of the big chamber.

"Did you see that!" cried Ned. "He lifted him as easily as you or I would a cat, and I'll bet that fellow weighed close to four hundred pounds, Tom."

"I should say so! It's great!"

The audience was now at an end, and Tom thought it was about time to make some sort of a present to the king to get on good terms with him. He looked out of the palace hut and saw that their pack animals were close at hand. Nearby was one that had on its back a box containing a phonograph and some records.

Making signs that he wanted to bring in some of his baggage, Tom stepped out of the hut, telling his friends to wait for him. The king and the other giants watched the lad curiously, but did not endeavor to stop him.

"I'm going to give him a little music," went on the young inventor as he adjusted the phonograph, and slipped in a record of a lively dance air. His motions were curiously watched, and when the phonograph started and there was a whirr of the mechanism, some of the giants who had crowded into the king's audience chamber, showed a disposition to run. But a word of command from their ruler stopped them.

Suddenly the music started and, coming forth as it did from the phonograph horn, in the midst of that hut, in which stood the silence-awed giants, it was like a bolt of lightning from the clear sky.

At first the king and all the others seemed struck dumb, and then there arose a mighty shout, and one word was repeated over and over again. It sounded like "Chackalok! Chackalok!" and later Tom learned that it meant wizard, magician or something like that.

Shout after shout rent the air, and was taken up by those outside, for through the open door the strains of music floated. The giants seemed immensely pleased, after their first fright, and suddenly the king, coming down from his throne, stood with his big ear as nearly inside the horn as he could get it.

A great grin spread over his face and then, approaching Tom, he leaned over, touched him once on the forehead, and uttered a word. At this sign of royal favor the other giants at once bowed to Tom.

"Say," cried Ned, "you've got his number all right! You're one of the royal family now, Tom."

"It looks like it. Well, I'm glad of it, for I want to be on friendly terms with His Royal Highness."

Once more the king addressed Tom, and the head hunter, motioning to Tom and his friends, led them out of the palace, and to a large hut not far off. This, he made himself understood by signs, was to be their resting place, and truly it was not a bad home, for it was well made. It had simple furniture in it, low couches covered with skins, stools, and there were several rooms to it.

Calling in authorative tones to his fellow hunters, Tom had them take the packs off the beasts of burdens and soon the boxes, bales and packages were carried into the big hut, which was destined to be the abiding place of our friends for some time. The animals were then led away.

"Well, here we are, safe and sound, with all our possessions about us," commented Tom, when all but Oom had withdrawn. "I guess we'll make out all right in giant land. I wonder what they have to eat? Or perhaps we'd better tackle some of our own grub."

He looked at Oom, who laughed gleefully. Then Tom rubbed his stomach, opened his mouth and pointed to it and said: "We'd like to eat—we're hungry!"

Oom boomed out something in his bass voice, grinned cheerfully, and hurried out. A little later he came back, and following him, a number of giant women. Each one bore a wooden platter or slab of bark which answered for a plate. The plates were covered with broad palm leaves, and when they had been set down on low benches, and the coverings removed, our friends saw they had food in abundance.

There was some boiled lamb, some roasted fowls, some cereal that looked like boiled rice, some sweet potatoes, a number of other things which could only be guessed at, and a big gourd filled with something that smelled like sweet cider.

"Say, this is a feast all right, after what we've been living on!" cried Tom.

Once more Oom laughed joyfully, pointing to the food and to our friends in turn.

"Oh, we'll eat all right!" exclaimed Tom. "Don't worry about that!"

The good-natured giant showed them where they could find rude wooden dishes and table implements, and then he left them alone. It was rather awkward at first, for though the bench or table looked low in comparison to the size of the room, yet it was very high, to allow for the long legs of the giants getting under it.

"If we stay here long enough we can saw off the table legs," said the young inventor. "Now for our first meal in giant land."

They were just helping themselves when there arose a great shouting outside.

"I wonder what's up now?" asked Tom, pausing with upraised fork.

"Maybe the king is coming to see us," suggested Ned.

"I'll look," volunteered Mr. Damon, as he went to the door. Then he called quickly:

"Tom! Ned! Look! It's that minister we met on the ship—Reverend Josiah Blinderpool! How in the world did he ever get here? And how strangely he's dressed!"

Well might Mr. Damon say this, for the supposed clergyman was attired in a big checked suit, a red vest, a tall hat and white canvas shoes. In fact he was almost like some theatrical performer.

The gaudily-dressed man was accompanied by two natives, and all rode mules, and there were three other animals, laden with packs on either side.

"What's his game?" mused Ned.

The answer came quickly and from the man himself. Riding forward toward the king's hut or palace, while the populace of wondering giants followed behind, the man raised his voice in a triumphant announcement.

"Here at last!" he cried. "In giant land! And I'm ahead of Tom Swift for all his tricks. I've got Tom Swift beat a mile."

"Oh, you have!" shouted our hero with a sudden resolve, as he stepped into view. "Well, you've got another guess coming. I'm here ahead of you, and there's standing room only."

"Tom Swift!" gasped the rival circus man. "Tom Swift here in ahead of me!"

HELD CAPTIVES

There was a great commotion among the giants. Men, women and children ran to and fro, and a number of the largest of the big men could be seen hurrying into the palace hut of King Kosk. If the arrival of Tom and his friends had created a surprise it was more than doubled when the circus man, and his small caravan, advanced into the giants' city. His approach had been unheralded because the giants were so taken up with Tom and his party that no one thought to guard the paths leading into the village. And, as a matter of fact, the giants were so isolated, they were so certain of their own strength, and they had been unmolested so many years, that they did not dream of danger.

As for our hero, he stood in the hut gazing at his rival, while Hank Delby, in turn, stared at the young inventor. Then Hank dismounted from his mule and approached Tom's hut.

"Bless my railroad ticket!" exclaimed Mr. Damon. "This is a curious state of affairs! What in the world are we to do, Tom?"

"I don't know, I'm sure. We'll have to wait until we see what HE does. He's been following us all along. He was that fake minister on the boat. It's a wonder we didn't get on to him. I believe he's been trying to learn our secret ever since Mr. Preston warned us about him. Now he's here and he'll probably try to spoil our chances for getting a giant so that he may get one for himself. Perhaps Andy Foger gave him a tip about our plans."

"But can't we stop him?" asked Ned.

"I'm going to try!" exclaimed Tom grimly.

"Here he comes," spoke Mr. Damon quickly. "I wonder what he wants?"

Hank Delby had started toward the big hut that sheltered our friends, while the gathered crowd of curious giants looked on and wondered what the arrival of two white parties so close together could mean.

"Well, what do you want?" asked Tom, when, his rival had come within speaking distance.

"There's no use beating about the bush with you, Tom Swift," was the frank answer. "I may as well out with it. I came after a giant, and I'm going to get one for Mr. Waydell."

"Then you took advantage of our trail, and followed us?" asked the young inventor.

"Oh, you can put it that way if you like," replied Delby calmly. "I HAVE followed you, and a hard time I've had of it. I tried to do it quietly, but you got on to my tricks. However it doesn't matter. I'm here now, and I'm going to beat you out if I can."

"I remember now!" exclaimed Ned whispering in Tom's ear, "he was disguised as one of the mule drivers and you fired him because he had a revolver. Don't you remember, Tom?"

"That's right!" exclaimed the young inventor as he noted the face and form of Delby more closely. Then our hero added: "You played a low-down trick, Mr. Delby, and it won't do you any good. I caught you trying to sneak along in my company and I'll catch you again. I'm here first, and I've got the best right to try and get a giant for Mr. Preston, and if you had any idea of fair play—"

"All's fair in this business, Tom Swift," was the quick answer. "I'm going to do my best to beat you, and I expect you to do your best to beat me. I can't speak any fairer than that. It's war between us, from now on, and you might as well know it. One thing I will promise you, though, if there's any danger of you or your party getting hurt by these big men I'll fight on your side. But I guess they are too gentle to fight."

"We can look after ourselves," declared Tom. "And since it's to be war between us look out for yourself."

"Don't worry!" exclaimed Tom's rival with a laugh. "I've gone through a lot to get here, and I'm not going to give up without a struggle. I guess—"

But he did not finish his sentence for at that moment Oom, the big hunting giant, came up behind him, tapped him on the shoulder, and pointed to the king's hut, motioning to indicate that Mr. Delby was wanted there.

"Very good," said the circus agent in what he tried to make sound like a jolly voice, "I'm to call on his majesty; am I? Here's where I beat you to it, Tom Swift."

Tom did not answer, but there was a worried look on his face, as he turned to join his friends in the big hut. And, as he looked from a window, and saw Delby being led into the presence of Kosk, Tom could hear the strains of the big phonograph he had presented to the king.

"I guess his royal highness will remain friends with us," said Ned with a smile, as he heard the music. "He can see what a lot of presents and other things we have, and as for that Delby, he doesn't seem to have much of anything."

"Oh, I haven't shown half the things I have as yet," spoke Tom. "But I don't like this, just the same. Those giants may turn from us, and favor him on the slightest pretense. I guess we've got our work cut out for us."

"Then let's plan some way to beat him," suggested Mr. Damon. "Look over your goods, Tom, and make the king a present that will bind his friendship to us."

"I believe I will," decided the young inventor and then he and Ned began overhauling the boxes and bales, while a crowd of curious giants stood without their hut, and another throng surrounded the palace of the giant king.

"There goes Delby out to get something from his baggage," announced Ned, looking from the window. Tom saw his rival taking something from one of the packs slung across the back of a mule. Soon the circus agent hurried back into the king's hut, and a moment later there was heard the strains of a banjo being picked by an unpracticed hand. It was succeeded by a rattling tune played in good style.

"Bless my fiddlestick!" exclaimed Mr. Damon, "Does your phonograph have a banjo record, Tom?"

"No." was the somewhat hesitating answer of the young inventor. "Delby who can play a banjo himself must have given Kosk one for a present, and, like a child, the king is amused by the latest novelty. So far he has scored one on us," he added, as once more they heard the unmelodious strains of the banjo slowly picked. "The king is evidently learning to play the instrument, and he'd rather have that than a phonograph, which only winds up."

"But haven't you some other things you can give the king to off-set the banjo?" asked Mr. Damon.

"Plenty of them," replied Tom. "But if I give him—say a toy steam engine, for I have one among our things—what is to prevent Delby giving him some other novelty that will take his attention? In that way we'll sea-saw back and forth, and I guess Delby has had more experience in this business than I have. It's going to be a question which of us gets a giant."

"Bless my reserved seat ticket!" exclaimed Mr. Damon. "I never heard of such a thing! But, Tom, I'm sure we'll win out."

"Get something startling to give the king," advised Ned, and Tom began opening one of the boxes that had been transported with such labor from the coast.

"Delby had much better luck with his mule drivers than we did Tom," remarked Ned as he saw the two natives standing by the pack animals of the rival circus man. "They evidently didn't get scared off by the giants."

"No, but probably he didn't tell them where they were headed for. Though, as a matter of fact, I don't believe any one has anything to fear from these big men. All they ask is to be let alone. They're not at all warlike, and I don't believe they'd attack the other natives. But probably their size makes them feared, and when our drivers heard the word 'giant' they simply wilted."

"Guess you're right. But come on, Tom. If we're going to make the king a present that will open his eyes, and get him on our side instead of Delby's, we'd better be getting at it."

"I will. This is what I'm going to give him," and Tom brought out from a box a small toy circus, with many performing animals and acrobats, the whole being worked by a small steam engine that burned alcohol for fuel. A little water put in the boiler of the toy engine, a lighting of the alcohol wick and there would be a toy that even a youngster of the United States might be proud to own.

"Mah land a massy!" exclaimed Eradicate as Tom got the apparatus ready to work. "Dat shore will please him!"

"It ought to," replied the young inventor. "Come on, now I'm ready."

Delby had not yet come from the king's hut, and as Tom and his friends, bearing the new toy, were about to leave the structure that had been set aside for their use, they saw a crowd of the giant men approaching. Each of the big men carried a club and a spear.

"Bless my eye glasses!" gasped Mr. Damon. "Something is wrong. What can it be?"

He had his answer a moment later. With a firm but gentle motion the chief giant shoved our four friends back into the hut, and then pulled the grass mat over the opening. Then, as Tom and the others could see by looking from a crack, he and several others took their position in front, while other giants went to the various windows, stationing themselves outside like sentries around a guard house.

"Bless my—" began Mr. Damon, but words failed him.

"We're prisoners!" gasped Ned.

"It looks like it," admitted Tom grimly. "Evidently Delby has carried out his threat and set the king against us. We are to be held captives here, and he can do as he pleases. Oh, why didn't I think sooner."

TOM'S MYSTERIOUS BOX

The young inventor walked slowly back to the middle of the hut—a prison now it was—and sat down on a bench. The others followed his example, and the elaborate toy, with which they had hoped to win the king's favor, was laid aside. For a moment there was silence in the structure—a silence broken only by the pacing up and down of the giant guards outside. Then Eradicate spoke.

"Massa Tom," began the aged negro, "can't we git away from heah?"

"It doesn't seem so, Rad."

"Can't we shoot some of dem giants wif de 'lectric guns, an' carry a couple ob 'em off after we stun 'em like?"

"No, Rad; I'm afraid violent measures won't do, though now that you speak of the guns I think that we had better get them ready."

"You're not going to shoot any of them, are you, Tom?" asked Mr. Damon quickly.

"No, but if they continue to turn against us as easily as they have, there is no telling what may happen. If they attack us we will have to defend ourselves. But I think they are too gentle for that, unless they are unduly aroused by what misstatements Hank Delby may make against us."

"Misstatements?" inquired Ned.

"Yes. I don't doubt but what he told the king a lot of stuff that isn't true, to cause his majesty to make us captives here. Probably he said we came to destroy the giant city with magic, or something like that, and he represented himself as a simple traveler. He's used to that sort of business, for he has often tried to get ahead of Mr. Preston in securing freaks or valuable animals for the circus. He wants to make it look bad for us, and good for himself. So far he has succeeded. But I've got a plan."

"What is it?" asked Mr. Damon.

"I'll tell you when I've got it more worked out. The thing to do now is to get in shape to stand off the giants if they should attack us. This hut is pretty strong, and we can risk a siege in here. Let's arrange the boxes and bales into a sort of breastwork, and then we'll take the electric rifles inside."

This was soon done, and, though there was considerable noise attending the moving about of the boxes and bales, the giant guards did not seem at all alarmed. They did not even take the trouble to stop the work, though they looked in the windows. In a short time there was a sort of hollow square formed in the middle of the big main room, and inside of this our friends could give battle.

"And now for my plan of teaching these giants a lesson," said Tom, when this work was finished. "Ned, help me open this box," and he indicated one with his initials on in red letters.

"That's the same one you saved from the fire in the ship," commented Ned.

"Yes, and I can't put it to just exactly the use I intended, as the situation has changed—for the worse I may say. But this box will answer a good purpose," and Tom and Ned proceeded to open the mysterious case which the young inventor had transported with such care.

"Bless my cannon cracker!" exclaimed Mr. Damon who watched them. "You're as careful of that as if it contained dynamite."

"It does contain something like that," answered Tom. "It has some blasting powder in, and I was going to use it to show the giants how little their strength would prevail against the power which the white man could secure from some harmless looking powder. There are also a lot of fireworks in the box, and I intend to use them to scare these big men. That's why I was so afraid when I heard that there was a blaze near my box. I was worried for fear the ship would be blown up. But I can't use the blasting powder—at least not now. But we'll give these giants an idea of what Fourth of July looks like. Come on, Ned, we'll take a look and see from which window it will be safest to set off the rockets and other things, as I don't want to set fire to any of the grass huts."

Eradicate and Mr. Damon looked on wonderingly while Tom and his chum got out the packages of fireworks which had been kept safe and dry. As for the giant guards, if they saw through the windows what was going on, they made no effort to stop Tom.

Tom had brought along a good collection of sky rockets, aerial bombs, Roman candles and similar things, together with the blasting powder. The latter was put in a safe place in a side room, and then, with some boards, the young inventor and his chum proceeded to make a sort of firing stand. One big window opened out toward a vacant stretch of woods into which it would not be dangerous to aim the fireworks.

Building the stand took some time, and they knocked off to make a meal from the food that had been brought, and which they had been about to eat when the circus man had appeared. The food was good, and it made them feel better.

"I hope they won't forget us to-morrow," observed Tom, for there was enough of the first meal left for supper. "But if they do we have some food of our own."

"Oh, I don't think they mean to starve us," remarked Ned. "I think they are just acting on suggestions from that circus man."

"Perhaps," agreed Tom. "Well, they may sing another tune when we get through with them."

As night approached the giant guards about the hut were changed, and again the women came, bearing platters of food. There was plenty of it, showing that the king, however fickle his friendship might be, did not intend to starve his captives. Tom and his friends had not seen Delby come out of the royal palace, and they concluded that he was still with his giant majesty.

"Is it dark enough now, Tom?" asked Ned of his chum, as they sat about the rude wooden platform which they had made to hold the fireworks. "Shall we set them off?"

"Pretty soon now. Wait until it gets a little darker, and the effect will be better." The room was dimly lighted by a small portable electric lamp, one of several Tom had brought along in his mysterious box. The lamps were operated by miniature but powerful dry batteries. The giant guards were still outside, but they showed no disposition to interfere with our friends.

"There's something going on at the palace," reported Mr. Damon, who was watching the big hut. "There are a lot of giants around it with torches."

"Maybe they're going to escort Delby to a hut with the same honors they paid us," suggested Tom. "If they do, we'll set off the fireworks as he comes out and maybe they'll think he is afflicted with bad magic, and they'll give us our freedom."

"Good idea!" cried Ned. "Say, that's what they're going to do," he added a moment later as, in the glare of a number of torches, there could be seen issuing from the king's palace, the two big giants, evidently his brothers. Between them was the figure of the circus man, looking like a dwarf. He was not so far away but what the smile of triumph on his face could be seen as he glanced in the direction of the darkened hut where Tom and his friends were captives.

"Now's our chance!" cried the young inventor. "Set 'em off, Ned. You help, Mr. Damon. The more noise and fuss we make at once, the more impressive it will be. Set off everything in sight!"

There was a flicker of matches as they were applied to the fuses, and then a splutter of sparks. An instant later it seemed as if the whole heavens had been lighted up.

Sky rockets shot screaming toward the zenith, aerial bombs went whirling slantingly upward amid a shower of sparks, then to burst with deafening reports, sending out string after string of colored lights. Red and green fire gleamed, and the hot balls from Roman candles burst forth. There was a whizz, a rush and a roar. Blinding flashes and startling reports followed each other as Tom and his friends set off the fireworks. It was like the Independence Day celebration of some little country village, and to the simple giants it must have seemed as if a volcano had suddenly gone into action.

For several minutes the din and racket, the glare and explosions, kept up, pouring out of the big window of the hut. And then, as the last of the display was shot off, and darkness seemed to settle down blacker than ever over the giant village, there arose howls of fear and terror from the big men and their women and children. They cried aloud in their thunderous voices, and there was fear in every cry.

WEAK GIANTS

A great silence followed the setting off of the fireworks—silence and darkness—and even the circus man ceased to shout. He wanted to see what the effect would be. So did Tom and the others. When their eyes had become used to the gloom again, after the glare of the rockets and bombs, the young inventor said:

"Look out of the windows, Ned, and see if our guards have run away."

Ned did as requested, but for a few seconds he could make out nothing. Then he cried out:

"They've gone, but they're coming back again, and there are twice as many. I guess they don't want us to escape, Tom, for fear we may do a lot of damage."

"Bless my hitching post!" cried Mr. Damon. "The guards doubled? We ARE in a predicament, Tom."

"Yes, I'm afraid so. The fireworks didn't just have the effect I expected. I thought they'd be glad to let us go, fearing that we could work magic, and might turn it on them. Most of the natives are deadly afraid of magic, the evil eye, witch doctors, and stuff like that. But evidently we've impressed the giants in the wrong way. If we could only speak their language now, we could explain that unless they let us go we might destroy their village, though of course we wouldn't do anything of the kind. If we could only speak their language but we can't."

"Do you suppose they understood what Delby said?" asked Ned.

"Not a bit of it! He was just desperate when he yelled out that way. He saw that we had an advantage on him—or at least I thought we did, but I guess we didn't," and Tom gazed out of the windows in front of each of which stood two of the largest giants. By means of the torches it could be seen that the circus man was being taken to another hut, some distance away from the royal one. Then, after an awed silence, there broke out a confused talking and shouting among the giant population, that was drawn up in a circle a respectful distance from the hut where the captives were confined. Doubtless they were discussing what had taken place, hoping and yet fearing, that there might be more fireworks.

"Well, we might as well go to bed," declared Tom at length. "We can't do any more to-night, and I'm dead tired. In the morning we can talk over new plans. My box of tricks isn't exhausted yet."

In spite of their strange captivity our friends slept well, and they did not awaken once during the night, for they had worked hard that day, and were almost exhausted. In the morning they looked out and saw guards still about the hut.

"Now for a good breakfast, and another try!" exclaimed Tom, as he washed in a big earthen jar of water that had been provided. Freshened by the cool liquid, they were made hungry for the meal which was brought to them a little later. They noticed that the women cooks looked at them with fear in their eyes, and did not linger as they had done before. Instead they set down the trays of food and hurried away.

"They're getting to be afraid of us," declared Tom. "If we could only talk their language—"

"By Jove!" suddenly interrupted Ned. "I've just thought of something. Jake Poddington you know—the agent for Mr. Preston who so mysteriously disappeared."

"Well, what about him?" asked Tom. "Did you see him?"

"No, but he may be here—a captive like ourselves. If he is he's been here long enough to have learned the language of the giants, and if he could translate for us, we wouldn't have any trouble. Why didn't we think of it before? If we could only find Mr. Poddington!"

"Yes, IF we only could," put in Tom. "But it's a slim chance. I declare I've forgotten about him in the last few days, so many things have happened. But what makes you think he is here, Ned?"

"Why he started for giant land, you'll remember, and he may have reached here. Oh, if we could only find him, and save him and save ourselves!"

"It would be great!" admitted Tom. "But I'm afraid we can't do it. There's a chance, though, that Mr. Poddington may be here, or may have been here. If we could only get out and make some explorations or some inquiries. It's tough to be cooped up here like chickens."

Tom looked from the window, vainly hoping that the guards might have been withdrawn. The giants were still before the windows and doors.

For a week this captivity was kept up, and in that time Tom and his friends had occasional glimpses of Hank Delby going to and from the king's hut. His majesty himself was not seen, but there appeared to be considerable activity in the giant village.

From their prison-hut the captives could see the native market held in the big open space, and giants from surrounding towns and the open country came in to trade. There were also curious about the white captives, and there was a constant throng around the big hut, peering in. So also there was about the hut where the circus man had his headquarters. Delby seemed to be free to come and go as he choose.

"I guess he's laying his plans to take a giant or two away with him," remarked Tom one day. "I wonder what will become of us, when he does go?"

It was a momentous question, and no one could answer it. Tom was doing some hard thinking those days. Two weeks passed and there was no change. Our friends were still captives in giant land. They had tried, by signs, to induce their guards to take some message to the king, but the giants refused with shakes of their big heads.

Yet the adventurers could not complain of bad treatment. They were well fed, and the guards seemed good natured, laughing among themselves, and smiling whenever they saw any of the captives. But let Tom or some of the others, step across the threshold of the door, and they were kindly, but firmly, shoved back.

"It's of no use!" exclaimed Tom in despair one day, after a bold attempt to walk out. "We've got to do something. If we can't get word to the king we've got to plan some way to gain the friendship, or work on the fear of the guards. We have about the same crowd every time. If we can scare them they may keep far enough off so we can have a chance to escape."

"Escape! That's the thing!" cried Mr. Damon. "Why can't we put the airship together in this hut, Tom, and fly away in it?"

"We can, when the right time comes—if it ever does—but first we've got to work on the guards. Let me see what I can do? Ha! I have it. Ned, come here, I want your help. I'm going to show these giants that, with all their strength, I can make each of them as weak as a baby, and, at the same time prove that they can't lift even a light weight."

"How you going to do it?" asked Mr. Damon.

"I'll soon show you. Come on, Ned."

Tom and his chum were busy for several days among the various boxes and bales that formed the baggage. They rigged up two pieces of apparatus which I will describe in due time. They also opened several boxes of trinkets and trading goods, which had been brought along for barter. These they distributed among the guards, and, though the giants were immensely pleased, they did not get friendly enough to walk off and leave our friends free to do as they pleased.

"Well, I guess we're ready for the lesson now," remarked Tom one afternoon, when they had been held captives for about three weeks. "If they won't respond to gentle treatment we'll try some other kind of persuasion."

The guards had become so friendly of late that some of them often spent part of the day inside the hut, looking at the curious things Tom and his party had brought with them. This was just what the young inventor wanted, as he was now ready to give them a second lesson in white man's magic.

Tom and Ned had learned a few words of the giant's language, which was quite simple, though it sounded hard, and one day, after he had shown them simple toys, the young inventor brought forth a simple-looking box, with two shining handles.

"Here is a little thing," explained Tom, partly by words, and partly by using signs, "a simple little thing which, if one of you will but take hold of, you cannot let go of again until I move my finger. Do you believe that a small white man like myself can make this little thing stronger than a giant?" he asked.

One of the biggest of the guards shook his head.

"Try," invited Tom. "Take hold of the handles. At first you will be able to let go easily. But, when I shall move my finger though but a little, you will be held fast. Then, another movement, and you will be loose again. Can I do it?"

Once more the giant shook his head.

"Try," urged Tom, and he put the two shining handles into the big palms of the giant. The native grinned and some of his companions laughed. Then to show how easy it was he let go. He took hold again.

"Now!" cried Tom, and he moved his finger.

Instantly the giant leaped up into the air. He uttered a howl that seemed to shake the very roof of the hut, and his arms were as rigid as poles. They were drawn up in knots, and though he tried with all his great might, he could not loose his fingers from the shiny handles. He howled in terror, and his companions murmured in amazement.

"It is as I told you!" exclaimed Tom. "Is it enough?"

"Loose me! Loose me! Loose me from the terrible magic!" cried the giant, and, with a movement of his finger, Tom switched off the current from the electric battery. Instantly the giant's arms dropped to his side, his hands relaxed and the handles dropped clattering to the floor.

With a look of fear, and a howl of anguish, the big guard fled, but to the surprise and gratification of Tom and his friends the others seemed only amused, and they nodded in a friendly fashion to the captives. They all pressed forward to try the battery.

One and all endeavored to loose their hands after Tom, by a movement of his forefinger, had turned the switch of the battery, and one and all of the giant guards were unable to stir, as the electricity gripped their muscles. They were evidently awed.

"This is working better than the fireworks did," murmured Tom. "Now if I can only keep up the good work, and get ahead of Delby I'll be all right. Now for the other test, Ned."

Ned brought from a box what looked to be a small iron bar, with a large handle on the top. The bottom was ground very smooth.

"This is very small and light," explained Tom, partly by signs, and partly by words. "I can easily lift it by one finger, and to a giant it is but a feather's weight."

He let the giants handle it, and of course they could feel scarcely any weight at all, for it tipped the scales at only a pound. But it was shortly to be much heavier.

"See," went on the young inventor. "I place the weight on the floor, and lift it easily. Can you do it?"

The giants laughed at such a simple trick. Tom set the iron bar down and raised it several times. So did several of the giants.

"Now for the test!" cried Tom with a dramatic gesture. "I shall put my magic upon you, and you shall all become as weak as babies. You cannot lift the bar of iron!"

As he spoke he made a signal to Ned, who stood in a distant corner of the room. Then Tom carefully placed the weight on a sheet of white paper on a certain spot on the floor of the hut and motioned to the largest giant to pick up the iron bar.

With a laugh of contempt and confidence, the big man stooped over and grasped the handle. But he did not arise. Instead, the muscles of his naked arm swelled out in great bunches.

"See, you are as a little babe!" taunted Tom. "Another may try!"

Another did, and another and another, until it came the turn of the mightiest giant of all the guard that day. With a sudden wrench he sought to lift the bar. He tugged and strained. He bent his back and his legs; his shoulders heaved with the terrific effort he made—but the bar still held to the floor of the hut as though a part of the big beams themselves.

"Now!" cried Tom. "I shall show you how a white man's magic makes him stronger than the biggest giant."

Once more he made a hidden sign to Ned, and then, stooping over, Tom crooked his little finger in the handle of the iron bar and lifted it as easily as if it was a feather.

THE LONE CAPTIVE

The murmurs of astonishment that greeted Tom's seemingly marvelous feat of strength was even greater than that which had marked his trick with the electric battery. The giants stared at him as though they feared the next moment he might suddenly turn upon them and hurl them about like ten-pins.

"You see, it is easy when one knows the white man's magic," spoke Tom, making many gestures to help along. "Go tell your king that it is not well that he keeps us prisoners here, for if he does not soon let us go the magic may break loose and destroy his palace!"

There was a gasp of dismay from the giants at this bold talk.

"Better go easy, Tom," counseled Ned.

"I'm tired of going easy," replied the young inventor. "Something has got to happen pretty soon, or it will be all up with us. I'm getting weary of being cooped up here. Not that the king doesn't treat us well, but I don't want to be a prisoner. I want to get out and see if we can't arrange to take a couple of these giants back for Mr. Preston. That Delby sneak has things all his own way."

And this was so, for the circus man had poisoned the king's mind against Tom and his friends, representing (as our hero learned later) that the first arrivals in giant land were dangerous people, and not to be trusted. On his own part, Hank Delby intimated that he would always be a friend to the king, would teach him many of the white man's secrets, and would make him powerful. Thus the circus man was making plans for his own ends, and he was scheming to get a couple of giants for himself, who he intended to hurry away, leaving Tom and his friends to escape as best they could.

And Delby had brought with him some novelties in the way of toys and machinery that seemed greatly to take the fancy of the king. Tom realized this when he saw his rival free to come and go, and one reason why our hero did the experiments just related was so that the king might hear of them, and wonder.

"Go tell the king that, strong as he is, I am stronger," went on Tom boldly to the giant guards. "I am not afraid of him."

"Bless my war club, Tom, aren't you a little rash to talk that way?" asked Mr. Damon.

"No. As I said, I want things to happen. If I can only get the king curious enough to come here I can show him things to open his eyes. I'll work the miniature circus, and explain that some of his subjects can take part in a real one if they will come with us. I want to beat this Delby at his own game."

"That's the stuff!" cried Ned. "Stick to it, Tom. I'll help you, and we'll get a giant or two yet. And maybe we can get some news of poor Jake Poddington."

"I intend to make inquiries about him, now that these guards are a little more friendly," said Tom. "It may be that he is a prisoner in this very village."

The giant guards, now that they had gotten over their fright at their own inability to raise the bar while Tom had lifted it with one finger, again crowded around, asking that the trick be repeated. Tom did it, with the same result.

None of the giants could move the iron, yet Tom had no difficulty in doing so. Of course my readers have already guessed how the trick was done. It was worked by a strong magnet, hidden in the floor. At a signal from Tom, Ned would switch on the current. The iron would be held fast and immovable, but when Tom himself went to raise it Ned would cut off the electricity and the bar was lifted as easily as an ordinary piece of iron. But simple as the trick was, it impressed the giants. Then Tom did some other stunts for them, simple experiments in physics, that every High School lad has done in class.

"I want to get these guards friendly with me," he explained. "In time the news will reach the king and he'll be so curious that he'll come here and then—well, we'll see what will happen."

But this did not take place as soon as Tom desired. In fact, the giants were very slow to act. The guards did get quite friendly, and every day they wanted the same two first tricks performed over again. Tom did them many times, wondering when the king would come.

Then he played a bold game, and made open inquiries about a white man, one like the king's captives, who might have come to giant land about a year previous.

"Is there a lone white captive here?" asked Tom.

The giant guard to whom he directed his question gave a start, for Tom could now speak the language fairly well, and, after the first indication of surprise, the guard muttered something to his companions. There was a startled ejaculation, a curious glance at the captives, and then—silence. The guards filed silently away, and, a little later, could be seen going in the king's big hut.

"By Jove, Tom!" cried Ned. "You touched 'em that time. There's something up, as sure as you're born!"

"I believe so myself," agreed the young inventor. "And now to throw a real scare into these giants," he added, as he went to a distant room of the hut where he had hidden some of the things he had taken from his "box of tricks," as Ned dubbed it.

"Bless my necktie!" cried Mr. Damon. "What's up now, Tom."

"I'm going to show these giants that they'd better make friends with us soon, or we may blow their whole town sky-high!" cried Tom. "I'm going to use some of the blasting powder—just a pinch, so to speak—and knock an empty hut into slivers. I think that will impress these fellows. If I can only—"

"Look, Tom!" suddenly cried Ned. "The king's two brothers are coming here. Something's up. He's sent some of the family to interview us. Get ready to receive them."

"Couldn't be better!" cried the young inventor. "I've been waiting for this. Now I'll give them a surprise party."

The two big brothers of the king, for such Tom and his friends had recently learned was the relationship the giants on either side of the "throne" bore to the ruler, were indeed headed toward the hut of the captives. They came alone, in their royal garments of jaguar skins, and, standing about the palace hut, could be seen the giant guards who had doubtless carried the news of the question Tom had asked.

"Come on, Ned, we've got to get busy!" exclaimed Tom. "Connect the electric battery, and get that magnet in shape. I'm going to make a fuse for this blasting powder bomb, and if I can get those royal brothers to plant it for me, there'll be some high jinks soon."

Tom busied himself in making an improvised bomb, while Ned attended to the electrical attachments, and Mr. Damon and Eradicate acted as general assistants.

The two giant brothers entered the hut and greeted Tom and the others calmly. Then they explained that the king had sent them to investigate certain stories told by the guard.

"I'll show you!" exclaimed Tom, and he induced them to take hold of the handles of the battery. The current was turned on full strength, and from the manner in which the royal brothers writhed and howled Tom judged that the experiment was a success.

"With all your strength you can not let go until I move my finger," the young inventor explained, and it was so. Even the skeptical giants agreed on that.

"Now I shall show you that I am stronger than you!" exclaimed Tom, and though the giants smiled increduously so it was, for the magnet trick worked as well as before. There were murmurs of surprise from the two immense brothers, and they talked rapidly together.

"I will now show you that I can call the lightning from the sky to do my bidding," went on Tom. "Is that possible to any of you giants?"

"Never! Never! No man can do it!" cried Tola and Koku together.

"Then watch me!" invited Tom. "Is there an empty hut near here?" he asked. "One that it will do no harm to destroy?"

Tola pointed to one visible from the window of the prison of our friends.

"Then take this little ball, with the string attached to it, and place it in the hut," went on Tom. "Then flee for your lives, for standing from here, I shall call the lightning down, and you shall see the hut destroyed."

"Why don't you ask them something about Jake Poddington?" asked Ned.

"Time enough for that after I've shown them what a little powder will do, when I attach electric wires to it and press a button," replied Tom. "I've got that bomb fixed so it will go off by an electric fuse. If they'll only put it in the hut for me. I'd do it myself, only they won't let me go out."

The brothers conferred for a moment and then, seeming to arrive at a decision, Koku, who was slightly the larger, took the bomb, looked curiously at it, and walked with it toward the empty hut, the electric wire being reeled out behind him by Tom.

The bomb was left inside the frail structure, the two brothers hurried away, and, standing at a safe distance from the hut of the captives, as well as the one that Tom had promised to destroy by lightning, they waved their hands to show that they were ready.

"Bless my admission ticket!" exclaimed Mr. Damon. "You've got quite an audience, Tom."

And so he had, for there was a crowd in the market square, another throng about the king's palace, while all about, hidden behind trees or huts, was nearly the whole population of the giant town.

"That's what I want," said the young inventor. "It will be all the more impressive."

"And there's the king himself!" exclaimed Ned. "He's standing in the door of his royal hut."

"Better yet!" cried Tom. "Are those wires all connected, Ned?"

"Yes," answered his chum, after a quick inspection.

"Then here she goes!" cried Tom, as he pressed the button.

Instantly the hut, in which the bomb had been placed, arose in the air. The roof was lifted off, the sides spread out and there was a great flash of fire and a puff of smoke.

Then as the smoke cleared away Ned cried out:

"Look, Tom! Look! You've blown a hole in the hut next to the one you destroyed!"

"Yes, and bless my check book!" exclaimed Mr. Damon, "some one is running out of it. A white man, Tom! A white man!"

"It's Poddington! Poor Jake Poddington. We've found him at last! This way, Mr. Poddington! This way! Mr. Preston sent us to rescue you!" cried Tom.

A ROYAL CONSPIRACY

Howls of terror, cries of anger, and a rushing to and fro on the part of the giants, followed the latest trick of Tom Swift to impress them with his power. But to all this the young inventor and his friends paid no attention. Their eyes were fixed on the ragged figure of the white man who was rushing toward their hut as fast as his legs, manacled as they were, would let him.

"Come on! Come on!" cried Tom.

"Look out!" yelled Ned. "Some of the giants are after him, Tom!"

Several of the big men, after their first fright, had recovered sufficiently to pursue the captive so strangely released by the explosion.

"Hand me an electric rifle, Ned!" cried Tom,

"Bless my shoe laces!" cried Mr. Damon. "You're not going to kill any of the giants; are you, Tom?"

"Well, I'm not going to let them capture Jake Poddington again," was the quick answer, "but I guess if I stun a few of them with the electric bullets that will answer."

Poddington (for later the white captive did prove to be the missing circus man) ran on, and close behind him came two of the giants, taking long strides. Tom aimed his electric rifle at the foremost and pulled the trigger. There was no sound, but the big man crumpled up and fell, rolling over and over. With a yell of rage his companion pressed on, but a moment later, he, too, went down, and then the others, who had started in pursuit of their recent captive, turned back.

"I thought that would fix 'em," murmured Tom gleefully.

In another five seconds Poddington was inside the hut, gasping from his run. He was very thin and pale, and the sudden exertion had been too much for him.

"Water—water!" he gasped, and Mr. Damon gave him some. He sank on one of the skin-covered benches, and his half-exhausted breath slowly came back to him.

"Boys," he gasped. "I don't know who you are, but thank heaven you came just in time. I couldn't have stood it much longer. I heard you yell something about Preston. Is it possible he sent you to find me?"

"Partly that and partly to get a giant," explained Tom. "We didn't know you were in that hut, or we'd never have blown up the one next to it, though we suspected you might be held captive somewhere around here, from the queer way the giants acted when we asked about you."

"And so you blew up that hut?" remarked the circus agent. "I thought it was struck by lightning. But it did me a good turn. I was chained to the wall of the hut next door, and your explosion split the beam to which my chains were fastened. I didn't lose any time running out, I can tell you. Oh, but it's good to be free once more and to see someone my own size!"

"How did you get here, and why did they keep you a prisoner?" asked Tom. Then Poddington told his story, while Ned and Mr. Damon aided Tom in filing off the rude iron shackles from his wrists and ankles.

As Mr. Preston had heard, Jake Poddington had started for giant land. But he lost his way, his escort of natives deserted him, just as Tom's did, and he wandered on in the jungle, nearly dying. Then, merely by accident, he came upon giant land, but he had the misfortune to incur the anger of the big men who took him for an enemy. They at once made him a prisoner, and had kept him so ever since, though they did not harm him otherwise, and gave him good food.

"I think they were a bit afraid of me in spite of my small size," explained the circus man. "I never thought to be rescued, for, though I figured that Mr. Preston might hear of my plight, he could never find this place. How did you get here?"

Then Tom told his story, and of how they themselves were held captives because of the treachery of Hank Delby.

"That's just like him!" cried Poddington. "He was always mean, and always trying to get the advantage of his rivals. But I'm glad I'm with you. With what stuff you have here it oughtn't to be difficult to get away from giant land."

"But I want a giant," insisted Tom. "I told Mr. Preston I'd bring him back one, and I'm going to do it."

"You can't!" cried the circus man. "They won't come with you, and it's almost impossible to make a prisoner of one. You'd better escape. I want to get away from giant land. I've had enough."

"We'll get away," said Tom confidently, "and we'll have a giant or two when we go."

"You'll have some before you go I guess!" suddenly interrupted Ned. "There's a whole crowd of 'em headed this way, and they've got clubs, bows and arrows and those blow guns! I guess they're going to besiege us."

"All right!" cried Tom. "If they want to fight we can give 'em as good as they send. Ned, you and Mr. Damon and I will handle the electric rifles. Eradicate, use your shotgun, and fire high. We don't want to hurt any of the big men. We'll merely stun them with the electric bullets, but the noise of Rad's gun will help some."

"What can I do?" asked Mr. Poddington.

"You're too weak to do much," replied Tom. "You just keep on the lookout, and tell us if they try any surprises. I guess we can handle 'em all right."

With shouts and yells the big men came on. Evidently their indifference toward their captives had turned to anger because of the freeing of Poddington, and now they were determined to use harsh measures. They advanced with wild yells, brandishing their clubs and other weapons, while the weird sound of the tom-toms and natives drums added to the din.

When a short distance from the hut the giants stopped, and began firing arrows and darts from the blow guns.

"Look out for those!" warned Tom. "They probably are poisoned, and a scratch may mean death. Give 'em a few shots now, Ned and Mr. Damon! Rad, give 'em a salute, but fire high!"

"Dat's what I will, Massa Tom!"

The gun of the colored man barked out a noisy welcome, and, at the same time three giants fell, stunned by the electric bullets, for the rifles were adjusted to send out only mild charges.

Thrice they charged, and each time they were driven back, and then, finding that the captives were ever ready for them, they gave up the attempt to overwhelm them, and hurried away, many going into the king's hut. His royal majesty did not show himself during the fight.

"Well, I guess they won't try that right away again," remarked Tom, as he saw the stunned giants slowly arouse themselves and crawl away. "We've taught them a lesson."

They felt better after that, and then, when they had eaten and drank, they began to consider ways and means of escape. But Tom would not hear of going until he could get at least one giant for the circus.

"But you can't!" insisted Mr. Poddington.

"Well, it's too soon to give up yet," declared Tom. "I'd like to take the king's two brothers with me."

"By Jove!" exclaimed Mr. Poddington, "I never thought of that. There is just a bare chance. Did you know that the two brothers, who are twins, dislike the king, for he is younger than they, and he practically took the throne away from them. They should rule jointly by rights. If we could enlist Tola and Koku on our side we might win out yet."

"Then we'll try!" exclaimed Tom.

Jake Poddington, who had been a captive in the giant city long enough to know something of its history, and had learned to talk the language, explained how Kosk had ursurped the throne. His brothers were subject to him, he said, but several times they had tried in vain to start a revolution. To punish them for their rebellious efforts the king made them his personal servants, and this explained why he sent them to see the tricks Tom performed.

"If we could only get into communication with the big twins," went on the circus man, "we could offer to take them with us to a country where they would be bigger kings than their brother is here. It's a royal conspiracy worth trying."

"Then we'll try it!" cried Tom enthusiastically.

THE TWIN GIANTS

Daring indeed was the scheme decided on by the captives, and yet its very boldness might make it possible for them to carry it out. The king would never suspect them of plotting to carry off his two royal brothers, and this made it all the easier to lay their plans. In this they were much helped by Poddington, who knew the language and who had made a few friends among the more humble people of the village, though none dared assist him openly.

"The first thing to do," said the circus man, "is to get into communication with the twins."

That proved harder than they expected, for a week passed, and they did not have a glimpse of Tola and Koku. Meanwhile the giant guard was still maintained about the hut night and day. No more food was given the prisoners, and they would have starved had not Tom possessed a good supply of his own provisions. It was evidently the intention of the king to starve his captives into submission.

"Suppose you do get those big brothers to accompany you, Tom?" asked Ned one day. "How are you going to manage to get away, and take them with you?"

"My aeroplane!" answered Tom quickly. "I've got it all planned out. You and I with Mr. Damon, Mr. Poddington and Eradicate will skip away in the aeroplane. We can put it together in here, and I've got enough gasolene to run it a couple of hundred miles if necessary."

"But the giants—you can't carry them in it."

"No, and I'm not going to try. If they'll agree to go they can set off through the woods afoot. We'll meet them in a certain place— where there's a good land mark which we can easily distinguish from the aeroplane. We'll take what stuff we can with us, and leave the rest here. Oh, it can be done, Ned."

"But when you start out with the aeroplane they'll make a rush and overwhelm us."

"No, for I'll do it so quickly that they won't have a chance. I'm going to saw through the beams of one side of this hut. To the rear there is level ground that will make a fine starting place. When everything is ready, say some night, we'll pull the side wall down, start the aeroplane out as it falls, and sail away. Then we'll pick up the giant brothers out in the woods, and travel to civilization again."

"By Jove! I believe that will work!" cried the circus man.

"Bless my corn plaster, I think so myself!" added Mr. Damon.

"But first we've got to get the brothers to agree," went on Tom, "and that is going to be hard work."

It was not so difficult as it was tedious. Through an aged woman, with whom he had made friends when a captive, Jake Poddington managed to get word to the royal twins that he and the other captives would like to see them privately. Then they had to wait for an answer.

In the meanwhile the giants tried several times to surprise Tom and his friends by attacks, but the captives were on the alert, and the electric rifles drove them back.

One night nearly all the guards were observed to be absent. There were not more than half a dozen scattered about the hut.

"I wonder what that means?" asked Tom, who was puzzled.

"I know!" exclaimed Jake Poddington after a moment's thought. "It's their big annual feast. Even the king goes to it. They were just getting over it when I struck here last year, and maybe that's what set them so against me. Boys, this may be our chance!"

"How?" asked Ned.

"The king's brothers may find an opportunity to come and talk to us when the feast is at its height," was the reply.

Anxiously they waited, and in order that the royal brothers might come in unobserved, if they did conclude to speak to the captives, Tom and his companions hung some pieces of canvas over the windows and doors, and had only a single light burning.

It was at midnight that a cautious knock sounded at the side of the hut and Tom glided to the main door. In the shadows he saw the two royal brothers, Tola and Koku.

"Here they are!" whispered Tom to Jake Poddington, who came forward.

"Come!" invited the circus man in the giants' tongue, and the brothers entered the hut.

How Jake persuaded them to throw in their fortunes with the captives the circus man hardly knew himself. Perhaps it was due as much as anything to the dislike they felt toward the king, and the mean way he had treated them.

"Come, and you will be kings among the small men in our country," invited Poddington. The brothers looked at each other, talked together in low tones, and then Koku exclaimed:

"We will come, and we will help you to escape. We have spoken, and we will talk with you again."

Then they glided out into the darkness, while from afar came the sounds of revelry at the big feast.

A Surprise in the Night

Tom and his friends could scarcely believe their good fortune. It seemed incredible that they should have induced two of the biggest giants to accompany them back, and, not only that, but that they had the promise of the strong men to aid them.

"Now we must get busy," declared Tom, when their visitors had gone. "We've got lots of work to do on the aeroplane, and we must try out the engine. Then we've got to fix the side of the hut so it will fall out when we're ready for it. And we've got to plan how to meet the giants later in the forest."

"Yes," agreed the circus man, "and we must take care that Hank Delby doesn't spoil our plans."

Then ensued busy days. In the seclusion of their hut the prisoners could work undisturbed at the aeroplane, which had been almost assembled.

The engine was installed and tried, and, when the motor began its thundering explosions, there was consternation among the giants, who had again surrounded the hut to see that the prisoners did not escape.

Meanwhile Delby seemed to be unusually active. He could be observed going in and out from his hut to that of the king, and he often carried large bundles.

"He's making himself solid with his royal highness," declared Tom. "Well, if all goes right, we won't have to worry much longer about what he does."

"If only those twin giants don't fail us," put in Ned.

"Oh, you can depend on them," said Mr. Poddington. "These giants are curious creatures, but once they give their word they stick to it."

He told much about the strange big men, confirming Tom's theory that favorable natural conditions, for a number of generations, had caused ordinary South American natives to develope into such large specimens.

Our friends were under quite a nervous tension, for they could not be sure of what would happen from day to day. They continued to work on the aeroplane, and then, finding that it would work in the seclusion of the hut, they were anxious for the time to come when they could try it in the open.

"Do you think it will carry the five of us with safety?" asked the circus man, as he gazed rather dubiously at the somewhat frail-appearing affair.

"Sure!" exclaimed Tom. "We'll get away all right if I can get enough of a start. Now we must see to opening the side of the hut."

This work had to be done cautiously, yet the prisoners had a certain freedom, for the guards were afraid to approach too closely.

The supporting and cross beams were sawed through, for Tom had brought a number of carpenter tools along with him. Then, in the silence of the night, the two royal brothers brought other beams that could be put in place temporarily to hold up the roof when the others were pulled out to allow the aeroplane to rush forth.

In due time all was in readiness for the attempt to escape. The royal twins had agreed to slip off at a certain signal, and await Tom and his party in the forest at the foot of a very large hill, that was a landmark for miles around. The giants could travel fast, but not as fast as the aeroplane, so it was planned that they were to have a day and night's start. They would take along food, and would arrange to have a number of Tom's mules hidden in the woods, so that our hero and his friends would have means of transportation back to the coast, after they had ended their flight in the airship.

"I wish we had brought along the larger one, so we could take the giants with us," said Tom, "but I guess they're strong enough to walk to the coast. We'll take what provisions we can carry, our electric rifles, and the rest of the things we'll leave here for the king, though he doesn't deserve them."

"What do you think Delby will do?" asked Ned.

"Give it up. He's got some plan though. I only hope he doesn't get a giant. Then ours will be a greater attraction."

Several days passed, and the last of the preparations had been made.

"The giant twins will pretend to go off on a hunting trip to-morrow morning," said the circus man one night, "but they won't come back. They'll wait for us at the big hill."

"Then we must escape the following morning," decided Tom. "Well, I'm ready for it."

From their hut, surrounded as it was still by the giant guards, our friends watched the royal brothers start off, seemingly on a hunting expedition.

The day passed slowly. Tom went carefully over the aeroplane, to see that it was in shape for a quick flight, and he looked to the wall of the hut—the wall that was to be pulled from place to afford egress for the air craft.

They went to bed early that night—the night they hoped would be their last in giant land. It must have been about midnight when Tom suddenly awoke. He thought he heard a noise outside the hut and in a moment he had jumped up.

"Repel boarders!" cried Tom.

THE AIRSHIP FLIGHT

For a few moments there was confusion inside the hut that was to be the last stronghold of our friends against the approaching force of giants. Confusion and not a little fear were mingled, for Tom's words sent a chill to every heart. Then, after the first panic, there came a calmer feeling—a feeling that each one would do his duty in the face of danger and, if he had to die, he would die fighting.

"Everyone take a window!" yelled Tom. "Don't kill any one if you can help it. Shoot to disable, Rad. Mr. Poddington, there's an extra shotgun somewhere about! See if you can find it. We'll use the electric rifles. Get those Roman candles somebody!"

Tom was like a general giving orders, and once his friends realized that he was managing things they felt more confidence. Ned grasped his electric rifle, as did Mr. Damon, and they stood ready to use them.

"The strongest stunning charge!" ordered the young inventor. "Something that will lay 'em out for a good while. We'll teach 'em a lesson!"

Bang!

That was Eradicate's shotgun going off. It had a double load in it, and the wonder of it was that the barrel did not burst. It sounded like a small cannon, but it had the good effect of checking the first rush of giants, for the electric rifles had not yet been adjusted, and Mr. Poddington, in the light of the single electric torch that had been left burning, could find neither the spare shotgun nor the Roman candles.

Bang!

Eradicate let the other barrel go, almost in the faces of the advancing giants, but over their heads, for he bore in mind Tom's words not to injure.

"That's the stuff!" cried Tom. "Come on now, Ned, we're ready for 'em!"

But the giants had retreated, and could be seen standing in groups about the hut, evidently planning what to do next. Then from back in the village there shone a glare of light.

"Bless my insurance policy! It's a fire!" cried Mr. Damon. "They're going to burn us out!"

"Jove! If they do!" exclaimed Ned.

"We mustn't let 'em!" shouted Tom. "Fire, Ned!"

Together the chums discharged their electric rifles at the enemy and a number of them fell, stunned, and were carried away by their companions.

The glaring light approached and now it could be seen that it was caused by a number of the big men carrying torches of some kind of blazing wood. It did look as though they intended to fire the prison hut.

"Give 'em another taste of it!" shouted Ned, and this time the three electric rifles shot out their streaks of blue flame, for Mr. Damon had his in action. It was still dark in the hut, for to set aglow more of the electric torches meant that Tom and his friends would be exposed to view, and would be the targets for the arrows, or darts from the deadly blow guns.

Several more of the giants toppled over, and then began a retreat to some distance, the first squad of fighters going to meet the men who had come up with the torches. There was no sign of women or children.

"Shall we fire again?" asked Ned.

"No," answered Tom. "Save your ammunition until they are closer, and we'll be surer of our marks. Besides, if they let us alone that's all we ask. We don't want to hurt 'em."

"Bless my gizzard!" exclaimed Mr. Damon. "I wonder why they attacked us, anyhow?"

"Maybe it's about the two giant brothers who have not come back," suggested Mr. Poddington. "They may imagine that we have them captive, and they want to rescue them."

"That's so," admitted Tom. "Well, if they had only postponed this reception for a few hours we'd have been out of their way, and they wouldn't have had this trouble," and he glanced at the aeroplane, that stood in the big hut, ready for instant flight.

"They're coming back!" suddenly shouted Ned, and a look from the half-opened windows showed the giants again advancing.

"I've got the Roman candles!" called Mr. Poddington from a corner where he had been rummaging in that box of Tom's which contained so many surprises. "What shall I do with 'em?"

"Let 'em go right in their faces!" yelled Tom. "They won't do much damage, but they'll throw a scare into the big fellows! Get ready, Ned!"

"They're dividing!" shouted his chum. "They're coming at us from two sides!"

"They're only trying to confuse us," decided Tom. "Fire at the main body!" And with that he opened up with his electric rifle, an example followed by Mr. Damon and Ned.

With a whizz, and several sharp explosions, the circus man got the Roman candles into action. The glaring fire of them lighted up the scene better than did the flaming torches of the giants, and truly it was a wonderful sight. There, in that lonely hut, in the midst of a South American jungle, four intrepid white persons, and an aged but brave negro, stood against hundreds of giants—mighty men, who, had they come to a personal contact, any one of which would have been more than a match for the combined strength of Tom and his party. It was a weird picture that the young inventor looked out upon, but his heart did not quail.

Giant after giant went down under the fierce rain of the electric bullets, stunned, but not otherwise injured. There was a shower of sparks, and a hail of burning balls from the Roman candles, but still the advance was kept up. Eradicate was banging away with his shotgun.

"Dis suah am hot work!" cried the colored man, as his hand came in contact with the barrel. "Wow! It's most RED hot!" he added with a cry of pain.

"Use the other gun," advised Tom, never turning his head from the window through which he was aiming. "That one may get choked, and explode in here."

"All right," answered Eradicate.

"Duck!" yelled Ned with sudden energy. "They're going to fire!" A number of the giants could be seen fitting arrows to bow strings, while others raised to their lips the long hollow reeds, from which the blow guns were made. It was the first time the enemy had fired and doubtless they had held back because they hoped to capture Tom and his friends alive. But they did not count on such a stubborn resistance.

Every one moved away from the windows, and not an instant too soon, for, a moment later, a shower of arrows and darts came in, fortunately injuring no one.

Then, above the shouting and yelling of the giants, whose deep, bass voices had a terrorizing effect, there came the din of the tom-toms, making a weird combination of sound.

"We've got 'em on the run again!" cried Ned, and so it proved, for the larger body of giants, who had approached the hut from the front and two sides, were running back.

"Guess they've given it up," exclaimed Tom. "I'm glad of it, too, for—"

He paused and glanced behind him. A tiny spurt of flame at the base of the rear wall of the hut had caught his eye. Instantly the flame grew larger, and a puff of smoke followed.

"Fire!" cried Ned. "We're on fire!"

"Bless my water bucket!" gasped Mr. Damon. "They've set fire to the hut!"

It was but too true. While Tom and the others had been standing off the giants in front, a smaller force had crept around to the rear, and set the inflamable side of the hut ablaze.

Desperately Tom looked around. There was no means at hand of fighting fire. Hardly a bucket of water was in the place, and the structure was filled with quick-burning stuff, while the fireworks that remained, and the blasting powder, made it doubly dangerous. Then Tom's eyes lighted on the big aeroplane, ready for instant service.

"That's it!" he cried suddenly. "It's our only hope, and the last one! Come on, everybody! Down with that wall! Pull on the ropes and it will come! We've got to go now. In another minute it will be too late. Climb up, Mr. Poddington, Mr. Damon, Ned, and I will start the machine."

"The wall first! The wall!" cried Ned.

"Sure," answered Tom. He and his friends grasped the two ropes that had been attached to the key-beams in the structure. It had been so arranged that when the supports were pulled out the wall would fall outward, making a fairly smooth and level gangplank, on which the aeroplane could rush from the hut.

There was a creaking of timbers, a straining of ropes, and then, with a crash, the wall fell. Instantly there was a yell of surprise from the giants, and a brighter glare from the torches, as those carrying them rushed up to see what had happened. The din of the tom-toms was well-nigh deafening. Fortunately the enemy forgot to take advantage of the opening and pour in a flight of arrows or darts.

"Start the motor!" cried Tom to his chum.

There was a rattling, banging noise, like a salvo of small arms, and the big propellers revolved with incredible swiftness. The two white men were already in place, and now Eradicate, still carrying his shotgun, clambered up.

"Up with you, Ned!" yelled Tom. "I'm going to head her around and make a flying start."

Tom's Giant—Conclusion

"I don't see anything of them, do you?"

"No, and yet this is the place where they said they'd meet us."

It was Tom who asked the question, and Ned who answered it. It was the day after their sensational escape from the giants' prison, and they were circling about in the aeroplane which had been the means of getting them away from giant land. For they were safely away from that strange and terrible place, and they were now seeking the two giant brothers who had promised to meet them at a certain big hill.

For an hour that night Tom and his friends had traveled on the wings of the Lark and when a rising moon showed them a level spot for a landing, they had gone down and made a camp. They had provisions with them, and plenty of blankets and it was so warm that more shelter was not necessary.

The next day, leaving Mr. Damon, Eradicate and the circus man in the temporary camp, Tom and Ned had gone aloft to see if they could pick up the giant twins, who were to meet them and have some mules ready for the journey back to civilization.

"Well, we're in no great hurry," went on Tom, after vainly scanning the ground below. "They may not have traveled as fast as we thought they could, and the mules may have given trouble. We'll stick around here a day or so, and—"

"Look!" suddenly exclaimed Ned. "Didn't you see something moving then."

"Where?"

"By that big dead tree."

Tom took a look through a pair of field glasses, while Ned steered the aeroplane. Then the young inventor cried:

"It's all right. It's one of the giants, but I can't tell which one. Ned, I believe they're hiding because they're afraid of us. They've never seen an aeroplane in action before. I'm going down."

Quickly and gracefully the Lark was volplaned to a level place near the dead tree. No one was in sight, and Tom, after looking about, called:

"Tola! Koku! Where are you? It is I, Tom Swift! We have escaped! Where are you? Don't be afraid!"

There was a moment's silence, and then two big forms rushed from the dense bushes, one of them—Koku—advancing to Tom, and catching him up in what was meant for a loving hug.

"Oh, I say now, Koku!" cried the young inventor, with a laugh. "I've got ribs, you know. Easy on that squeeze!"

The two giant twins laughed too, and they were immensely pleased to see their friends again, both talking at once and so fast that not even the circus man could catch what they said.

"Have you got the mules?" asked Tom, for he knew that much depended on the animals. "Is everything all right?"

"All right," answered Koku, the talk being conducted in the language of the giants of which Tom was now fairly a master when it was spoken slowly. Then the brothers explained that they had gotten safely away, had gathered up the mules, and with a supply of food, had hidden the beasts in a nearby valley. The giant twins were waiting for Tom to arrive, but, though they had seen the areoplanes in the hut they had no idea that it could fly so nearly like a bird, and when they saw it hovering over them they had become frightened, and hidden, until Tom's voice had reassured them.

"Well, get the animals," advised Tom, after he had told of the fight of the night before, and the escape. "I'll go find the others and we'll start from here. Then we'll hike for the United States as fast as we can."

Mr. Damon, Eradicate and the circus man were soon brought to the place where the giant brothers had made their camp, and it was decided to remain there a few days until the aeroplane could be taken apart for transportation, for Tom had no idea of abandoning it. Of course it could not be packed up very well, as there were no boxes or bales at hand. But it was made small enough so that the parts could be slung across the backs of several mules, there being a number of the pack animals available, some being the same ones Tom had purchased after his native escort had deserted him.

It was the morning they had decided to begin their march for the coast. Everything was in readiness, they had some food, and with the shotguns and the electric rifles which they had brought along, they could get game. All their other things, save a few necessaries, had been left behind. Eradicate, as he had always done, rode his mule up beside Tom, to look after his young master.

Suddenly Koku, who seemed to have become very fond of Tom, strode forward and took his place on the other side of the mule ridden by the young inventor.

"Me stay by you," he said with a grin on his big face. "Me like you! Me take care of you, Tom—be your servant. Him too old," and he motioned to Eradicate.

"Eh! What's dat yo' done said?" gasped the colored man. "Me too old? Looky heah, giant man, I'd hab yo' know dat I's been in de Swift fambly a good many years, an' I's jest as spry as I eber was. I kin look after Massa Tom as good as eber. Now yo' git back where yo' belongs, giant man, an' doan't let me heah no mo' ob dat foolishness talk. Nobody waits on Massa Tom Swift but me. Does yo' heah dat, giant man?"

"Me Tom's man!" exclaimed the big fellow, and in fairly good English. Tom laughed. He had no idea the giant had picked up any words.

"Go on away!" cried Eradicate.

Koku gave the colored man one look, then, with a good natured grin on his face, he reached over one hand, calmly lifted Eradicate from his mule and set him on the ground. Then, with a push, he shoved the mule galloping ahead, and took his place at the side of the young inventor.

"Well, what do you know about that?" gasped Ned.

"Bless my coffee cup!" cried Mr. Damon.

Eradicate stood still for a moment, gazing first at his master and then at the big being who had so ruthlessly plucked him from the mule's back, as easily as he would have lifted a child. Then Eradicate, with a trace of tears in his eyes, stretched forth his hands toward Tom, and turned aside. That was too much for our hero.

With one leap he was off his animal, and the next minute he had his arms around the faithful old colored man.

"By Jove, Rad!" cried Tom, and his own eyes were not dry. "I'm not going to be deserted by you in that way. You're just the same as ever to me, giant or no giant, and don't you forget it!" and he patted the old man on the back affectionately.

"Praise de Lord fo' heahin' yo' say dat, Massa Tom," gasped Eradicate. "Praise de dear Lord!"

And then, knowing that he still held a place in his young master's heart, the colored man was content. And from then on he rode on one side of Tom, while the giant, Koku, strode along on the other. He had established himself as Tom's bodyguard and even though Eradicate insisted on remaining, Koku would not go away.

"I guess I'll have to keep 'em both," said Tom, with a grin, "but I'm going to change Koku's name."

"What are you going to call him?" asked Ned.

"Let's see, what month is this?"

"August," said Mr. Damon.

"Then August is his name!" exclaimed Tom. "Koku sounds too much like a cocoanut cake. Here, August, shift that package on the white mule," he called, "it's cutting her back," and the giant, with a pleased grin, did as he was bid. And August he was called from then on.

But my story is getting too long, so I must bring it to a close. And really there is not much to tell. The march back to the coast was full of hardships, danger and difficulties, but they accomplished it. The two giants seemed glad that they had left their own country behind and they were simple and affectionate beings. Tom made up his mind he would let the circus man have one and keep the other for his personal attendant.

They traveled by day, and slept at night, shooting game as they needed it. Several times they narrowly escaped getting mixed up in the native conflicts. Tom had one striking evidence of his giant servant's usefulness.

One day he was stalking a small beast, like a deer, when, from a tree overhead, a jaguar sprang down at him. But Koku—I beg his pardon—August was at hand, and, like Sampson of old, the giant slew the beast bare-handed, choking it to death.

In fine time our friends reached a native town and the wonder caused by the giants was no less than the amusement of the big men at the things they saw. They wondered more when they got to a city, and saw more marvels of the white man's progress.

Then Tom and his friends reached the coast, and took a steamer for New York. The giants created a great sensation, the more when it was known that Tom intended to keep one for himself. With this arrangement Mr. Preston agreed, for he only wanted one as an attraction.

"Couldn't have done it better myself!" the circus proprietor said to Tom when he heard the story, and this was high praise from Mr. Preston.

"And you rescued old Jake, too! Well, well! Couldn't have done it better myself! I really couldn't!"

"I wonder how our old enemy Delby made out?" asked Mr. Poddington. They heard later that he was driven from giant land, not even being allowed to take a boy as a specimen. He had worked on the "tip" Andy Foger had given Mr. Waydell, but it failed. When Tom escaped, the king confiscated all the things in the hut, and he was so taken up with the novelties that he paid no more attention to the circus agent, who had all his trouble, plotting and scheming against Tom for his pains.

"A giant in the house!" cried Mrs. Baggert, when Tom got home with August. "I never heard of such a thing in all my life! Where will he sleep? Not a bed is big enough!"

"We'll give him two beds then," laughed Tom.

And so they did, and August was immensely pleased with his new life. He proved to be very useful, and readily adapted himself to civilized ways.

Tola, the other giant, made a big sensation when exhibited, and Mr. Preston said he was well worth the fifteen thousand dollars he had cost.

"Well, Tom, what next?" asked Ned one day, when they had been home several weeks and had told their story over and over again.

"No where!" exclaimed Tom. "I'm going to take a long rest."

But Tom Swift wasn't that kind of a young man, and he was soon active again. If you care to learn more of his doings you may do so in the next volume of this series, to be called, "Tom Swift and His Electric Camera; Or Thrilling Adventures While Taking Moving Pictures."

And now, for a time, we will take leave of the young inventor and his new giant servant, to meet them again a little later.

TOM SWIFT AND HIS WIZARD CAMERA
Or Thrilling Adventures While Taking Moving Pictures

TABLE OF CONTENTS:

A Strange Offer

"Some one to see you, Mr. Tom."

It was Koku, or August, as he was sometimes called, the new giant servant of Tom Swift, who made this announcement to the young inventor.

"Who is it, Koku?" inquired Tom, looking up from his work-bench in the machine shop, where he was busy over a part of the motor for his new noiseless airship. "Any one I know? Is it the 'Blessing Man?'" for so Koku had come to call Mr. Damon, an eccentric friend of Tom's.

"No, not him. A strange man. I never see before. He say he got quick business."

"Quick business; eh? I guess you mean important, Koku," for this gigantic man, one of a pair that Tom had brought with him after his captivity in "Giant Land," as he called it, could not speak English very well, as yet. "Important business; eh, Koku? Did he send in his card?"

"No, Mr. Tom. Him say he have no card. You not know him, but he very much what you call—recited."

"Excited I guess you mean, Koku. Well, tell him to wait a few minutes, and I'll see him. You can show him in then. But I say, Koku," and Tom paused as he looked at the big man, who had attached himself to our hero, as a sort of personal helper and bodyguard.

"Yes, Mr. Tom; what is it?"

"Don't let him go poking around the shop. He might look at some of my machines that I haven't got fully patented yet. Is he in the front office?"

"That's where him am. He be lookin' at pictures on the walls."

"Oh, that's all right then. Just keep him there. And, Koku, don't let him come back in the shop here, until I get ready to see him. I'll ring the bell when I am."

"All right, Mr. Tom."

Koku, very proud of his, mission of keeping guard over the strange visitor, marched from the room with his big strides, his long arms and powerful hands swinging at his sides, for Koku, or August, as Tom had rechristened him, and as he often called him (for it was in the month of August that he had located the giants) was a very powerful man. A veritable giant, being extremely tall, and big in proportion.

"Be sure. Don't let him in here, Koku!" called Tom, in an additional warning, as his new servant left the main shop.

"Sure not!" exclaimed Koku, very earnestly.

"I don't know who he may be," mused Tom, as he began putting away the parts to his new noiseless motor, so that the stranger could not see them, and profit thereby. "It looks rather funny, not sending in his name.

It may be some one who thinks he can spring a trick on me, and get some points about my inventions, or dad's.

"It may even be somebody sent on by Andy Foger, or his father. I can't be too careful. I'll just put everything away that isn't fully covered by patents, and then if he wants to infringe on any of the machines I can sue him."

Tom looked about the shop, which was filled with strange machinery, most of which had been made by himself, or his father, or under their combined directions. There was a big biplane in one corner, a small monoplane in another, parts of a submarine boat hanging up overhead, and a small, but very powerful, electric auto waiting to have some repairs made to it, for on his last trip in it Tom Swift had suffered a slight accident.

"There, I guess he can't see anything but what I want him to," mused Tom, as he put away the last part of a new kind of motor, from which he hoped great things. "Let's see, yes, it's out of sight now. I wish Ned Newton, or Mr. Damon were here to be a witness in case he starts anything. But then I have Koku, even if he doesn't speak much English yet. If it comes to blows—well, I wouldn't want that giant to hit me," finished Tom with a laugh, as he rang the bell to announce to his servant that the visitor might be shown in.

There was a sound outside the door that separated the business office from the main shop, and Tom heard Koku exclaim:

"Hold on! Wait! I go first. You wait!"

"What's the matter with me going ahead?" demanded a quick, snappy voice. "I'm in a hurry, and—"

"You wait! I go first," was the giant's reply, and then came the sound of a scuffle.

"Ouch! Say! Hold on there, my man! Take your hand off my shoulder! You're crushing me with those big fingers of yours!"

This was evidently the visitor remonstrating with the giant.

"Humph! I guess Koku must have grabbed him," said Tom softly. "I don't like that sort of a visitor. What's his hurry getting in here?" and our hero looked about, to see if he had a weapon at hand in case of an attack. Often cranks had forced their way into his shop, with pet inventions which they wanted him to perfect after they had themselves failed. Tom saw a heavy iron bar at hand, and knew this would serve to protect him.

"You come after me!" exclaimed Koku, when the voice of the other had ceased. "Do you stand under me?"

"Oh, yes, I understand all right. I'll keep back. But I didn't mean anything. I'm just in a hurry to see Tom Swift, that is all. I'm always in a hurry in fact. I've lost nearly a thousand dollars this morning, just by this delay. I want to see Mr. Swift at once; and have a talk with him."

"Another crank, I guess," mused Tom. "Well, I'm not going to waste much time on him."

A moment later the door opened, and into the shop stepped Koku, followed by a short, stout, fussy little man, wearing a flaming red tie, but otherwise his clothes were not remarkable.

"Is this Mr. Tom Swift?" asked the stranger, as he advanced and held out his hand to the young man.

"Yes," answered Tom, looking carefully at the visitor. He did not seem to be dangerous, he had no weapon, and, Tom was relieved to note that he did not carry some absurd machine, or appliance, that he had made, hoping to get help in completing it. The youth was trying to remember if he had ever seen the stranger before, but came to the conclusion that he had not.

"Sorry to take up your time," went on the man, "but I just had to see you. No one else will do. I've heard lots about you. That was a great stunt you pulled off, getting those giants for the circus. This is one; isn't he?" and he nodded toward Koku.

"Yes," replied Tom, wondering if the little man was in such a hurry why he did not get down to business.

"I thought so," the caller went on, as he shook hands with Tom. "Once you felt his grip you'd know he was a giant, even if you didn't see him. Yes, that was a great stunt. And going to the caves of ice, too, and that diamond-making affair. All of 'em great. I—"

"How did you know about them?" interrupted Tom, wishing the man would tell his errand.

"Oh, you're better known than you have any idea of, Tom Swift. As soon as I got this idea of mine I said right away, to some of the others in my business, I says, says I, 'Tom Swift is the boy for us. I'll get him to undertake this work, and then it will be done to the Queen's taste. Tom's the boy who can do it,' I says, and they all agreed with me. So I came here today, and I'm sorry I had to wait to see you, for I'm the busiest man in the world, I believe, and, as I said, I've lost about a thousand dollars waiting to have a talk with you. I—"

"I am sorry," interrupted Tom, and he was not very cordial. "But I was busy, and—"

"All right! All right! Don't apologize!" broke in the man in rapid tones, while both Tom, and his servant, Koku, looked in surprise at the quick flow of language that came from him. "Don't apologize for the world. It's my fault for bothering you. And I'll lose several thousand dollars, willingly, if you'll undertake this job. I'll make money from it as it is. It's worth ten thousand dollars to you, I should say, and I'm willing to pay that."

He looked about, as though for a seat, and Tom, apologizing for his neglect in offering one, shoved a box forward.

"We don't have chairs in here," said the young inventor with a smile. "Now if you will tell me what you—"

"I'm coming right to it. I'll get down to business in a moment," interrupted the man as he sat down on the box, not without a grunt or two, I for he was very stout. "I'm going to introduce myself in just a second, and then I'm going to tell you who I am. And I hope you'll take up my offer, though it may seem a strange one."

The man took out a pocketbook, and began searching through it, evidently for some card or paper.

"He's as odd as Mr. Damon is, when he's blessing everything," mused Tom, as he watched the man.

"I thought I had a card with me, but I haven't," the visitor went on. "No matter. I'm James Period—promoter of all kinds of amusement enterprises, from a merry-go-'round to a theatrical performance. I want you to—"

"No more going after giants," interrupted. Tom. "It's too dangerous, and I haven't time—"

"No, it has nothing to do with giants," spoke Mr. Period, as he glanced up at Koku, who towered over him as he sat on the box near Tom.

"Well?" returned Tom.

"This is something entirely new. It has never been done before, though if you should happen to be able to get a picture of giants don't miss the opportunity."

"Get a picture?" exclaimed Tom, wondering if, after all, his visitor might not be a little insane.

"Pictures, yes. Listen. I'm James Period. Jim, if you like it better, or just plain 'Spotty.' That's what most of my friends call me. Get the idea? A period is a spot. I'm a Period, therefor I'm a spot. But that isn't the real reason. It's because I'm always Johnny on the Spot when anything is happening. If it's a big boxing exhibition, I'm there. If it's a coronation, I'm there, or some of my men are. If it's a Durbar in India, you'll find Spotty on the spot. That's me. If there's going to be a building blown up with dynamite—I'm on hand; or some of my men. If there's a fire I get there as soon as the engines do—if it's a big one. Always on the spot—that's me—James Period—Spotty for short. Do you get me?" and he drew a long breath and looked at Tom, his head on one side.

"I understand that you are—"

"In the moving picture business," interrupted Mr. Period, who never seemed to let Tom finish a sentence. "I'm the biggest moving picture man in the world—not in size, but in business. I make all the best films. You've seen some of 'em I guess. Every one of 'em has my picture on the end of the film. Shows up great. Advertising scheme—get me?"

"Yes," replied Tom, as he recalled that he had seen some of the films in question, and good ones they were too. "I see your point, but—"

"You want to know why I come to you; don't you?" again interrupted "Spotty," with a laugh. "Well, I'll tell you. I need you in my business. I want you to invent a new kind of moving picture camera. A small light one—worked by electricity—a regular wizard camera. I want you to take it up in an airship with you, and then go to all sorts of wild and strange countries, Africa, India—the jungles—get pictures of wild animals at peace and fighting—herds of elephants—get scenes of native wars— earthquakes—eruptions of volcanoes—all the newest and most wonderful pictures you can. You'll have to make a new kind of camera to do it. The kind we use won't do the trick.

"Now do you get me? I'm going to give you ten thousand dollars, above all your expenses, for some films such as I've been speaking of. I want novelty. Got to have it in my business! You can do it. Now will you?"

"I hardly think—" began Tom.

"Don't answer me now," broke in Mr. Period. "Take four minutes to think it over. Or even five. I guess I can wait that long. Take five minutes. I'll wait while you make up your mind, but I know you'll do it. Five minutes—no more,' and hastily getting up off the box Mr. Period began impatiently pacing up and down the shop.

A Man in the Snow Bank

Tom Swift looked somewhat in surprise at his strange visitor. It had all happened so suddenly, the offer had been such a strange one, the man himself—Mr. Period—was so odd, that our hero hardly knew what to think. The moving picture agent continued pacing up and down the room now and then looking at his watch as if to note when the five minutes had passed.

"No," said Tom to himself. "I'm not going to take this offer. There's too much work and risk attached to it. I want to stay at home and work on my noiseless motor for the airship. After that— well—I don't know what I'll do. I'll tell Mr. Period that he needn't wait the five minutes. My mind is made up now!"

But as Tom was about to make this announcement, and dismiss his caller, he looked again at the visitor. There was something attractive about him—about his hasty way of talking, about his manner of interrupting, about the way he proposed matters. Tom was interested in spite of himself.

"Well," he reflected, "I may as well wait until the five minutes are up, anyhow."

Koku, the giant servant, glanced at his young master, as if to ask if there was anything that he could do. Tom shook his head, and then the big man strolled over to the other side of the machine shop, at the same time keeping a careful eye on Mr. Period.

While Tom is waiting for the time to expire, I will take a few minutes to tell you something more about him. Those of my friends who have read the previous books in this series need no introduction to my hero, but those who may chance upon this as their first book in the Tom Swift series, will like to be more formally introduced.

Tom, whose mother had been dead some years, lived with his father, Barton Swift, in the town of Shopton. Mr. Swift was an inventor of prominence, and his son was fast following in his footsteps. A Mrs. Baggert kept house for the Swifts, and another member of the household was Eradicate Sampson, an aged colored man, who said he used to "eradicate" the dirt. He had been with Tom on many trips, but of late was getting old and feeble. Then there was Garret Jackson, an engineer employed by the Swifts. These were all the immediate members of the household.

Tom had a chum, Ned Newton, who used to work in a bank, and there was a girl, Mary Nestor, a daughter of Amos Nestor, in which young lady Tom was much interested.

Eradicate Sampson had a mule, Boomerang, of whom he thought almost as much as he did of Tom. Eradicate was a faithful friend and servant, but, of late, Koku, or August, the giant, had rather supplanted him. I must not forget Mr. Wakefield Damon, of Waterfield, a village near Shopton. Mr. Damon was an odd man, always blessing everything. He and Tom were good friends, and had been on many trips together.

The first book of the series was called "Tom Swift and His Motor-Cycle," and related how Tom bought the cycle from Mr. Damon, after the latter had met with an accident on it, and it was in this way that our hero became acquainted with the odd man.

Tom had many adventures on his motor-cycle, and, later on he secured a motor-boat, in which he beat his enemy, Andy Foger, in a race. Next Tom built an airship, and in this he went on a wonderful trip. Returning from this he and his father heard about a treasure sunken under the ocean. In his submarine boat Tom secured the valuables, and made a large sum for himself.

In his electric runabout, which was the swiftest car on the road, Tom was able to save from ruin a bank in which his father was interested, and, a short time after that, he went on a trip in an airship, with a man who had invented a new kind. The airship was smashed, and fell to Earthquake Island, where there were some refugees from a shipwreck, among them being the parents of Mary Nestor. In the volume called "Tom Swift and His Wireless Message," I told how he saved these people.

When Tom went among the diamond makers he had more strange adventures, on that trip discovering the secret of phantom mountain. He had bad luck when he went to the caves of ice, for there his airship was wrecked.

When Tom made the trip in his sky racer he broke all records for an aerial flight, incidentally saving his father's life. It was some time after this when he invented an electric rifle, and went to elephant land, to rescue some missionaries from the red pygmies.

The eleventh volume of the series is called "Tom Swift in the Land of Gold," and relates his adventures underground, while the next one tells of a new machine he invented—an air-glider— which he used to save the exiles of Siberia, incidentally, on that trip, finding a valuable deposit of platinum.

As I have said, it was on his trip to giant land that Tom got his big servant. This book, the thirteenth of the series, is called "Tom Swift in Captivity," for the giants captured him and his friends, and it was only by means of their airship that they made their daring escape.

Tom had been back from the strange land some time now. One giant he had turned over to the circus representative for whom he had undertaken the mission, and the other he retained to work around his shop, as Eradicate was getting too old. It was now winter, and there had been quite a fall of snow the day before Mr. Period, the odd moving picture man, called on Tom. There were many big drifts outside the building.

Tom had fitted up a well-equipped shop, where he and his father worked on their inventions. Occasionally Ned Newton, or Mr. Damon, would come over to help them, but of late Tom had been so busy on his noiseless motor that he had not had time to even see his friends.

"Well, I guess the five minutes have passed, and my mind is made up," thought Tom, as he looked at his watch. "I might as well tell Mr. Period that I can't undertake his commission. In the first place it isn't going to be an easy matter to make an electric moving picture camera. I'd have to spend a lot of time studying up the subject, and then I might not be able to get it to work right.

"And, again, I can't spare the time to go to all sorts of wild and impossible places to get the pictures. It's all well enough to talk about getting moving pictures of natives in battle, or wild beasts fighting, or volcanoes in action, but it isn't so easy to do it. Then, too, I'd have to make some changes in my airship if I went on that trip. No, I can't go. I'll tell him he'll have to find some one else."

Mr. Period pulled out his watch, opened it quickly, snapped it shut again, and exclaimed:

"Well, how about it, Tom Swift? When can you start! The sooner the better for me! You'll want some money for expenses I think. I brought my check book along, also a fountain pen. I'll give you a thousand dollars now, for I know making an electric moving picture camera isn't going to be cheap work. Then, when you get ready to start off in your airship, you'll need more money. I'll be Johnny-on-the-spot all right, and have it ready for you. Now when do you think you can start?"

He sat down at a bench, and began filling out a check.

"Hold on!" cried Tom, amused in spite of himself. "Don't sign that check, Mr. Period. I'm not going."

"Not going?" The man's face showed blank amazement.

"No," went on Tom. "I can't spare the time. I'm sorry, but you'll have to get some one else."

"Some one else? But who can I get?"

"Why, there are plenty who would be glad of the chance."

"But they can't invent an electric moving picture camera, and, if they could, they wouldn't know enough to take pictures with it. It's got to be you or no one, Tom Swift. Look here, I'll make it fifteen thousand dollars above expenses."

"No, I'm sorry, but I can't go. My work here keeps me too busy.

"Oh, pshaw! Now, look here, Tom Swift! Do you know who sent me to see you?"

"It was Mr. Nestor, who has a daughter named Mary, I believe. Mr. Nestor is one of the directors in our company, and one day, when he told me about you sending a wireless message from Earthquake Island, I knew you would be the very man for me. So now you see you'll be doing Mr. Nestor a favor, as well as me, if you go on this trip."

Tom was somewhat surprised, yet he realized that Mr. Period was speaking the truth. Mr. Nestor was identified with many new enterprises. Yet the youth was firm.

"I really can't go," said our hero. "I'd like to, but I can't. I'd like to oblige Mr. Nestor, for—well, for more reasons than one," and Tom blushed slightly. "But it is out of the question. I really can't go."

"But you must!" insisted the camera man. "I won't take 'no' for an answer. You've got to go, Tom Swift, do you hear that? You've go to go?"

Mr. Period was apparently very much excited. He strode over to Tom and smote his hands together to emphasize what he said. Then he shook his finger at Tom, to impress the importance of the matter on our hero.

"You've just got to go!" he cried. "You're the only one who can help me, Tom. Do go! I'll pay you well, and—oh, well, I know you don't need the money, exactly, but—say, you've got to go!"

In his earnestness Mr. Period laid his hand on Tom's arm. The next instant something happened.

With a few big strides Koku was beside the picture man. With great quickness he grasped Mr. Period by the coat collar, lifted him off his feet with one hand, and walked over to a window with him, easily lifting him above the floor.

With one fling the giant tossed the short, stout gentleman out into a snow bank, while Tom looked on, too surprised to do anything, even if he had had the chance.

"There. You touch Tom Swift again, and I sit on you and keep you under snow!" cried the giant, while Mr. Period kicked and squirmed about in the drift, as Tom made a leap forward to help him out.

TOM MAKES UP HIS MIND

"Great Scott!" yelled the picture man. "What in the world happened to me? Did I get kicked by that mule Boomerang of Eradicate's, that I've heard so much about? Or was it an earthquake, such as I want to get a picture of? What happened?"

He was still floundering about in the deep bank of snow that was just outside the window. Fortunately the sash had been up, and Koku had tossed Mr. Period through the open window. Otherwise, had there been glass, the well-meaning, but unreasoning giant would probably have thrown his victim through that, and he might have been badly cut. Tom had the window open for fresh air, as it was rather close in the shop.

"Why, Koku!" exclaimed the young inventor, as he leaned out of the window, and extended his hand to the moving picture man to help him out of the drift. "What do von mean by that?" Have you gone crazy?"

"No, but no one shall lay hands on my master!" declared the giant half savagely. "I have vowed to always protect you from danger, in return for what you did for me. I saw this man lay his hand on you. In another moment he might have killed you, had not Koku been here. There is no danger when I am by," and he stretched out his huge arms, and looked ferocious. "I have turned over that man, your enemy!" he added.

"Yes, you overturned me all right," admitted Mr. Period, as he got to his feet, and crawled in through the window to the shop again. "I went head over heels. I'm glad it was clean snow, and not a mud bank, Tom. What in the world is the matter with him?"

"I guess he thought you were going to harm me, said Tom in a low voice, as the picture man came in the shop. "Koku is very devoted to me, and sometimes he makes trouble," the youth went on. "But he means it all for the best. I am very sorry for what happened," and Tom aided Mr. Period in brushing the snow off his garments. "Koku, you must beg the pardon of this gentleman," Tom directed.

"What for?" the giant wanted to know.

"For throwing him into the snow. It is not allowed to do such things in this country, even though it is in Giant Land. Beg his pardon.

"I shall not," said the giant calmly, for Tom had taught him to speak fairly good English, though sometimes he got his words backwards.

"The man was about to kill you, and I stopped him—I will stop him once more, though if he does not like the snow, I can throw him somewhere else."

"No! No! You must not do it!" cried Tom. "He meant no harm. He is my friend."

"I am glad to hear you say that," exclaimed the picture man. "I have hopes that you will do what I want."

"He your friend?" asked Koku wonderingly. "Certainly; and you must beg his pardon for what you did," insisted Tom.

"Very well. I am glad you did not hurt yourself," said the giant, and with that "apology" he stalked out of the room, his feelings evidently very much disturbed.

"Ha! Ha!" laughed Mr. Period. "I guess he can't see any one but you, Tom. But never mind. I know he didn't mean anything, and, as I'm none the worse I'll forgive him. My necktie isn't spotted; is it?"

"No, the snow didn't seem to do that any harm," replied the young inventor, as he looked at the brilliant piece of red silk around Mr. Period's collar.

"I am very particular about my neckties," went on the picture man. "I always wear one color. My friends never forget me then."

Tom wondered how they could ever forget him, even though he wore no tie, for his figure and face were such as to not easily be forgotten.

"I'm glad it's not soiled," went on "Spotty" as he liked to be called. "Now, Tom, you said you were my friend. Prove it by accepting my offer. Build that wizard camera, and get me some moving pictures that will be a sensation. Say you will!"

He looked appealingly at Tom, and, remembering the rather rude and unexpected treatment to which Koku had submitted the gentleman, Tom felt his mind changing. Still he was not yet ready to give in. He rather liked the idea the more he thought of it, but he felt that he had other duties, and much to occupy him at home, especially if he perfected his silent motor.

"Will you go?" asked Mr. Period, picking up his fountain pen and check book, that he had laid aside when he walked over to Tom, just before the giant grasped him. "Say you will."

The young inventor was silent a moment. He thought over the many adventures he had gone through—in the caves of ice, in the city of gold, escaping from the giants, and the red pygmies—He went over the details of his trips through the air, of the dangers under the seas, of those he had escaped from on Earthquake Island. Surely e was entitled to a little rest at home.

And yet there was a lure to it all. A certain fascination that was hard to resist. Mr. Period must have seen what was going on in Tom's mind, for he said:

"I know you're going. I can see it. Why, it will be just the very thing you need. You'll get more fame out of this thing than from any of your other inventions. Come, say you'll do it.

"I'll tell you what I'll do !" he went on eagerly. "After you make the camera, and take a lot of films, showing strange and wonderful scenes, I'll put at the end of each film, next to my picture, your name, and a statement showing that you took the originals. How's that? Talk about being advertised! Why you can't beat it! Millions of people will read your name at the picture shows every night."

"I am not looking for advertisements," said Tom, with a laugh.

"Well, then, think of the benefit you will be to science," went on Mr. Period quickly. "Think of the few people who have seen wild animals as they are, of those who have ever seen an earth-quake, or a volcano in action. You can go to Japan, and get pictures of earthquakes. They have them on tap there. And as for volcanoes, why the Andes mountains are full of 'em. Think of how many people will be thankful to you for showing them these wonderful scenes."

"And think of what might happen if I should take a tumble into a crack in the earth, or down a hot volcano, or fall into a jungle when there was a fight on among the elephants," suggested Tom. "My airship might take a notion to go down when I was doing the photographing," he added.

"No. Nothing like that will happen to Tom Swift," was the confident answer of the picture man. "I've read of your doings. You don't have accidents that you can't get the better of. But come, I know you're thinking of it, and I'm sure you'll go. Let me make you out this check, sign a contract which I have all ready, and then get to work on the camera."

Tom was silent a moment. Then he said:

"Well, I admit that there is something attractive about it. I hoped I was going to stay home. for a long time. But—"

"Then you'll go!" cried Mr. Period eagerly. "Here's the money," and he quickly filled out a check for Tom's first expenses, holding the slip of paper toward the young inventor.

"Wait a minute! Hold on!" cried Tom. "Not so fast if you please. I haven't yet made up my mind."

"But you will; won't you?" asked Mr. Period.

"Well, I'll make up my mind, one way or the other," replied the young man. "I won't say I'll go, but—"

"I'll tell you what I'll do!" interrupted Mr. Period. "I'm a busy man, and every second is worth money to me. But I'll wait for you to make up your mind. I'll give you until to-morrow night. How's that? Fair, isn't it?"

"Yes—I think so. I am afraid—"

"I'm not!" broke in the picture man. "I know you'll decide to go. Think of the fun and excitement you'll have. Now I've taken up a lot of your time, and I'm going to leave you alone. I'll be back tomorrow evening for my answer. But I know you're going to get those moving pictures for me. Is that giant of yours anywhere about?" he asked, as he looked cautiously around before leaving the shop. "I don't want to fall into his hands again."

"I don't blame you," agreed Tom. "I never knew him to act that way before. But I'll go to the gate with you, and Koku will behave him self. I am sorry—"

"Don't mention it !" broke in the picture man. "It was worth all I suffered, if you go, and I know you will. Don't trouble yourself to come out. I can find my way, and if your giant comes after me, I'll call for help."

He hurried out before Tom could follow, and, hearing the gate click a little later, and no call for help coming, our hero concluded that his visitor had gotten safely away.

"Well, what am I going to do about it?" mused Tom, as he resumed work on his silent motor. He had not been long engaged in readjusting some of the valves, when he was again interrupted.

This time it was his chum, Ned Newton, who entered, and, as Ned was well known to the giant, nothing happened.

"Well, what's up, Tom?" asked Ned.

"Why, did you notice anything unusual?" asked Tom.

"I saw Koku standing at the gate a while ago, looking down the road at a short stout man, with a red tie. Your giant seemed rather excited about something."

"Oh, yes. I'll tell you about it," and Tom related the details of Mr. Period's visit.

"Are you going to take his offer?" asked Ned.

"I've got until tomorrow to make up my mind. What would you do, Ned?"

"Why, I'd take it in a minute, if I knew how to make an electric camera. I suppose it has to be a very speedy one, to take the kind of pictures he wants. Wait, hold on, I've just thought of a joke. It must be a swift camera—catch on—you're Swift, and you make a swift camera; see the point?"

"I do," confessed Tom, with a laugh. "Well, Ned, I've been thinking it over, but I can't decide right away. I will tomorrow night, though."

"Then I'm coming over, and hear what it is. If you decide to go, maybe you'll take me along."

"I certainly will, and Mr. Damon, too."

"How about the giant?"

"Well, I guess there'll be room for him. But I haven't decided yet. Hand me that wrench over there; will you," and then Tom and Ned began talking about the new apparatus on which the young inventor was working.

True to his promise Mr. Period called the next evening. He found Tom, Ned and Mr. Swift in the library, talking over various matters.

"Well, Tom, have you made up your mind?" asked the caller, when Mrs. Baggert, the housekeeper, had shown him into the room. "I hope you have, and I hope it is favorable to me."

"Yes," said Tom slowly, "I've thought it all over, and I have decided that I will—"

At that moment there was a loud shouting outside the house, and the sound of some one running rapidly through the garden that was just outside the low library window—a garden now buried deep under snow.

"What's that?" cried Ned, jumping to his feet.

"That was Koku's voice," replied Tom, "and I guess he was chasing after some one."

"They'll need help if that giant gets hold of them," spoke Mr. Period solemnly, while the noise outside increased in volume.

HELD FAST

"Here, Tom! Come back! Where are you going?" cried aged Mr. Swift, as his son started toward the window.

"I'm going to see what's up, and who it is that Koku is chasing," replied the young inventor.

As he spoke he opened the window, which went all the way down to the floor. He stepped out on a small balcony, put his hand on the railing, and was about to leap over. Back of him was his father, Mr. Period and Ned.

"Come back! You may get hurt!" urged Mr. Swift. He had aged rapidly in the last few months, and had been obliged to give up most of his inventive work. Naturally, he was very nervous about his son.

"Don't worry, dad; replied the youth. "I'm not in much danger when Koku is around."

"That's right, agreed the moving picture man. "I'd sooner have that giant look after me than half a dozen policemen."

The noise had now grown fainter, but the sound of the pursuit could still be heard. Koku was shouting in his hearty tones, and there was the noise of breaking twigs as the chase wound in and out of the garden shrubbery.

Tom paused a moment, to let his eyes get somewhat used to the darkness. There was a crescent moon, that gave a little light, and the snow on the ground made it possible to notice objects fairly well.

"See anything?" asked Ned, as he joined his chum on the balcony.

"No, but I'm going to have a closer look. Here goes!" and Tom leaped to the ground.

"I'm with you," added Ned, as he followed.

Then came another voice, shouting:

"Dat's de way! Catch him! I'se comm', I is! Ef we gits him we'll tie him up, an' let Boomerang walk on him!"

"Here comes Eradicate," announced Tom, with a look back toward his chum, and a moment later the aged colored man, who had evidently started on the chase with Koku, but who had been left far behind, swung totteringly around the corner of the house.

"Did ye cotch him, Massa Tom?" asked Eradicate. "Did ye cotch de raskil?"

"Not yet, Rad. But Koku is after him. Who was he, and what did he do?"

"Didn't do nuffin yit, Massa Tom, 'case as how he didn't git no chance," replied the colored man, as he hurried along as rapidly as he could beside the two youths. "Koku and I was too quick for him. Koku an' me was a-sittin' in my shack, sort of talkin' togedder, when we hears a racket neah de chicken house. I'se mighty partial t' de chickens, an' I didn't want nobody t' 'sturb 'em. Koku was jes' de same, an' when we hears dat noise, up we jumps, an' gits t' chasm.' He runned dis way, an' us was arter him, but land lub yo', ole Eradicate ain't so spry as he uster be an' Koku an' de chicken thief got ahead ob me. Leastwise he ain't no chicken thief yit, 'case as how he didn't git in de coop, but he meant t' be one, jes' de same."

"Are you sure he was after the chickens?" asked Tom, with quick suspicion in his mind, for, several times of late, unscrupulous persons had tried to enter his shop, to get knowledge of his valuable inventions before they were patented.

"Course he were arter de chickens," replied Eradicate. "But he didn't git none."

"Come on, Ned!" cried Tom, breaking into a run. "I want to catch whoever this was. Did you see him, Rad?"

"Only jes' had a glimpse ob his back."

"Well, you go back to the house and tell father and Mr. Period about it. Ned and I will go on with Koku. I hope to get the fellow."

"Why, Tom?" asked his chum.

"Because I think he was after bigger game than chickens. My noiseless motor, for the new airship, is nearly complete, and it may have been some one trying to get that. I received an offer from a concern the other day, who wished to purchase it, and, when I refused to sell, they seemed rather put out."

The two lads raced on, while Eradicate tottered back to the house, where he found Mr. Swift and the picture man awaiting him.

"I guess he got away," remarked Ned, after he and his chum had covered nearly the length of the big garden.

"I'm afraid so," agreed Tom. "I can't hear Koku any more. Still, I'm not going to give up."

Pantingly they ran on, and, a little later, they met the big man coming back.

"Did he get away?" asked Tom.

"Yes, Mr. Tom, he scaped me all right."

"Escaped you mean, Koku. Well, never mind. You did your best."

"I would like to have hold of him," spoke the giant, as he stretched out his big arms.

"Did you know who he was?" inquired Ned.

"No, I couldn't see his face," and he gave the same description of the affair as had Eradicate.

"Was it a full grown man, or some one about my size?" Tom wanted to know.

"A man," replied the giant.

"Why do you ask that?" inquired Ned, as the big fellow went on to resume his talk with Eradicate, and the two chums turned to go into the house, after the fruitless chase.

"Because, I thought it might be Andy Foger," was Tom's reply. "It would be just like him, but if it was a man, it couldn't be him. Andy's rather short."

"Besides, he doesn't live here any more," said Ned.

"I know, but I heard Sam Snedecker, who used to be pretty thick with him, saying the other day that he expected a visit from Andy. I hope he doesn't come back to Shopton, even for a day, for he always tries to make trouble for me. Well, let's go in, and tell 'em all about our chase after a chicken thief."

"And so he got away?" remarked Mr. Swift, when Tom had completed his story.

"Yes," answered the young inventor, as he closed, and locked, the low library window, for there was a chilly breeze blowing. "I think I will have to rig up the burglar alarm on my shop again. I don't want to take any chances."

"Do you remember what we were talking about, when that interruption came?" asked Mr. Period, after a pause. "You were saying, Tom, that you had made up your mind, and that was as far as you got. What is your answer to my offer?"

"Well," spoke the lad slowly, and with a smile, "I think I will—"

"Now don't say 'no'"; interrupted the picture man. "If you are going to say 'no' take five minutes more, or even ten, and think it over carefully. I want you—"

"I wasn't going to say 'no,'" replied Tom. "I have decided to accept your offer, and I'll get right at work on the electrical camera, and see what I can do in the way of getting moving pictures for you."

"You will? Say, that's great! That's fine! I knew you would accept, but I was the least bit afraid you might not, without more urging."

"Of course," began Tom, "it will take—"

"Not another word. Just wait a minute," interrupted Mr. Period in his breezy fashion. "Take this."

He quickly filled out a check and handed it to Tom.

"Now sign this contract, which merely says that you will do your best to get pictures for me, and that you won't do it for any other concern, and everything will be all right. Sign there," he added, pointing to a dotted line, and thrusting a fountain pen into Tom's hand. The lad read over the agreement, which was fair enough, and signed it, and Ned affixed his name as a witness.

"Now when can you go?" asked Mr. Period eagerly.

"Not before Spring, I'm afraid," replied Torn. "I have first to make the camera, and then my airship needs overhauling if I am to go on such long trips as will be necessary in case I am to get views of wild beasts in the jungle."

"Well, make it as soon as you can," begged Mr. Period. "I can have the films early next Fall then, and they will be in season for the Winter runs at the theatres. Now, I'm the busiest man in the world, and I believe I have lost five hundred dollars by coming here to-night. Still, I don't regret it. I'm going back now, and I'll expect to hear from you when you are ready to start. There's my address. Good-bye," and thrusting a card into Tom's hand he hurried out of the room.

"Won't you stop all night?" called Mr. Swift after him.

"Sorry. I'd like to but can't. Got a big contract I must close in New York to-morrow morning. I've ordered a special train to be at the Shopton station in half an hour, and I must catch that. Good night!" and Mr. Period hurried away.

"Say, he's a hustler all right!" exclaimed Ned.

"Yes, and I've got to hustle if I invent that camera," added Tom. "It's got to be a specially fast one, and one that can take pictures from a long distance. Electricity is the thing to use, I guess."

"Then you are really going off on this trip. Tom?" asked his father, rather wistfully.

"I'm afraid I am," replied his son. "I thought I could stay at home for a while, but it seems not."

"I was in hopes you could give me a little time to help me on my gyroscope invention," went on the aged man. "But I suppose it will keep until you come back. It is nearly finished."

"Yes, and I don't like stopping work on my noiseless motor," spoke Tom. "But that will have to wait, too."

"Do you know where you are going?" inquired Ned.

"Well, I'll have to do considerable traveling I suppose to get all the films he wants. But once I'm started I'll like it I guess. Of course you're coming, Ned."

"I hope so."

"Of course you are!" insisted Tom, as if that settled it. "And I'm sure Mr. Damon will go also. I haven't seen him in some time. I hope he isn't ill."

Tom started work on his Wizard Camera, as he called it, the next day—that is he began drawing the designs, and planning how to construct it. Ned helped him, and Koku was on hand in case he was needed, but there was little he could do, as yet. Tom made an inspection of his shop the morning after the chicken thief scare, but nothing seemed to have been disturbed.

A week passed, and Tom had all the plans drawn for the camera. He had made several experiments with different forms of electricity for operating the mechanism, and had decided on a small, but very powerful, storage battery to move the film, and take the pictures.

This storage battery, which would be inside the camera, would operate it automatically. That is, the camera could be set up any place, in the jungle, or on the desert, it could be left alone, and would take pictures without any one being near it. Tom planned to have it operate at a certain set time, and stop at a certain time, and he could set the dials to make this time any moment of the day or night. For there was to be a powerful light in connection with the camera, in order that night views might be taken. Besides being automatic the camera could be worked by hand.

When it was not necessary to have the camera operate by the storage battery, it could be connected to wires and worked by an ordinary set of batteries, or by a dynamo. This was for use on the airship, where there was a big electrical machine. I shall tell you more about the camera as the story proceeds.

One afternoon Tom was alone in the shop, for he had sent Koku on an errand, and Eradicate was off in a distant part of the grounds, doing some whitewashing, which was his specialty. Ned had not come over, and Mr. Swift, having gone to see some friends, and Mrs. Baggert being at the store, Tom, at this particular time, was rather isolated.

He was conducting some delicate electrical experiments, and to keep the measuring instruments steady he had closed all the windows and doors of his shop. The young inventor was working at a bench in one corner, and near him, standing upright, was a heavy shaft of iron, part of his submarine, wrapped in burlap, and padded, to keep it from rusting.

"Now," said Tom to himself, as he mixed two kinds of acid in a jar, to produce a new sort of electrical current, "I will see if this is any better than the first way in which I did it."

He was careful about pouring out the powerful stuff, but, in spite of this, he spilled a drop on his finger. It burned like fire, and, instinctively, he jerked his hand back.

The next instant there was a series of happenings. Tom's elbow came in contact with another jar of acid, knocking it over, and spilling it into the retort where he had been mixing the first two liquids. There was a hissing sound, as the acids combined, and a thick, white vapor arose, puffing into Tom's face, and making him gasp.

He staggered back, brushed against the heavy iron shaft in the corner, and it fell sideways against him, knocking him to the floor, and dropping across his thighs. The padding on it saved him from broken bones, but the shaft was so heavy, that after it was on him, Tom could not move. He was held fast on the floor of his shop, unable to use his legs, and prevented from getting up.

For a moment Tom was stunned, and then he called:

"Help! Help! Eradicate! Koku! Help!"

He waited a moment, but there was only a silence.

And then Tom smelled a strange odor—an odor of a choking gas that seemed to smother him.

"It's the acids!" he cried. "They're generating gas! And I'm held fast here! The place is closed up tight, and I can't move! Help! Help!"

But there was no one at hand to aid Tom, and every moment the fumes of the gas became stronger. Desperately the youth struggled to rid himself of the weight of the shaft, but he could not. And then he felt his senses leaving him, for the powerful gas was making him unconscious.

TOM GETS A WARNING

"Bless my shoe buttons!" exclaimed a voice, as a man came toward Tom's shop, a little later. "Bless my very necktie! This is odd. I go to the house, and find no one there. I come out here, and not a soul is about. Tom Swift can't have gone off on another one of his wonderful trips, without sending me word. I know he wouldn't do that. And yet, bless my watch and chain, I can't find any one!"

It was Mr. Damon who spoke, as my old readers have already guessed. He peered into one of the shop windows, and saw something like a fog filling the place.

"That's strange," he went on. "I don't see Tom there, and yet it looks as if an experiment was going on. I wonder—"

Mr. Damon heard some one coming up behind him, and turned to see Koku the giant, who was returning . from the errand on which Tom had sent him.

"Oh, Koku, it's you; is it?" the odd man asked. "Bless my cuff buttons! Where is Tom?"

"In shop I guess."

"I don't see him. Still I had better look. There doesn't seem to be any one about."

Mr. Damon opened the shop door, and was met by such an outward rush of choking gas that he staggered back.

"Bless my—" he began but he had to stop, to cough and gasp. "There must have been some sort of an accident," he cried, as he got his lungs full of fresh air. "A bad accident! Tom could never work in that atmosphere. Whew!"

"Accident! What is matter?" cried Koku stepping to the doorway. He, too choked and gasped, but his was such a strong and rugged nature, and his lungs held such a supply of air, that it took more than mere gas to knock him out. He peered in through the wreaths of the acid vapor, and saw the body of his master, lying on the floor—held down by the heavy iron.

In another instant Koku had rushed in, holding his breath, for, now that he was inside the place, the gas made even him feel weak.

"Come back! Come back!" cried Mr. Damon. 'You'll be smothered! Wait until the gas escapes!"

"Then Mr. Tom die!" cried the giant. "I get him—or I no come out."

With one heave of his powerful right arm, Koku lifted the heavy shaft from Tom's legs. Then, gathering the lad up in his left arm, as if he were a baby, Koku staggered out into the fresh air, almost falling with his burden, as he neared Mr. Damon, for the giant was, well-nigh overcome.

"Bless my soul!" cried the odd man. "Is he—is he—"

He did not finish the sentence, but, as Koku laid Tom down on the overcoat of Mr. Damon, which the latter quickly spread on the snow, the eccentric man put his hand over the heart of the young inventor.

"It beats!" he murmured. "He's alive, but very weak. We must get a doctor at once. I'll do what I can. There's no time to spare. Bless my—"

But Mr. Damon concluded that there was no time for blessing anything, and so he stopped short.

"Carry him up to the house, Koku," he said. "I know where there are some medicines, and I'll try to revive him while we're waiting for the doctor Hurry!"

Tom was laid on a lounge, and, just then, Mrs. Baggert came in.

"Telephone for the doctor!" cried Mr. Damon to the housekeeper, who kept her nerve, and did not get excited. "I'll give Tom some ammonia, and other stimulants, and see if I can bring him around. Koku, get me some cold water."

The telephone was soon carrying the message to the doctor, who promised to come at once. Koku, in spite of his size, was quick, and soon brought the water, into which Mr. Damon put some strong medicine, that he found in a closet. Tom's eyelids fluttered as the others forced some liquid between his lips.

"He's coming around!" cried the eccentric man. "I guess he'll be all right, Koku."

"Koku glad," said the giant simply, for he loved Tom with a deep devotion.

"Yes, Koku, if it hadn't been for you, though, I don't believe that he would be alive. That was powerful gas, and a few seconds more in there might have meant the end of Tom. I didn't see him lying on the floor, until after you rushed in. Bless my thermometer! It is very strange."

They gave Tom more medicine, rubbed his arms and legs, and held ammonia under his nose. Slowly he opened his eyes, and in a faint voice asked:

"Where—am—I?"

"In your own house," replied Mr. Damon, cheerfully. "How do you feel?"

"I'm—all—right—now," said Tom slowly. He, felt his strength coming gradually back, and he remembered what had happened, though he did not yet know how he had been saved. The doctor came in at this moment, with a small medical battery, which completed the restorative work begun by the others. Soon Tom could sit up, though he was still weak and rather sick.

"Who brought me out?" he asked, when he had briefly told how the accident occurred.

"Koku did," replied Mr. Damon. "I guess none of the rest of us could have lifted the iron shaft from your legs."

"It's queer how that fell," said Tom, with a puzzled look on his face. "I didn't hit it hard enough to bring it down. Beside, I had it tied to nails, driven into the wall, to prevent just such an accident as this. I must see about it when I get well."

"Not for a couple of days," exclaimed the doctor grimly. "You've got to stay in bed a while yet. You had a narrow escape, Tom Swift."

"Well, I'm glad I went to Giant Land," said the young inventor, with a wan smile. "Otherwise I'd never have Koku," and he looked affectionately at the big man, who laughed happily. In nature Koku was much like a child.

Mr. Swift came home a little later, and Ned Newton called, both being very much surprised to hear of the accident. As for Eradicate, the poor old colored man was much affected, and would have sat beside Tom's bed all night, had they allowed him.

Our hero recovered rapidly, once the fumes of the gas left his system, and, two days later, he was able to go out to the shop again. At his request everything had been left just as it was after he had been brought out. Of course the fumes of the gas were soon dissipated, when the door was opened, and the acids, after mingling and giving off the vapor, had become neutralized, so that they were now harmless.

"Now I'm going to see what made that shaft fall," said Tom to Ned, as the two chums walked over to the bench where the young inventor had been working. "The tap I gave it never ought to have brought it down."

Together they examined the thin, but strong, cords that had been passed around the shaft, having been fastened to two nails, driven into the wall.

"Look!" cried Tom, pointing to one of the cords.

"What is it?" asked Ned.

"The strands were partly cut through, so that only a little jar was enough to break the remaining ones," went on Tom. "They've been cut with a knife, too, and not frayed by vibration against the nail, as might be the case. Ned, someone has been in my shop, meddling, and he wanted this shaft to fall. This is a trick!"

"Great Scott, Tom! You don't suppose any one wanted that shaft to fall on you; do you?"

"No, I don't believe that. Probably some one wanted to damage the shaft, or he might have thought it would topple over against the bench, and break some of my tools, instruments or machinery. I do delicate experiments here, and it wouldn't take much of a blow to spoil them. That's why those cords were cut."

"Who did it? Do you think Andy Foger—"

"No, I think it was the man Koku thought was a chicken thief, and whom we chased the other night. I've got to be on my guard. I wonder if—"

Tom was interrupted by the appearance of Koku, who came out of the shop with a letter the postman had just left.

"I don't know that writing very well, and yet it looks familiar," said Tom, as he tore open the missive. "Hello, here's more trouble!" he exclaimed as he hastily read it.

"What's up now?" asked Ned.

"This is from Mr. Period, the picture man," went on the young inventor. It's a warning."

"A warning?"

"Yes. He says:

"'Dear Tom. Be on your guard. I understand that a rival moving picture concern is after you. They want to make you an offer, and get you away from me. But I trust you. Don't have anything to do with these other fellows. And, at the same time, don't give them a hint as to our plans. Don't tell them anything about your new camera. There is a lot of jealousy and rivalry in this business and they are all after me. They'll probably come to see you, but be on your guard. They know that I have been negotiating with you. Remember the alarm the other night."

TRYING THE CAMERA

"Well, what do you think of that?" cried Ned, as his chum finished.

"It certainly isn't very pleasant," replied Tom. "I wonder why those chaps can't let me alone? Why don't they invent cameras of their own? Why are they always trying to get my secret inventions?"

"I suppose they can't do things for themselves," answered Ned. "And then, again, your machinery always works, Tom, and some that your rivals make, doesn't."

"Well, maybe that's it," admitted our hero, as he put away the letter. "I will be on the watch, just as I have been before. I've got the burglar alarm wires adjusted on the shop now, and when these rival moving picture men come after me they'll get a short answer."

For several days nothing happened, and Tom and Ned worked hard on the Wizard Camera. It was nearing completion, and they were planning, soon, to give it a test, when, one afternoon, two strangers, in a powerful automobile, came to the Swift homestead. They inquired for Tom, and, as he was out in the shop, with Ned and Koku, and as he often received visitors out there, Mrs. Baggert sent out the two men, who left their car in front of the house.

As usual, Tom had the inner door to his shop locked, and when Koku brought in a message that two strangers would like to see the young inventor, Tom remarked:

"I guess it's the rival picture men, Ned. We'll see what they have to say."

"Which of you is Tom Swift?" asked the elder of the two men, as Tom and Ned entered the front office, for our hero knew better than to admit the strangers to the shop.

"I am," replied Tom.

"Well, we're men of business," went on the speaker, "and there is no use beating about the bush. I am Mr. Wilson Turbot, and this is my partner, Mr. William Eckert. We are in the business of making moving picture films, and I understand that you are associated with Mr. Period in this line. 'Spotty' we call him."

"Yes, I am doing some work for Mr. Period," admitted Tom, cautiously.

"Have you done any yet?"

"No, but I expect to."

"What kind of a camera are you going to use?" asked Mr. Eckert eagerly.

"I must decline to answer that," replied Tom, a bit stiffly.

"Oh, that's all right," spoke Mr. Turbot, good naturedly. "Only 'Spotty' was bragging that you were making a new kind of film for him, and we wondered if it was on the market."

"We are always looking for improvements," added Mr. Eckert.

"This camera isn't on the market," replied Tom, on his guard as to how he answered.

The two men whispered together for a moment, and then Mr. Turbot said:

"Well, as I remarked, we're men of business, and there's no use beating about the bush. We've heard of you, Tom Swift, and we know you can do things. Usually, in this world, every man has his price, and we're willing to pay big to get what we want. I don't know what offer Mr. Period made to you, but I'll say this: We'll give you double what he offered, for the exclusive rights to your camera, whenever it's on the market, and we'll pay you a handsome salary to work for us."

"I'm sorry, but I can't consider the offer," replied Tom firmly. "I have given my word to Mr. Period. I have a contract with him, and I cannot break it."

"Offer him three times what Period did," said Mr. Eckert, in a hoarse whisper that Tom heard.

"It would be useless!" exclaimed our hero. "I wouldn't go back on my word for a hundred times the price I am to get. I am not in this business so much for the money, as I am for the pleasure of it."

The men were silent a moment. There were ugly looks on their faces. They looked sharply at Tom and Ned. Then Mr. Eckert said:

"You'll regret this, Tom Swift. We are the biggest firm of moving picture promoters in the world. We always get what we want."

"You won't get my camera," replied Tom calmly.

"I don't know about that!" exclaimed Mr. Turbot, as he made a hasty stride toward Tom, who stood in front of the door leading to the shop—the shop where his camera, almost ready for use, was on a bench. "I guess if we—"

"Koku!" suddenly called Tom.

The giant stepped into the front office. He had been standing near the door, inside the main shop. Mr. Turbot who had stretched forth his hand, as though to seize Tom, and his companion, who had advanced toward Ned, fairly jumped back in fright at the sight of the big man.

"Koku," went on Tom, in even tones, "just show these gentlemen to the front door—and lock it after them," he added significantly, as he turned back into the shop, followed by Ned.

"Yes, Mr. Tom," answered the giant, and then, with his big hand, and brawny fist, he gently turned the two men toward the outer door. They were gasping in surprise as they looked at the giant.

"You'll be sorry for this, Tom Swift!" exclaimed Mr. Turbot. "You'll regret not having taken our offer. This Period chat is only a small dealer. We can do better by you. You'll regret—"

"You'll regret coming here again," snapped Tom, as he closed the door of his shop, leaving Koku to escort the baffled plotters to their auto. Shortly afterward Tom and Ned heard the car puffing away.

"Well, they came, just as Mr. Period said they would," spoke Tom, slowly.

"Yes, and they went away again!" exclaimed Ned with a laugh. "They had their trip for nothing. Say, did you see how they stared at Koku?"

"Yes, he's a helper worth having, in cases like these."

Tom wrote a full account of what had happened and sent it to Mr. Period. He received in reply a few words, thanking him for his loyalty, and again warning him to be on his guard.

In the meanwhile, work went on rapidly on the Wizard Camera. Briefly described it was a small square box, with a lens projecting from it. Inside, however, was complicated machinery, much too complicated for me to describe. Tom Swift had put in his best work on this wonderful machine. As I have said, it could be worked by a storage battery, by ordinary electric current from a dynamo, or by hand. On top was a new kind of electric light. This was small and compact, but it threw out powerful beams. With the automatic arrangement set, and the light turned on, the camera could be left at a certain place after dark, and whatever went on in front of it would be reproduced on the moving roll of film inside.

In the morning the film could be taken out, developed, and the pictures thrown on a screen in the usual way, familiar to all who have been in a moving picture theatre. With the reproducing machines Tom had nothing to do, as they were already perfected. His task had been to make the new-style camera, and it was nearly completed.

A number of rolls of films could be packed into the camera, and they could be taken out, or inserted, in daylight. Of course after one film had been made, showing any particular scene any number of films could be made from this "master" one. Just as is done with the ordinary moving picture camera. Tom had an attachment to show when one roll was used, and when another needed inserting.

For some time after the visit of the rival moving picture men, Tom was on his guard. Both house and shop were fitted with burglar alarms, but they did not ring. Eradicate and Koku were told to be on watch, but there was nothing for them to do.

"Well," remarked Tom to Ned, one afternoon, when they had both worked hard, "I think it's about finished. Of course it needs polishing, and there may be some adjusting to do, but my camera is now ready to take pictures—at least I'm going to give it a test."

"Have you the rolls of films?"

"Yes, half a dozen of 'em And I'm going to try the hardest test first."

"Which one is that?"

"The night test. I'm going to place the camera out in the yard, facing my shop. Then you and I, and some of the others, will go out, pass in front of it, do various stunts, and, in the morning we'll develop the films and see what we have."

"Why, are you going to leave the camera out, all night?"

"Sure. I'm going to give it the hardest kind of a test."

"But are you and I going to stay up all night to do stunts in front of it?"

"No, indeed. I'm going to let it take what ever pictures happen to come along to be taken after we get through making some special early ones. You see my camera will be a sort of watch dog, only of course it won't catch any one—that is, only their images will be caught on the film.

"Oh, I see," exclaimed Ned, and then he helped Tom fix the machine for the test.

What the Camera Caught

"Well, is she working, Tom?" asked our hero's chum, a little later, when they had set the camera up on a box in the garden. It pointed toward the main shop door, and from the machine came a clicking sound. The electric light was glowing.

"Yes, it's all ready," replied Tom. "Now just act as if it wasn't there. You walk toward the shop. Do anything you please. Pretend you are coming in to see me on business. Act as if it was daytime. I'll stand here and receive you. Later, I'll get dad out here, Koku and Eradicate. I wish Mr. Period was here to see the test, but perhaps it's just as well for me to make sure it works before be sees it."

"All right, Tom, here I come."

Ned advanced toward the shop. He tried to act as though the camera was not taking pictures of him, at the rate of several a second, but he forgot himself, and turned to look at the staring lens. Then Tom, with a laugh, advanced to meet him, shaking hands with him. Then the lads indulged in a little skylarking. They threw snowballs at each other, taking care, however to keep within range of the lens. Of course when Tom worked the camera himself, he could point it wherever he wanted to, but it was now automatic.

Then the lads went to the shop, and came out again. They did several other things. Later Koku, and Eradicate did some "stunts," as Tom called them. Mr. Swift, too, was snapped, but Mrs. Baggert refused to come out.

"Well, I guess that will do for now," said Tom, as he stopped the mechanism. "I've just thought of something," he added. "If I leave the light burning, it will scare away, before they got in front of the lens, any one who might come along. I'll have to change that part of it."

"How can you fix it?" asked Ned.

"Easily. I'll rig up some flash lights, just ordinary photographing flashlights, you know. I'll time them to go off one after the other, and connect them with an electric wire to the door of my shop."

"Then your idea is—" began Ned.

"That some rascals may try to enter my shop at night. Not this particular night, but any night. If they come to-night we'll be ready for them."

"An' can't yo'-all take a picture ob de chicken coop?" asked Eradicate. "Dat feller may come back t' rob mah hens."

"With the lens pointing toward the shop," spoke Tom, "it will also take snap shots of any one who tries to enter the coop. So, if the chicken thief does come, Rad, we'll have a picture of him."

Tom and Ned soon had the flashlights in place, and then they went to bed, listening, at times, for the puff that would indicate that the camera was working. But the night passed without incident, rather to Tom's disappointment. However, in the morning, he developed the film of the first pictures taken in the evening. Soon they were dry enough to be used in the moving picture machine, which Tom had bought, and set up in a dark room.

"There we are!" he cried, as the first images were thrown on the white screen. "As natural as life, Ned! My camera works all right!"

"That's so. Look! There's where I hit you with a snowball!" cried his chum, as the skylarking scene was reached.

"Mah goodness!" cried Eradicate, when he saw himself walking about on the screen, as large as life. "Dat shorely am wonderful."

"It is spirits!" cried Koku, as he saw himself depicted.

"I wish we had some of the other pictures to show," spoke Tom. "I mean some unexpected midnight visitors."

For several nights in succession the camera was set to "snap" any one who might try to enter the shop. The flashlights were also in place. Tom and Ned, the latter staying at his chum's house that week, were beginning to think they would have their trouble for their pains. But one night something happened.

It was very dark, but the snow on the ground made a sort of glow that relieved the blackness. The camera had been set as usual, and Tom and Ned went to bed.

It must have been about midnight when they were both awakened by hearing the burglar alarm go off. At the same time there were several flashes of fire from the garden.

"There she goes!" cried Ned.

"Yes, they're trying to get into the shed," added Tom, as a glance at the burglar-alarm indicator on the wall of the room, showed that the shop door was being tried. "Come on!"

"I'm with you!" yelled Ned.

They lost little time getting into their clothes, for they had laid them out in readiness for putting on quickly. Down the stairs they raced, but ere they reached the garden they heard footsteps running along the wall toward the road.

"Who's there?" cried Tom, but there was no answer.

"Koku! Eradicate!" yelled Ned.

"Yais, sah, I'se comm'!" answered the colored man, and the voice of the giant was also heard. The flashlights had ceased popping before this, and when the two lads and their helpers had reached the shop, there was no one in sight.

"The camera's there all right!" cried Tom in relief as he picked it up from the box. "Now to see what it caught. Did you see anything of the fellows, Koku, or Eradicate?" Both said they had not, but Eradicate, after examining the chicken house door by the aid of a lighted match, cried out:

"Somebody's been tryin' t' git in heah, Massa Tom. I kin see where de do's been scratched."

"Well, maybe we'll have the picture for you to look at in the morning," said Tom.

The films were developed in the usual way in the morning, but the pictures were so small that Tom could not make out the features or forms of the men. And it was plain that at least three men had been around the coop and shop.

By the use of alcohol and an electric fan Tom soon had the films dry enough to use. Then the moving picture machine was set up in a dark room, and all gathered to see what would be thrown on the screen, greatly enlarged.

First came several brilliant flashes of light, and then, as the entrance to the shop loomed into view, a dark figure seemed to walk across the canvas. But it did not stop at the shop door. Instead it went to the chicken coop, and, as the man reached that door, he began working to get it open. Of course it had all taken place in a few seconds, for, as soon as the flashlights went off, the intruders had run away. But they had been there long enough to have their pictures taken.

The man at the chicken coop turned around as the lights flashed, and he was looking squarely at the camera. Of course this made his face very plain to the audience, as Tom turned the crank of the reproducing machine.

"Why, it's a colored man!" cried Ned in surprise.

"Yes, I guess it's only an ordinary chicken thief, after all," remarked Tom.

There was a gasp from Eradicate.

"Fo' de land sakes!" he cried. "De raskil! Ef dat ain't mah own second cousin, what libs down by de ribber! An' to t'ink dat Samuel 'Rastus Washington Jackson Johnson, mah own second cousin, should try t' rob mah chicken coop! Oh, won't I gib it t' him!"

"Are you sure, Rad?" asked Tom.

"Suah? Sartin I'se suah, Massa Tom," was the answer as the startled colored man on the screen stared at the small audience. "I'd know. dat face ob his'n anywhere."

"Well, I guess he's the only one we caught last night," said Tom, as the disappointed chicken thief ran away, and so out of focus But the next instant there came another series of flashlight explosions on the screen, and there, almost as plainly as if our friends were looking at them, they saw two men stealthily approaching the shop. They, too, as the chicken thief had done, tried the door, and then, they also, startled by the flashes, turned around.

"Look!" cried Ned.

"Great Scott !" exclaimed Tom. "Those are the two rivals of Mr. Period! They are Mr. Turbot and Mr. Eckert!"

"Same men I pushed out!" cried Koku, much excited.

There was no doubt of it, and, as the images faded from the screen, caused by the men running away, Tom and Ned realized that their rivals had tried to put their threat into execution—the threat of making Tom wish he had taken their offer.

"I guess they came to take my camera,—but, instead the camera took them," said the young inventor grimly.

PHOTOS FROM THE AIRSHIP

"Well, Tom, how is it going?" asked a voice at the door of the shop where the young inventor was working. He looked up quickly to behold Mr. Nestor, father of Mary, in which young lady, as I have said, Tom was much interested. "How is the moving picture camera coming on?"

"Pretty good, Mr. Nestor. Come in. I guess Koku knew you all right. I told him to let in any of my friends, but I have to keep him there on guard."

"So I understand. They nearly got in the other night, but I hear that your camera caught them."

"Yes, that proved that the machine is a success, even if we didn't succeed in arresting the men."

"Did you try?"

"Yes, I sent copies of the film, showing Turbot and Eckert trying to break into my shop, to Mr. Period, and he had enlarged photographs made, and went to the police. They said it was rather flimsy evidence on which to arrest anybody, and so they didn't act. However, we sent copies of the pictures to Turbot and Eckert themselves, so they know that we know they were here, and I guess they'll steer clear of me after this."

"I guess so, Tom," agreed Mr. Nestor with a laugh. "But what about the chicken thief?"

"Oh, Eradicate attended to his second cousin. He went to see him, showed him a print from the film, and gave him to understand that he'd be blown up with dynamite, or kicked by Boomerang, if he ever came around here again, and so Samuel 'Rastus Washington Jackson Johnson will be careful about visiting strange chicken coops, after this."

"I believe you, Tom. But how is the camera coming on?"

"Very well. I am making a few changes in it, and I expect to get my biggest airship in readiness for the trip in about a week, and then I'll try taking pictures from her. But I understand that you are interested in Mr. Period's business, Mr. Nestor?"

"Yes, I own some stock in the company, and, Tom, that's what I came over to see you about. I need a vacation. Mary and her mother are going away this Spring for a long visit, and I was wondering if you couldn't take me with you on the trips you will make to get moving pictures for our concern."

"Of. course I can, Mr. Nestor. "I'll be glad to do it."

"And there is another thing, Tom," went on Mr. Nestor, soberly. "I've got a good deal of my fortune tied up in this moving picture affair. I want to see you win out—I don't want our rivals to get ahead of us."

"They shan't get ahead of us."

"You see, Tom, it's this way. There is a bitter fight on between our concern and that controlled by our rivals. Each is trying to get the business of a large chain of moving picture theatres throughout the United States. These theatre men are watching us both, and the contracts for next season will go to the concern showing the best line of films. If our rivals get ahead of us—well, it will just about ruin our company,—and about ruin me too, I guess."

"I shall do my very best," answered our hero.

"Is Mr. Damon going along?"

"Well, I have just written to ask him. I sent the letter yesterday.

"Doesn't he know what you contemplate?"

"Not exactly. You see when he came, that time I was overcome by the fumes from the acids, everything was so upset that I didn't get a chance to tell him. He's been away on business ever since, but returned yesterday. I certainly hope that he goes with us. Ned Newton is coming, and with you, and Koku and myself, it will be a nicer party."

"Then you are going to take Koku?"

"I think I will. I'm a little worried about what these rival moving picture men might do, and if I get into trouble with them, my giant helper would come in very useful, to pick one up and throw him over a tree top, for instance."

"Indeed, yes," agreed Mr. Nestor, with a laugh. "But I hope nothing like that happens."

"Nothing like that happens?" suddenly asked a voice. "Bless my bookcase! but there always seems to be something going on here. What's up now, Tom Swift?"

"Nothing much, Mr. Damon," replied our hero, as he recognized his odd friend. "We were just talking about moving pictures, Mr. Damon, and about you. Did you get my letter?"

"I did, Tom."

"And are you going with us?"

"Tom, did you ever know me to refuse an invitation from you? I guess not! Of course I'm going. But, for mercy sakes, don't tell my wife! She mustn't know about it until the last minute, and then she'll be so surprised, when I tell her, that she won't think of objecting. Don't let her know."

Tom laughed, and promised, and then the three began talking of the prospective trip. After a bit Ned Newton joined the party.

Tom showed the two men how his new camera worked. He had made several improvements on it since the first pictures were taken, and now it was almost perfect. Mr. Period had been out to see it work, and said it was just the apparatus needed.

"You can get films with that machine," he said, "that will be better than any pictures ever thrown on a screen. My fortune will be made, Tom, and yours too, if you can only get pictures that are out of the ordinary. There will be some hair-raising work, I expect, but you can do it."

"I'll try," spoke Tom. "I have—"

"Hold on! I know what you are going to say," interrupted Mr. Period. "You are going to say that you've gone through some strenuous times already. I know you have, but you're going to have more soon. I think I'll send you to India first."

"To India!" exclaimed Tom, for Mr. Period had spoken of that as if it was but a journey downtown.

"Yes, India. I want a picture of an elephant drive, and if you can get pictures of the big beasts in a stampede, so much the better. Then, too, the Durbar is on now, and that will make a good film. How soon can you start for Calcutta?"

"Well, I've got to overhaul the airship," said Tom. "That will take about three weeks. The camera is practically finished. I can leave in a month, I guess."

"Good. We'll have fine weather by that time. Are you going all the way by your airship?"

"No, I think it will be best to take that apart, ship it by steamer, and go that way ourselves. I can put the airship together in India, and then use it to get to any other part of Europe, Asia or Africa you happen to want pictures from."

"Good! Well, get to work now, and I'll see you again."

In the days that followed, Tom and Ned were kept busy. There was considerable to do on the airship, in the way of overhauling it. This craft was Tom's largest, and was almost like the one in which he had gone to the caves of ice, where it was wrecked. It had been, however, much improved.

The craft was a sort of combined dirigible balloon, and aeroplane, and could be used as either. There was a machine on board for generating gas, to use in the balloon part of it, and the ship, which was named the Flyer, could carry several persons.

"Bless my shoe laces!" cried Mr. Damon one day as he looked at Koku. "If we take him along in the airship, will we be able to float, Tom?"

"Oh, yes. The airship is plenty big enough. Besides, we are not going to take along a very large party, and the camera is not heavy. Oh, we'll be all right. I suppose you'll be on hand tomorrow, Mr. Damon?"

"To-morrow? What for?"

"We're going to take the picture machine up in the airship, and get some photos from the sky. I expect to make some films from high in the air, as well as some in the regular way, on the ground, and I want a little practice. Come around about two o'clock, and we'll have a trial flight."

"All right. I will. But don't let my wife know I'm going up in an airship again. She's read of so many accidents lately, that she's nervous about having me take a trip."

"Oh, I won't tell," promised Tom with a laugh, and he worked away harder than ever, for there were many little details to perfect. The weather was now getting warm, as there was an early spring, and it was pleasant out of doors.

The moving picture camera was gotten in readiness. Extra rolls of films were on hand, and the big airship, in which they were to go up, for their first test of taking pictures from high in the air, had been wheeled out of the shed.

"Are you going up very far?" asked Mr. Nestor of Tom, and the young inventor thought that Mary's father was a trifle nervous. He had not made many flights, and then only a little way above the ground, with Tom.

"Not very high," replied our hero. "You see I want to get pictures that will be large, and if I'm too far away I can't do it."

"Glad to hear it, replied Mr. Nestor, with a note of relief in his voice. "Though I suppose to fall a thousand feet isn't much different from falling a hundred when you consider the results."

"Not much," admitted Tom frankly.

"Bless my feather bed!" cried Mr. Damon. "Please don't talk of falling, when we're going up in an airship. It makes me nervous."

"We'll not fall!" declared Tom confidently.

Mr. Period sent his regrets, that he could not be present at the trial, stating in his letter that he was the busiest man in the world, and that his time was worth about a dollar a minute just at present. He, however, wished Tom all success. Tom's first effort was to sail along, with the lens of the camera pointed straight toward the earth. He would thus get, if successful, a picture that, when thrown on the screen, would give the spectators the idea that they were looking down from a moving balloon. For that reason Tom was not going to fly very high, as he wanted to get all the details possible.

"All aboard!" cried the young inventor, when he had seen to it that his airship was in readiness for a flight. The camera had been put aboard, and the lens pointed toward earth through a hole in the main cabin floor. All who were expected to make the trip with Tom were on hand, Koku taking the place of Eradicate this time, as the colored man was too aged and feeble to go along.

"All ready?" asked Ned, who stood in the steering tower, with his hand on the starting lever, while Tom was at the camera to see that it worked properly.

"All ready," answered the young inventor, and, an instant later, they shot upward, as the big propellers whizzed around.

Tom at once started the camera to taking pictures rapidly, as he wanted the future audience to get a perfect idea of how it looked to go up in a balloon, leaving the earth behind. Then as the Flyer moved swiftly over woods and fields, Tom moved the lens from side to side, to get different views.

"Say! This is great!" cried Mr. Nestor, to whom air-riding was much of a novelty. "Are you getting good pictures, Tom?"

"I can't tell until we develop them. But the machine seems to be working all right. I'm going to sail back now, and get some views of our own house from up above."

They had sailed around the town of Shopton, to the neighboring villages, over woods and fields. Now they were approaching Shopton again.

"Bless my heart!" suddenly exclaimed Mr. Damon, who was looking toward the earth, as they neared Tom's house.

"What is it?" asked our hero, glancing up from the picture machine, the registering dial of which he was examining.

"Look there! At your shop, Tom! There seems to be a lot of smoke coming from it!"

They were almost over Tom's shop now, and, as Mr. Damon had said, there was considerable smoke rolling above it.

"I guess Eradicate is burning up papers and trash," was Ned's opinion.

Tom looked to where the camera pointed, he was right over his shop now, and could see a dense vapor issuing from the door.

That isn't Eradicate!" cried the young inventor. "My shop is on fire! I've got to make a quick drop, and save it! There are a lot of valuable models, and machines in there! Send us down, Ned, as fast as she'll go!"

OFF FOR INDIA

"Bless my hose reel!" cried Mr. Damon, as the airship took a quick lurch toward the earth. "Things are always happening to you, Tom Swift! Your shop on fire! How did it happen?"

"Look!" suddenly cried Ned, before Tom had a chance to answer. "There's a man running away from the shop, Tom!"

All saw him, and, as the airship rushed downward it could be seen that he was a fellow dressed in ragged garments, a veritable tramp.

"I guess that fire didn't happen," said Tom significantly. "It was deliberately set. Oh, if we can only get there before it gains too much headway!"

"I like to catch that fellow!" exclaimed Koku, shaking his big fist at the retreating tramp. "I fix him!"

On rushed the airship, and the man who had probably started the fire, glanced up at it. Tom suddenly turned the lens of his Wizard Camera toward him. The mechanism inside, which had been stopped, started clicking again, as the young inventor switched on the electric current.

"What are you doing?" cried Ned, as he guided the airship toward the shop, whence clouds of smoke were rolling.

"Taking his picture," replied Tom. "It may come in useful for evidence."

But he was not able to get many views of the fellow, for the latter must have suspected what was going on. He quickly made a dive for the bushes, and was soon lost to sight. Tom shut off his camera.

"Bless my life preserver!" cried Mr. Damon. "There comes your father, Tom, and Mrs. Baggert! They've got buckets! They're going to put out the fire!"

"Why don't they think to use the hose?" cried the young inventor, for he had his shop equipped With many hose lines, and an electrically driven pump. The hose! The hose, dad!" shouted Tom, but it is doubtful if his father or Mrs. Baggert heard him, for the engine of the airship was making much noise. However, the two with the buckets looked up, and waved their hands to those on the Flyer.

"There's Eradicate!" yelled Ned. "He's got the hose all right!" The colored man was beginning to unreel a line.

"That's what it needs!" exclaimed Tom. "Now there's some chance to save the shop."

"We'll be there ourselves to take a hand in a few seconds!" cried Mr. Damon, forgetting to bless anything.

"The scoundrel who started this fire, and those back of him, ought to be imprisoned for life!" declared Mr. Nestor.

A moment later Ned had landed the airship within a short distance of the shop. In an instant the occupants of the craft had leaped out, and

Tom, after a hasty glance to see that his valuable camera was safe, dashed toward the building crying:

"Never mind the pails, dad! Use the hose! there's a nozzle at the back door. Go around there, and play the water on from that end."

Eradicate, with his line of hose, had disappeared into the shop through the front door, and the others pressed in after him, heedless of the dense smoke.

"Is it blazing much, Rad?" cried Tom.

"Can't see no blaze at all, Massa Tom," replied the colored man. "Dere's a heap of suffin in de middle ob de flo', an' dat's what's raisin' all de rumpus."

They all saw it a moment later, a smoldering heap of rags and paper on the concrete floor of the shop. Eradicate turned his hose on it, there was a hissing sound, a cloud of steam arose, and the fire was practically out, though much smoke remained.

"Jove! that was a lucky escape!" exclaimed Tom, as he looked around when the vapor had partly cleared away. "No damage done at all, as far as I can see. I wonder what the game was? Did you see anything of a tramp around here?" he asked of his father.

"No, Tom. I have been busy in the house. So has Mrs. Baggert. Suddenly she called my attention to the smoke coming from the door, and we ran out."

"I seen it, too," added Eradicate. "I was doin' some whitewashin', an' I run up as soon as I could."

"We saw the tramp all right, but he got away," said Tom, and he told how he had taken pictures of him. "I don't believe it would be much use to look for him now, though."

"Me look," spoke Koku significantly, as he hurried off in the direction taken by the tramp. He came back later, not having found him.

"What do you think of it, Tom?" asked Ned, when the excitement had calmed down, and the pile of burned rags had been removed. It was found that oil and chemicals had been put on them to cause a dense smoke.

"I think it was the work of those fellows who are after my camera," replied the young inventor. "They are evidently watching me, and when they saw us all go off in the airship they thought probably that the coast was clear."

"But why should they start a fire?"

"I don't know, but probably to create a lot of smoke, and excitement, so that they could search, and not be detected. Maybe the fellow after he found that the camera was gone, wanted to draw those in the house out to the shop, so he could have a clear field to search in my room for any drawings that would give him a dew as to how my machine works. They certainly did not want to burn the shop, for that pile of rags could have smoldered all day on the concrete floor, without doing any harm. Robbery was the motive, I think."

"The police ought to be notified," declared Mr. Nestor. "Develop those pictures, Tom, and I'll take the matter up with the police. Maybe they can identify the tramp from the photographs."

But this proved impossible. Tom had secured several good films, not only in the first views he took, giving the spectators the impression that they were going up in an airship, but also those showing the shop on fire, and the tramp running away, were very plain.

The police made a search for the incendiary, but of course did not find him. Mr. Period came to Shopton, and declared it was his belief that his rivals, Turbot and Eckert, had had a hand in the matter. But it was only a suspicion, though Tom himself believed the same thing. Still nothing could be accomplished.

"The thing to do, now that the camera works all right, is for you to hit the trail for India at once," suggested the picture man. "They won't follow you there. Get me some pictures of the Durbar, of elephants being captured, of tiger fights, anything exciting."

"I'll do my—" began Tom.

"Wait, I'm not through," interrupted the excitable man. "Then go get some volcanoes, earthquakes—anything that you think would be interesting. I'll keep in touch with you, and cable occasionally. Get all the films you can. When will you start?"

"I can leave inside of two weeks," replied Tom.

"Then do it, and, meanwhile, be on your guard."

It was found that a few changes were needed on the camera. And some adjustments to the airship. Another trial flight was made, and some excellent pictures taken. Then Tom and his friends prepared to take the airship apart. and pack it for shipment to Calcutta. It was to go on the same steamer as themselves, and of course the Wizard Camera would accompany Tom. He took along many rolls of films, enough, he thought, for many views. He was also to send back to Mr. Period from time to time, the exposed rolls of film, so they could be developed, and printed in the United States, as Tom would not have very good facilities for this on the airship, and to reproduce them there was almost out of the question. Still he did fit up a small dark room aboard the Flyer, where he could develop pictures if he wished.

There was much to be done, but hard work accomplished it, and finally the party was ready to start for India. Tom said good-bye to Mary Nestor, of course, and her father accompanied our hero from the Nestor house to the Swift homestead, where the start was to take place.

Eradicate bade his master a tearful good-bye, and there was moisture in the eyes of Mr. Swift, as he shook hands with his son.

"Take care of yourself, Tom," he said. "Don't run too many risks. This moving picture taking isn't as easy as it sounds. It's more than just pointing your camera at things. Write if you get a chance, or send me a message."

Tom promised, and then bade farewell to Mrs. Baggert. All were assembled, Koku, Mr. Damon, who blessed everything he saw, and some things he did not, Ned, Mr. Nestor and Tom. The five were to go by train to New York, there to go aboard the steamer.

Their journey to the metropolis was uneventful. Mr. Period met them at the steamship dock, after Tom had seen to it that the baggage, and the parts of the airship were safely aboard.

"I wish I were going along!" exclaimed the picture man. "It's going to be a great trip. But I can't spare the time. I'm the busiest man in the world. I lose about a thousand dollars just coming down to see you off, but it's a good investment. I don't mind it. Now, Tom, good luck, and don't forget, I want exciting views."

"I'll try—" began our here,.

"Wait, I know what you're going to say!" interrupted Mr. Period. "You'll do it, of course. Well, I must be going. I will— Great Scott!" and Mr. Period interrupted himself. "He has the nerve to come here!"

"Who?" asked Tom.

"Wilson Turbot, the rascal! He's trying to balk me at the last minute, I believe. I'm going to see what he means!" and with this, the excited Mr. Period rushed down the gangplank, toward the man at whom he had pointed—one of the men who had tried to buy Tom's picture taking camera.

A moment later the steamer's whistle blew, the last belated passenger rushed up the gangplank, it was drawn in, and the vessel began to move away from the dock. Tom and his friends were on their way to India, and the last glimpse they had of Mr. Period was as he was chasing along the pier, after Mr. Turbot.

Unexpected Excitement

"Well, what do you know about that, Tom?" asked Ned, as they stood on deck watching the chase. "Isn't he the greatest ever— Mr. Period, I mean?"

"He certainly is. I'd like to see what happens when he catches that Turbot chap."

"Bless my pocket handkerchief!" cried Mr. Damon. "I don't believe he will. Mr. Period's legs aren't long enough for fast running."

"Those scoundrels were after us, up to the last minute," spoke Mr. Nestor, as the ship moved farther out from the dock. Tom and his friends could no longer see the excitable picture man after his rival, but there was a commotion in the crowd, and it seemed as if he had caught the fellow.

"Well, we're free of him now," spoke the young inventor, with a breath of relief. "That is, unless they have set some one else on our trail," and he looked carefully at the passengers near him, to detect, if possible, any who might look like spies in the pay of the rival moving picture concern, or any suspicious characters who might try to steal the valuable camera, that was now safely locked in Tom's cabin. Our hero, however, saw no one to worry about. He resolved to remain on his guard.

Friends and relatives were waving farewells to one another, and the band was playing, as the big vessel drew out into the North, or Hudson, river, and steamed for the open sea.

Little of interest marked the first week of the voyage. All save Koku had done much traveling before, and it was no novelty to them. The giant, however, was amused and delighted with everything, even the most commonplace things he saw. He was a source of wonder to all the other passengers, and, in a way, he furnished much excitement.

One day several of the sailors were on deck, shifting one of the heavy anchors. They went about it in their usual way, all taking hold, and "heaving" together with a "chanty," or song, to enliven their work. But they did not make much progress, and one of the mates got rather excited about it.

"Here, shiver my timbers!" he cried. "Lively now! Lay about you, and get that over to the side!"

"Yo! Heave! Ho!" called the leader of the sailor gang.

The anchor did not move, for it had either caught on some projection, or the men were not using their strength.

"Lively! Lively!" cried the mate.

Suddenly Koku, who was in the crowd of passengers watching the work, pushed his way to where the anchor lay. With a powerful, but not rough action, he shoved the sailors aside. Then, stooping over, he took a firm grip of the big piece of iron, planted his feet well apart on the deck, and lifted the immense mass in his arms. There was a round of applause from the group of passengers.

"Where you want him?" Koku calmly asked of the mate, as he stood holding the anchor.

"Blast my marlin spikes!" cried the mate. "I never see the like of this afore! Put her over there, shipmate. If I had you on a voyage or two you'd be running the ship, instead of letting the screw push her along. Put her over there," and he indicated where he wanted the anchor.

Koku calmly walked along the deck, laid the anchor down as if it was an ordinary weight, and passed over to where Tom stood looking on in amused silence. There were murmurs of surprise from the passengers at the giant's strength, and the sailors went forward much abashed.

"Say, I'd give a good bit to have a bodyguard like that," exclaimed a well-known millionaire passenger, who, it was reported, was in constant fear of attacks, though they had never taken place. "I wonder if I could get him."

He spoke to Tom about it, but our hero would not listen to a proposition to part with Koku. Besides, it is doubtful if the simple giant would leave the lad who had brought him away from his South American home. But, if Koku was wonderfully strong, and, seemingly afraid of nothing, there were certain things he feared.

One afternoon, for the amusement of the passengers, a net was put overboard, sunk to a considerable depth, and hauled up with a number of fishes in it. Some of the finny specimens were good for eating, and others were freaks, strange and curious.

Koku was in the throng that gathered on deck to look at the haul. Suddenly a small fish, but very hideous to look at, leaped from the net and flopped toward the giant. With a scream of fear Koku jumped to one side, and ran down to his stateroom. He could not be induced to come on deck until Tom assured him that the fishes had been disposed of. Thus Koku was a mixture of giant and baby. But he was a general favorite on the ship, and often gave exhibitions of his strength.

Meanwhile Tom and his friends had been on the lookout for any one who might be trailing them. But they saw no suspicious characters among the passengers, and, gradually, they began to feel that they had left their enemies behind.

The weather was pleasant, and the voyage very enjoyable. Tom and the others had little to do, and they were getting rather impatient for the time to come when they could put the airship together, and sail off over the jungle, to get moving pictures of the elephants.

"Have you any films in the camera now?" asked Ned of his chum on day, as they sat on deck together.

"Yes, it's all ready for instant use. Even the storage battery is charged. Why?"

"Oh, I was just wondering. I was thinking we might somehow see something we could take pictures of."

"Not much out here," said Tom, as he looked across the watery expanse. As he did so, he saw a haze of smoke dead ahead. "We'll pass a steamer soon," he went on, "but that wouldn't make a good picture. It's too common."

As the two lads watched, the smoke became blacker, and the cloud it formed grew much larger.

"They're burning a lot of coal on that ship," remarked Ned. "Must be trying for a speed record."

A little later a sailor stationed himself in the crow's nest, and focused a telescope on the smoke. An officer, on deck, seemed to be waiting for a report from the man aloft.

"That's rather odd," remarked Ned. "I never knew them to take so much interest in a passing steamer before; and we've gone by several of late."

"That's right," agreed Tom. "I wonder—"

At that moment the officer, looking up, called out:

"Main top!"

"Aye, aye, sir," answered the sailor with the glass. "She's a small steamer, sir, and she's on fire!"

"That's what I feared. Come down. I'll tell the captain. We must crowd on all steam, and go to the rescue."

"Did you hear that?" cried Ned to Tom, as the officer hurried to the bridge, where the captain awaited him. "A steamer on fire at sea, Tom! why don't you—"

"I'm going to!" interrupted the young inventor, as he started for his cabin on the run. "I'm going to get some moving pictures of the rescue! That will be a film worth having."

A moment later the Belchar, the vessel on which our friends had embarked, increased her speed, while sudden excitement developed on board.

As the Belchar approached the burning steamer, which had evidently seen her, and was making all speed toward her, the cloud of smoke became more dense, and a dull flame could be seen reflected in the water.

"She's going fast!" cried Mr. Nestor, as he joined Ned on deck.

"Bless my insurance policy!" cried Mr. Damon. "What a strange happening! Where's Tom Swift?"

"Gone for his camera," answered his chum. "He's going to get some pictures of the rescue."

"All hands man the life boats!" cried an officer, and several sailors sprang to the davits, ready to lower the boats, when the steamers should be near enough together.

Up on deck came Tom, with his wonderful camera.

"Here you go, Ned!" he called. "Give me a hand. I'm going to start the film now."

An Elephant Stampede

"Lower away!"

"Stand by the life boats!"

"Let go! Pull hearty!"

These and other commands marked the beginning of the rescue, as the sailors manned the davit-falls, and put the boats into the water. The burning steamer had now come to a stop, not far away from the Belchar, which was also lay-to. There was scarcely any sea running, and no wind, so that the work of rescuing was not difficult from an ordinary standpoint. But there was grave danger, because the fire on the doomed vessel was gaining rapidly.

"That's oil burning," remarked an officer, and it seemed so, from the dense clouds of smoke that rolled upward.

"Is she working, Tom?" asked Ned, as he helped his chum to hold the wonderful camera steady on the rail, so that a good view of the burning steamer could be had.

"Yes, the film is running. Say, I wonder if they'll get 'em all off?"

"Oh, I think so. There aren't many passengers. I guess it's a tramp freighter."

They could look across the gap of water, and see the terrified passengers and crew crowding to the rail, holding out their hands appealingly to the brave sailors who were lustily and rapidly, pulling toward them in life boats.

At times a swirl of smoke would hide those on the doomed vessel from the sight of the passengers on the Belchar, and on such occasions the frightened screams of women could be heard. Once, as the smoke cleared away, a woman, with a child in her arms, giving a backward glance toward the flames that were now enveloping the stern of the vessel, attempted to leap overboard.

Many hands caught her, however, and all this was registered on the film of Tom's camera, which was working automatically. As the two vessels drifted along, Tom and Ned shifted the lens so as to keep the burning steamer, and the approaching lifeboats, in focus.

"There's the first rescue!" cried Ned, as the woman who had attempted to leap overboard, was, with her child, carefully lowered into a boat. "Did you get that, Tom?"

"I certainly did. This will make a good picture. I think I'll send it back to Mr. Period as soon as we reach port."

"Maybe you could develop it on board here, and show it. I understand there's a dark room, and the captain said one of his officers, who used to be in the moving picture business, had a reproducing machine."

"Then that's what I'll do!" cried Tom. "I'll have our captain charge all the Belchar passengers admission, and we'll get up a fund for the fire sufferers. They'll probably lose all their baggage."

"That will be great!" exclaimed Ned.

The rescue was now in full swing, and, in a short time all the passengers and crew had been transferred to the life boats. Tom got a good picture of the captain of the burning steamer being the last to leave his vessel. Then the approaching life boats, with their loads of sailors, and rescued ones, were caught on the films.

"Are you all off?" cried the captain of the Belchar to the unfortunate skipper of the doomed ship.

"All off, yes, thank you. It is a mercy you were at hand. I have a cargo of oil. You had better stand off, for she'll explode in a few minutes."

"I must get a picture of that!" declared Tom as the Belchar got under way again. "That will cap the climax, and make a film that will be hard to beat."

A few moments later there was a tremendous explosion on the tramp oiler. A column of wreckage and black smoke shot skyward, and Tom secured a fine view of it. Then the wreck disappeared beneath the waves, while the rescuing steamer sailed on, with those who had been saved. They had brought off only the things they wore, for the fire had occurred suddenly, and spread rapidly. Kind persons aboard the Belchar looked after the unfortunates. Luckily there was not a large passenger list on the tramp. And the crew was comparatively small, so it was not hard work to make room for them, or take care of them, aboard the Belchar.

Tom developed his pictures, and produced then in one of the large saloons, on a machine he borrowed from the man of whom Ned had spoken. A dollar admission was charged, and the crowd was so large that Tom had to give two performances. The films, showing the burning steamer and the rescue, were excellent, and enough money was realized to aid, most substantially, the unfortunate passengers and crew.

A few days later a New York bound steamer was spoken, and on it Tom sent the roll of developed films to Mr. Period, with a letter of explanation.

I will not give all the details of the rest of the voyage. Sufficient to say that no accidents marred it, nor did Tom discover any suspicious characters aboard. In due time our friends arrived at Calcutta, and were met by an agent of Mr. Period, for he had men in all quarters of the world, making films for him.

This agent took Tom and his party to a hotel, and arranged to have the airship parts sent to a large open shed, not far away, where it could be put together. The wonderful scenes in the Indian city interested Tom and his companions for a time, but they had observed so many strange sights from time to time that they did not marvel greatly. Koku, however, was much delighted. He was like a child.

"What are you going to do first?" asked Ned, when they had recovered from the fatigue of the ocean voyage and had settled themselves in the hotel.

"Put the airship together," replied our hero, "and then, after getting some Durbar pictures, we'll head for the jungle. I want to get some elephant pictures, showing the big beasts being captured."

Mr. Period's agent was a great help to them in this. He secured native helpers, who aided Tom in assembling the airship, and in a week or two it was ready for a flight. The wonderful camera, too, was looked over, and the picture agent said he had never seen a better one.

"It can take the kind of pictures I never could," he said. "I get Calcutta street scenes for Mr. Period, and occasionally I strike a good one. But I wish I had your chance."

Tom invited him to come along in the airship, but the agent, who only looked after Mr. Period's interests as a side issue, could not leave his work.

The airship was ready for a flight, stores and provisions had been put on board, there was enough gasoline for the motor, and gas for the balloon bag, to carry the Flyer thousands of miles. The moving picture camera had been tested after the sea voyage, and had been found to work perfectly. Many rolls of films were taken along. Tom got some fine views of the Durbar of India, and his airship created a great sensation.

"Now I guess we're all ready for the elephants," said Tom one day as he came back from an inspection of the airship as it rested in the big shed. "We'll start to-morrow morning, and head for the jungle."

Amid the cries from a throng of wondering and awed natives, and with the farewells of Mr. Period's agent ringing in their ears, Tom and his party made an early start. The Flyer rose like a bird, and shot across the city, while on the house tops many people watches the strange sight. Tom did not start his camera working, as Mr. Period's agent said he had made many pictures of the Indian city, and even one taken from an airship, would not be much of a novelty.

Tom had made inquiries, and learned that by a day's travel in his airship (though it would have been much longer ordinarily) he could reach a jungle where elephants might be found. Of course there was nothing certain about it, as the big animals roamed all over, being in one district one day, and on the next, many miles off.

Gradually the city was left behind, and some time later the airship was sailing along over the jungle. After the start, when Ned and Tom, with Mr. Damon helping occasionally, had gotten the machinery into proper adjustment, the Flyer almost ran herself. Then Tom took his station forward, with his camera in readiness, and a powerful spyglass at hand, so that he might see the elephants from a distance.

He had been told that, somewhere in the district for which he was headed, an elephant drive was contemplated. He hoped to be on hand to get pictures of it, and so sent his airship ahead at top speed.

On and on they rode, being as much at ease in the air as they would have been if traveling in a parlor car. They did not fly high, as it was necessary to be fairly close to the earth to get good pictures.

"Well, I guess we won't have any luck today," remarked Ned, as night approached, and they had had no sight of the elephants. They had gone over mile after mile of jungle, but had seen few wild beasts in sufficient numbers to make it worth while to focus the camera on them.

"We'll float along to-night," decided Tom, "and try again in the morning."

It was about ten o'clock the next day, when Ned, who had relieved Tom on watch, uttered a cry:

"What is it?" asked his chum, as he rushed forward. "Has anything happened?"

"Lots!" cried Ned. "Look!" He pointed down below. Tom saw, crashing through the jungle, a big herd of elephants. Behind them, almost surrounding them, in fact, was a crowd of natives in charge of white hunters, who were driving the herd toward a stockade.

"There's a chance for a grand picture!" exclaimed Tom, as he got the camera ready. "Take charge of the ship, Ned. Keep her right over the big animals, and I'll work the camera."

Quickly he focused the lens on the strange scene below him. There was a riot of trumpeting from the elephants. The beaters and hunters shouted and yelled. Then they saw the airship and waved their hands to Tom and his friends, but whether to welcome them, or warn them away, could not be told.

The elephants were slowly advancing toward the stockade. Tom was taking picture after picture of them, when suddenly as the airship came lower, in response to a signal to Ned from the young inventor, one of the huge pachyderms looked up, and saw the strange sight. He might have taken it for an immense bird. At any rate he gave a trumpet of alarm, and the next minute, with screams of rage and fear, the elephants turned, and charged in a wild stampede on those who were driving them toward the stockade.

"Look!" cried Ned. "Those hunters and natives will be killed!"

"I'm afraid so!" shouted Tom, as he continued to focus his camera on the wonderful sight.

THE LION FIGHT

Crashing through the jungle the huge beasts turned against those who had, been driving them on toward the stockade. With wild shouts and yells, the hunters and their native helpers tried to turn back the elephant tide, but it was useless. The animals had been frightened by the airship, and were following their leader, a big bull, that went crashing against great trees, snapping them off as if they were pipe stems.

"Say, this is something like!" cried Ned, as he guided the airship over the closely packed body of elephants, so Tom could get good pictures, for the herd had divided, and a small number had gone off with one of the other bulls.

"Yes, I'll get some great pictures," agreed Tom, as he looked in through a red covered opening in the camera, to see how much film was left.

The airship was now so low down that Tom, and the others, could easily make out the faces of the hunters, and the native helpers. One of the hunters, evidently the chief, shaking his fist at our hero, cried:

"Can't you take your blooming ship out of the way, my man? It's scaring the beasts, and we've been a couple of weeks on this drive. We don't want to lose all our work. Take your bloody ship away!"

"I guess he must be an Englishman," remarked Mr. Nestor, with a laugh.

"Bless my dictionary, I should say so," agreed Mr. Damon. "Bloody, blooming ship! The idea!"

"Well, I suppose we have scared the beasts," said Tom. "We ought to get out of the way. Put her up, Ned, and we'll come down some distance in advance."

"Why, aren't you going to take any more views of the elephants?"

"Yes, but I've got enough of a view from above. Besides, I've got to put in a fresh reel of film, and I might as well get out of their sight to do it. Maybe that will quiet them, and the hunters can turn them back toward the stockade. If they do, I have another plan."

"What is it?" his chum wanted to know.

"I'm going to make a landing, set up my camera at the entrance to the stockade, and get a series of pictures as the animals come in. I think that will be a novelty.

"That certainly will," agreed Mr. Nestor. "I am sure Mr. Period will appreciate that. But won't it be dangerous, Tom?"

"I suppose so, but I'm getting used to danger," replied our hero, with a laugh.

Ned put the ship high into the air, as Tom shut off the power from the camera. Then the Flyer was sent well on in advance of the stampede of elephants, so they could no longer see it, or hear the throb of the powerful engines. Tom hoped that this would serve to quiet the immense creatures.

As the travelers flew on, over the jungle, they could still hear the racket made by the hunters and beaters, and the shrill trumpeting of the elephants, as they crashed through the forest.

Tom at once began changing the film in the camera, and Ned altered the course of the airship, to send it back toward the stockade, which they had passed just before coming upon the herd of elephants.

I presume most of my readers know what an elephant drive is like. A stockade, consisting of heavy trees, is made in the jungle. It is like the old fashioned forts our forefathers used to make, for a defense against the Indians. There is a broad entrance to it, and, when all is in readiness, the beaters go out into the jungle, with the white hunters, to round up the elephants. A number of tame pachyderms are taken along to persuade the wild ones to follow.

Gradually the elephants are gathered together in a large body, and gently driven toward the stockade. The tame elephants go in first, and the others follow. Then the entrance is closed, and all that remains to be done is to tame the wild beasts, a not very easy task.

"Are you all ready?" asked Ned, after a bit, as he saw Tom come forward with the camera.

"Yes, I'm loaded for some more excitement. You can put me right over the stockade now, Ned, and when we see the herd coming back I'll go down, and take some views from the ground."

"I think they've got 'em turned," said Mr. Damon. "It sounds as if they were coming back this way."

A moment later they had a glimpse of the herd down below. It was true that the hunters had succeeded in stopping the stampede, and once more the huge beasts were going in the right direction.

"There's a good place to make a landing," suggested Tom, as he saw a comparatively clear place in the jungle. "It's near the stockade, and, in case of danger, I can make a quick get-away."

"What kind of danger are you looking for?" asked Ned, as he shifted the deflecting rudder.

"Oh, one of the beasts might take a notion to chase me."

The landing was made, and Tom, taking Ned and Mr. Nestor with him, and leaving the others to manage the airship in case a quick flight would be necessary, made his way along a jungle trail to the entrance to the stockade. He carried his camera with him, for it was not heavy.

On came the elephants, frightened by the shouts and cries of the beaters, and the firing of guns. The young inventor took his place near the stockade entrance, and, as the elephants advanced through the forest, tearing up trees and bushes, Tom got some good pictures of them.

Suddenly the advance of the brutes was checked, and the foremost of them raised their trunks, trumpeted in anger, and were about to turn back again.

"Get away from that bloomin' gate!" shouted a hunter to Tom. "You're scaring them as bad as your airship did."

"Yes, they won't go in with you there!" added another man.

Tom slipped around the corner of the stockade, out of sight, and from that vantage point he took scores of pictures, as the tame animals led the wild ones into the fenced enclosure. Then began another wild scene as the gate was closed.

The terrified animals rushed about, trying in vain to find a way of escape. Tom managed to climb up on top of the logs, and got some splendid pictures. But this was nearly his undoing. For, just as the last elephant rushed in, a big bull charged against the stockade, and jarred Tom so that he was on the point of falling. His one thought was about his camera, and he looked to see if he could drop it on the soft grass, so it would not be damaged.

He saw Koku standing below him, the giant having slipped out of the airship, to see the beasts at closer range.

"Catch this, Koku!" cried Tom, tossing the big man his precious camera, and the giant caught it safely. But Tom's troubles were not over. A moment later, as the huge elephant again rammed the fence, Tom fell off, but fortunately outside. Then the large beast, seeing a small opening in the gate that was not yet entirely closed, made for it. A moment later he was rushing straight at Tom, who was somewhat stunned by his fall, though it was not a severe one.

"Look out!" yelled Ned.

"Take a tree, Tom!" cried Mr. Nestor.

The elephant paid no attention to any one but Tom, whom he seemed to think had caused all his trouble. The young inventor dashed to one side, and then started to run toward the airship, for which Ned and Mr. Nestor were already making. The elephant hunters at last succeeded in closing the gate, blocking the chance of any more animals to escape.

"Run, Tom! Run!" yelled Ned, and Tom ran as he had never run before. The elephant was close after him though, crashing through the jungle. Tom could see the airship just ahead of him.

Suddenly he felt something grasp him from behind. He thought surely it was the elephant's trunk, but a quick glance over his shoulder showed him the friendly face of Koku, the giant.

"Me run for you," said Koku, as he caught Tom up under one arm, and, carrying the camera under the other, he set off at top speed. Now Koku could run well at times, and this time he did. He easily outdistanced the elephant, and, a little later, he set Tom down on the deck of the airship, with the camera beside him. Then Ned and Mr. Nestor came up panting, having run to one side.

"Quick!" cried Tom. "We must get away before the elephant charges the Flyer."

"He has stopped," shouted Mr. Nestor, and it was indeed so. The big beast, seeing again the strange craft that had frightened him before, stood still for a moment, and then plunged off into the jungle, trumpeting with rage.

"Safe!" gasped Tom, as he looked at his camera to see if it had been damaged. It seemed all right.

"Bless my latch key!" cried Mr. Damon. "This moving picture business isn't the most peaceful one in the world."

"No, it has plenty of perils," agreed Mr. Nestor.

"Come on, let's get out of here while we have the chance," suggested Tom. "There may be another herd upon us before we know it."

The airship was soon ascending, and Tom and his companions could look down and see the tame elephants in the stockade trying to calm the wild ones. Then the scene faded from sight.

"Well, if these pictures come out all right I'll have some fine ones," exclaimed Tom as he carried his camera to the room where he kept the films. "I fancy an elephant drive and stampede are novelties in this line."

"Indeed they are," agreed Mr. Nestor. "Mr. Period made no mistake when he picked you out, Tom, for this work. What are you going to try for next?"

"I'd like to get some lion and tiger pictures," said the young inventor. "I understand this is a good district for that. As soon as those elephants get quieted down, I'm going back to the stockade and have a talk with the hunters."

This he did, circling about in the airship until nearly evening. When they again approached the stockade all was quiet, and they came to earth. A native showed them where the white hunters had their headquarters, in some bungalows, and Tom and his party were made welcome. They apologized for frightening the big beasts, and the hunters accepted their excuses.

"As long as we got 'em, it's all right," said the head man, "though for awhile, I didn't like your bloomin' machine." Tom entertained the hunters aboard his craft, at which they marvelled much, and they gave him all the information they had about the lions and tigers in the vicinity.

"You won't find lions and tigers in herds, like. elephants though," said the head hunter. "And you may have to photograph 'em at night, as then is when they come out to hunt, and drink."

"Well, I can take pictures at night," said Tom, as he showed his camera apparatus.

The next day, in the airship, they left for another district, where, so the natives reported, several lions had been seen of late. They had done much damage, too, carrying off the native cattle, and killing several Indians.

For nearly a week Tom circled about in his airship, keeping a sharp lookout down below for a sign of lions that he might photograph them. But he saw none, though he did get some pictures of a herd of Indian deer that were well worth his trouble.

"I think I'll have to try for a night photograph," decided Tom at last. "I'll locate a spring where wild beasts are in the habit of coming, set the camera with the light going, and leave it there."

"But will the lions come up if they see the light?" asked Ned.

"I think so," replied his chum. "I'll take a chance, anyhow. If that doesn't work then I'll hide near by, and see what happens."

"Bless my cartridge belt!" cried Mr. Damon. "You don't mean that; do you Tom?"

"Of course. Come to think of it, I'm not going to leave my camera out there for a lion to jump on, and break. As soon as I get a series of pictures I'll bring it back to the ship, I think."

By inquiry among the natives they learned the location of a spring where, it was said, lions were in the habit of coming nightly to drink.

"That's the place I want!" cried Tom.

Accordingly the airship was headed for it, and one evening it came gently to earth in a little clearing on the edge of the jungle, while Koku, as was his habit, got supper.

After the meal Tom and Ned set the camera, and then, picking out a good spot nearby, they hid themselves to wait for what might happen. The lens was focused on the spring, and the powerful electric light set going. It glowed brightly, and our hero thought it might have the effect of keeping the beasts away, but Tom figured that, after they had looked at it for a while, and seen that it did not harm them, they would lose their suspicions, and come within range of his machine.

"The camera will do the rest," he said. In order not to waste films uselessly Tom arranged a long electric wire, running it from the camera to where he and Ned were hid. By pressing a button he could start or stop the camera any time he wished, and, as he had a view of the spring from his vantage point, he could have the apparatus begin taking pictures as soon as there was some animal within focus.

"Well, I'm getting stiff," said Ned, after an hour or so had passed in silent darkness, the only light being the distant one on the camera.

"So am I," said Tom.

"I don't believe anything will come to-night," went on his chum. "Let's go back and—"

He stopped suddenly, for there was a crackling in the underbrush, and the next moment the jungle vibrated to the mighty roar of a lion.

"He's coming!" hoarsely whispered Tom.

Both lads glanced through the trees toward the camera, and, in the light, they saw a magnificent, tawny beast standing on the edge of the spring. Once more he roared, as if in defiance, and then, as if deciding that the light was not harmful, he stooped to lap up the water

Hardly had he done so than there was another roar, and a moment later a second lion leaped from the dense jungle into the clearing about the spring. The two monarchs of the forest stood there in the glare of the light, and Tom excitedly pressed the button that started the shutter to working, and the film to moving back of the lens.

There was a slight clicking sound in the camera, and the lions turned startledly. Then both growled again, and the next instant they sprang at each other, roaring mightily.

"A fight!" cried Tom. "A lion fight, and right in front of my camera! It couldn't be better. This is great! This will be a film."

"Quiet!" begged Ned. "They'll hear you, and come for us. I don't want to be chewed up!"

"No danger of them hearing me!" cried Tom. and he had to shout to be heard above the roaring of the two tawny beasts, as they bit and clawed each other, while the camera took picture after picture of them.

A SHOT IN TIME

"Tom, did you ever see anything like it in your life?"

"I never did, Ned! It's wonderful! fearful! And to think that we are here watching it, and that thousands of people will see the same thing thrown on a screen. Oh, look at the big one. The small lion has him down!"

The two lads, much thrilled, crouched down behind a screen of bushes, watching the midnight fight between the lions. On the airship, not far distant, there was no little alarm, for those left behind heard the terrific roars, and feared Tom and Ned might be in some danger. But the lions were too much occupied with their battle, to pay any attention to anything else, and no other wild beasts were likely to come to the spring while the two "kings" were at each other.

It was a magnificent, but terrible battle. The big cats bit and tore at each other, using their terrific claws and their powerful paws, one stroke of which is said to be sufficient to break a bullock's back. Sometimes they would roll out of the focus of the camera, and, at such times, Tom wished he was at the machine to swing the lens around, but he knew it would be dangerous to move. Then the beasts would roll back into the rays of light again, and more pictures of them would be taken.

"I guess the small one is going to win!" said Tom, after the two lions had fought for ten minutes, and the bigger one had been down several times.

"He's younger," agreed Ned, "and I guess the other one has had his share of fights. Maybe this is a battle to see which one is to rule this part of the jungle."

"I guess so," spoke the young inventor, as he pressed the button to stop the camera, as the lions rolled out of focus. "Oh, look!" he cried a moment later, as the animals again rolled into view. Tom started the camera once more. "This is near the end," he said.

The small lion had, by a sudden spring, landed on the back of his rival. There was a terrific struggle, and the older beast went down, the younger one clawing him terribly. Then, so quickly did it happen that the boys could not take in all the details, the older lion rolled over and over, and rid himself of his antagonist. Quickly he got to his feet, while the smaller lion did the same. They stood for a moment eyeing each other, their tails twitching, the hair on their backs bristling, and all the while they uttered frightful, roars.

An instant later the larger beast sprang toward his rival. One terrible paw was upraised. The small lion tried to dodge, but was not quick enough. Down came the paw with terrific force, and the boys could hear the back bone snap. Then, clawing his antagonist terribly, as he lay disabled, the older lion, with a roar of triumph, lapped up water, and sprang off through the jungle, leaving his dying rival beside the spring.

"That's the end," cried Tom, as the small lion died, and the young inventor pressed the button stopping his camera. There was a rustle in the leaves back of Tom and Ned, and they sprang up in alarm, but they need not have feared, for it was only Koku, the giant, who, with a portable electrical torch, had come to see how they had fared.

"Mr. Tom all right?" asked the big man, anxiously.

"Yes, and I got some fine pictures. You can carry the camera back now, Koku. I think that roll of film is pretty well filled."

The three of them looked at the body of the dead lion, before they went back to the airship. I have called him "small," but, in reality, the ;beast was small only in comparison with his rival, who was a tremendous lion in size. I might add that of all the pictures Tom took, few were more highly prized than that reel of the lion fight.

"Bless my bear cage!" cried Mr. Damon, as Tom came back, "you certainly have nerve, my boy."

"You have to, in this business," agreed Tom with a laugh. "I never did this before, and I don't know that I would want it for a steady position, but it's exciting for a change."

They remained near the "lion spring" as they called it all night, and in the morning, after Koku had served a tasty breakfast, Tom headed the airship for a district where it was said there were many antelope, and buffaloes, also zebus.

"I don't want to get all exciting pictures," our hero said to Mr. Nestor. "I think that films showing wild animals at play, or quietly feeding, will be good."

"I'm sure they will," said Mary's father. "Get some peaceful scenes, by all means."

They sailed on for several days, taking a number of pictures from the airship, when they passed over a part of the country where the view was magnificent, and finally, stopping at a good sized village they learned that, about ten miles out, was a district where antelope abounded.

"We'll go there," decided Tom, "and I'll take the camera around with me on a sort of walking trip. In that way I'll get a variety of views, and I can make a good film."

This plan was followed out. The airship came to rest in a beautiful green valley, and Ned and Tom, with Mr. Damon, who begged to be taken along, started off.

"You can follow me in about half an hour, Koku," said Tom, "and carry the camera back. I guess you can easily pick up our trail."

"Oh, sure," replied the giant. Indeed, to one who had lived in the forest, as he had all his life, before Tom found him, it was no difficult matter to follow a trail, such as the three friends would leave.

Tom found signs that showed him where the antelopes were in the habit of passing, and, with Ned and Mr. Damon, stationed himself in a secluded spot.

He had not long to wait before a herd of deer came past. Tom took many pictures of the graceful creatures, for it was daylight now, and he needed no light. Consequently there was nothing to alarm the herd.

After having made several films of the antelope, Tom and his two companions went farther on. They were fortunate enough to find a place that seemed to be a regular playground of the deer. There was a large herd there, and, getting as near as he dared, Tom focused his camera, and began taking pictures.

"It's as good as a play," whispered Mr. Damon, as he and Ned watched the creatures, for they had to speak quietly. The camera made scarcely any noise. "I'm glad I came on this trip."

"So am I," said Ned. "Look, Tom, see the mother deer all together, and the fawns near them. It's just as if it was a kindergarten meeting."

"I see," whispered Tom. "I'm getting a picture of that."

For some little time longer Tom photographed the deer, and then, suddenly, the timid creatures all at once lifted up their heads, and darted off. Tom and Ned, wondering what had startled them, looked across the glade just in time to see a big tiger leap out of the tall grass. The striped animal had been stalking the antelope, but they had scented him just in time.

"Get him, Tom," urged Ned, and the young inventor did so, securing several fine views be. fore the tiger bounded into the grass again, and took after his prey.

"Bless my china teacup! What's that!" suddenly cried Mr. Damon. As he spoke there was a crashing in the bushes and, an instant later as two-horned rhinoceros sprang into view, charging straight for the group.

"Look out!" yelled Ned.

"Bless my—" began Mr. Damon, but he did not finish, for, in starting to run his foot caught in the grass, and he went down heavily.

Tom leaped to one side, holding his camera so as not to damage it. But he stumbled over Mr. Damon, and went down.

With a "wuff" of rage the clumsy beast, came on, moving more rapidly than Tom had any idea he was capable of. Hampered by his camera our hero could not arise. The rhinoceros was almost upon him, and Ned, catching up a club, was just going to make a rush to the rescue, when the brute seemed suddenly to crumple up. It fell down in a heap, not five feet from where Tom and Mr. Damon lay.

"Good!" cried Ned. "He's dead. Shot through the heart! Who did it?"

"I did," answered Koku quietly, stepping out of the bushes, with one of Tom's Swift's electric rifles in his hand.

In a Great Gale

Tom Swift rose slowly to his feet, carefully setting his camera down, after making sure that it was not injured. Then he looked at the huge beast which lay dead in front of him, and, going over to the giant he held out his hand to him.

"Koku, you saved my life," spoke Tom. "Probably the life of Mr. Damon also. I can't begin to thank you. It isn't the first time you've done it, either. But I want to say that you can have anything you want, that I've got."

"Me like this gun pretty much," said the giant simply.

"Then it's yours!" exclaimed Tom. "And you're the only one, except myself, who has ever owned one." Tom's wonderful electric rifle, of which I have told you in the book bearing that name, was one of his most cherished inventions.

He guarded jealously the secret of how it worked, and never sold or gave one away, for fear that unscrupulous men might learn how to make them, and to cause fearful havoc. For the rifle was a terrible weapon. Koku seemed to appreciate the honor done him, as he handled the gun, and looked from it to the dead rhinoceros.

"Bless my blank cartridge!" exclaimed Mr. Damon, as he also got up and came to examine the dead beast. It was the first thing he had said since the animal had rushed at him, and he had not moved after he fell down. He had seemingly been in a daze, but when the others heard him use one of his favorite expressions they knew that he was all right again. "Bless my hat!" went on the odd man. "What happened, Tom? Is that beast really dead? How did Koku come to arrive in time?"

"I guess he's dead all right," said Tom, giving the rhinoceros a kick. "But I don't know how Koku happened to arrive in the nick of time, and with the gun, too."

"I think maybe I see something to shoot when I come after you, like you tell me to do," spoke the giant. "I follow your trail, but I see nothing to shoot until I come here. Then I see that animal run for you, and I shoot."

"And a good thing you did, too," put in Ned. "Well let's go back. My nerves are on edge, and I want to sit quiet for a while."

"Take the camera, Koku," ordered Tom, "and I'll carry the electric rifle—your rifle, now," he added, and the giant grinned in delight. They reached the airship without further incident, and, after a cup of tea, Tom took out the exposed films and put a fresh roll in his camera, ready for whatever new might happen.

"Where is your next stopping place, Tom?" asked Ned, as they sat in the main room of the airship that evening, talking over the events of the day. They had decided to stay all night anchored on the ground, and start off in the morning.

"I hardly know, answered the young inventor. "I am going to set the camera to-night, near a small spring I saw, to get some pictures of deer coming to drink. I may get a picture of a lion or a tiger attacking them. If I could it would be another fine film. To-morrow I think we will start for Switzerland. But now I'm going to get the camera ready for a night exposure.

"Bless my check book!" cried Mr. Damon. "You don't mean to say that you are going to stay out at a spring again, Tom, and run the chance of a tiger getting you."

"No, I'm merely going to set the camera, attach the light and let it work automatically this time. I've put in an extra long roll of film, for I'm going to keep it going for a long while, and part of the time there may be no animals there to take pictures of. No, I'm not going to sit out to-night. I'm too tired. I'll conceal the camera in the bushes so it won't be damaged if there's a fight. Then, as I said, we'll start for Switzerland to-morrow."

"Switzerland!" cried Ned. "What in the world do you want to go make a big jump like that for? And what do you expect to get in that mountain land?"

"I'm going to try for a picture of an avalanche," said Tom. "Mr. Period wants one, if I can get it. It is quite a jump, but then we'll be flying over civilized countries most of the time, and if any accident happens we can go down and easily make repairs. We can also get gasolene for the motor, though I have quite a supply in the tanks, and perhaps enough for the entire trip. At the same time we won't take any chances. So we'll be off for Switzerland in the morning.

"I think some avalanche pictures will be great, if you can get them," remarked Mr. Nestor. "But, Tom, you know those big slides of ice, snow and earth aren't made to order."

"Oh, I know," agreed the young inventor with a smile. "I'll just have to take my chances, and wait until one happens."

"Bless my insurance policy!" exclaimed Mr. Damon. "And when it does happen, Tom, are you going to stand in front of it, and snap-shot it?"

"Indeed I'm not. This business is risky and dangerous enough, without looking for trouble. I'm going to the mountain region, and hover around in the air, until we see an avalanche 'happen' if that is the right word. Then I'll focus the camera on it, and the films and machinery will do the rest."

"Oh, that's different," remarked the odd man, with an air of relief.

Tom and Ned soon had the camera set near the spring and then, everyone being tired with the day's work and excitement, they retired. In the morning there were signs around the spring that many animals had been there in the night. There were also marks as if there had been a fight, but of course what sort, or how desperate, no one could say.

"If anything happened the camera got it, I'm sure of that much," remarked Tom, as he brought in the apparatus. "I'm not going to develop the roll, for I don't want to take the time now. I guess we must have something, anyhow."

"If there isn't it won't so much matter for you have plenty of other good views," said Mr. Nestor.

I will not go into details of the long trip to Switzerland, where, amid the mountains of that country, Tom hoped to get the view he wanted.

Sufficient to say that the airship made good time after leaving India. Sometimes Tom sent the craft low down, in order to get views, and again, it would be above the clouds.

"Well, another day will bring us there," said Tom one evening, as he was loading the camera with a fresh roll of films. "Then we'll have to be on the lookout for an avalanche."

"Yes, we're making pretty good time," remarked Ned, as he looked at the speed gage. "I didn't know you had the motor working so fast, Tom."

"I haven't," was the young inventor's answer, as he looked up in surprise. "Why, we are going quite fast! It's the wind, Ned. It's right with us, and it's carrying us along."

Tom arose and went to the anemometer, or wind-registering instrument. He gave a low whistle, half of alarm.

"Fifty miles an hour she's blowing now," he said. "It came on suddenly, too, for a little while ago it was only ten."

"Is there any danger?" asked Mr. Nestor, for he was not very familiar with airship perils.

"Well, we've been in big blows before, and we generally came out all right," returned Tom. "Still, I don't like this. Why she went up five points since I've been looking at it!" and he pointed to the needle of the gage, which now registered fifty-five miles an hour.

"Bless my appendix!" gasped Mr. Damon. "It's a hurricane Tom!"

"Something like that," put in Ned, in a low voice.

With a suddenness that was startling, the wind increased in violence still more. Tom ran to the pilot house.

"What are you going to do?" Ned called.

"See if we can't go down a bit," was Tom's answer. "I don't like this. It may be calmer below. We're up too high as it is."

He tried to throw over the lever controlling the deflecting rudder, which would send the Flyer down, but he could not move it.

"Give me a hand!" he called to Ned, but even the strength of the two lads was not sufficient to shift it.

"Call Koku!" gasped Tom. "If anybody can budge it the giant can!"

Meanwhile the airship was being carried onward in the grip of a mighty wind, so strong that its pressure on the surface of the deflecting rudder prevented it from being shifted.

Snapping an Avalanche

"Bless my thermometer!" gasped Mr. Damon. "This is terrible!" The airship was plunging and swaying about in the awful gale. "Can't something be done, Tom?"

"What has happened?" cried Mr. Nestor. "We were on a level keel before. What is it?"

"It's the automatic balancing rudder!" answered Tom. "Something has happened to it. The wind may have broken it! Come on, Ned!" and he led the way to the engine room.

"What are you going to do? Don't you want Koku to shift the deflecting rudder? Here he is," Ned added, as the giant came forward, in response to a signal bell that Tom's chum had rung.

"It's too late to try the deflecting rudder!" tried Tom. "I must see what is the matter with our balancer." As he spoke the ship gave a terrific plunge, and the occupants were thrown sideways. The next moment it was on a level keel again, scudding along with the gale, but there was no telling when the craft would again nearly capsize.

Tom looked at the mechanism controlling the equalizing and equilibrium rudder. It was out of order, and he guessed that the terrific wind was responsible for it.

"What can we do?" cried Ned, as the airship nearly rolled over. "Can't we do anything, Tom?"

"Yes. I'm going to try. Keep calm now. We may come out all right. This is the worst blow we've been in since we were in Russia. Start the gas machine full blast. I want all the vapor I can get."

As I have explained the Flyer was a combined dirigible balloon and aeroplane. It could be used as either, or both, in combination. At present the gas bag was not fully inflated, and Tom had been sending his craft along as an aeroplane.

"What are you going to do?" cried Ned, as he pulled over the lever that set the gas generating machine in operation.

"I'm going up as high as I can go!" cried Tom. "If we can't go down we must go up. I'll get above the hurricane instead of below it. Give me all the gas you can, Ned!"

The vapor hissed as it rushed into the big bag overhead. Tom carried aboard his craft the chemicals needed to generate the powerful lifting gas, of which he alone had the secret. It was more powerful than hydrogen, and simple to make. The balloon of the Flyer was now being distended.

Meanwhile Tom, with Koku, Mr. Damon and Mr. Nestor to help him, worked over the deflecting rudder, and also on the equilibrium mechanism. But they could not get either to operate.

Ned stood by the gas machine, and worked it to the limit. But even with all that energy, so powerful was the wind, that the Flyer rose slowly, the gale actually holding her down as a water-logged craft is held below the waves. Ordinarily, with the gas machine set at its limit the craft would have shot up rapidly.

At times the airship would skim along on the level, and again it would be pitched and tossed about, until it was all the occupants could do to keep their feet. Mr. Damon was continually blessing everything he could remember.

"Now she's going!" suddenly cried Ned, as he looked at the dials registering the pressure of the gas, and showing the height of the airship above the earth.

"Going how?" gasped Tom, as he looked over from where he was working at the equilibrium apparatus. "Going down?"

"Going up!" shouted Ned. "I guess we'll be all right soon!"

It was true. Now that the bag was filled with the powerful lifting gas, under pressure, the Flyer was beginning to get out of the dangerous predicament into which the gale had blown her, Up and up she went, and every foot she climbed the power of the wind became less.

"Maybe it all happened for the best," said Tom, as he noted the height gage. "If we had gone down, the wind might have been worse nearer the earth."

Later they learned that this was so. The most destructive wind storm ever known swept across the southern part of Europe, over which they were flying that night, and, had the airship gone down, she would probably have been destroyed. But, going up, she got above the wind-strata. Up and up she climbed, until, when three miles above the earth, she was in a calm zone. It was rather hard to breathe at this height, and Tom set the oxygen apparatus at work.

This created in the interior of the craft an atmosphere almost like that on the earth, and the travelers were made more at their ease. Getting out of the terrible wind pressure made it possible to work the deflecting rudder, though Tom had no idea of going down, as long as the blow lasted.

"We'll just sail along at this height until morning," he said, "and by then the gale may be over, or we may be beyond the zone of it. Start the propellers, Ned. I think I can manage to repair the equilibrium rudder now."

The propellers, which gave the forward motion to the airship, had been stopped when it was found that the wind was carrying her along, but they were now put in motion again, sending the Flyer forward. In a short time Tom had the equilibrium machine in order, and matters were now normal again.

"But that was a strenuous time while it lasted," remarked the young inventor, as he sat down.

"It sure was," agreed Ned.

"Bless my pen wiper!" cried Mr. Damon. "That was one of the few times when I wish I'd never come with you, Tom Swift," and everyone laughed at that.

The Flyer was now out of danger, going along high in the air through the night, while the gale raged below her. At Tom's suggestion, Koku got a lunch ready, for they were all tired with their labors, and somewhat nervous from the danger and excitement.

"And now for sleep!" exclaimed Tom, as he pushed back his plate. "Ned, set the automatic steering gear, and we'll see where we bring up by morning."

An examination, through a powerful telescope in the bright light of morning, showed the travelers that they were over the outskirts of a large city, which, later, they learned was Rome, Italy.

"We've made a good trip," said Tom. "The gale had us worried, but it sent us along at a lively clip. Now for Switzerland, and the avalanches!"

They made a landing at a village just outside the "Holy City," as Rome is often called, and renewed their supply of gasolene. Naturally they attracted a crowd of curious persons, many of whom had never seen an airship before. Certainly few of them had ever seen one like Tom Swift's.

The next day found them hovering over the Alps, where Tom hoped to be able to get the pictures of snow slides. They went down to earth at a town near one of the big mountain ranges, and there made inquiries as to where would be the best location to look for big avalanches. If they went but a few miles to the north, they were told, they would be in the desired region, and they departed for that vicinity.

"And now we've just got to take our time, and wait for an avalanche to happen," remarked Tom, as they were flying along over the mountain ranges. "As Mr. Damon said, these things aren't made to order. They just happen."

For three days they sailed in and out over the great snow-covered peaks of the Alps. They did not go high up, for they wanted to be near earth when an avalanche would occur, so that near-view pictures could be secured. Occasionally they saw parties of mountain climbers ascending some celebrated peak, and for want of something better to photograph, Tom "snapped" the tourists.

"Well, I guess they're all out of avalanches this season," remarked Ned one afternoon, when they had circled back and forth over a mountain where, so it was said, the big snow slides were frequent.

"It does seem so," agreed Tom. "Still, we're in no hurry. It is easier to be up here, than it is walking around in a jungle, not knowing what minute a tiger may jump out at you."

"Bless my rubbers, yes!" agreed Mr. Damon.

The sky was covered with lowering clouds, and there were occasionally flurries of snow. Tom's airship was well above the snow line on the mountains. The young inventor and Ned sat in the pilot house, taking observations through a spyglass of the mountain chain below them.

Suddenly Ned, who had the glass focused on a mighty peak, cried out: "There she is, Tom!"

"What?"

"The avalanche! The snow is beginning to slide down the mountain! Say, it's going to be a big one, too. Got your camera ready?"

"Sure! I've had it ready for the last three days. Put me over there, Ned. You look after the airship, and I'll take the pictures!"

Tom sprang to get his apparatus, while his chum hurried to the levers, wheels and handles that controlled the Flyer. As they approached the avalanche they could see the great mass of ice, snow, big stones, and earth sliding down the mountain side, carrying tall trees with it.

"This is just what I wanted!" cried Tom, as he set his camera working. "Put me closer, Ned."

Ned obeyed, and the airship was now hovering directly over the avalanche, and right in its path. The big landslide, as it would have been called in this country, met no village in its path, fortunately, or it would have wiped it out completely. It was in a wild and desolate region that it occurred.

"I want to get a real close view!" cried Tom, as he got some pictures showing a whole grove of giant trees uprooted and carried off. "Get closer Ned, and—"

Tom was interrupted by a cry of alarm from his chum.

"We're falling!" yelled Ned. "Something has gone wrong. We're going down into the avalanche!"

TELEGRAPH ORDERS

There was confusion aboard the airship. Tom, hearing Ned's cry, left his camera, to rush to the engine room, but not before he had set the picture apparatus to working automatically. Mr. Damon, Mr. Nestor and Koku, alarmed by Ned's cries, ran back from the forward part of the craft, where they had been watching the mighty mass of ice and earth as it rushed down the side of the mountain.

"What's wrong, Ned?" cried Tom excitedly.

"I don't know! The propellers have stopped! We were running as an aeroplane you know. Now we're going down!"

"Bless my suspenders!" shouted Mr. Damon. "If we land in the midst of that conglomeration of ice it will be the end of us."

"But we're not going to land there!" cried Tom.

How are you going to stop it?" demanded Mr. Nestor.

"By the gas machine!" answered Tom. "That will stop us from falling. Start it up, Ned!"

"That's right! I always forget about that! I'll have it going in a second!"

"Less than a second," called Tom, as he saw how near to the mighty, rushing avalanche they were coming.

Ned worked rapidly, and in a very short time the downward course of the airship was checked. It floated easily above the rushing flood of ice and earth, and Tom, seeing that his craft, and those on it, were safe, hurried back to his camera. Meanwhile the machine had automatically been taking pictures, but now with the young inventor to manage it, better results would be obtained.

Tom aimed it here and there, at the most spectacular parts of the avalanche. The others gathered around him, after Ned had made an inspection, and found that a broken electrical wire had caused the propellers to stop. This was soon repaired and then, as they were hanging in the air like a balloon, Tom took picture after picture of the wonderful sight below them. Forest after forest was demolished.

"This will be a great film!" Tom shouted to Ned, as the latter informed him that the machinery was all right again. "Send me up a little. I want to get a view from the top, looking down."

His chum made the necessary adjustments to the mechanism and then, there being nothing more to slide down the mountainside the avalanche was ended. But what a mass of wreck and ruin there was! It was as if a mighty earthquake had torn the mountain asunder.

"It's a good thing it wasn't on a side of the mountain where people lived," commented Ned, as the airship rose high toward the clouds. "If it had been, there'd be nothing left of 'em. What hair-raising stunt are you going to try next, Tom?"

"I don't know. I expect to hear from Mr. Period soon.

"Hear from Mr. Period?" exclaimed Mr. Nestor. "How are you going to do that, Tom?"

"He said he would telegraph me at Berne, Switzerland, at a certain date, as he knew I was coming to the Alps to try for some avalanche pictures. It's two or three days yet, before I can expect the telegram, which of course will have to come part way by cable. In the meanwhile, I think we'll take a little rest, and a vacation. I want to give the airship an overhauling, and look to my camera. There's no telling what Mr. Period may want next."

"Then he didn't make out your programme completely before you started?" asked Mr. Nestor.

"No, he said he'd communicate with me from time to time. He is in touch with what is going on in the world, you know, and if he hears of anything exciting at any place, I'm to go there at once. You see he wants the most sensational films he can get."

"Yes, our company is out to give the best pictures we can secure," spoke Mary's father, "and I think we are lucky to have Tom Swift working for us. We already have films that no other concern can get. And we need them."

"I wonder what became of those men who started to make so much trouble for you, Tom?" asked Mr. Damon.

"Well, they seem to have disappeared," replied our hero. "Of course they may be after me any day now, but for the time being, I've thrown them off my track."

"So then you don't know where you're going next?" asked Ned.

"No, it may be to Japan, or to the North Pole. Well, I'm ready for anything. We've got plenty of gasolene, and the Flyer can certainly go," said Tom.

They went down to earth in a quiet spot, just outside of a little village, and there they remained three days, to the no small wonder of the inhabitants. Tom wanted to see if his camera was working properly. So he developed some of the avalanche pictures, and found them excellent. The rest of the time was spent in making some needed repairs to the airship, while the young inventor overhauled his Wizard machine, that he found needed a few adjustments.

Their arrival in Berne created quite a sensation, but they were used to that. Tom anchored his airship just outside the city, and, accompanied by Ned, made his way to the telegraph office. Some of the officials there could speak English, though not very well.

"I am expecting a message," said Tom.

"Yes? Who for?" asked the clerk.

"Tom Swift. It will be from America."

As Tom said this he observed a man sitting in the corner of the office get up hurriedly and go out. All at once his suspicions were aroused. He thought of the attempts that had been made to get his Wizard Camera away from him.

"Who was that man?" he quickly asked the agent.

"Him? Oh, he, too, is expecting a message from America. He has been here some time."

"Why did he go out so quickly?" Ned wanted to know.

"Why, I can not tell. He is an Englishman. They do strange things."

"My telegram? Is it here?" asked Tom impatiently. He wanted to get whatever word there was from Mr. Period, and be on his way to whatever destination the picture man might select. Perhaps, after all, his suspicions, against the man who had so suddenly left, were unfounded.

"Yes, there is a cablegram here for you, Monsieur Swift," said the man, who was French. "There are charges on it, however."

"Pay 'em, Ned, while I see what this is," directed the young inventor, as he tore open the envelope.

"Whew!" he whistled a moment later. "This is going some."

"Where to now?" asked Ned. "The North Pole?"

"No, just the opposite. Mr. Period wants me to go to Africa— the Congo Free State. There's an uprising among the natives there, and he wants some war pictures. Well, I guess I'll have to go."

As Tom spoke he looked toward the door of the telegraph office, and he saw the man, who had so hurriedly gone out a few moments before, looking in at him.

Suspicious Strangers

"Off to Africa; eh?" remarked Ned, as Tom put the envelope in his pocket. "That's another long jump. But I guess the Flyer can do it,

"Yes, I think so. I say Ned, not so loud," said Tom, who had hurried to the side of his chum, whispered the last words.

"What's up?" inquired Ned quickly. "Anything wrong?"

"I don't know. But I think we are being watched. Did you notice that fellow who was in here a minute ago, when I asked for a telegram?"

"Yes, what about him?"

"Well, he's looking in the door now I think. Don't turn round. Just look up into that mirror on the wall, and you can see his reflection."

"I understand," whispered Ned, as he turned his gaze toward the mirror in question, a large one, with advertisements around the frame. "I see him," he went on. "There's some one with him."

"That's what I thought," replied Tom. "Take a good look. Whom do you think the other chap is?"

Ned looked long and earnestly. By means of the mirror, he could see, perfectly plain, two men standing just outside the door of the telegraph office. The portal was only partly open. Ned drew an old letter from his pocket, and pretended to be showing it to Tom. But, all the while he was gazing earnestly at the two men. Suddenly one of them moved, giving Tom's chum a better view of his face.

"By Jove, Tom!" the lad exclaimed in a tense whisper. "If it isn't that Eckert fellow I'm a cow."

"That's what I thought," spoke Tom coolly. "Not that you're a cow, Ned, but I believe that this man is one of the moving picture partners, who are rivals of Mr. Period. I wasn't quite sure myself after the first glance I had of him, so I wanted you to take a look. Do you know the other chap—the one who ran out when I asked for my telegram?"

"No, I've never seen him before as far as I know."

"Same here. Come on."

"What are you going to do?"

"Go back to the airship, and tell Mr. Nestor. As one of the directors in the concern I'm working for. I want his advice."

"Good idea," replied Ned, and they turned to leave the office. The spying stranger, and William Eckert, were not in sight when the two lads came out.

"They got away mighty quick," remarked Tom, as he looked up and down the street.

"Yes, they probably saw us turn to come out, and made a quick get-away. They might be in any one of these places along here," for the street, on either side of the telegraph office, contained a number of hotels, with doors opening on the sidewalk.

"They must be on your trail yet," decided Mr. Nestor when Tom, reaching the anchored airship, told what had happened. "Well, my advice is to go to Africa as soon as we can. In that way we'll leave them behind, and they won't have any chance to get your camera."

"But what I can't understand," said Tom, "is how they knew I was coming here. It was just as if that one man had been waiting in the telegraph office for me to appear. I'm sorry, now, that I mentioned to Ned where we were ordered to. But I didn't think."

"They probably knew, anyway," was Mr. Nestor's opinion. "I think this may explain it. The rival concern in New York has been keeping track of Mr. Period's movements. Probably they have a paid spy who may be in his employ. They knew when he sent you a telegram, what it contained, and where it was directed to. Then, of course, they knew you would call here for it. What they did not know was when you would come, and so they had to wait. That one spy was on guard, and, as soon as you came, he went and summoned Eckert, who was waiting somewhere in the neighborhood."

"Bless my detective story!" cried Mr. Damon. "What a state of affairs! They ought to be arrested, Tom."

"It would be useless," said Mr. Nestor. "They are probably far enough away by this time. Or else they have put others on Tom's track."

"I'll fight my own battles!" exclaimed the young inventor. "I don't go much on the police in a case like this, especially foreign police. Well, my camera is all right, so far," he went on, as he took a look at it, in the compartment where he kept it. "Some one must always remain near it, after this. But we'll soon start for Africa, to get some pictures of a native battle. I hope it isn't the red pygmies we have to photograph."

"Bless my shoe laces! Don't suggest such a thing," begged Mr. Damon, as he recalled the strenuous times when the dwarfs held the missionaries captive.

It was necessary to lay in some stores and provisions, and for this reason Tom could not at once head the airship for the African jungles. As she remained at anchor, just outside the city, crowds of Swiss people came out to look at the wonderful craft. But Tom and his companions took care that no one got aboard, and they kept a strict lookout for Americans, or Englishmen, thinking perhaps that Mr. Eckert, or the spy, might try to get the camera. However, they did not see them, and a few days after the receipt of the message from Mr. Period, having stocked up, they rose high into the air, and set out to cross the Mediterranean Sea for Africa. Tom laid a route over Tripoli, the Sahara Desert, the French Congo, and so into the Congo Free State. In his telegram, Mr. Period had said that the expected uprising was to take place near Stanley Falls, on the Congo River.

"And supposing it does not happen?" asked Mr. Damon. "What if the natives don't fight, Tom? You'll have your trip for nothing, and Will run a lot of risk besides."

"It's one of the chances I'm taking," replied the young inventor, and truly, as he thought of it, he realized that the perils of the moving picture business were greater than he had imagined. Tom hoped to get a quick trip to the Congo, but, as they were sailing over the big desert, there was an accident to the main motor, and the airship suddenly began shooting toward the sands. She was easily brought up, by means of the gas bags, and allowed to settle gently to the ground, in the vicinity of a large oasis. But, when Tom looked at the broken machinery, he said:

"This means a week's delay. It will take that, and longer, to fix it so we can go on."

"Too bad!" exclaimed Mr. Nestor. "The war may be over when we get there. But it can't be helped."

It took Tom and his friends even longer than he had thought to make the repairs. In the meanwhile they camped in the desert place, which was far from being unpleasant. Occasionally a caravan halted there, but, for the most part, they were alone.

"No danger of Eckert, or any of his spies coming here, I guess," said Tom grimly as he blew on a portable forge, to weld two pieces of iron together.

In due time they were again on the wing, and without further incident they were soon in the vicinity of Stanley Falls. They managed to locate a village where there were some American missionaries established. They were friends of Mr. and Mrs. Illington, the missionaries whom Tom had saved from the red pygmies, as told in the "Electric Rifle" volume of this series, and they made our hero and his friends welcome.

"Is it true?" asked Tom, of the missionaries who lived not far from Stanley Falls, "that there is to be a native battle? Or are we too late for it?"

"I am sorry to say, I fear there will be fighting among the tribesmen," replied Mr. Janeway, one of the Christian workers. "It has not yet taken place, though."

"Then I'm not too late!" cried Tom, and there was exultation in his voice. "I don't mean to be barbarous," he went on, as he saw that the missionaries looked shocked, "but as long as they are going to fight I want to get the pictures."

"Oh, they'll fight all right," spoke Mrs. Janeway. "The poor, ignorant natives here are always ready to fight. This time I think it is about some cattle that one tribe took from another."

"And where will the battle take place?" asked Tom.

"Well, the rumors we have, seem to indicate that the fight will take place about ten miles north of here. We will have notice of it before it starts, as some of the natives, whom we have succeeded in converting, belong to the tribe that is to be attacked. They will be summoned to the defense of their town and then it will be time enough for you to go. Oh, war is a terrible thing! I do not like to talk about it. Tell me how you rescued our friends from the red pygmies," and Tom was obliged to relate that story, which I have told in detail elsewhere.

Several days passed, and Tom and his friends spent a pleasant time in the African village with the missionaries. The airship and camera were in readiness for instant use, and during this period of idleness our hero got several fine films of animal scenes, including a number of night-fights among the beasts at the drinking pools. One tiger battle was especially good, from a photographic standpoint.

One afternoon, a number of native bearers came into the town. They preceded two white men, who were evidently sportsmen, or explorers, and the latter had a well equipped caravan. The strangers sought the advice of the missionaries about where big game might be found, and Tom happened to be at the cottage of Mr. Janeway when the strangers arrived.

The young inventor looked at them critically, as he was introduced to them. Both men spoke with an English accent, one introducing himself as Bruce Montgomery, and the other as Wade Kenneth. Tom decided that they were of the ordinary type of globe-trotting Britishers, until, on his way to his airship, he passed the place where the native bearers had set down the luggage of the Englishmen.

"Whew!" whistled Tom, as he caught sight of a peculiarly shaped box. "See that, Ned?"

"Yes, what is it? A new kind of magazine gun?"

"It's a moving picture camera, or I lose my guess!" whispered Tom. "One of the old fashioned kind. Those men are no more tourists, or after big game, than I am! They're moving picture men, and they're here to get views of that native battle! Ned, we've got to be on our guard. They may be in the pay of that Turbot and Eckert firm, and they may try to do us some harm!"

"That's so!" exclaimed Ned. "We'll keep watch of them, Tom."

As they neared their airship, there came, running down what served as the main village street, an African who showed evidence of having come from afar. As he ran on, he called out something in a strange tongue. Instantly from their huts the other natives swarmed.

"What's up now?" cried Ned.

"Something important, I'll wager," replied Tom. "Ned, you go back to the missionaries house, and find out what it is. I'm going to stand guard over my camera."

"It's come!" cried Ned a little later, as he hurried into the interior of the airship, where Tom was busy working over a new attachment he intended putting on his picture machine.

"What has?"

"War! That native, whom we saw running in, brought news that the battle would take place day after to-morrow. The enemies of his tribe are on the march, so the African spies say, and he came to summon all the warriors from this town. We've got to get busy!"

"That's so. What about those Englishmen?"

"They were talking to the missionaries when the runner came in. They pretended to have no interest in it, but I saw one wink to the other, and then, very soon, they went out, and I saw them talking to their native bearers, while they were busy over that box you said was a picture machine."

"I knew it, Ned! I was sure of it! Those fellows came here to trick us, though how they ever followed our trail I don't know. Probably they came by a fast steamer to the West Coast, and struck inland, while we were delayed on the desert. I don't care if they are only straight out-and-out rivals—and not chaps that are trying to take an unfair advantage. I suppose all the big picture concerns have a tip about this war, and they may have representatives here. I hope we get the best views. Now come on, and give me a hand. We've got our work cut out for us, all right."

"Bless my red cross bandage!" cried Mr. Damon, when he heard the news. "A native fight, eh? That will be something I haven't seen in some time. Will there be any danger, Tom, do you think?"

"Not unless our airship tumbles down between the two African forces," replied our hero, "and I'll take care that it doesn't do that. "We'll be well out of reach of any of their blow guns, or arrows."

"But I understand that many of the tribes have powder weapons," said Mr. Nestor.

"They have," admitted Tom, "but they are 'trader's' rifles, and don't carry far. We won't run any risk from such old-fashioned guns."

"A big fight; eh?" asked Koku when they told him what was before them. "Me like to help."

"Yes, and I guess both sides would give a premium for your services," remarked Tom, as he gazed at his big servant. "But we'll need you with us, Koku."

"Oh, me stay with you, Mr. Tom," exclaimed the big man, with a grin.

Somewhat to Tom's surprise the two Englishmen showed no further interest in him and his airship, after the introduction at the missionaries' bungalow.

With the stolidity of their race the Britishers did not show any surprise, as, some time afterward, they strolled down toward Tom's big craft, after supper, and looked it over. Soon they went back to their own camp, and a little later, Koku, who walked toward it, brought word that the Englishmen were packing up.

"They're going to start for the seat of war the first thing in the morning," decided Tom. "Well, we'll get ahead of them. Though we can travel faster than they can, we'll start now, and be on the ground in good season. Besides, I don't like staying all night in the same neighborhood with them. Get ready for a start, Ned."

Tom did not stop to say good-bye to the Englishmen, though he bade farewell to the missionaries, who had been so kind to him. There was much excitement in the native town, for many of the tribesmen were getting ready to depart to help their friends or relatives in the impending battle.

As dusk was falling, the big airship arose, and soon her powerful propellers were sending her across the jungle, toward Stanley Falls in the vicinity of which the battle was expected to take place.

THE NATIVE BATTLE

"By Jove, Tom, here they come!"

"From over by that drinking pool?"

"Yes, just as the spies said they would. Wow, what a crowd of the black beggars there are! And some of 'em have regular guns, too. But most of 'em have clubs, bows and arrows, blow guns, or spears."

Tom and Ned were standing on the forward part of the airship, which was moving slowly along, over an open plateau, in the jungle where the native battle was about to take place. Our friends had left the town where the missionaries lived, and had hovered over the jungle, until they saw signs of the coming struggle. They had seen nothing of their English rivals since coming away, but had no doubt but that the Britishers were somewhere in the neighborhood.

The two forces of black men, who had gone to war over a dispute about some cattle, approached each other. There was the beating of tom-toms, and skin drums, and many weird shouts. From their vantage point in the air, Tom and his companions had an excellent view. The Wizard Camera was loaded with a long reel of film, and ready for action.

"Bless my handkerchief!" cried Mr. Damon, as he looked down on the forces that were about to clash. "I never saw anything like this before!"

"I either," admitted Tom. "But, if things go right, I'm going to get some dandy films!"

Nearer and nearer the rival forces advanced. At first they had stared, and shouted in wonder at the sight of the airship, hovering above them, but their anger soon drew their attention to the fighting at hand, and, after useless gestures toward the craft of the air, and after some of them had vainly fired their guns or arrows at it, they paid no more attention, but rushed on with their shouts and cries and amid the beating of their rude drums.

"I think I'll begin to take pictures now," said Tom, as Ned, in charge of the ship, sent it about in a circle, giving a general view of the rival forces. "I'll show a scene of the two crowds getting ready for business, and, later on, when they're actually giving each other cats and dogs, I'll get all the pictures possible."

The camera was started while, safe in the a those on the Flyer watched what went on below them.

Suddenly the forward squads of the two small armies of blacks met. With wild, weird yells they rushed at each other. The air was filled with flying arrows and spears. The sound of the old-fashioned muzzle-loading guns could he heard, and clouds of smoke arose. Tilting his camera, and arranging the newly attached reflecting mirrors so as to give the effect as if a spectator was looking at the battle from in front, instead of from above, Tom Swift took picture after picture.

The fight was now on. With yells of rage and defiance the Africans came together, giving blow for blow. It was a wild melee, and those on the airship looked on fascinated, though greatly wishing that such horrors could be stopped.

"How about it, Tom?" cried Ned.

"Everything going good! I don't like this business, but now I'm in it I'm going to stick. Put me down a little lower," answered the young inventor.

"All right. I say Tom, look over there."

"Where?"

"By that lightning-struck gum tree. See those two men, and some sort of a machine they've got stuck up on stilts? See it?"

"Sure. Those are the two Englishmen—my rivals! They're taking pictures, too!"

And then, with a crash and roar, with wild shouts and yells, with volley after volley of firearms, clouds of smoke and flights of arrows and spears, the native battle was in full swing, while the young inventor, sailing above it in his airship, reeled off view after view of the strange sight.

A Heavy Loss

"Bless my battle axe, but this is awful!" cried Mr. Damon.

"War is always a fearful thing," spoke Mr. Nestor. "But this is not as bad as if the natives fought with modern weapons. See! most of them are fighting with clubs, and their fists. They don't seem to hurt each other very much."

"That's so," agreed Mr. Damon. The two gentlemen were in the main cabin, looking down on the fight below them, while Tom, with Ned to help him change the reels of films, as they became filled with pictures, attended to the camera. Koku was steering the craft, as he had readily learned how to manage it.

"Are those Englishmen taking pictures yet?" asked Tom, too busy to turn his head, and look for himself.

"Yes, they're still at," replied Ned. "But they seem to be having trouble with their machine," he added as he saw one of the men leave the apparatus, and run hurriedly back to where they had made a temporary camp.

"I guess it's an old-fashioned kind," commented Tom. "Say, this is getting fierce!" he cried, as the natives got in closer contact with each other. It was now a hand-to-hand battle.

"I should say so!" yelled Ned. "It's a wonder those Englishmen aren't afraid to be down on the same level with the black fighters."

"Oh, a white person is considered almost sacred by the natives here, so the missionaries told me," said Tom. "A black man would never think of raising his hand to one, and the Englishmen probably know this. They're safe enough. In fact I'm thinking of soon going down myself, and getting some views from the ground."

"Bless my gizzard, Tom!" cried Mr. Damon. "Don't do it!"

"Yes, I think I will. Why, it's safe enough. Besides, if they attack us we have the electric rifles. Ned, you tell Koku to get the guns out, to have in readiness, and then you put the ship down. I'll take a chance."

"Jove! You've been doing nothing but take chances since we came on this trip!" exclaimed Ned, admiringly. "All right! Here we go," and he went to relieve Koku at the wheel, while the giant, grinning cheerfully at the prospect of taking part in the fight himself, got out the rifles, including his own.

Meanwhile the native battle went on fiercely. Many on both sides fell, and not a few ran away, when they got the chance, their companions yelling at them, evidently trying to shame them into coming back.

As the airship landed, Mr. Damon, Mr. Nestor, Ned and Koku stood ready with the deadly electric rifles, in case an attack should be made on them. But the fighting natives paid no more attention to our friends than they did to the two Englishmen. The latter moved their clumsy camera from place to place, in order to get various views of the fighting.

"This is the best yet!" cried Tom, as, after a lull in the fight, when the two opposing armies had drawn a little apart, they came together again more desperately than before. "I hope the pictures are being recorded all right. I have to go at this thing pretty much in the dark. Say, look at the beggars fight!" he finished.

But a battle, even between uncivilized blacks, cannot go on for very long at a time. Many had fallen, some being quite severely injured it seemed, being carried off by their friends. Then, with a sudden rush, the side which, as our friends learned later, had been robbed of their cattle, made a fierce attack, overwhelming their enemies, and compelling them to retreat. Across the open plain the vanquished army fled, with the others after them. Tom, meanwhile, taking pictures as fast as he could.

"This ends it!" he remarked to Ned, when the warriors were too far away to make any more good views. "Now we can take a rest."

"The Englishmen gave up some time ago," said his chum, motioning to the two men who were taking their machine off the tripod.

"Guess their films gave out," spoke Tom. "Well, you see it didn't do any harm to come down, and I got some better views here."

"Here they come back!" exclaimed Ned, as a horde of the black fellows emerged f row the jungle, and came on over the plain.

"Hear 'em sing!" commented Tom, as the sound of a rude chant came to their ears. "They must be the winners all right."

"I guess so," agreed Ned. "But what about staying here now? Maybe they won't be so friendly to us when they haven't any fighting to occupy their minds."

"Don't worry," advised Tom. "They won't bother us."

And the blacks did not. They were caring for their wounded, who had not already been taken from the field, and they paid no attention to our friends, save to look curiously at the airship.

"Bless my newspaper!" cried Mr. Damon, with an air of relief. "I'm glad that's over, and we didn't have to use the electric rifles, after all."

"Here come the Englishmen to pay us a visit," spoke Ned a little later, as they sat about the cabin of the Flyer. The two rival picture men soon climbed on deck.

"Beg pardon," said the taller of the two, addressing our hero, "but could you lend us a roll of film? Ours are all used up, and we want to get some more pictures before going back to our main camp."

"I'm sorry," replied Tom, "but I use a special size, and it fits no camera but my own."

"Ah! might we see your camera?" asked the other Englishman. "That is, see how it works?"

"I don't like to be disobliging," was Tom's answer, "but it is not yet patented and—well—" he hesitated.

"Oh, I see!" sneered the taller visitor. "You're afraid we might steal some of your ideas. Hum!" Come on Montgomery," and, swinging on his heels, with a military air, he hurried away, followed by his companion.

"They don't like that, but I can't help it," remarked Tom to his friends a little later. "I can't afford to take any chances."

"No, you did just right," said Mr. Nestor. "Those men may be all right, but from the fact that they are in the picture taking business I'd be suspicious of them."

"Well, what's next on the programme?" asked Ned as Tom put his camera away.

"Oh, I think we'll stay here over night," was our hero's reply. "It's a nice location, and the gas machine needs cleaning. We can do it here, and maybe I can get some more pictures."

They were busy the rest of the day on the gas generator, but the main body of natives did not come back, and the Englishmen seemed to have disappeared.

Everyone slept soundly that night. So soundly, in fact, that the sun was very high when Koku was the first to awaken, His head felt strangely dizzy, and he wondered at a queer smell in the room he had to himself.

"Nobody up yet," he exclaimed in surprise, as he staggered into the main cabin. There, too, was the strange, sweetish, sickly smell. "Mr. Tom, where you be? Time to get up!" the giant called to his master, as he went in, and gently shook the young inventor by the shoulder.

"Eh? What's that? What's the matter?" began Tom, and then he suddenly sat up. "Oh, my head!" he exclaimed, putting his hands to his aching temples.

"And that queer smell!" added Ned, who was also awake now.

"Bless my talcum powder!" cried Mr. Damon. "I have a splitting headache."

"Hum! Chloroform, if I'm any judge!" called Mr. Nestor from his berth.

"Chloroform!" cried Tom, staggering to his feet. "I wonder" He did not finish his sentence, but made his way to the room where his camera was kept. "It's gone!" he cried. "We have been chloroformed in the night, and some one has taken my Wizard Camera."

AFTER THE ENGLISHMEN

"The camera gone!" gasped Ned.

"Did they chloroform us?" exclaimed Mr. Damon. "Bless my—" but for one of the few times in his life, he did not know what to bless.

"Get all the fresh air you can," hastily advised Mr. Nestor. "Koku, open all the doors and windows," for, though it was hot during the day in the jungle, the nights were cool, and the airship was generally closed up. With the inrush of the fresh air every one soon felt better.

"Is anything else gone?" asked Ned, as he followed Tom into the camera room.

"Yes, several rolls of unexposed films. Oh, if only they haven't got too much of a start! I'll get it away from them!" declared Tom with energy.

"From who? Who took it?" asked Ned.

"Those Englishmen, of course! Who else? I believe they are in the pay of Turbot and Eckert. Their taking pictures was only a bluff! They got on my trail and stuck to it. The delays we had, gave them a chance to catch up to us. They came over to the airship, to pretend to borrow films, just to get a look at the place, and size it up, so they could chloroform us, and get the camera."

"I believe you're right," declared Mr. Nestor. "We must get after those scoundrels as quickly as possible!"

"Bless my shoulder braces!" cried Mr. Damon. "How do you imagine they worked that trick on us?"

"Easily enough," was Mr. Nestor's opinion. "We were all dead tired last night, and slept like tops. They watched their chance, sneaked up, and got in. After that it was no hard matter to chloroform each one of us in turn, and they had the ship to themselves. They looked around, found the camera, and made off with it."

"Well, I'm going to get right after them!" cried Tom. "Ned, start the motor. I'll steer for a while."

"Hold on! Wait a minute," suggested Mr. Nestor. "I wouldn't go off in the ship just yet,~ Tom."

"Why not?"

"Because you don't know which way to go. We must find out which trail the Englishmen took. They have African porters with them, and those porters doubtless know some of the blacks around here. We must inquire of the natives which way the porters went, in carrying the goods of our rivals, for those Englishmen would not abandon camp without taking their baggage with them."

"That's so," admitted the young inventor. "That will be the best plan. Once I find which way they have gone I can easily overtake them in the airship. And when I find 'em—" Tom paused significantly.

"Me help you fix 'em!" cried Koku, clenching his big fist.

"They will probably figure it out that you will take after them," said Mr. Nestor, "but they may not count on you doing it in the Flyer, and so they may not try to hide. It isn't going to be an easy matter to pick a small party out of the jungle though, Tom."

"Well, I've done more difficult things in my airships," spoke our hero. "I'll fly low, and use the glass. I guess we can pick out their crowd of porters, though they won't have many. Oh, my camera! I hope they won't damage it."

"They won't," was Ned's opinion. "It's too valuable. They want it to take pictures with, themselves."

"Maybe. I hope they don't open it, and see how it's made. And I'm glad I thought to hide the picture films I've taken so far. They didn't get those away from us, only some of the blank. ones," and Tom looked again in a secret closet. where he kept the battle-films, and the others, in the dark, to prevent them from being light-struck, by any possible chance.

"Well, if we're going to make some inquiries, let's do it," suggested Mr. Nestor. "I think I see some of the Africans over there. They have made a temporary camp, it seems, to attend to some of their wounded."

"Do you think we can make them understand what we want?" asked Ned. "I don't believe they speak English."

"Oh these blacks have been trading with white men," said Tom, "for they have 'trader's' guns, built to look at, and not to shoot very well. I fancy we can make ourselves understood. If not, we can use signs."

Leaving Koku and Mr. Damon to guard the airship, Tom, Ned and Mr. Nestor went to the African camp. There was a large party of men there, and they seemed friendly enough. Probably winning the battle the day before had put them in good humor, even though many of them were hurt.

To Tom's delight he found one native who could speak a little English, and of him they made inquiries as to what direction the Englishmen had taken. The black talked for a while among his fellows, and then reported to our friends that, late in the night, one of the porters, hired by Montgomery and Kenneth, had come to camp to bid a brother good-bye. This porter had said that his masters were in a hurry to get away, and had started west.

"That's it!" cried Mr. Nestor. "They're going to get somewhere so they can make their way to the coast. They want to get out of Africa as fast as they can."

"And I'm going to get after 'em as fast as I can!" cried Tom grimly. "Come on!"

They hurried back to the airship, finding Koku and Mr. Damon peacefully engaged in talk, no one having disturbed them.

"Start the motor, Ned!" called his chum. "We'll see what luck we have!"

Up into the air went the Flyer, her great propellers revolving rapidly. Over the jungle she shot, and then, when he found that everything was working well, and that the cleaned gas generator was operating as good as when it was new, the young inventor slowed up, and brought the craft down to a lower level.

"For we don't want to run past these fellows, or shoot over their heads in our hurry," Tom explained. "Ned, get out the binoculars. They're easier to handle than the telescope. Then go up forward, and keep a sharp lookout. There is something like a jungle trail below us, and it looks to be the only one around here. They probably took that." Soon after leaving the place where they had camped after the battle, Tom had seen a rude path through the forest, and had followed that lead.

On sped the Flyer, after the two Englishmen, while Tom thought regretfully of his stolen camera.

The Jungle Fire

"Well, Tom, I don't seem to see anything of them," remarked Ned that afternoon, as he sat in the bow of the air craft, gazing from time to time through the powerful glasses.

"No, and I can't understand it, either," responded the young inventor, who had come for-ward to relieve his chum. "They didn't have much the start of us, and they'll have to travel very slowly. It isn't as if they could hop on a train; and, even if they did, I could overtake them in a short time. But they have to travel on foot through the jungle, and can't have gone far."

"'Maybe they have bullock carts," suggested Mr. Damon.

'~The trail isn't wide enough for that," declared Tom. "We've come quite a distance now, even if we have been running at low speed, and we haven't seen even a black man on the trail," and he motioned to the rude path below them.

"They may have taken a boat and slipped down that river we crossed a little while ago," suggested Ned.

"That's so!" cried Tom. "Why didn't I think of it? Say! I'm going to turn back."

"Turn back?"

"Yes, and go up and down the stream a way. We have time, for we can easily run at top speed on the return trip. Then, if we don't see anything of them on the water, we'll pick up the trail again. Put her around, Ned, and I'll take the glasses for a while."

The Flyer was soon shooting back over the same trail our friends had covered, and, as Ned set the propellers going at top speed, they were quickly hovering over a broad but shallow river, which cut through the jungle.

"Try it down stream first," suggested Tom, who was peering through the binoculars. "They'd be most likely to go down, as it would be easier."

Along over the stream swept the airship, covering several miles.

"There's a boat!" suddenly exclaimed Mr. Nestor, pointing to a native canoe below them.

"Bless my paddle wheel! So it is!" cried Mr. Damon. "I believe it's them, Tom!"

"No, there are only natives in that craft," answered the young inventor a moment later, as he brought the binoculars into focus. "I wish it was them, though."

A few more miles were covered down stream, and then Tom tried the opposite direction. But all to no purpose. A number of boats were seen, and several rafts, but they had no white men on them.

"Maybe the Englishmen disguised themselves like natives, Tom," suggested Ned.

Our hero shook his head.

"I could see everything in the boats, through these powerful glasses," he replied, "and there was nothing like my camera. "I'd know that a mile off. No, they didn't take to this stream, though they probably crossed it. We'll have to keep on the way we were going. It will soon be night, and we'll have to camp. Then we'll take up the search to-morrow."

It was just getting dusk, and Tom was looking about for a good place to land in the jungle, when Ned, who was standing in the bow, cried:

"I say, Tom, here's a native village just ahead. There's a good place to stop, and we can stay there over night."

"Good!" exclaimed Tom. "And, what's more, we can make some inquiries as to whether or not the Englishmen have passed here. This is great! Maybe we'll come out all right, after all! They can't travel at night—or at least I don't believe they will—and if they have passed this village we can catch them to-morrow. We'll go down."

They were now over the native town, which was in a natural clearing in the jungle. The natives had by this time caught sight of the big airship over them, and were running about in terror. There was not a man, woman or child in sight when the Flyer came down, for the inhabitants had all fled in fright.

"Not much of a chance to make inquiries of these folks," said Mr. Nestor.

"Oh, they'll come back," predicted Tom. "They are naturally curious, and when they see that the thing isn't going to blow up, they'll gather around. I've seen the same thing happen before."

Tom proved a true prophet. In a little while some of the men began straggling back, when they saw our friends walking about the airship, as it rested on the ground. Then came the children, and then the women, until the whole population was gathered about the airship, staring at it wonderingly. Tom made signs of friendship, and was lucky enough to find a native who knew a few French words. Tom was not much of a French scholar, but he could frame a question as to the Englishmen.

"Oui!" exclaimed the native, when he understood. Then he rattled off something, which Tom, after having it repeated, and making signs to the man to make sure he understood, said meant that the Englishmen had passed through the village that morning.

"We're on the right trail!" cried the young inventor. "They're only a day's travel ahead of us. We'll catch them to-morrow, and get my camera back."

The natives soon lost all fear of the airship, and some of the chief men even consented to come aboard. Tom gave them a few trifles for presents, and won their friendship to such an extent that a great feast was hastily gotten up in honor of the travelers. Big fires were lighted, and fowls by the score were roasted.

"Say, I'm glad we struck this place!" exclaimed Ned, as he sat on the ground with the others, eating roast fowl. "This is all to the chicken salad!"

"Things are coming our way at last," remarked Tom. "We'll start the first thing in the morning. I wish I had my camera now. I'd take a picture of this scene. Dad would enjoy it, and so would Mrs. Baggert. Oh, I almost wish I was home again. But if I get my camera I've got a lot more work ahead of me."

"What kind?" asked Ned.

"I don't know. I'm to stop in Paris for the next instructions from Mr. Period. He is keeping in touch with the big happenings of the world, and he may send us to Japan, to get some earthquake pictures."

The night was quiet after the feast, and in the morning Tom and his friends sailed off in their airship, leaving behind the wondering and pleased natives, for our hero handed out more presents, of small value to him, but yet such things as the blacks prized highly.

Once more they were flying over the trail, and they put on more speed now, for they were fairly sure that the men they sought were ahead of them about a day's travel. This meant perhaps twenty miles, and Tom figured that he could cover fifteen in a hurry, and then go over the remaining five slowly, so as not to miss his quarry.

"Say, don't you smell something?" asked Ned a little later, when the airship had been slowed down. "Something like smoke?"

"Humph! I believe I do get an odor of something burning," admitted Tom, sniffing the atmosphere.

"Bless my pocket book!" exclaimed Mr. Damon, "look down there, boys!" He pointed below, and, to the surprise of the lads, and no less of himself, he saw many animals hurrying back along the jungle trail.

There were scores of deer, leaping along, here and there a tawny lion, and one or two tigers. Off to one side a rhinoceros crashed his way through the tangle, and occasionally an elephant was seen.

"That's queer," cried Ned. "And they're not paying any attention to each other, either."

"Something is happening," was Mr. Nestor's opinion. "Those animals are running away from something."

"Maybe it's an elephant drive," spoke Tom. "I think—"

But he did not finish. The smell of smoke suddenly became stronger, and, a moment later, as the airship rose higher, in response to a change in the angle of the deflecting rudder, which Ned shifted, all on board saw a great volume of black smoke rolling toward the sky.

"A jungle fire!" cried Tom. "The jungle is burning! That's why the animals are running back this way."

"We'd better not go on!" shouted Ned, choking a bit, as the smoke rolled nearer.

"No, we've got to turn back!" decided Tom. "Say, this will stop the Englishmen! They can't go on. We'll go back to the village we left, and wait for them. They're trapped!" And then he added soberly: "I hope my camera doesn't get burnt up!"

A Dangerous Commission

"Look at that smoke!" yelled Ned, as he sent the airship about in a great circle on the backward trail.

"And there's plenty of blaze, too," added Tom. "See the flames eating away! This stuff is as dry as tinder for there hasn't been any rain for months."

"Much hot!" was the comment of the giant, when he felt the warm wind of the fire.

"Bless my fountain pen!" gasped Mr. Damon, as he looked down into the jungle. "See all those animals!"

The trail was now thick with deer, and many small beasts, the names of which Tom did not know. On either side could be heard larger brutes, crashing their way forward to escape the fire behind them.

"Oh, if you only had your camera now!" cried Ned. "You could get a wonderful picture, Tom."

"What's the use of wishing for it. Those Englishmen have it, and—"

"Maybe they're using it!" interrupted Ned. "No, I don't think they would know how to work it. Do you see anything of them, Ned?"

"Not a sight. But they'll surely have to come back, just as you said, unless they got ahead of the fire. They can't go on, and it would be madness to get off the trail in a jungle like this."

"I don't believe they could have gotten ahead of the fire," spoke Tom. "They couldn't travel fast enough for that, and see how broad the blaze is."

They were now higher up, well out of the heat and smoke of the conflagration, and they could see that it extended for many miles along the trail, and for a mile or so on either side of it.

"We're far enough in advance, now, to go down a bit, I guess," said Tom, a little later. "I want to get a good view of the path, and I can't do that from up here. I have an idea that—"

Tom did not finish, for as the airship approached nearer the ground, he caught up a pair of binoculars, and focused them on something on the trail below.

"What is it?" cried Ned, startled by something in his chum's manner.

"It's them! The Englishmen!" cried Tom. "See, they are racing back along the trail. Their porters have deserted them. But they have my camera! I can see it! I'm going down, and get it! Ned, stand by the wheel, and make a quick landing. Then we'll go up again!"

Tom handed the glasses to his chum, and Ned quickly verified the young inventor's statement. There were the two rascally Englishmen. The fire was still some distance in the rear, but was coming on rapidly. There were no animals to be seen, for they had probably gone off on a side trail, or had slunk deeper into the jungle. Above the distant roar of the blaze sounded the throb of the airship's motor. The Englishmen heard it, and looked up. Then, suddenly, they motioned to Tom to descend.

"That's what I'm going to do," he said aloud, but of course they could not hear him.

"They're waiting for us!" cried Ned. "I wonder why?" for the rascals had come to a halt, setting down the packs they carried on the trail. One of the things they had was undoubtedly Tom's camera.

"They probably want us to save their lives," said Tom. "They know they can't out-run this fire. They've given up! We have them now!"

"Are you going to save them?" asked Mr. Damon.

"Of course. I wouldn't let my worst enemy run the chances of danger in that terrible blaze. I'd save them even if they had smashed my camera. I'll go down, and get them, and take them back to the native village, but that's as far as I will carry them. They'll have to get away as best they can, after that."

It was the work of but a few minutes to lower the airship to the trail. Fortunately it widened a bit at this point, or Tom could never have gotten his craft down through the trees.

"Hand up that camera!" ordered our hero curtly, when he had stopped near the Englishmen.

"Yes, my dear chap," spoke the tall Britisher, "but will you oblige us, by taking us—"

"Hand up the camera first!" sharply ordered Tom again.

They passed it to him.

"I know we treated you beastly mean," went on Kenneth, "but, my dear chap—"

"Get aboard," was all Tom said, and when the rascals, with fearful glances back into the burning jungle, did so, our hero sent his craft high into the air again.

"Where are you taking us, my dear chap?" asked the tall rascal.

"Don't 'dear chap' me!" retorted Tom. "I don't want to talk to you. I'm going to drop you at the native village."

"But that will burn!" cried the Englishman.

"The wind is changing," was our hero's answer. "The fire won't get to the village. You'll be safe. Have you damaged my camera?" he asked as he began to examine it, while Ned managed the ship.

"No, my dear chap. You mustn't think too hard of us. We were both down on our luck, and a chap offered us a big sum to get on your trail, and secure the camera. He said you had filched it from him, and that he had a right to it. Understand, we wouldn't have taken it had we known—"

"Don't talk to me!" interrupted Tom, as he saw that his apparatus had not been damaged. "The man who hired you was a rascal—that's all I'll say. Put on a little more speed, Ned. I want to get rid of these 'dear chaps' and take some pictures of the jungle fire."

As Tom had said, the wind had changed, and was blowing the flames away off to one side, so that the native village would be in no danger. It was soon reached, and the Africans were surprised to see Tom's airship back again. But he did not stay long, descending only to let the Englishmen alight. They pleaded to be taken to the coast, making all sorts of promises, and stating that, had they known that Turbot and Eckert (for whom they admitted they had acted) were not telling the truth, they never would have taken Tom's camera.

"Don't leave us here!" they pleaded.

"I wouldn't have you on board my airship another minute for a fortune!" declared Tom, as he signalled to Ned to start the motor. Then the Flyer ascended on high, leaving the plotters and started back for the fire, of which Tom got a series of fine moving pictures.

A week later our friends were in Paris, having made a quick trip, on which little of incident occurred, though Tom managed to get quite a number of good views on the way.

He found a message awaiting him, from Mr. Period.

"Well, where to now?" asked Ned, as his chum read the cablegram.

"Great Scott!" cried our hero. "Talk about hair-raising jobs, this certainly is the limit!"

"Why, what's the matter?"

"I've got to get some moving pictures of a volcano in action," was the answer. "Say, if I'd known what sort of things 'Spotty' wanted, I'd never have consented to take this trip. A volcano in action, and maybe an earthquake on the side! This is certainly going some!"

At the Volcano

"And you've got to snap-shot a volcano?" remarked Ned to his chum, after a moment of surprised silence. "Any particular one? Is it Vesuvius? If it is we haven't far to go. But how does Mr. Period know that it's going to get into action when we want it to?"

"No, it isn't Vesuvius," replied Tom. "We've got to take another long trip, and we'll have to go by steamer again. The message says that the Arequipa volcano, near the city of the same name, in Peru, has started to 'erupt,' and, according to rumor, it's acting as it did many years ago, just before a big upheaval."

"Bless my Pumice stones!" cried Mr. Damon. "And are you expected to get pictures of it shooting out flames and smoke, Tom?"

"Of course. An inactive volcano wouldn't make much of a moving picture. Well, if we go to Peru, we won't be far from the United States, and we can fly back home in the airship. But we've got to take the Flyer apart, and pack up again."

"Will you have time?" asked Mr. Nestor. "Maybe the volcano will get into action before you arrive, and the performance will be all over with."

"I think not," spoke Tom, as he again read the cablegram. "Mr. Period says he has advices from Peru to the effect that, on other occasions, it took about a month from the time smoke was first seen coming from the crater, before the fireworks started up. I guess we've got time enough, but we won't waste any."

"And I guess Montgomery and Kenneth won't be there to make trouble for us," put in Ned. "It will be some time before they get away from that African town, I think."

They began work that day on taking the airship apart for transportation to the steamer that was to carry them across the ocean. Tom decided on going to Panama, to get a series of pictures on the work of digging that vast canal. On inquiry he learned that a steamer was soon to sail for Colon, so he took passage for his friends and himself on that, also arranging for the carrying of the parts of his airship.

It was rather hard work to take the Flyer apart, but it was finally done, and, in about a week from the time of arriving in Paris, they left that beautiful city. The pictures already taken were forwarded to Mr. Period, with a letter of explanation of Tom's adventures thus far, and an account of how his rivals had acted.

Just before sailing, Tom received another message from his strange employer. The cablegram read:

"Understand our rivals are also going to try for volcano pictures. Can't find out who will represent Turbot and Eckert, but watch out. Be suspicious of strangers."

"That's what I will!" cried Tom. "If they get my camera away from me again, it will be my own fault."

The voyage to Colon was not specially interesting. They ran into a terrific storm, about half way over, and Tom took some pictures from the steamer's bridge, the captain allowing him to do so, but warning him to be careful.

"I'll take Koku up there with me," said the young inventor, "and if a wave tries to wash me overboard he'll grab me."

And it was a good thing that he took this precaution, for, while a wave did not get as high as the bridge, one big, green roller smashed over the bow of the vessel, staggering her so that Tom was tossed against the rail. He would have been seriously hurt, and his camera might have been broken, but for the quickness of the giant.

Koku caught his master, camera and all, in a mighty arm, and with the other clung to a stanchion, holding Tom in safety until the ship was on a level keel once more.

"Thanks, Koku!" gasped Tom. "You always seem to be around when I need you." The giant grinned happily.

The storm blew out in a few days, and, from then on, there was pleasant sailing. When Tom's airship had been reassembled at Colon, it created quite a sensation among the small army of canal workers, and, for their benefit, our hero gave several flying exhibitions.

He then took some of the engineers on a little trip, and in turn, they did him the favor of letting him get moving pictures of parts of the work not usually seen.

"And now for the volcano!" cried Tom one morning, when having shipped to Mr. Period the canal pictures, the Flyer was sent aloft, and her nose pointed toward Arequipa. "We've got quite a run before us."

"How long?" asked Ned.

"About two thousand miles. But I'm going to speed her up to the limit." Tom was as good as his word, and soon the Flyer was shooting along at her best rate, reeling off mile after mile, just below the clouds.

It was a wild and desolate region over which the travelers found themselves most of the time, though the scenery was magnificent. They sailed over Quito, that city on the equator, and, a little later, they passed above the Cotopaxi and Chimbarazo volcanoes. But neither of them was in action. The Andes Mountains, as you all know, has many volcanoes scattered along the range. Lima was the next large city, and there Tom made a descent to inquire about the burning mountain he was shortly to photograph.

"It will soon be in action," the United States counsel said. "I had a letter from a correspondent near there only yesterday, and he said the people in the town were getting anxious. They are fearing a shower of burning ashes, or that the eruption may be accompanied by an earthquake."

"Good!" cried Tom. "Oh, I don't mean it exactly that way," he hastened to add, as he saw the counsel looking queerly at him. "I meant that I could get pictures of both earthquake and volcano then. I don't wish the poor people any harm."

"Well, you're the first one I ever saw who was anxious to get next door to a volcano," remarked the counsel. "Hold on, though, that's not quite right. I heard yesterday that a couple of young fellows passed through here on their way to the same place. Come to think of it, they were moving picture men, also."

"Great Scott!" cried Tom. "Those must be my rivals, I'll wager. I must get right on the job. Thanks for the information," and hurrying front the office he joined his friends on the airship. and was soon aloft again.

"Look, Tom, what's that?" cried Ned, about noon the next day when the Flyer, according to their calculations must be nearing the city of Arequipa. "See that black cloud over there. I hope it isn't a tornado, or a cyclone, or whatever they call the big wind storms down here."

Tom, and the others, looked to where Ned pointed. There was a column of dense smoke hovering in the air, lazily swirling this way and that. The airship was rapidly approaching it.

"Why that—" began Tom, but before he could complete the sentence the smoke was blown violently upward. It became streaked with fire, and, a moment later, there was the echo of a tremendous explosion.

"The volcano!" cried Tom. "The Arequipa volcano! We're here just in time, for she's in eruption now! Come on, Ned, help me get out the camera! Mr. Damon, you and Mr. Nestor manage the airship! Put us as close as you dare! I'm going to get some crackerjack pictures!"

Once more came a great report.

"Bless my toothpick!" gasped Mr. Damon. "This is awful!" And the airship rushed on toward the volcano which could be plainly seen now, belching forth fire, smoke and ashes.

THE MOLTEN RIVER

"Whew!" gasped Ned, as he stood beside Tom in the bow of the airship. "What's that choking us, Tom?"

"Sulphur, I guess, and gases from the volcano. The wind blew 'em over this way. They're not dangerous, as long as there is no carbonic acid gas given off, and I don't smell any of that, yet. Say, Ned, it's erupting all right, isn't it?"

"I should say so!" cried his chum.

"Put us a little to one side, Mr. Damon," called Tom to his friend, who was in the pilot house. "I can't get good pictures through so much smoke. "It's clearer off to the left."

"Bless my bath robe!" cried the odd man. "You're as cool about it, Tom, as though you were just in an ordinary race, at an aeroplane meet."

"And why shouldn't I be?" asked our hero with a laugh, as he stopped the mechanism of the camera until he should have a clearer view of the volcano. "There's not much danger up here, but I want to get some views from the level, later, and then—"

"You don't get me down there!" interrupted Mr. Nestor, with a grim laugh.

They were now hovering over the volcano, but high enough up so that none of the great stones that were being thrown out could reach them. The column of black smoke, amid which could be seen the gleams of the molten fires in the crater, rolled toward them, and the smell of sulphur became stronger.

But when, in accordance with Tom's suggestion, the airship had been sent over to one side, they were clear of the vapor and the noxious gas. Then, too, a better view could be had of the volcano below them.

"Hold her down!" cried Tom, as he got in a good position, and the propellers were slowed down so that they just overcame the influence of a slight wind. Thus the Flyer hovered in the air, while below her the volcano belched forth red-hot rocks, some of them immense in size, and quantities of hot ashes and cinders. Tom had the camera going again now, and there was every prospect of getting a startling and wonderful, as well as rare series of moving pictures.

"Wow! That was a big one!" cried Ned, as an unusually large mass of rocks was thrown out, and the column of fire and smoke ascended nearly to the hovering craft. A moment later came an explosion, louder than any that had preceded. "We'd better be going up; hadn't we Tom?" his chum asked.

"A little, yes, but not too far. I want to get as many near views as I can."

"Bless my overshoes!" gasped Mr. Damon, as he heard Tom say that. Then he sent some of the vapor from the generating machine into the gas bag, and the Flyer arose slightly.

Ned looked in the direction of the town, but could not see it, on account of the haze. Then he directed his attention to the terrifying sight below him.

"It's a good thing it isn't very near the city," he said to Tom, who was engaged in watching the automatic apparatus of the camera, to see when he would have to put in a fresh film. "It wouldn't take much of this sort of thing to destroy a big city. But I don't see any streams of burning lava, such as they always say come out of a volcano."

"It isn't time for that yet," replied Tom. "The lava comes out last, after the top layer of stones and ashes have been blown out. They are a sort of stopper to the volcano, I guess, like the cork of a bottle, and, when they're out of the way, the red-hot melted rock comes out. Then there's trouble. I want to get pictures of that."

"Well, keep far enough away," advised Mr. Nestor, who had come forward. "Don't take any chances. I guess your rivals won't get here in time to take any pictures, for they can't travel as fast as we did."

"No," agreed the young inventor, "unless some other party of them were here ahead of us. They'll have their own troubles, though, making pictures anything like as good as we're getting."

"There goes another blast!" cried Ned, as a terrific explosion sounded, and a shower of hot stuff was thrown high into the air. "If I lived in Arequipa I'd be moving out about now."

"There isn't much danger I guess, except from showers of burning ashes, and volcanic dust," spoke Mr. Nestor, "and the wind is blowing it away from the town. If it continues this way the people will be saved."

"Unless there is so much of the red-hot lava that it will bury the city," suggested Tom. "I hope that doesn't happen," and he could not repress a shudder as he looked down on the awful scene below him.

After that last explosion the volcano appeared to subside somewhat, though great clouds of smoke and tongues of fire leaped upward.

"I've got to put in a new reel of film!" suddenly exclaimed Tom. "While I stop the camera, Mr. Damon, I think you and Mr. Nestor might put the airship down to the ground. I want some views on the level."

"What! Go down to earth with this awful volcano spouting fire?" cried Mr. Damon. "Bless my comb and brush!"

"We can get well down the side of the mountain," said Tom. "I won't go into any danger, much less ask any one else to do so, and I certainly don't want my ship damaged. We can land down there," he said, pointing to a spot on the side of the volcanic mountain, that was some distance removed from the mouth of the crater. It won't take me long to get one reel of views, and then I'll come up again."

The two men finally gave in to Tom's argument, that there was comparatively little danger, for they admitted that they could quickly rise up at the first sign of danger, and accordingly the Flyer descended. Tom quickly had a fresh reel of film inserted, and started his camera to working, standing it on a tripod some distance from the airship.

Once more the volcano was "doing its prettiest," as Tom expressed it. He glanced around, as another big explosion took place, to see if any other picture men were on hand, but the terrible mountain seemed deserted, though of course someone might be on the other side.

"What's that?" suddenly cried Ned, looking apprehensively at his chum. At the same time Tom jumped to his feet, for he had been kneeling near the camera.

"Bless my—" began Mr. Damon, but he got no farther, for suddenly the solid ground began to tremble and shake.

"An earthquake!" shouted Mr. Nestor. "Come, Tom! Get back to the ship!" The young inventor and Ned had been the only ones to leave it, as it rested on a spur of the mountain.

As Tom and Ned leaped forward to save the camera which was toppling to one side, there came a great fissure in the side of the volcano, and a stream of molten rock, glowing white with heat, gushed out. It was a veritable river of melted stone, and it was coming straight for the two lads.

"Run! Run!" cried Mr. Nestor. "We have everything ready for a quick flight. "Run, Tom! Ned!"

The lads leaped for the Flyer, the molten rock coming nearer and nearer, and then with a cry Koku sprang overboard and made a dash toward his master.

THE EARTHQUAKE—CONCLUSION

"Here, Mr. Tom. Me carry you an' Ned. You hold picture machine!" cried the giant. "Me run faster."

As he spoke he lifted Ned up under one arm, and caught Tom in the other. For they were but as children to his immense strength. Tom held on to his camera, and, thus laden down, Koku ran as he had never run before, toward the waiting airship.

"Come on! Come on!" shouted Mr. Damon, for he could see what Tom, Ned and Koku could not, that the stream of lava was nearing them rapidly.

"It's hot!" cried Ned, as a wave of warm air fanned his cheek.

"I should say so!" cried Tom. "The volcano is full of red-hot melted stone."

There came a sickening shake of the earth. Koku staggered as he ran on, but he kept his feet, and did not fall. Again came a tremendous explosion, and a shower of fine ashes sifted over the airship, and on Koku and his living burdens.

"This is the worst ever!" gasped Tom. "But I've got some dandy pictures, if we ever get away from here alive to develop them."

"Hurry, Koku! Hurry!" begged Mr. Nestor. "Bless my shoe laces!" yelled Mr. Damon, who was fairly jumping up and down on the deck of the Flyer. "I'll never go near a volcano again!"

Once more the ground shook and trembled, as the earthquake rent it. Several cracks appeared in Koku's path, but he leaped over them with tremendous energy. A moment later he had thrust Tom and Ned over the rail, to the deck, and leaped aboard himself.

"Let her go!" cried Tom. "I'll do the rest of my moving picture work, around volcanoes and earthquakes, from up in the air!"

The Flyer shot upward, and scarcely a moment too soon, for, an instant after she left the ground, the stream of hot, burning and bubbling lava rolled beneath her, and those on board could feel the heat of it ascending.

"Say, I'm glad we got out of that when we did," gasped Ned, as he looked down. "You're all right, Koku."

"That no trouble," replied the giant with a cheerful grin. "Me carry four fellows like you," and he stretched out his big arms. Tom had at once set his camera to working again, taking view after view.

It was a terrifying but magnificent sight that our friends beheld, for the earth was trembling and heaving. Great fissures opened in many places. Into some of them streams of lava poured, for now the volcano had opened in several places, and from each crack the melted rocks belched out. The crater, however, was not sending into the air such volumes of smoke and ashes as before, as most of the tremendous energy had passed, or was being used to spout out the lava.

The earthquake was confined to the region right about the volcano, or there might have been a great loss of life in the city. As it was, the damage done was comparatively slight.

Tom continued to take views, some showing the earth as it was twisted and torn, and other different aspects of the crater. Then, as suddenly as the earthquake had begun, it subsided, and the volcano was less active.

"My! I'm glad to see that!" exclaimed Mr. Damon. "I've had about enough of horrors!"

"And I have too," added Tom. "I'm on my last roll of film, and I can't take many more pictures. But I guess I have all Mr. Period needs, and we'll start for home, as soon as I finish the next roll. But I'm going to save that for a night view. That will he a novelty."

The volcano became active again after dark, and presented a magnificent though terrifying aspect. As the airship hovered above it, Tom got some of his best pictures, and then, as the last bit of film slipped along back of the lens, the airship was headed north.

"Now for Shopton!" cried Tom. "Our trip is ended."

"It's too had you didn't have more film," said Ned. "I thought you had plenty."

"Well, I used more than I counted on, but there are enough pictures as it is."

"Plenty," agreed Mr. Nestor. "I'm sure our company will be very well satisfied with them, Tom. We can't get home any too soon to suit me. I've had enough excitement."

"And we didn't see anything of those other fellows whom we heard about," spoke Mr. Damon, as the big airship flew on.

"No," said Tom. "But I'm not worrying about them."

They made another stop in Lima, on their homeward trip, to renew their supply of gasolene, and there learned that the rival picture men had arrived at the volcano too late to see it in operation. This news came to a relative of one of the two men who lived in Lima.

"Then our views of the earthquake and the smoking mountain will be the only ones, and your company can control the rights," said Tom to Mr. Nestor, who agreed with him.

In due time, and without anything out of the ordinary happening the Flyer reached Shopton, where Tom found a warm welcome awaiting him, not only from his father, but from a certain young lady, whose name I do not need to mention.

"And so you got everything you went after, didn't you, Tom," exclaimed Mr. Period, a few days later, when he had come from New York to get the remainder of the films.

"Yes, and some things I didn't expect," replied Tom. "There was—"

"Yes! Yes! I know!" interrupted the odd picture man. "It was that jungle fire. That's a magnificent series. None better. And those scoundrels took your camera; eh?"

"Yes. Could you connect them with Turbot and Eckert?" asked Tom.

"No, but I'm sure they were acting for them just the same. I had no legal evidence to act on, however, so I had to let it go. Turbot and Eckert won't be in it when I start selling duplicates of the films you have. And these last ought to be the best of all. I didn't catch that fellow when I raced after him on the dock. He got away, and has steered clear of me since," finished Mr. Period.

"And our rivals didn't secure any views like ours," said Tom.

"I'm glad of it," spoke Mr. Period. "Turbot and Eckert bribed one of my men, and so found out where I was sending messages to you. They even got a copy of my cablegram. But it did them no good."

"Were all the films clear that I sent you?" asked our hero.

"Every one. Couldn't be better. The animal views were particularly fine. You must have had your nerve with you to get some of 'em."

"Oh, Tom always has his nerve," laughed Ned.

"Well, how soon will you be ready to start out again?" asked the picture man, as he packed up the last of the films which Tom gave him. "I'd like to get some views of a Japanese earthquake, and we haven't any polar views. I want some of them, taken as near the North Pole as you can get."

Tom gently shook his head.

"What! You don't mean to say you won't get them for me?" cried Mr. Period. "With that wonderful camera of yours you can get views no one else ever could."

"Then some one else will have to take them," remarked the young inventor. "I'll lend you the camera, and an airship, and you can go yourself, Mr. Period. I'm going to stay home for a while. I did what I set out to do, and that's enough."

"I'm glad you'll stay home, Tom," said his father. "Now perhaps I'll get my gyroscope finished."

"And I, my noiseless airship," went on our hero. "No, Mr. Period, you'll have to excuse me this time. Why don't you go yourself?" he asked. "You would know just what kind of pictures you wanted."

"No, I'm a promoter of the moving picture business, and I sell films, but I don't know hew to take them," was the answer. "Besides I—er—well, I don't exactly care for airships, Tom Swift," he finished with a laugh. "Well, I can't thank you enough for what you did for me, and I've brought you a check to cover your expenses, and pay you as I agreed. All the same I'm sorry you won't start for Japan, or the North Pole."

"Nothing doing," said Tom with a laugh; and Mr. Period departed.

"Have you any idea what you will do next?" asked Ned, a day or so later, when he and Tom were in the workshop.

"I can't tell until I finish my noiseless airship," was the answer. "Then something may happen."

Something did, as I shall have the pleasure of telling you about in the next volume of this series, to be called, "Tom Swift and His Great Searchlight; or, On the Border for Uncle Sam," and in it will be given an account of a great lantern our hero made, and how he baffled the smugglers with it.

"Oh, Tom, weren't you dreadfully frightened when you saw that burning river of lava coming toward you?" asked Mary Nestor, when the young inventor called on her later and told her some of his adventures. "I should have been scared to death."

"Well, I didn't have time to get scared," answered Tom. "It all happened so quickly, and then, too I was thinking of my camera. Next I knew Koku grabbed me, and it was all over."

"But those wild beasts! Didn't they frighten you, especially when the rhinoceros charged you?"

"If you won't let it get out, I'll make a confession to you," said Tom, lowering his voice. "I was scared stiff that time, but don't let Ned know it."

"I won't," promised Mary with a laugh. And now, when Tom is in such pleasant company, we will take leave of him for a while, knowing that. sooner or later, he will be seeking new adventures as exciting as those of the past.

Tom Swift and His Great Searchlight
Or On the Border for Uncle Sam

TABLE OF CONTENTS:

A Scrap of Paper

"Tom, did you know Andy Foger was back in town?"

"Great Scott, no, I didn't Ned! Not to stay, I hope."

"I guess not. The old Foger homestead is closed up, though I did see a man working around it today as I came past. But he was a carpenter, making some repairs I think. No, I don't believe Andy is here to stay."

"But if some one is fixing up the house, it looks as if the family would come back," remarked Tom, as he thought of the lad who had so long been his enemy, and who had done him many mean turns before leaving Shopton, where our hero lived.

"I don't think so," was the opinion of Ned Newton, who was Tom Swift's particular chum. "You know when Mr. Foger lost all his money, the house was supposed to be sold. But I heard later that there was some flaw in the title, and the sale fell through. It is because he couldn't sell the place that Mr. Foger couldn't get money to pay some of his debts. He has some claim on the house, I believe, but I don't believe he'd come back to live in it."

"Why not?"

"Because it's too expensive a place for a poor man to keep up, and Mr. Foger is now poor."

"Yes, he didn't get any of the gold, as we did when we went to the underground city," remarked Tom. "Well, I don't wish anybody bad luck but I certainly hope the Fogers keep poor enough to stay away from Shopton. They bothered me enough. But where did you see Andy?"

"Oh, he was with his crony, Sam Snedecker. You know Sam said, some time ago, that Andy was to pay him a visit, but Andy didn't come then, for some reason or other. I suppose this call makes up for it. I met them down near Parker's drug store."

"You didn't hear Andy say anything about coming back here?" and the young inventor's voice was a trifle anxious.

"No," replied Ned. "What makes you so nervous about it?"

"Well, Ned, you know what Andy is—always trying to make trouble for me, even sneaking in my shop sometimes, trying to get the secret of some of my airships and machinery. And I admit I think it looks suspicious when they have a carpenter working on the old homestead. Andy may come back, and—"

"Nonsense, Tom! If he does you and I can handle him. But I think perhaps the house may be rented, and they may be fixing it up for a tenant. It's been vacant a long time you know, and I heard the other day that it was haunted."

"Haunted, Ned! Get out! Say, you don't believe in that sort of bosh, do you?"

"Of course not. It was Eradicate who told me, and he said when he came past the place quite late the other night he heard groans, and the clanking of chains coming from it, and he saw flashing lights."

"Oh, wow! Eradicate is geting batty in his old age, poor fellow! He and his mule Boomerang are growing old together, and I guess my colored helper is 'seeing things,' as well as hearing them. But, as you say, it may be that the house is going to be rented. It's too valuable a property to let stand idle. Did you hear how long Andy was going to stay?"

"A week, I believe."

"A week! Say, one day would be enough I should think."

"You must have some special reason for being afraid Andy will do you some harm," exclaimed Ned. "Out with it, Tom."

"Well, I'll tell you what it is, Ned," and Tom led his chum inside the shop, in front of which the two lads had been talking. It was a shop where the young inventor constructed many of his marvelous machines, aircraft, and instruments of various sorts.

"Do you think some one may hear you?" asked Ned.

"They might. I'm not taking any chances. But the reason I want to be especially careful that Andy Foger doesn't spy on any of my inventions is that at last I have perfected my noiseless airship motor!"

"You have!" cried Ned, for he knew that his chum had been working for a long time on this motor, that would give out no sound, no matter at how high a speed it was run. "That's great, Tom! I congratulate you. I don't wonder you don't want Andy to get even a peep at it."

"Especially as I haven't it fully patented," went on the young inventor. He had met with many failures in his efforts to perfect this motor, which he intended to install on one of his airships. "If any one saw the finished parts now it wouldn't take them long to find out the secret of doing away with the noise."

"How do you do it?" asked Ned, for he realized that his chum had no secrets from him.

"Well, it's too complicated to describe," said Tom, "but the secret lies in a new way of feeding gasolene into the motor, a new sparking device, and an improved muffler. I think I could start my new airship in front of the most skittish horse, and he wouldn't stir, for the racket wouldn't wake a baby. It's going to be great."

"What are you going to do with it, when you get it all completed?"

"I haven't made up my mind yet. It's going to be some time before I get it all put together, and installed, and in that time something may turn up. Well, let's talk about something more pleasant than Andy Foger. I guess I won't worry about him."

"No, I wouldn't. I'd like to see the motor run."

"You can, in a day or so, but just now I need a certain part to attach to the sparker, and I had to send to town for it. Koku has gone after it."

"What, that big giant servant? He might break it on the way back, he's so strong. He doesn't realize how much muscle he has."

"No, that's so. Well, while we're waiting for him, come on in the house, and I'll show you some new books I got."

The two lads were soon in the Swift homestead, a pleasant and large old-fashioned residence, in the suburbs of Shopton. Tom brought out the books, and he and his chum poured over them.

"Mr. Damon gave me that one on electricity," explained the young inventor, handing Ned a bulky volume.

"'Bless my bookmark!' as Mr. Damon himself would say if he were here," exclaimed Ned with a laugh. "That's a dandy. But Mr. Damon didn't give you THIS one," and Ned picked up a dainty volume of verse. "'To Tom Swift, with the best wishes of Mary—'" but that was as far as he read, for Tom grabbed the book away, and closed the cover over the flyleaf, which bore some writing in a girl's hand. I think my old readers can guess whose hand it was.

"Wow! Tom Swift reading poetry!" laughed Ned.

"Oh, cut it out," begged his chum. "I didn't know that was among the books. I got it last Christmas. Now here's a dandy one on lion hunting, Ned," and to cover his confusion Tom shoved over a book containing many pictures of wild animals.

"Lion hunting; eh," remarked Ned. "Well, I guess you could give them some points on snapping lions with your moving picture camera, Tom."

"Yes, I got some good views," admitted the young inventor modestly. "I may take the camera along on some trips in my noiseless airship. Hello! here comes Koku back. I hope he got what I wanted."

A man, immense in size, a veritable giant, one of two whom Tom Swift had brought away from captivity with him, was entering the front gate. He stopped to speak to Mr. Swift, Tom's father, who was setting out some plants in a flower bed, taking them from a large wheel barrow filled with the blooms.

Mr. Swift, who was an inventor of note, had failed in his health of late, and the doctor had recommended him to be out of doors as much as possible. He delighted in gardening, and was at it all day.

"Look!" suddenly cried Ned, pointing to the giant. Then Tom and his chum saw a strange sight.

With a booming laugh, Koku picked up Mr. Swift gently and set him on a board that extended across the front part of the wheel barrow. Then, as easily as if it was a pound weight, the big man lifted Mr. Swift, barrow, plants and all, in his two hands, and carried them across the garden to another flower bed, that was ready to be filled.

"No use to walk when I can carry you, Mr. Swift," exclaimed Koku with a laugh. "I overtook you quite nice; so?"

"Yes, you took me over in great shape, Koku!" replied the aged inventor with a smile at Koku's English, for the giant frequently got his words backwards. "That barrow is quite heavy for me to wheel."

"You after this call me," suggested Koku.

"Say, but he's strong all right," exclaimed Ned, "and that was an awkward thing to carry."

"It sure was," agreed Tom. "I haven't yet seen any one strong enough to match Koku. And he's gentle about it, too. He's very fond of dad."

"And you too, I guess," added Ned.

"Well, Koku, did you get that attachment?" asked Tom, as his giant servant entered the room.

"Yes, Mr. Tom. I have it here," and from his pocket Koku drew a heavy piece of steel that would have taxed the strength of either of the boys to lift with one hand. But Koku's pockets were very large and made specially strong of leather, for he was continually putting odd things in them.

Koku handed over the attachment, for which his master had sent him. He held it out on a couple of fingers, as one might a penknife, but Tom took both hands to set it on the ground.

"I the female get, also," went on Koku, as he began taking some letters and papers from his pocket. "I stop in the office post, and the female get."

"Mail, Koku, not female," corrected Tom with a laugh. "A female is a lady you know."

"For sure I know, and the lady in the post office gave me the female. That is I said what, did I not?"

"Well, I guess you meant it all right," remarked Ned. "But letter mail and a male man and a female woman are all different."

"Oh such a language!" gasped the giant. "I shall never learn it. Well, then, Mr. Tom, here is your mail, that the female lady gave to me for you, and you are a male. It is very strange."

Koku pulled out a bundle of letters, which Tom took, and then the giant continued to delve for more. One of the papers, rolled in a wrapper, stuck on the edge of the pocket.

"You must outcome!" exclaimed Koku, giving it a sudden yank, and it "outcame" with such suddenness that the paper was torn in half, tightly wrapped as it was, and it was considerable of a bundle.

"Koku, you're getting too strong!" exclaimed Tom, as scraps of paper were scattered about the room. "I think I'll give you less to eat."

"I am your forgiveness," said Koku humbly, as he stooped over to pick up the fragments. "I did not mean."

"It's all right," said Tom kindly. "That's only a big bundle of Sunday papers I guess."

"I'll give him a hand," volunteered Ned, stooping over to help Koku clear the rug of the litter. As he did so Tom's chum gave a gasp of surprise.

"Hello, Tom!" Ned cried. "Here's something new, and I guess it will interest you."

"What is it?"

"It's part of an account of some daring smugglers who are working goods across the Canadian border into the northern part of this state. The piece is torn, but there's something here which says the government agents suspect the men of using airships to transport the stuff."

"Airships! Smugglers using airships!" cried Tom. "It doesn't seem possible!"

"That's what it says here, Tom. It says the custom house authorities have tried every way to catch them, and when they couldn't land 'em, the only theory they could account for the way the smuggling was going on was by airships, flying at night."

"That's odd. I wonder how it would seem to chase a smuggler in an airship at night? Some excitement about that; eh, Ned? Let's see that scrap of paper."

Ned passed it over, and Tom scanned it closely. Then in his turn, he uttered an exclamation of surprise.

"What is it?" inquired his chum.

"Great Scott, Ned, listen to this! 'It is suspected that some of the smugglers have'—then there's a place where the paper is torn-'in Shopton, N.Y.'" finished Tom. "Think of that, Ned. Our town here, is in some way connected with the airship smugglers! We must find the rest of this scrap of paper, and paste it together. This may be a big thing! Find that other scrap! Koku, you go easy on papers next time," cautioned Tom, good naturedly, as he and his chum began sorting over the torn parts of the paper.

A Spy in Town

Tom Swift, Ned Newton and Koku, the giant, are busy trying to piece together the torn parts of the paper, containing an account of the airship smugglers. I will take the opportunity of telling you something about the young inventor and his work, for, though many of my readers have made Tom's acquaintances in previous books of this series, there may be some who pick up this one as their first volume.

Tom lived with his father, also an inventor of note, in the town of Shopton, New York state. His mother was dead, and a Mrs. Baggert kept house. Eradicate was an eccentric, colored helper, but of late had become too old to do much. Mr. Swift was also quite aged, and had been obliged to give up most of his inventive work.

Ned Newton was Tom Swift's particular chum, and our hero had another friend, a Mr. Wakefield Damon, of the neighboring town of Waterford. Mr. Damon had the odd habit of blessing everything he saw or could think of. Another of Tom's friends was Miss Mary Nestor, whom I have mentioned, while my old readers will readily recognize in Andy Foger a mean bully, who made much trouble for Tom.

The first book of the series was called "Tom Swift and His Motor-Cycle," and on that machine Tom had many advances on the road, and not a little fun. After that Tom secured a motor boat, and had a race with Andy Foger. In his airship our hero made a stirring cruise, while in his submarine boat he and his father recovered a sunken treasure.

When Tom Swift invented a new electric run-about he did not realize that it was to be the speediest car on the road, but so it proved, and he was able to save the bank with it. In the book called "Tom Swift and His Wireless Message," I told you how he saved the castaways of Earthquake Island, among whom were Mr. and Mrs. Nestor, the parents of Mary.

Tom Swift had not been long on the trail of the diamond makers before he discovered the secret of Phantom Mountain, and after that adventure he went to the caves of ice, where his big airship was wrecked. But he got home, and soon made another, which he called a sky racer, and in that he made the quickest flight on record.

With his electric rifle Tom went to elephant land, where he succeeded in rescuing two missionaries from the red pygmies. A little later he set out for the city of gold, and had marvelous adventures underground.

Hearing of a deposit of valuable platinum in Siberia, Tom started for that lonely place, and, to reach a certain part of if, he had to invent a new machine, called an air glider. It was an aeroplane without means of propulsion save the wind.

In the book, "Tom Swift in Captivity," I related the particulars of how he brought away two immense men from giant land. One, Koku, he kept for himself, while the other made a good living by being exhibited in a circus.

When the present story opens Tom had not long been home after a series of strange adventures. A moving picture concern, with which Mr. Nestor was associated, wanted some views of remarkable scenes, such as fights among wild beasts, the capture of herds of elephants, earthquakes, and volcanos in action, and great avalanches in the Alps. Tom invented a wizard camera, and got many good views, though at times he was in great danger, even in his airship. Especially was this so at the erupting volcano.

But our hero came swiftly hack to Shopton, and there, all Winter and Spring, he busied himself perfecting a new motor for an airship—a motor that would make no noise. He perfected it early that Summer, and now was about to try it, when the incident of the torn newspaper happened.

"Have you got all the pieces, Tom?" asked Ned, as he passed his chum several scraps, which were gathered up from the floor.

"I think so. Now we'll paste them together, and see what it says. We may be on the trail of a big mystery, Ned."

"Maybe. Go ahead and see what you can make of it."

Tom fitted together, as best he could, the ragged pieces, and then pasted them on a blank sheet of paper.

"I guess I've got it all here now," he said finally. "I'll skip the first part. You read me most of that, Ned. Just as you told me, it relates how the government agents, having tried in vain to get a clue to the smugglers, came to the conclusion that they must be using airships to slip contraband goods over the border at night."

"Now where's that mention of Shopton? Oh, here it is," and he read:

"'It is suspected that some of the smugglers have been communicating with confederates in Shopton, New York. This came to the notice of the authorities today, when one of the government agents located some of the smuggled goods in a small town in New York on the St. Lawrence. The name of this town is being kept secret for the present."

"'It was learned that the goods were found in a small, deserted house, and that among them were letters from someone in Shopton, relating to the disposal of the articles. They refuse to say who the letters were from, but it is believed that some of Uncle Sam's men may shortly make their appearance in the peaceful burg of Shopton, there to follow up the clue. Many thousands of dollars worth of goods have been smuggled, and the United States, as well as the Dominion of Canada custom authorities, say they are determined to put a stop to the daring efforts of the smugglers. The airship theory is the latest put forth.'"

"Well, say, that's the limit!" cried Ned, as Tom finished reading. "What do you know about that?"

"It brings it right home to us," agreed the young inventor. "But who is there in Shopton who would be in league with the smugglers?"

"That's hard to say."

"Of course we don't know everyone in town," went on Tom, "but I'm pretty well acquainted here, and I don't know of a person who would dare engage in such work."

"Maybe it's a stranger who came here, and picked out this place because it was so quiet," suggested Ned.

"That's possible. But where would he operate from?" asked Tom. "There are few in Shopton who would want to buy smuggled goods."

"They may only ship them here, and fix them so they can't be recognized by the custom authorities, and then send them away again," went on Ned. "This may be a sort of clearing-house for the smugglers."

"That's so. Well, I don't know as we have anything to do with it. Only if those fellows are using an airship I'd like to know what kind it is. Well, come on out to the shop now, and we'll see how the silent motor works."

On the way Tom passed his father, and, telling him not to work too hard in the sun, gave his parent the piece of paper to read, telling about the smugglers.

"Using airships! eh?" exclaimed Mr. Swift. "And they think there's a clue here in Shopton? Well, we'll get celebrated if we keep on, Tom," he added with a smile.

Tom and Ned spent the rest of the day working over the motor, which was set going, and bore out all Tom claimed for it. It was as silent as a watch.

"Next I want to get it in the airship, and give it a good test," Tom remarked, speeding it up, as it was connected on a heavy base in the shop.

"I'll help you," promised Ned, and for the next few days the chums were kept busy fitting the silent motor into one of Tom's several airships.

"Well, I think we can make a flight to-morrow," said the young inventor, about a week later. "I need some new bolts though, Ned. Let's take a walk into town and get them. Oh, by the way, have you seen anything more of Andy Foger?"

"No. and I don't want to. I suppose he's gone back home after his visit to Sam. Let's go down the street, where the Foger house is, and see if there's anything going on."

As the two lads passed the mansion, they saw a man, in the kind of suit usually worn by a carpenter, come out of the back door and stand looking across the garden. In his hand he held a saw.

"Still at the repairs, I guess," remarked Ned. "I wonder what—"

"Look there! Look! Quick!" suddenly interrupted Tom, and Ned, looking, saw someone standing behind the carpenter in the door. "If that isn't Andy Foger, I'll eat my hat!" cried Tom.

"It sure is," agreed Ned. "What in the world is he doing there?"

But his question was not answered, for, a moment later, Andy turned, and went inside, and the carpenter followed, closing the door behind them.

"That's queer," spoke Tom.

"Very," agreed Ned. "He didn't go back after all. I'd like to know what's going on in there."

"And there's someone else who would like to know, also, I think," said Tom in a low voice.

"Who?" asked Ned.

"That man hiding behind the big tree across the street. I'm sure he's watching the Foger house, and when Andy came to the door that time, I happened to look around and saw that man focus a pair of opera glasses on him and the carpenter."

"You don't mean it, Tom!" exclaimed Ned.

"I sure do. I believe that man is some sort of a spy or a detective."

"Do you think he's after Andy?"

"I don't know. Let's not get mixed up in the affair, anyhow. I don't want to be called in as a witness. I haven't the time to spare."

As if the man behind the tree was aware that he had attracted the attention of our friends, he quickly turned and walked away. Tom and Ned glanced up at the Foger house, but saw nothing, and proceeded on to the store.

"I'll wager anything that Andy has been getting in some sort of trouble in the town he moved to from here," went on Tom, "and he daren't go back. So he came here, and he's hiding in his father's old house. He could manage to live there for a while, with the carpenter bringing him in food. Say, did you notice who that man was, with the saw?"

"Yes, he's James Dillon, a carpenter who lives down on our street," replied Ned. "A nice man, too. The next time I see him, I'm going to ask him what Andy is doing in town, and what the repairs are that he's making on the house."

"Well, of course if Andy has been doing anything wrong, he wouldn't admit it," said Tom. "Though Mr. Dillon may tell you about the carpenter work. But I'm sure that man was a detective from the town where Andy moved to. You'll see."

"I don't think so," was Ned's opinion. "If Andy was hiding he wouldn't show himself as plainly as he did."

The two chums argued on this question, but could come to no decision. Then, having reached Tom's home with the bolts, they went hard at work on the airship.

"Well, now to see what happens!" exclaimed Tom the next day, when everything was ready for a trial flight. "I wish Mr. Damon was here. I sent him word, but I didn't hear from him."

"Oh, he may show up any minute," replied Ned, as he helped Tom and Koku wheel the newly-equipped airship out of the shed. "The first thing you'll hear will be him blessing something. Is this far enough out, Tom?"

"No, a little more, and then head her up into the wind. I say, Ned, if this is a success, and—"

Tom stopped suddenly and looked out into the road. Then, in a low voice, he said, to Ned:

"Don't move suddenly, or he'll suspect that we're onto his game, but turn around slowly, and look behind that big sycamore tree in front of our house Ned. Tell me what you see."

"There's a man hiding there, Tom," reported his chum, a little later, after a cautious observation.

"I thought so. What's he doing?"

"Why he—by Jove! Tom, he's looking at us through opera glasses, like that other—"

"It isn't *another*, it's the same fellow!" whispered Tom. "It's the spy who was watching Andy! I'm going to see what's up," and he strode rapidly toward the street, at the curb of which was the tree that partly screened the man behind it.

QUEER REPAIRS

Quickly Tom Swift crossed the space between the airship, that was ready for a flight, and the tree. The man behind it had apparently not seen Tom coming, being so interested in looking at the airship, which was a wonderful craft. He was taken completely by surprise as Tom, stepping up to him, asked sharply:

"Who are you and what are you doing here?"

The man started so that he nearly dropped the opera glasses, which he had held focused on the aeroplane. Then he stepped back, and eyed Tom sharply.

"What do you want?" repeated our hero. "What right have you to be spying on that airship—on these premises?" The man hesitated a moment, and then coolly returned the glasses to his pocket. He did not seem at all put out, after his first start of surprise.

"What are you doing?" Tom again asked. He looked around to see where Koku, the giant, was, and beheld the big man walking slowly toward him, for Ned had mentioned what had taken place.

"What right have you to question my actions?" asked the man, and there was in his tones a certain authority that made Tom wonder.

"Every right," retorted our hero. "That is my airship, at which you have been spying, and this is where I live."

"Oh, it is; eh?" asked the man calmly. "And that's your airship, too?"

"I invented it, and built the most of it myself. If you are interested in such things, and can assure me that you have no spying methods in view, I can show you—"

"Have you other airships?" interrupted the man quickly.

"Yes, several," answered Tom. "But I can't understand why you should be spying on me. If you don't care to accept my offer, like a gentleman, tell me who you are, and what your object is, I will have my assistant remove you. You are on private property, as this street is not a public one, being cut through by my father. I'll have Koku remove you by force, if you won't go peaceably, and I think you'll agree with me that Koku can do it. Here Koku," he called sharply, and the big man advanced quickly.

"I wouldn't do anything rash, if I were you," said the man quietly. "As for this being private property, that doesn't concern me. You're Tom Swift, aren't you; and you have several airships?"

"Yes, but what right have you to—"

"Every right!" interrupted the man, throwing back the lapel of his coat, and showing a badge. "I'm Special Agent William Whitford, of the United States Customs force, and I'd like to ask you a few questions, Tom Swift." He looked our hero full in the face.

"Customs department!" gasped Tom. "You want to ask me some questions?"

"That's it," went on the man, in a business-like voice.

"What about?"

"Smuggling by airship from Canada!"

"What!" cried Tom. "Do you mean to say you suspect me of being implicated in—"

"Now go easy," advised the man calmly. "I didn't say anything, except that I wanted to *question* you. If you'd like me to do it out here, why I can. But as someone might hear us—"

"Come inside," said Tom quietly, though his heart was beating in a tumult. "You may go, Koku, but stay within call," he added significantly. "Come on, Ned," and he motioned to his chum who was approaching. "This man is a custom officer and not a spy or a detective, as we thought."

"Oh, yes, I am a *sort* of a detective," corrected Mr. Whitford. "And I'm a spy, too, in a way, for I've been spying on you, and some other parties in town. But you may be able to explain everything," he added, as he took a seat in the library between Ned and Tom. "I only know I was sent here to do certain work, and I'm going to do it. I wanted to make some observations before you saw me, but I wasn't quite quick enough."

"Would you mind telling me what you want to know?" asked Tom, a bit impatiently. "You mentioned smuggling, and—"

"Smuggling!" interrupted Ned.

"Yes, over from Canada. Maybe you have seen something in the papers about our department thinking airships were used at night to slip the goods over the border."

"We saw it!" cried Tom eagerly. "But how does that concern me?"

"I'll come to that, presently," replied Mr. Whitford. "In the first place, we have been roundly laughed at in some papers for proposing such a theory. And yet it isn't so wild as it sounds. In fact, after seeing your airship, Tom Swift, I'm convinced—"

"That I've been smuggling?" asked Tom with a laugh.

"Not at all. As you have read, we confiscated some smuggled goods the other day, and among them was a scrap of paper with the words Shopton, New York, on it."

"Was it a letter from someone here, or to someone here?" asked Ned. "The papers intimated so."

"No. they only guessed at that part of it. It was just a scrap of paper, evidently torn from a letter, and it only had those three words on it. Naturally we agents thought we could get a clue here. We imagined, or at least I did, for I was sent to work up this end, that perhaps the airships for the smugglers were made here. I made inquiries, and found that you, Tom Swift, and one other, Andy Foger, had made, or owned, airships in Shopton."

"I came here, but I soon exhausted the possibility of Andy Foger making practical airships. Besides he isn't at home here any more, and he has no facilities for constructing the craft as you have. So I came to look at your place, and I must say that it looks a bit suspicious, Mr. Swift. Though, of course, as I said," he added with a smile, "you may be able to explain everything."

"I think I can convince you that I had no part in the smuggling," spoke Tom, laughing. "I never sell my airships. If you like you may talk with my father, the housekeeper, and others who can testify that since my return from taking moving pictures, I have not been out of town, and the smuggling has been going on only a little while."

"That is true," assented the custom officer. "I shall be glad to listen to any evidence you may offer. This is a very baffling case. The government is losing thousands of dollars every month, and we can't seem to stop the smugglers, or get much of a clue to them. This one is the best we have had so far."

It did not take Tom many hours to prove to the satisfaction of Mr. Whitford that none of our hero's airships had taken any part in cheating Uncle Sam out of custom duties.

"Well, I don't know what to make of it," said the government agent, with a disappointed air, as he left the office of the Shopton chief of police, who, with others, at Tom's request, had testified in his favor. "This looked like a good clue, and now it's knocked into a cocked hat. There's no use bothering that Foger fellow," he went on, "for he has but one airship, I understand."

"And that's not much good." put in Ned. "I guess it's partly wrecked, and Andy has kept it out in the barn since he moved away."

"Well, I guess I'll be leaving town then," went on the agent. "I can't get any more clues here, and there may be some new ones found on the Canadian border where my colleagues are trying to catch the rascals. I'm sorry I bothered you, Tom Swift. You certainly have a fine lot of airships," he added, for he had been taken through the shop, and shown the latest, noiseless model. "A fine lot. I don't believe the smugglers, if they use them, have any better."

"Nor as good!" exclaimed Ned. "Tom's can't be beat."

"It's too late for our noiseless trial now," remarked Tom, after the agent had gone. "Let's put her back in the shed, and then I'll take you down street, and treat you to some ice cream, Ned. It's getting quite summery now."

As the boys were coming out of the drug store, where they had eaten their ice cream in the form of sundaes, Ned uttered a cry of surprise at the sight of a man approaching them.

"It's Mr. Dillon, the carpenter whom we saw in the Foger house, Tom!" exclaimed his chum. "This is the first chance I've had to talk to him. I'm going to ask him what sort of repairs he's making inside the old mansion." Ned was soon in conversation with him.

"Yes, I'm working at the Foger house," admitted the carpenter, who had done some work for Ned's father. "Mighty queer repairs, too. Something I never did before. If Andy wasn't there to tell me what he wanted done I wouldn't know what to do."

"Is Andy there yet?" asked Tom quickly.

"Yes, he's staying in the old house. All alone too, except now and then, he has a chum stay there nights with him. They get their own meals. I bring the stuff in, as Andy says he's getting up a surprise and doesn't want any of the boys to see him, or ask questions. But they are sure queer repairs I'm doing," and the carpenter scratched his head reflectively.

"What are you doing?" asked Ned boldly.

"Fixing up Andy's old airship that was once busted," was the unexpected answer, "and after I get that done, if I ever do, he wants me to make a platform for it on the roof of the house, where he can start it swooping through the air. Mighty queer repairs, I call 'em. Well, good evening, boys," and the carpenter passed on.

Searching for Smugglers.

"Well, of all things!"

"Who in the world would think such a thing?"

"Andy going to start out with his airship again!"

"And going to sail it off the roof of his house!"

These were the alternate expressions that came from Tom and Ned, as they stood gazing at each other after the startling information given them by Mr. Dillon, the carpenter.

"Do you really think he means it?" asked Tom, after a pause, during which they watched the retreating figure of the carpenter. "Maybe he was fooling us."

"No, Mr. Dillon seldom jokes," replied Ned, "and when he does, you can always tell. He goes to our church, and I know he wouldn't deliberately tell an untruth. Oh. Andy's up to some game all right."

"I thought he must be hanging around here the way he has been, instead of being home. But I admit I may have been wrong about the police being after him. If he'd done something wrong, he would hardly hire a man to work on the house while he was hiding in it. I guess he just wants to keep out of the way of everybody but his own particular cronies. But I wonder what he is up to, anyhow; getting his airship in shape again?"

"Give it up, unless there's an aero meet on somewhere soon," replied Ned. "Maybe he's going to try a race again."

Tom shook his head.

"I'd have heard about any aviation meets, if there were any scheduled," he replied. "I belong to the national association, and they send out circulars whenever there are to be races. None are on for this season. No, Andy has some other game."

"Well, I don't know that it concerns us," spoke Ned.

"Not as long as he doesn't bother me," answered the young inventor. "Well, Ned, I suppose you'll be over in the morning and help me try out the noiseless airship?"

"Sure thing. Say, it was queer, about that government agent, wasn't it? suspecting you of supplying airships to the smugglers?"

"Rather odd," agreed Tom. "He might much better suspect Andy Foger."

"That's so, and now that we know Andy is rebuilding his old airship, maybe we'd better tell him."

"Tell who?"

"That government agent. Tell him he's wrong in thinking that Andy is out of the game. We might send him word that we just learned that Andy is getting active again. He has as much right to suspect and question him, as he had you."

"Oh, I don't know," began Tom slowly. He was not a vindictive youth, nor, for that matter, was Ned. And Tom would not go out of his way to give information about an enemy, when it was not certain that the said enemy meant anything wrong. "I don't believe there's anything in it," finished our hero. "Andy may have a lot of time on his hands, and, for want of something better to do, he's fixing up his aeroplane."

"Look!" suddenly exclaimed Ned. "There's that agent now! He's going to the depot to get a train, I guess," and he pointed to the government man, who had so lately interviewed Tom. "I'm going to speak to him!" impulsively declared Ned.

"I wouldn't," objected Tom, but his chum had already hastened on ahead, and soon was seen talking excitedly to Mr. Whitford. Tom sauntered up in time to hear the close of the conversation.

"I'm much obliged to you for your information," said the custom officer. "but I'm afraid, just as you say your chum felt about it, that there's nothing in it. This Foger chap may have been bad in the past, but I hardly think he's in with the smugglers. What I'm looking for is not a lad who has one airship, but someone who is making a lot of them, and supplying the men who are running goods over the border. That's the sort of game I'm after, and if this Andy Foger only has one aeroplane I hardly think he can be very dangerous."

"Well, perhaps not," admitted Ned. "But I thought I'd tell you."

"And I'm glad you did. If you hear anything more. I'll be glad to have you let me know. Here's my card," and thanking the boys for their interest Mr. Whitford passed on.

Tom and Ned gave the noiseless airship a test the next day. The craft, which was the stanch Falcon, remodeled, was run out of the shed, Koku the giant helping, while Mr. Swift stood looking on, an interested spectator of what his son was about to do. Eradicate, the old colored man, who was driving his mule Boomerang, hitched to a wagon in which he was carting away some refuse that had been raked up in the garden, halted his outfit nearby.

"I say, Massa Tom!" he called, as the young inventor passed near him, in making a tour of the ship.

"Well, Rad, what is it?"

"Doan't yo'-all want fo' ma an' Boomerang t' gib yo'-all a tow? Mebby dat new-fangled contraption yo'-all has done put on yo' ship won't wuk, an' mebby I'd better stick around t' pull yo'-all home."

"No, Rad, I guess it will work all right. If it doesn't, and we get stuck out a mile or two, I'll send you a wireless message."

"Doan't do dat!" begged the colored man. "I neber could read dem wireless letters anyhow. Jest gib a shout, an' me an' Boomerang will come a-runnin'."

"All right, Rad, I will. Now, Ned, is everything in shape?"

"I think so, Tom."

"Koku, just put a little more wind in those tires. But don't pump as hard as you did the other day," Tom cautioned.

"What happened then?" asked Ned.

"Oh, Koku forgot that he had so much muscle, and he kept on pumping air into the bicycle wheel tires until he burst one. Go easy this time, Koku."

"I will, Mr. Tom," and the giant took the air pump.

"Is he going along?" asked Ned, as he looked to see that all the guy wires and stays were tight.

"I guess so," replied Tom. "He makes good ballast. I wish Mr. Damon was here. If everything goes right we may take a run over, and surprise him."

In a little while the noiseless airship was ready for the start. Tom, Ned and Koku climbed in, and took their positions.

"Good luck!" Mr. Swift called after them. Tom waved his hand to his father, and the next moment his craft shot into the air. Up and up it went, the great propeller blades beating the air, but, save for a soft whirr, such as would be made by the wings of a bird, there was absolutely no sound.

"Hurrah!" cried Tom. "She works! I've got a noiseless airship at last!"

"Say, don't yell at a fellow so," begged Ned, for Tom had been close to his chum when he made his exulting remark.

"Yell! I wasn't yelling," replied Tom. "Oh, I see what happened. I'm so used to speaking loud on the other airships, that make such a racket, that I didn't realize how quiet it was aboard the new Falcon. No wonder I nearly made you deaf, Ned. I'll be careful after this," and Tom lowered his voice to ordinary tones. In fact it was as quiet aboard his new craft, as if he and Ned had been walking in some grass-grown country lane.

"She certainly is a success," agreed Ned. "You could creep up on some other airship now, and those aboard would never know you were coming."

"I've been planning this for a long time," went on our hero, as he shifted the steering gear, and sent the craft around in a long, sweeping curve. "Now for Waterford and Mr. Damon."

They were soon above the town where the odd man lived, and Tom, picking out Mr. Damon's house, situated as it was in the midst of extensive grounds, headed for it.

"There he is, walking through the garden," exclaimed Ned, pointing to their friend down below. "He hasn't heard us, as he would have done if we had come in any other machine."

"That's so!" exclaimed Tom. "I'm going to give him a sensation. I'll fly right over his head, and he won't know it until he sees us. I'll come up from behind."

A moment later he put this little trick into execution. Along swept the airship, until, with a rush, it passed right over Mr. Damon's head. He never heard it. and was not aware of what was happening until he saw the shadow it cast. Then, jumping aside, as if he thought something was about to fall on him, he cried:

"Bless my mosquito netting! What in the world—"

Then he saw Tom and Ned in the airship, which came gently to earth a few yards further on.

"Well of all things!" cried Mr. Damon. "What are you up to now, Tom Swift?"

"It's my noiseless airship," explained our hero. "She doesn't make a sound. Get aboard, and have a ride."

Mr. Damon looked toward the house.

"I guess my wife won't see me," he said with a chuckle. "She's more than ever opposed to airships, Tom, since we went on that trip taking moving pictures. But I'll take a chance." And in he sprang, when the two lads started up again. They made quite a flight, and Tom found that his new motor exceeded his expectations. True, it needed some adjustments, but these could easily be made.

"Well, what are you going to do with it, now that you have it?" asked Mr. Damon, as Tom once more brought the machine around to the odd man's house, and stopped it. "What's it for?"

"Oh, I think I'll find a use for it," replied the young inventor. "Will you come back to Shopton with us?"

"No, I must stay here. I have some letters to write. But I'll run over in a few days, and see you. Then I'll go on another trip, if you've got one planned."

"I may have," answered Tom with a laugh. "Good-bye."

He and Ned made a quick flight home, and Tom at once started on making some changes in the motor. He was engaged at this work the next day, when he noticed a shadow pass across an open window. He looked up to see Ned.

"Hello, Tom!" cried his chum. "Have you heard the news?"

"No, what news? Has Andy Foger fallen out of his airship?"

"No, but there are a whole lot of Custom House detectives in town, looking for clues to the smugglers."

"Still at it, eh? Shopton can't seem to keep out of the limelight. Has anything new turned up?"

"Yes. I just met Mr. Whitford. He's back on the case and he has several men with him. They received word that some smuggled goods came to Shopton, and were shipped out of here again."

"How, by airship?"

"No, by horse and wagon. A lot of cases of valuable silks imported from England to Canada, where the duty is light, were slipped over the border somehow, in airships, it is thought. Then they came here by freight, labeled as calico, and when they reached this town they were taken away in a wagon."

"But how did they get here?"

"On the railroad, of course, but the freight people had no reason to suspect them."

"And where were they taken from the freight station?"

"That's what the customs authorities want to find out. They think there's some secret place here, where the goods are stored and reshipped. That's why so many detectives are here. They are after the smugglers hot-footed."

THE RAID

Tom Swift dropped the tool he was using, and came over to where Ned stood, his chum having vaulted in through the open window.

"Ned," said the young inventor, "there's something queer about this business."

"I'm beginning to think so myself, Tom. But just what do you mean?"

"I mean it's queer that the smugglers should pick out a place like Shopton—a small town—for their operations, or part of them, when there are so many better places. We're quite a distance from the Canadian border. Say, Ned, where was it that Mr. Foger moved to? Hogan's alley, or some such name as that; wasn't it?"

"Logansville, this state, was the place. I once saw Tom Snedecker mail Andy a letter addressed to there. But what has that to do with it?"

Tom's answer was to turn to a large map on the wall of his shop. With a long stick he pointed out the city of Logansville.

"That isn't very far from the Canadian border; is it, Ned?" he asked.

"Say, what are you driving at, Tom? It's right on the border between New York and Canada, according to that map."

"Well, that's a good map, and you can be sure it is nearly right. And, look here. There's the town of Montford, in Canada, almost opposite Logansville."

"Well?"

"Oh, nothing, only I'm going to see Mr. Whitford."

"What do you mean, Tom?"

"I mean that the something queer part about this business may be explained. They have traces of the smugglers sending their goods to Shopton to be re-shipped here, to avoid suspicion, probably. They have a suspicion that airships are used to get the goods over the Canadian border at night."

"But," broke in Ned, "the government agent said that it was across the St. Lawrence River they brought them. Montford is quite a distance from the river. I suppose the smugglers take the goods from the river steamers, land them, pack them in airships, and fly across with them. But if you're trying to connect the Fogers, and Logansville, and Montford with the smugglers, I don't see where it comes in with the St. Lawrence, and the airships, Tom."

"Forget that part of it for a while, Ned. Maybe they are all off on airships, anyhow. I don't take much stock in that theory, though it may be true."

"Just think of the Fogers," went on Tom. "Mr. Foger has lost all his money, he lives in a town near the Canadian border, it is almost certain that smuggled goods have been shipped here. Mr. Foger has a deserted house here, and—see the connection?"

"By Jove, Tom, I believe you're right!" cried his chum. "Maybe the airships aren't in it after all, and Andy is only making a bluff at having his repaired, to cover up some other operations in the house."

"I believe so."

"But that would mean that Mr. Dillon, the carpenter is not telling the truth, and I can't believe that of him."

"Oh, I believe he's honest, but I think Andy is fooling him. Mr. Dillon doesn't know much about airships, and Andy may have had him doing something in the house, telling him it was repair work on an airship, when, as a matter of fact, the carpenter might be making boxes to ship the goods in, or constructing secret places in which to hide them."

"I don't believe it, Tom. But I agree with you that there is something queer going on in Shopton. The Fogers may, or may not, be connected with it. What are you going to do?"

"I'm first going to have a talk with Mr. Whitford. Then I'm going to see if I can't prove, or disprove, that the Fogers are concerned in the matter. If they're not, then some one else in Shopton must be guilty. But I'm interested, because I have been brought into this thing in a way, and I want it sifted to the bottom."

"Then you're going to see Mr. Whitford?"

"I am, and I'm going to tell him what I think. Come on, we'll look him up now."

"But your noiseless airship?"

"Oh, that's all right. It's nearly finished anyhow, I've just got a little more work on the carburetor. That will keep. Come on, we'll find the government agent."

But Mr. Whitford was not at the hotel where he and the other custom inspectors had put up. They made no secret of their presence in Shopton, and all sorts of rumors were flying about regarding them. Mr. Whitford, the hotel clerk said, had gone out of town for the day, and, as Ned and Tom did not feel like telling their suspicions to any of the other agents, they started back home.

"I understand they're going to search every house in Shopton, before they go away," said the clerk to the boys. "They are going to look for smuggled goods."

"They are; eh?" exclaimed Colonel Henry Denterby, who had fought in the Civil War. "Search my house; eh? Well I guess not! A man's house is his castle, sir! That's what it is. No one shall enter mine, no matter if he is a government official, unless I give him permission, sir! And I won't do that, sir! I'll be revolutionized if I do! No, sir!"

"Why, you haven't any smuggled goods concealed, have you, Colonel?" slyly asked a hotel lounger.

"Smuggled goods? What do you mean, sir?" cried the veteran, who was something of a fire-eater. "No, sir! Of course not, sir! I pay my taxes, sir; and all my debts. But no government spy is going to come into my house, and upset everything, sir, looking for smuggled goods, sir. No, sir!"

Some were of one opinion, and some another, and there was quite a discussion underway concerning the rights of the custom officers, as the boys came out of the hotel.

Likewise there was talk about who might be the guilty ones, but no names were mentioned, at least openly.

"Let's go past the Foger house on our way back," proposed Ned, and as he and Tom came in front of it, they heard a pounding going on within, but saw no signs of Andy or the carpenter.

"They're keeping mighty close," commented Tom.

The two boys worked that afternoon on the new airship, and in the evening, when Ned came over, Tom proposed that they make another attempt to see Mr. Whitford.

"I want to get this thing off my mind," spoke the young inventor, and he and his chum started for the hotel. Once more they passed the Foger house. It was in darkness, but, as the two lads stood watching, they saw a flash of a light, as if it came through a crack in a shutter or a shade.

"Some one is in there," declared Tom.

"Yes, probably Andy is getting his own supper. It's queer he wants to lead that sort of a life. Well, everyone to their notion, as the old lady said when she kissed the cow."

They stood for a few minutes watching the old mansion, and then went on. As they passed down a lane, to take a short cut, they approached a small house, that, in times past, had been occupied by the gardener of the Foger estate. Now, that too, was closed. But, in front of it stood a wagon with a big canvas cover over it, and, as the lads came nearer, the wagon drove off quickly, and in silence. At the same time a door in the gardener's house was heard to shut softly.

"Did you see that?" cried Ned.

"Yes, and did you hear that?" asked Tom.

"They're carting stuff away from the old gardener's house," went on Ned. "Maybe it's there that the smugglers are working from! Let's hurry to see Mr. Whitford."

"Hold on!" exclaimed Tom in a whisper. "I've got one suggestion. Ned. Let's tell all we know, and what we think may be the case, but don't make any rash statements. We might be held responsible. Tell what we have seen, and let the government men do the rest."

"All right. I'm willing."

They watched the wagon as it passed on out of sight in the darkness, and then hurried on to see Mr. Whitford. To say that the custom officer was astonished at what the boys related to him, is putting it mildly. He was much excited.

"I think we're on the right trail!" he exclaimed. "You may have done a big service for Uncle Sam. Come on!"

"Where?" the boys asked him.

"We'll make a raid on the old Foger home, and on the gardener's house at once. We may catch the rascals red-handed. You can have the honor of representing Uncle Sam. I'll make you assistant deputies for the night. Here are some extra badges I always carry," and he pinned one each on the two young men.

Mr. Whitford quietly summoned several of his men to his hotel room, and imparted to them what he had learned. They were eager for the raid, and it was decided to go to the Foger home, and the other house at once, first seeking to gain an entrance to the mansion.

Accompanied by Tom and Ned, Mr. Whitford left the hotel. There were few persons about, and no attention was attracted. The other agents left the hotel one by one, and in the darkness gathered about the seemingly deserted mansion.

"Stand ready now, men," whispered Mr. Whitford. "Tom, Ned and I will go up the steps first, and knock. If they don't let us in I'm going to smash the door. Then you follow."

Rather excited by what was about to take place, the two chums accompanied the chief custom agent. He rapped loudly on the door of the house, where only darkness showed.

There was a moment of silence, and then a voice which Tom and Ned recognized as that of Andy Foger, asked:

"What do you want?"

"We want to come in," replied Mr. Whitford.

"But who are you?"

"Uncle Sam's officers, from the custom house."

Tom distinctly heard a gasp of surprise on the other side of the portal, and then a bolt was drawn. The door was thrown back, and there, confronting the two lads and Mr. Whitford, were Andy Foger and his father.

THE APPEAL TO TOM

"Well, what does this mean?" asked Mr. Foger in indignant tones, as he faced the custom officer and Tom and Ned. "What do you mean by coming to my house at this hour, and disturbing me? I demand an answer!"

"And you shall have it," replied Mr. Whitford calmly. He was used to dealing with "indignant" persons, who got very much on their dignity when accused of smuggling. "We are here, Mr. Foger, because of certain information we have received, and we must ask you to submit to some questions, and allow your house to be searched."

"What! You question me? Search this house? That is an indignity to which I will not submit!"

"You will have to, Mr. Foger. I have ample authority for what I am doing, and I am backed by the most powerful government in the world. I also have plenty of help with me."

Mr. Whitford blew his whistle, and at once his several deputies came running up.

"You see I am well prepared to meet force with force, Mr. Foger," said the chief agent, calmly.

"Force! What do you mean, sir?"

"I mean that I have certain information against you. There has been smuggling going on from Canada into the United States."

"Canada? What have I to do with Canada?"

"You don't live far from there," said Mr. Whitford significantly. "Airships have been used. Your son has one, but I don't believe that figured in the game. But two friends of mine saw something to-night that made me decide on this raid. Tom and Ned, tell Mr. Foger what you saw."

The agent stepped back, so that the two lads could be seen. There was another gasp of surprise, this time from Andy Foger, who had remained in the background.

"Tom Swift!" gasped the bully.

"Tell them what you saw. Tom," went on the agent, and Tom and Ned by turns, relayed the incident of the wagon load of goods driving away from the gardener's house.

"This, with what has gone before, made us suspicious," said Mr. Whitford. "So we decided on a raid. If you are not willing to let us in peaceably, we will come by force."

"By all means come in!" was the unexpected reply of Mr. Foger, as he stepped back, and opened wider the door. "Andy, these are some friends of yours, are they not?"

"Friends? I guess not!" exclaimed Andy with a sneer. "I won't even speak to them."

"Not much lost," commented Tom with a laugh.

"Search the house!" ordered Mr. Whitford sharply.

"I'll show you around," offered Mr. Foger.

"We can find our way," was the curt rejoinder of the chief agent.

"The place is deserted," went on Mr. Foger. "My son and I are just living here until certain repairs are made, when I am going to make another effort to sell it."

"Yes, we knew it was being repaired, and that your son was staying here," said Mr. Whitford, "But we did not expect to see you."

"I—er—that is—I came on unexpectedly," said Mr. Foger. "You may look about all you wish. You will find nothing wrong here."

And they did not, strange to say. There was considerable litter in many of the rooms, and in one was Andy's airship in parts. Clearly work was being done on that, and Mr. Dillon's story was confirmed, for tools, with his initials burned in the handles, were lying about.

The custom men, with Tom and Ned, went all over the house. Andy scowled blackly at our hero, but said nothing. Mr. Foger seemed anxious to show everything, and let the men go where they would. Finally a tour of the house had been completed, and nothing of a suspicious nature was found.

"I guess we'll just take a look at the roof, and see that airship platform your son is going to use," said Mr. Whitford, in rather disappointed tones, when he had found nothing.

"It isn't started yet," said Andy.

But they all went up through a scuttle, nevertheless, and saw where some posts had been made fast to the roof, to provide a platform foundation.

"I'll beat you all to pieces when I get flying," said the bully to Tom, as they went down the scuttle again.

"I'm not in the racing game any more," replied Tom coldly. "Besides I only race with my *friends*."

"Huh! Afraid of getting beat!" sneered Andy.

"Well. I guess there's nothing here," said Mr. Whitford to Mr. Foger, as they stood together in the front room.

"No, I knew you'd find nothing, and you have had your trouble for your pains."

"Oh, Uncle Sam doesn't mind trouble."

"And you have caused me much annoyance!" said Mr. Foger sharply.

"I'm afraid we'll have to cause you more," was the agent's comment. "I want to have a look in the gardener's house, from where Tom Swift saw the load going away."

"There is nothing there!" declared Mr. Foger quickly. "That is, nothing but some old furniture. I sold a lot of it, and I suppose the man who bought it came for it to-night."

"We'll take a look," repeated the agent, "I am very fond of old furniture."

"Very well," responded the bully's father, as he eyed Tom and Ned blackly.

He led the way out of the house, and soon they stood before the small cottage. It was dark, and when Mr. Foger unlocked the door he turned on the gas, and lighted it.

"I left the gas on until all the furniture should be taken out," he explained. "But you will find nothing here."

It needed but a glance about the place to show that only some odds and ends of furniture was all that it contained.

"Where does this door lead to," asked Mr. Whitford, when he had made a tour of the place.

"Nowhere. Oh, that is only down into the cellar." was the reply. "There is nothing there."

"We can't take anything for granted," went on the agent with a smile. "I'll take a look down there."

He descended with some of his men. Tom and Ned remained in the kitchen of the cottage, while Andy and his father conversed in low tones, occasionally casting glances at our heroes. Once Tom thought Mr. Foger looked apprehensively toward the door, through which the custom men had descended. He also appeared to be anxiously listening.

But when Mr. Whitford came back, with a disappointed look on his face, and said there was nothing to be found, Mr. Foger smiled:

"What did I tell you?" he asked triumphantly.

"Never mind," was the retort of Uncle Sam's man. "We are not through with Shopton yet."

"I'm sorry we gave you so much trouble on a false clue," said Tom, as he and Ned left the Foger premises with Mr. Whitford, the other deputies following.

"That's all right, Tom. We have to follow many false clues. I'm much obliged to you. Either we were on the wrong track, or the Fogers are more clever than I gave them credit for. But I am not done yet. I have something to propose to you. It has come to me in the last few minutes. I saw you in your airship once, and I know you know how to manage such craft. Now there is no question in my mind but what the smugglers are using airships. Tom, will you undertake a mission for Uncle Sam?"

"What do you mean?"

"I mean will you go to the border, in your airship, and try to catch the smugglers? I can promise you a big reward, and much fame if we catch them. An airship is just what is needed. You are the one to do it. Will you?"

A Searchlight Is Needed

For a few moments after the custom officer had made his appeal, Tom Swift did not reply. His thoughts were busy with many things. Somehow, it seemed of late, there had been many demands on him, demands that had been hard and trying.

In the past he had not hesitated, but in those cases friendship, as well as a desire for adventures, had urged him. Now he thought he had had his fill of adventures.

"Well?" asked Mr. Whitford, gently. "What's your answer, Tom? Don't you think this is a sort of duty-call to you?"

"A duty-call?" repeated the young inventor.

"Yes. Of course I realize that it isn't like a soldier's call to battle, but Uncle Sam needs you just the same. When there is a war the soldiers are called on to repel an enemy. Now the smugglers are just as much an enemy of the United States, in a certain way, as an armed invader would be."

"One strikes at the life and liberty of the people, while the smugglers try to cheat Uncle Sam out of money that is due him. I'm not going to enter into a discussion as to the right of the government to impose duties. People have their own opinion as to that. But, as long as the law says certain duties are to be collected, it is the duty of every citizen, not only to pay those dues, but to help collect them. That's what I'm asking you to do, Tom."

"I don't want to get prosy, or deliver a lecture on the work of the custom house, Tom, but, honestly, I think it is a duty you owe to your country to help catch these smugglers. I admit I'm at the end of my rope. This last clue has failed. The Fogers seem to be innocent of wrong doing. We need your help, Tom."

"But I don't see how I can help you."

"Of course you can! You're an expert with airships. The smugglers are using airships, of that I'm sure. You tell me you have just perfected a noiseless aircraft. That will be just the thing. You can hover on the border, near the line dividing New York State from Canada, or near the St. Lawrence, which is the natural division for a certain distance, and when you see an airship coming along you can slip up in your noiseless one, overhaul it, and make them submit to a search."

"But I won't have any authority to do that," objected Tom, who really did not care for the commission.

"Oh, I'll see that you get the proper authority all right," said Mr. Whitford significantly. "I made you a temporary deputy to-night, but if you'll undertake this work, to catch the smugglers in their airships, you will be made a regular custom official."

"Yes, but supposing I can't catch them?" interposed our hero. "They may have very fast airships, and—"

"I guess you'll catch 'em all right!" put in Ned, who was at his chum's side as they walked along a quiet Shopton street in the darkness. "There's not an aeroplane going that can beat yours, Tom."

"Well, perhaps I *could* get them," admitted the young inventor. "But—"

"Then you'll undertake this work for Uncle Sam?" interrupted Mr. Whitford eagerly. "Come, Tom, I know you will."

"I'm not so sure of that," spoke Tom. "It isn't going to be as easy as you think. There are many difficulties in the way. In the first place the smuggling may be done over such a wide area that it would need a whole fleet of airships to capture even one of the others, for they might choose a most unfrequented place to cross the border."

"Oh, we would be in communication with you," said the agent. "We can come pretty near telling where the contrabrand goods will be shipped from, but the trouble is, after we get our tips, we can't get to the place before they have flown away. But with your airship, you could catch them, after we sent you, say a wireless message, about where to look for them. So that's no objection. You have a wireless outfit on your airships, haven't you, Tom?"

"Yes, that part is all right."

"Then you can't have any more objections, Tom."

"Well, there are some. For instance you say most of this smuggling is done at night."

"Practically all of it, yes."

"Well, it isn't going to be easy to pick out a contraband airship in the dark, and chase it. But I'll tell you what I'll do, Mr. Whitford, I feel as if I had sort of 'fallen down' on this clue business, as the newspaper men say, and I owe it to you to make good in some way."

"That's what I want—not that I think you haven't done all you could," interposed the agent.

"Well, if I can figure out some way, by which I think I can come anywhere near catching these smugglers, I'll undertake the work!" exclaimed Tom. "I'll do it as a duty to Uncle Sam, and I don't want any reward except my expenses. It's going to cost considerable, but—"

"Don't mind the expense!" interrupted Mr. Whitford. "Uncle Sam will stand that. Why, the government is losing thousands of dollars every week. It's a big leak, and must be stopped, and you're the one to stop it, Tom."

"Well, I'll try. I'll see you in a couple of days, and let you know if I have formed any plan. Now come on, Ned. I'm tired and want to get to bed."

"So do I," added the agent. "I'll call on you day after to-morrow, Tom, and I expect you to get right on the job," he added with a laugh.

"Have you any idea what you are going to do, Tom?" asked his chum, as they turned toward their houses.

"Not exactly. If I go I'll use my noiseless airship. That will come in handy. But this night business rather stumps me. I don't quite see my way to get around that. Of course I could use an ordinary searchlight, but that doesn't give a bright enough beam, or carry far enough. It's going to be quite a problem and I've got to think it over."

"Queer about the Fogers; wasn't it, Tom?"

"Yes, I didn't think they were going to let us in."

"There's something going on there, in spite of the fact that they were willing for an inspection to be made," went on Ned.

"I agree with you. I thought it was funny the way Mr. Foger acted about not wanting the men to go down in the cellar."

"So did I, and yet when they got down there they didn't find anything."

"That's so. Well, maybe we're on the wrong track, after all. But I'm going to keep my eyes open. I don't see what Andy wants with an airship platform on the roof of his house. The ground is good enough to start from and land on."

"I should think so, too. But then Andy always did like to show off, and do things different from anybody else. Maybe it's that way now."

"Perhaps," agreed Tom. "Well, here's your house, Ned. Come over in the morning," and, with a good-night, our hero left his chum, proceeding on toward his own home.

"Why, Koku, haven't you gone to bed yet?" asked the young inventor, as, mounting the side steps, he saw his giant servant sitting there on a bench he had made especially for his own use, as ordinary chairs were not substantial enough. "What is the matter?"

"Nothing happen YET," spoke Koku significantly, "but maybe he come pretty soon, and then I get him."

"Get who, Koku?" asked Tom, with quick suspicion.

"I do not know, but Eradicate say he hear someone sneaking around his chicken coop, and I think maybe it be same man who was here once before."

"Oh, you mean the rivals, who were trying to get my moving picture camera?"

"That's what!" exclaimed Koku.

"Hum!" mused Tom. "I must be on the look-out. I'll tell you what I'll do, Koku. I'll set my automatic camera to take the moving pictures of any one who tries to get in my shop, or in the chicken coop. I'll also set the burglar alarm. But you may also stay on the watch, and if anything happens—"

"If anything happens, I will un-happen him!" exclaimed the giant, brandishing a big club he had beside him.

"All right," laughed Tom. "I'm sleepy, and I'm going to bed, but I'll set the automatic camera, and fix it with fuse flashlights, so they will go off if the locks are even touched."

This Tom did, fixing up the wizard camera, which I have told you about in the book bearing that title. It would take moving pictures automatically, once Tom had set the mechanism to unreel the films back of the shutter and lens. The lights would instantly flash, when the electrical connections on the door locks were tampered with, and the pictures would be taken.

Then Tom set the burglar alarm, and, before going to bed he focused a searchlight, from one of his airships, on the shed and chicken coop, fastening it outside his room window.

"There!" he exclaimed, as he got ready to turn in, not having awakened the rest of the household, "when the burglar alarm goes off, if it does, it will also start the searchlight, and I'll get a view of who the chicken thief is. I'll also get some pictures."

Then, thinking over the events of the evening, and wondering if he would succeed in his fight with the smugglers, providing he undertook it, Tom fell asleep.

It must have been some time after midnight that he was awakened by the violent ringing of a bell at his ear. At first he thought it was the call to breakfast, and he leaped from bed crying out:

"Yes, Mrs. Baggert, I'm coming!"

A moment later he realized what it was.

"The burglar alarm!" he cried. "Koku, are you there? Someone is trying to get into the chicken coop!" for a glance at the automatic indicator, in connection with the alarm, had shown Tom that the henhouse, and not his shop, had been the object of attack.

"I here!" cried Koku, "I got him!"

A series of startled cries bore eloquent testimony to this.

"I'm coming!" cried Tom. And then he saw a wonderful sight. The whole garden, his shop, the henhouse and all the surrounding territory was lighted up with a radiance almost like daylight. The beams of illumination came from the searchlight Tom had fixed outside his window, but never before had the lantern given such a glow.

"That's wonderful!" cried Tom, as he ran to examine it. "What has happened? I never had such a powerful beam before. There must be something that I have stumbled on by accident. Say, that is a light all right! Why it goes for miles and miles, and I never projected a beam as far as this before."

As Tom looked into a circle of violet-colored glass set in the side cf the small searchlight, to see what had caused the extraordinary glow, he could observe nothing out of the ordinary. The violet glass was to protect the eyes from the glare.

"It must be that, by accident, I made some new connection at the dynamo," murmured Tom.

"Hi! Lemme go! Lemme go, Massa giant! I ain't done nuffin'!" yelled a voice.

"I got you!" cried Koku.

"It's an ordinary chicken thief this time I guess," said Tom. "But this light—this great searchlight—"

Then a sudden thought came to him.

"By Jove!" he cried. "If I can find out the secret of how I happened to project such a beam, it will be the very thing to focus on the smugglers from my noiseless airship! That's what I need—a searchlight such as never before has been made—a terrifically powerful one. And I've got it, if I can only find out just how it happened. I've got to look before the current dies out."

Leaving the brilliant beams on in full blast, Tom ran down the stairs to get to his shop, from which the electrical power came.

TOM'S NEWEST INVENTION

"I got him, Mr. Tom!"

"Oh, please, good Massa Swift! Make him leggo me! He suah am squeezin' de liber outer me!"

"Shall I conflict the club upon him, Mr. Tom?"

It was Koku who asked this last question, as Tom came running toward the giant. In the strange glare from the searchlight, the young inventor saw his big servant holding tightly to a rather small, colored man, while the camera, which was focused full on them, was clicking away at a great rate, taking picture after picture on the roll of films.

"No, don't *inflict* nor *conflict* the club on him, Koku," advised Tom. "Who is he?"

"I don't know, Mr. Tom. I was in hiding, in the darkness, waiting for him to come back. He had been here once before in the evening, Eradicate says. Well, he came while I was waiting and I detained him. Then the lights went up. They are very bright lights, Mr. Tom."

"Yes, brighter than I expected they would be. I must look and see what causes it. So you detained him, did you, Koku?"

"Yes, and what exposition shall I make of him?"

"What *Disposition*?" corrected Tom, with a laugh. "Well, did he get any chickens, Koku?"

"Oh, no, I was too tight for him."

"Oh, you mean too fast, or quick. Well, if he didn't get any, I guess you might let him go. I have too much to attend to, to bother with him."

"Oh, bress yo' for dat, Massa Tom!" cried the negro, whom Tom recognized as a worthless character about the town. "I didn't go fo' to do nuffin', Massa Tom. I were jest goin' t' look in de coop, t' count an' see how many fowls mah friend Eradicate had, an' den—"

"Yes, and then I tie you!" broke in Koku.

"You collared him, I guess you mean to say," spoke Tom with a laugh. "Well, I guess, Sam," speaking to the negro, "if *you* had counted Rad's chickens HE couldn't have counted as many in the morning. But be off, and don't come around again, or you might have to count the bars in a jail cell for a change."

"Bress yo' honey. I won't neber come back."

"Shall release him?" asked Koku doubtfully.

"Yes," said Tom.

"And not reflect the club on him?"

The giant raised his club longingly.

"Oh, Massa Tom, protect me!" cried Sam.

"No, don't even *reflect* the club on him," advised the young inventor with a laugh. "He hasn't done any harm, and he may have been the means of a great discovery. Remember Sam," Tom went on sternly, "I have your picture, as you were trying to break into the coop, and if you come around again, I'll use it as evidence against you."

"Oh, I won't come. Not as long as dat giant am heah, anyhow," said the negro earnestly. "Besides, I were only goin' t' count Eradicate's chickens, t' see ef he had as many as I got."

"All right," responded Tom. "Now, Koku, you may escort him off the premises, and be on the lookout the rest of the night, off and on. Where's Rad?"

"He has what he says is 'de misery' in his back so that he had to go to bed," explained the giant, to account for the faithful colored man not having responded to the alarm.

"All right, get rid of Sam, and then come back."

As Tom turned to go in his shop he saw his aged father coming slowly toward him. Mr. Swift had hastily dressed.

"What is the matter, Tom?" he asked. "Has anything happened? I heard your alarm go off, and I came as quickly as I could."

"Nothing much has happened, father, excepting a chicken thief. But something great may come of it. Do you notice that searchlight, and how powerful it is?"

"I do, Tom. I never knew you had one as big as that."

"Neither did I, and I haven't, really. That's one of my smallest ones, but something seems to have happened to it to make it throw out a beam like that. I'm just going to look. Come on in the shop."

The two inventors, young and old, entered, and Tom quickly crossed to where the wires from the automatic dynamo, extended to the searchlight outside the window of his room. He made a quick inspection.

"Look, father!" he cried. "The alternating current from the automatic dynamo has become crossed with direct current from the big storage battery in a funny way. It must have been by accident, for never in the world would I think of connecting up in that fashion. I would have said it would have made a short circuit at once."

"But it hasn't. On the contrary, it has given a current of peculiar strength and intensity—a current that would seem to be made especially for searchlights. Dad, I'm on the edge of a big discovery."

"I believe you, Tom," said his father. "That certainly is a queer way for wires to be connected. How do you account for it?"

"I can't. That is unless some one meddled with the connections after I made them. That must be it. I'll ask Rad and Koku." Just then the giant came in. "Koku, did you touch the wires?" asked Tom.

"Well, Mr. Tom, I didn't mean to. I accidentally pulled one out a while ago, when I was waiting for the thief to come, but I put it right back again. I hope I did no damage."

"No, on the contrary, you did a fine thing, Koku. I never would have dared make such connections myself, but you, not knowing any better, did just the right thing to make an almost perfect searchlight current. It is wonderful! Probably for any other purpose such a current would be useless, but it is just the thing for a great light."

"And why do you need such a powerful light, Tom?" asked Mr. Swift.

"Why, it is of extraordinary brilliancy, and it goes for several miles. Look how plainly you can pick out the trees on Nob's Hill," and he pointed to an elevation some distance away from the Swift homestead, across the woods and meadows.

"I believe I could see a bird perched there, if there was one!" exclaimed Tom enthusiastically. "That certainly is a wonderful light. With larger carbons, better parabolic mirrors, a different resistance box, better connections, and a more powerful primary current there is no reason why I could not get a light that would make objects more plainly visible than in the daytime, even in the darkest night, and at a great distance."

"But what would be the object of such a light, Tom?"

"To play upon the smugglers, dad, and catch them as they come over the border in the airship."

"Smugglers, Tom! You don't mean to tell me you are going away again, and after smugglers?"

"Well, dad, I've had an offer, and I think I'll take it. There's no money in it, but I think it is my duty to do my best for Uncle Sam. The one thing that bothered me was how to get a view of the airship at night. This searchlight has solved the problem—that is if I can make a permanent invention of this accident, and I think I can."

"Oh, Tom, I hate to think of you going away from home again," said his father a bit sadly.

"Don't worry, father. I'm not going far this time. Only to the Canadian border, and that's only a few hundred miles. But I want to see if I can cut the current off, and turn it on again. When a thing happens by accident you never know whether you can get just exactly the same conditions again."

Tom shut off the current from the dynamo, and the powerful beam of light died out. Then he turned it on once more, and it glowed as brightly as before. He did this several times, and each time it was a success.

"Hurrah!" cried Tom. "To-morrow I'll start on my latest invention, a great searchlight!"

"Beware of the Comet!"

"Well, Tom, what are you up to now?"

Ned Newton peered in the window of the shop at his chum, who was busy over a bench.

"This is my latest invention, Ned. Come on in."

"Looks as though you were going to give a magic lantern show. Or is it for some new kinds of moving pictures? Say, do you remember the time we gave a show in the barn, and charged a nickel to come in? You were the clown, and—"

"I was not! You were the clown. I was part of the elephant. The front end, I think."

"Oh. so you were. I'm thinking of another one. But what are you up to now? Is it a big magic lantern?"

Ned came over toward the bench, in front of which Tom stood, fitting together sheets of heavy brass in the form of a big square box. In one side there was a circular opening, and there were various wheels and levers on the different sides and on top. The interior contained parobolic curved mirrors.

"It's a SORT of a lantern, and I hope it's going to do some MAGIC work," explained Tom with a smile. "But it isn't the kind of magic lantern you mean. It won't throw pictures on a screen, but it may show some surprising pictures to us—that is if you come along, and I think you will."

"Talking riddles; eh?" laughed Ned. "What's the answer?"

"Smugglers."

"I thought you were talking about a lantern."

"So I am, and it's the lantern that's going to show up the smugglers, so you can call it a smuggler's magic lantern if you like."

"Then you're going after them?"

This conversation took place several days after the raid on the Foger house, and after Tom's accidental discovery of how to make a new kind of searchlight. In the meantime he had not seen Ned, who had been away on a visit.

"Yes, I've made up my mind to help Uncle Sam," spoke Tom, "and this is one of the things I'll need in my work. It's going to be the most powerful searchlight ever made—that is, I never heard of any portable electric lights that will beat it."

"What do you mean, Tom?"

"I mean that I'm inventing a new kind of searchlight, Ned. One that I can carry with me on my new noiseless airship, and one that will give a beam of light that will be visible for several miles, and which will make objects in its focus as plain as if viewed by daylight."

"And it's to show up the smugglers?"

"That's what. That is it will if we can get on the track of them."

"But what did you mean when you said it would be the most powerful portable light ever made."

"Just what I said. I've got to carry this searchlight on an airship with me, and, in consequence, it can't be very heavy. Of course there are stationary searchlights, such lights as are in lighthouses, that could beat mine all to pieces for candle power, and for long distance visibility. But they are the only ones."

"That's the way to do things, Tom! Say, I'm going with you all right after those smugglers. But where are some of those powerful stationary searchlights you speak of?"

"Oh, there are lots of them. One was in the Eiffel Tower, during the Paris Exposition. I didn't see that, but I have read about it. Another is in one of the twin lighthouses at the High-lands, on the Atlantic coast of New Jersey, just above Asbury Park. That light is of ninety-five million candle power, and the lighthouse keeper there told me it was visible, on a clear night, as far as the New Haven, Connecticut, lighthouse, a distance of fifty miles."

"Fifty miles! That's some light!" gasped Ned.

"Well, you must remember that the Highlands light is up on a very high hill, and the tower is also high, so there is quite an elevation, and then think of ninety-five million candle power—think of it!"

"I can't!" cried Ned. "It gives me a head-ache."

"Well, of course I'm not going to try to beat that," went on Tom with a laugh, "but I am going to have a very powerful light." And he then related how he had accidently discovered a new way to connect the wires, so as to get, from a dynamo and a storage battery a much stronger, and different, current than usual.

"I'm making the searchlight now," Tom continued, "and soon I'll be ready to put in the lens, and the carbons."

"And then what?"

"Then I'm going to attach it to my noiseless airship, and we'll have a night flight. It may work, and it may not. If it does, I think we'll have some astonishing results."

"I think we will, Tom. Can I do anything to help you?"

"Yes, file some of the rough edges off these sheets of brass, if you will. There's an old pair of gloves to put on to protect your hands, otherwise you'll be almost sure to cut 'em, when the file slips. That brass is extra hard."

The two boys were soon working away, and were busy over the big lantern when Mr. Whitford came along. Koku was, as usual, on guard at the outer door of the shop, but he knew the custom officer, and at once admitted him.

"Well, Tom, how you coming on?" he asked.

"Pretty good. I think I've got just what I want. A powerful light for night work."

"That's good. You'll need it. They've got so they only smuggle the goods over in the night now. How soon do you think you'll be able to get on the border for Uncle Sam?"

"Why, is there any great rush?" asked Tom, as he noticed a look of annoyance pass over the agent's face.

"Yes, the smugglers have been hitting us pretty hard lately. My superiors are after me to do something, but I can't seem to do it. My men are working hard, but we can't catch the rascals."

"You see, Tom, they've stopped, temporarily, bringing goods over the St. Lawrence. They're working now in the neighborhood of Huntington, Canada, and the dividing line between the British possessions and New York State, runs along solid ground there. It's a wild and desolate part of country, too, and I haven't many men up there."

"Don't the Canadian custom officers help?" asked Ned.

"Well, they haven't been of any aid to us so far," was the answer. "No doubt they are trying, but it's hard to get an airship at night when you're on the ground, and can't even see it."

"How did they come to use airships?" asked Tom.

"Well, it was because we were too sharp after them when they tried to run things across the line afoot, or by wagons," replied the agent. "You must know that in every principal city, at or near the border line, there is a custom house. Goods brought from Canada to the United States must pass through there and pay a duty."

"Of course if lawless people try to evade the duty they don't go near the custom house. But there are inspectors stationed at the principal roads leading from the Dominion into Uncle Sam's territory, and they are always on the lookout. They patrol the line, sometimes through a dense wilderness, and again over a desolate plain, always on the watch. If they see persons crossing the line they stop them and examine what they have. If there is nothing dutiable they are allowed to pass. If they have goods on which there is a tax, they either have to pay or surrender the goods."

"But don't the smugglers slip over in spite of all the precautions?" asked Ned. "Say at some lonely ravine, or stretch of woods?"

"I suppose they do, occasionally," replied Mr. Whitford. "Yet the fact that they never can tell when one of the inspectors or deputies is coming along, acts as a stop. Yon see the border line is divided up into stretches of different lengths. A certain man, or men, are held responsible for each division. They must see that no smugglers pass. That makes them on the alert."

"Why, take it out west, I have a friend who told me that he often travels hundreds of miles on horseback, with pack ponies carrying his camping outfit, patroling the border on the lookout for smugglers."

"In fact Uncle Sam has made it so hard for the ordinary smuggler to do business on foot or by wagon, that these fellows have taken to airships. And it is practically impossible for an inspector patroling the border to be on the lookout for the craft of the air. Even if they saw them, what could they do? It would be out of the question to stop them. That's why we need some one with a proper machine who can chase after them, who can sail through the air, and give them a fight in the clouds if they have to."

"Our custom houses on the ground, and our inspectors on horse back, traveling along the border, can't meet the issue. We're depending on you, Tom Swift, and I hope you don't disappoint us."

"Well," spoke Tom, when Mr. Whitford had finished. "I'll do my best for you. It won't take very long to complete my searchlight, and then I'll give it a trial. My airship is ready for service, and once I find we're all right I'll start for the border."

"Good! And I hope you'll catch the rascals!" fervently exclaimed the custom official. "Well, Tom, I'm leaving it all to you. Here are some reports from my deputies. I'll leave them with you, and you can look them over, and map out a campaign. When you are ready to start I'll see you again, and give you any last news I have. I'll also arrange so that you can communicate with me, or some of my men."

"Have you given up all suspicion of the Fogers?" asked the young inventor.

"Yes. But I still think Shopton is somehow involved in the custom violations. I'm going to put one of my best men on the ground here, and go to the border myself."

"Well, I'll be ready to start in a few days," said Tom, as the government agent departed.

For the next week our hero and his chum were busy completing work on the great searchlight, and in attaching it to the airship. Koku helped them, but little of the plans, or of the use to which the big lantern was to be put, were made known to him, for Koku liked to talk, and Tom did not want his project to become known.

"Well, we'll give her a trial to-night," said Tom one afternoon, following a day of hard work. "We'll go up, and flash the light down."

"Who's going?"

"Just us two. You can manage the ship, and I'll look after the light."

So it was arranged, and after supper Tom and his chum, having told Mr. Swift were they were going, slipped out to the airship shed, and soon were ready to make an ascent. The big lantern was fastened to a shaft that extended above the main cabin. The shaft was hollow and through it came the wires that carried the current. Tom, from the cabin below, could move the lantern in any direction, and focus it on any spot he pleased. By means of a toggle joint, combined with what are known as "lazy-tongs," the lantern could be projected over the side of the aircraft and be made to gleam on the earth, directly below the ship.

For his new enterprise Tom used the Falcon in which he had gone to Siberia after the platinum. The new noiseless motor had been installed in this craft.

"All ready, Ned?" asked Tom after an inspection of the searchlight.

"All ready, as far as I'm concerned, Tom."

"Then let her go!"

Like a bird of the night, the great aeroplane shot into the air, and, with scarcely a sound that could be heard ten feet away, she moved forward at great speed.

"What are you going to do first?" asked Ned.

"Fly around a bit, and then come back over my house. I'm going to try the lantern on that first, and see what I can make out from a couple of miles up in the air."

Up and up went the Falcon, silently and powerfully, until the barograph registered nearly fourteen thousand feet.

"This is high enough." spoke Tom.

He shifted a lever that brought the searchlight into focus on Shopton, which lay below them. Then, turning on the current, a powerful beam of light gleamed out amid the blackness.

"Jove! That's great!" cried Ned. "It's like a shaft of daylight!"

"That's what I intended it to be!" cried Tom in delight.

With another shifting of the lever he brought the light around so that it began to pick up different buildings in the town.

"There's the church!" cried Ned. "It's as plain as day, in that gleam."

"And there's the railroad depot," added Tom.

"And Andy Foger's house!"

"Yes, and there's my house!" exclaimed Tom a moment later, as the beam rested on his residence and shops. "Say, it's plainer than I thought it would be. Hold me here a minute, Ned."

Ned shut off the power from the propellers, and the airship was stationary. Tom took a pair of binoculars, and looked through them at his home in the focus of light.

"I can count the bricks in the chimney!" he cried in eagerness at the success of his great searchlight. "It's even better than I thought it was! Let's go down, Ned."

Slowly the airship sank. Tom played his light all about, picking up building after building, and one familiar spot after another. Finally he brought the beam on his own residence again, when not far above it.

Suddenly there arose a weird cry. Tom and Ned knew at once that it was Eradicate.

"A comet! A comet!" yelled the colored man. "De end ob de world am comin'! Run, chillens, run! Beware ob de comet!"

"Eradicate's afraid!" cried Tom with a laugh.

"Oh good mistah comet! Doan't take me!" went on the colored man. "I ain't neber done nuffin', an' mah mule Boomerang ain't needer. But ef yo' has t' take somebody, take Boomerang!"

"Keep quiet, Rad! It's all right!" cried Tom. But the colored man continued to shout in fear.

Then, as the two boys looked on, and as the airship came nearer to the earth, Ned, who was looking down amid the great illumination, called to Tom:

"Look at Koku!"

Tom glanced over, and saw his giant servant, with fear depicted on his face, running away as fast as he could. Evidently Eradicate's warning had frightened him.

"Say, he can run!" cried Ned. "Look at him leg it!"

"Yes, and he may run away, never to come back," exclaimed Tom. "I don't want to lose him, he's too valuable. I know what happened once when he got frightened. He was away for a week before I could locate him, and he hid in the swamp. I'm not going to have that happen again."

"What are you going to do?"

"I'm going to chase after him in the airship. It will be a good test for chasing the smugglers. Put me after him, Ned, and I'll play the searchlight on him so we can't lose him!"

Off for the Border

"There he goes, Tom!"

"Yes, I see him!"

"Look at him run!"

"No wonder. Consider his long legs, Ned. Put on a little more speed, and keep a little lower down. It's clear of trees right here."

"There he goes into that clump of bushes."

"I see him. He'll soon come out," and Tom flashed the big light on the fleeing giant to whom fear seemed to lend more than wings.

But even a giant, long legged though he be, and powerful, cannot compete with a modern airship—certainly not such a one as Tom Swift had.

"We're almost up to him, Tom!" cried Ned a little later.

"Yes! I'm keeping track of him. Oh, why doesn't he know enough to stop? Koku! Koku!" called Tom. "It's all right! I'm in the airship! This is a searchlight, not a comet. Wait for us!"

They could see the giant glance back over his shoulder at them, and, when he saw how close the gleaming light was he made a desperate spurt. But it was about his last, for he was a heavy man, and did not have any too good wind.

"We'll have him in another minute," predicted Tom. "Give me a bit more speed, Ned."

The lad who was managing the Falcon swung the accelerating lever over another notch, and the craft surged ahead. Then Ned executed a neat trick. Swinging the craft around in a half circle, he suddenly opened the power full, and so got ahead of Koku. The next minute, sliding down to earth, Tom and Ned came to a halt, awaiting the oncoming of Koku, who, finding the glaring light full in his face, came to a halt.

"Why, Koku, what's the matter?" asked Tom kindly, as he turned off the powerful beams, and switched on some ordinary incandescents, that were on the outside of the craft. They made an illumination by which the giant could make out his master and the latter's chum. "Why did you run, Koku?" asked Tom.

"Eradicate say to," was the simple answer. "He say comet come to eat up earth. Koku no want to be eaten."

"Eradicate is a big baby!" exclaimed Tom. "See, there is no danger. It is only my new searchlight," and once more the young inventor switched it on. Koku jumped back, but when he saw that nothing happened he did not run.

"It's harmless," said Tom, and briefly he explained how the big lantern worked.

Koku was reassured now, and consented to enter the airship. He was rather tired from his run, and was glad to sit down.

"Where to now; back home?" asked Ned, as they made ready to start.

"No, I was thinking of going over to Mr. Damon's house. I'd like him to see my searchlight. And I want to find out if he's going with us on the trip to the border."

"Of course he will!" predicted Ned. "He hasn't missed a trip with you in a long while. He'll go if his wife will let him," and both boys laughed, for Mr. Damon's wife was nearly always willing to let him do as he liked, though the odd man had an idea that she was violently opposed to his trips.

Once more the Falcon went aloft, and again the searchlight played about. It brought out with startling distinctness the details of the towns and villages over which they passed, and distant landmarks were also made plainly visible.

"We'll be there in a few minutes now," said Tom, as he flashed the light on a long slant toward the town of Waterford, where Mr. Damon lived.

"I can see his house," spoke Ned a moment later. He changed the course of the craft, to bring it to a stop in the yard of the eccentric man, and, shortly afterward, they landed. Tom who had shut off the searchlight for a minute, turned it on again, and the house and grounds of Mr. Damon were enveloped in a wonderful glow.

"That will bring him out," predicted Tom.

A moment later they heard his voice.

"Bless my astronomy!" cried Mr. Damon. "There's a meteor fallen in our yard. Come out, wife—everybody—call the servants. It's a chance of a lifetime to see one, and they're valuable, too! Bless my star dust! I must tell Tom Swift of this!"

Out into the glare of the great searchlight ran Mr. Damon, followed by his wife and several of the servants.

"There it is!" cried the odd man. "There's the meteor!"

"First we're a comet and then we're a meteor," said Ned with a laugh.

"Oh. I hope it doesn't bury itself in the earth before I can get Tom Swift here!" went on Mr. Damon, capering about. "Bless my telephone book. I must call him up right away!"

"I'm here now, Mr. Damon!" shouted Tom, as he alighted from the airship. "That's my new searchlight you're looking at."

"Bless my—" began Mr. Damon, but he couldn't think of nothing strong enough for a moment, until he blurted out "dynamite cartridge! Bless my dynamite cartridge! Tom Swift! His searchlight! Bless my nitro-glycerine!"

Then Tom shut off the glare, and, as Mr. Damon and his wife came aboard he showed them how the light worked. He only used a part of the current, as he knew if he put on the full glare toward Mr. Damon's house, neighbors might think it was on fire.

"Well, that's certainly wonderful," said Mrs. Damon. "In fact this is a wonderful ship."

"Can't you take Mrs. Damon about, and show her how it works," said Mr. Damon suddenly. "Show her the ship."

"I will," volunteered Tom.

"No, let Ned," said the eccentric man. "I—er—I want to speak to you, Tom."

Mrs. Damon, with a queer glance at her husband, accompanied Ned to the motor room. As soon as she was out of hearing the odd gentleman came over and whispered to the young inventor.

"I say, Tom, what's up?"

"Smugglers. You know. I told you about 'em. I'm going after 'em with my big searchlight."

"Bless my card case! So you did. But, I say, Tom, I—I want to go!"

"I supposed you would. Well, you're welcome, of course. We leave in a few days. It isn't a very long trip this time, but there may be plenty of excitement. Then I'll book you for a passage, and—"

"Hush! Not another word! Here she comes, Tom. My wife! Don't breathe a syllable of it to her. She'll never let me go." Then, for the benefit of Mrs. Damon, who came back into the main cabin with Ned at that moment, her husband added in loud tones:

"Yes, Tom it certainly is a wonderful invention. I congratulate you," and, at the same time he winked rapidly at our hero. Tom winked in return.

"Well, I guess we'll start back," remarked Tom, after a bit. "I'll see you again, I suppose, Mr. Damon?"

"Oh yes, of course. I'll be over—soon," and once more he winked as he whispered in Tom's ear: "Don't leave me behind, my boy."

"I won't," whispered the young inventor in answer.

Mrs. Damon smiled, and Tom wondered if she had discovered her husband's innocent secret.

Tom and Ned, with Koku, made a quick trip back to Shopton, using the great searchlight part of the way. The next day they began preparations for the journey to the border.

It did not take long to get ready. No great amount of stores or supplies need be taken along, as they would not be far from home, not more than a two days' journey at any time. And they would be near large cities, where food and gasolene could easily be obtained.

About a week later, therefore, Mr. Whitford the government agent, having been communicated with in the meanwhile, Tom and Ned, with Koku and Mr. Damon were ready to start.

"I wonder if Mr. Whitford is coming to see us off?" mused Tom, as he looked to see if everything was aboard, and made sure that the searchlight was well protected by its waterproof cover.

"He said he'd be here," spoke Ned.

"Well, it's past time now. I don't know whether to start, or to wait."

"Wait a few minutes more," advised Ned. "His train may be a few minutes behind time."

They waited half an hour, and Tom was on the point of starting when a messenger boy came hurrying into the yard where the great airship rested on its bicycle wheels.

"A telegram for you, Tom," called the lad, who was well acquainted with our hero.

Hastily the young inventor tore open the envelope.

"Here's news!" he exclaimed,

"What is it?" asked Ned.

"It's from Mr. Whitford," answered his chum. "He says: 'Can't be with you at start. Will meet you in Logansville. Have new clue to the Fogers!'"

"Great Scott!" cried Ned, staring at his chum.

ANDY'S NEW AIRSHIP

Tom Swift tossed a quarter to the messenger boy, and leaped over the rail to the deck of his airship, making his way toward the pilot house.

"Start the motor, Ned," he called. "Are you all ready, Mr. Damon?"

"Bless my ancient history, yes. But—"

"Are you going, Tom?" asked Ned.

"Of course. That's why we're here; isn't it? We're going to start for the border to catch the smugglers. Give me full speed, I want the motor to warm up."

"But that message from Mr. Whitford? He says he has a new clue to the Fogers."

"That's all right. He may have, but he doesn't ask us to work it up. He says he will meet us in Logansville, and he can't if we don't go there. We're off for Logansville. Good-bye dad. I'll bring you back a souvenir, Mrs. Baggert," he called to the housekeeper. "Sorry you're not coming, Rad, but I'll take you next time."

"Dat's all right, Massa Tom. I doan't laik dem smugger-fellers, nohow. Good-bye an' good luck!"

"Bless my grab bag!" gasped Mr. Damon. "You certainly do things, Tom."

"That's the only way to get things done," replied the young inventor. "How about you, Ned? Motor all right?"

"Sure."

"Then let her go!"

A moment later Ned had started the machinery, and Tom, in the pilot house, had pulled the lever of the elevating rudder. Whizzing along, but making scarcely any sound, the noiseless airship mounted upward, and was off on her flight to capture the men who were cheating Uncle Sam.

"What are you going to do first, when you get there, Tom?" asked Ned, as he joined his chum in the pilot house, having set the motor and other apparatus to working automatically. "I mean in Logansville?"

"I don't know. I'll have to wait and see how things develop."

"That's where Mr. Foger lives, you know."

"Yes, but I doubt if he is there now. He and Andy are probably still in the old house here, though what they are doing is beyond me to guess."

"What do you suppose this new clue is that Mr. Whitford wired you about?"

"Haven't any idea. If he wants us to get after it he'll let us know. It won't take us long to get there at this rate. But I think I'll slow down a bit, for the motor is warmed up now, and there's no use racking it to pieces. But we're moving nicely; aren't we, Ned?"

"I should say so. This is the best all-around airship you've got."

"It is since I put the new motor in. Well, I wonder what will happen when we get chasing around nights after the smugglers? It isn't going to be easy work, I can tell you."

"I should say not. How you going to manage it?"

"Well, I haven't just decided. I'm going to have a talk with the customs men, and then I'll go out night after night and cruise around at the most likely place where they'll rush goods across the border. As soon as I see the outlines of an airship in the darkness, or hear the throb of her motor, I'll take after her, and—"

"Yes, and you can do it, too, Tom, for she can't hear you coming and you can flash the big light on her and the smugglers will think the end of the world has come. Cracky! Its going to be great, Tom! I'm glad I came along. Maybe they'll fight, and fire at us! If they have guns aboard, as they probably will have, we'll—"

"Bless my armor plate!" interrupted Mr. Damon. "Please don't talk about such hair-raising things, Ned! Talk about something pleasant."

"All right," agreed Tom's chum, and then, as the airship sailed along, high above the earth, they talked of many things.

"I think when we sight Logansville." said Tom, after a while, "that I will come down in some quiet spot, before we reach the city."

"Don't you want to get into a crowd?" asked Ned.

"No, it isn't that. But Mr. Foger lives there you know, and, though he may not be at home, there are probably some men who are interested in the thing he is working at."

"You mean smuggling?"

"Well, I wouldn't say that. At the same time it may have leaked out that we are after the smugglers in an airship and it may be that Mr. Whitford doesn't want the Fogers to know I'm on the ground until he has a chance to work up his clue. So I'll just go slowly, and remain in the background for a while."

"Well, maybe it's a good plan," agreed Tom.

"Of course," began Tom, "it would be—"

He was interrupted by a shout from Koku, who had gone to the motor room, for the giant was as fascinated over machinery as a child. As he yelled there came a grinding, pounding noise, and the big ship seemed to waver, to quiver in the void, and to settle toward the earth.

"Something's happened!" cried Ned, as he sprang for the place where most of the mechanism was housed.

"Bless my toy balloon!" shouted Mr. Damon. "We're falling, Tom!"

It needed but a glance at the needle of the barograph, to show this. Tom followed Ned at top speed, but ere either of them reached the engine room the pounding and grinding noises ceased, the airship began to mount upward again, and it seemed that the danger had passed.

"What can have happened?" gasped Tom.

"Come on, we'll soon see," said Ned, and they rushed on, followed by Mr. Damon, who was blessing things in a whisper.

The chums saw a moment later—saw a strange sight—for there was Koku, the giant, kneeling down on the floor of the motor room, with his big hands clasped over one of the braces of the bed-plate of the great air pump, which cooled the cylinders of the motor. The pump had torn partly away from its fastenings. Kneeling there, pressing down on the bed-plate with all his might, Koku was in grave danger, for the rod of the pump, plunging up and down, was within a fraction of an inch of his head, and, had he moved, the big taper pin, which held the plunger to the axle, would have struck his temple and probably would have killed him, for the pin, which held the plunger rigid, projected several inches from the smooth side of the rod.

"Koku, what is the matter? Why are you there?" cried Tom, for he could see nothing wrong with the machinery now. The airship was sailing on as before.

"Bolt break," explained the giant briefly, for he had learned some engineering terms since he had been with Tom. "Bolt that hold pump fast to floor crack off. Pump him begin to jump up. Make bad noise. Koku hold him down, but pretty hard work. Better put in new bolt, Mr. Tom."

They could see the strain that was put upon the giant in his swelling veins and the muscles of his hands and arms, for they stood out knotted, and in bunches. With all his great strength it was all Koku could do to hold the pump from tearing completely loose.

"Quick, Ned!" cried Tom. "Shut off all the power! Stop the pump! I've got to bolt it fast. Start the gas machine, Mr. Damon. You know how to do it. It works independent of the motor. You can let go in a minute, Koku!"

It took but a few seconds to do all this. Ned stopped the main motor, which had the effect of causing the propellers to cease revolving. Then the airship would have gone down but for the fact that she was now a balloon, Mr. Damon having started the generating machine which sent the powerful lifting gas into the big bag over head.

"Now you can let go, Koku," said Tom, for with the stooping of the motor the air pump ceased plunging, and there was no danger of it tearing loose.

"Bless my court plaster!" cried Mr. Damon. "What happened, Tom?"

As the giant arose from his kneeling position the cause of the accident could easily be seen. Two of the big belts that held down one end of the pump bed-plate to the floor of the airship, had cracked off, probably through some defect, or because of the long and constant vibration on them.

This caused a great strain on the two forward bolts, and the pump starter! to tear itself loose. Had it done so there would have been a serious accident, for there would have been a tangle in the machinery that might never have been repairable. But Koku, who, it seems, had been watching the pump, saw the accident as soon as it occurred. He knew that the pump must be held down, and kept rigid, and he took the only way open to him to accomplish this.

He pressed his big hands down over the place where the bolts had broken off, and by main strength of muscle he held the bed-plate in place until the power was shut off.

"Koku, my boy, you did a great thing!" cried Tom, when he realized what had happened. "You saved all our lives, and the airship as well."

"Koku glad," was the simple reply of the giant.

"But, bless my witch hazel!" cried Mr. Damon. "There's blood on your hands, Koku!"

They looked at the giant's palms. They were raw and bleeding.

"How did it happen?" asked Ned.

"Where belts break off, iron rough-like," explained Koku.

"Rough! I should say it was!" cried Tom. "Why, he just pressed with all his might on the jagged end of the belts. Koku you're a hero!"

"Hero same as giant?" asked Koku, curiously.

"No, it's a heap sight better," spoke Tom, and there was a trace of tears in his eyes.

"Bless my vaseline!" exclaimed Mr. Damon, blowing his nose harder than seemed necessary. "Come over here, Koku, and I'll bandage up your hands. Poor fellow, it must hurt a lot!"

"Oh, not so bad," was the simple reply.

While Mr. Damon gave first aid to the injured, Tom and Ned put new bolts in place of the broken ones on the bed-plate, and they tested them to see that they were perfect. New ones were also substituted for the two that had been strained, and in the course of an hour the repairs were made.

"Now we can run as an aeroplane again," said Tom. "But I'm not going to try such speed again. It was the vibration that did it I guess."

They were now over a wild and desolate stretch of country, for the region lying on either side of the imaginary line dividing Canada and New York State, at the point where the St. Lawrence flows north-east, is sparsely settled.

There were stretches of forest that seemed never to have been penetrated, and here and there patches of stunted growth, with little lakes dotted through the wilderness. There were hills and valleys, small streams and an occasional village.

"Just the place for smuggling," observed Tom, as he looked at a map, consulted a clock and figured out that they must be near Logansville. "We can go down here in one of these hollows, surrounded by this tangled forest, and no one would ever know we were here. The smugglers could do the same."

"Are you going to try it?" asked Ned.

"I think I will. We'll go up to quite a height now, and I'll see if I can pick out Logansville. That isn't much of a place I guess. When I sight it I'll select a good place to lay hidden for a day or two, until Mr. Whitford has had a chance to work up his clue."

The airship machinery was now working well again, and Tom sent his craft up about three miles. From there, taking observations through a powerful telescope, he was able, after a little while, to pick out a small town. From its location and general outline he knew it to be Logansville.

"We'll go down about three miles from it," he said to his chum. "They won't be likely to see us then, and we'll stay concealed for a while."

This plan was put into operation, and, a little later the Falcon came to rest in a little grassy clearing, located in among a number of densely wooded hills. It was an ideal place to camp, though very lonesome.

"Now, Ned, let's cut a lot of branches, and pile them over the airship," suggested Tom.

"Cover over the airship? What for?"

"So that in case anyone flies over our heads they won't look down and see us. If the Fogers, or any of the smugglers, should happen to pass over this place, they'd spot us in a minute. We've got to play foxy on this hunt."

"That's so," agreed his chum; and soon the three of them were busy making the airship look like a tangled mass of underbrush. Koku helped by dragging big branches along under his arm, but he could not use his hands very well.

They remained in the little grassy glade three days, thoroughly enjoying their camp and the rest. Tom and Ned went fishing in a nearby lake and had some good luck. They also caught trout in a small stream and broiled the speckled beauties with bacon inside them over live coals at a campfire.

"My! But that's good!" mumbled Ned, with his mouth full of hot trout, and bread and butter.

"Yes, I'd rather do this than chase smugglers," said Tom, stretching out on his back with his face to the sky. "I wish—"

But he did not finish the sentence. Suddenly from the air above them came a curious whirring, throbbing noise. Tom sat up with a jump! He and Ned gazed toward the zenith. The noise increased and, a moment later, there came into view a big airship, sailing right over their heads.

"Look at that!" cried Tom.

"Hush! They'll hear you," cautioned Ned.

"Nonsense! They're too high up," was Tom's reply. "Mr. Damon, bring me the big binoculars, please!" he called.

"Bless my spectacles, what's up?" asked the odd gentleman as he ran with the glasses toward Tom.

Our hero focused them on the airship that was swiftly sailing across the open space in the wilderness but so high up that there was no danger of our friends being recognized. Then the young inventor uttered a cry of astonishment.

"It's Andy Foger!" he cried. "He's in that airship, and he's got two men with him. Andy Foger, and it's a new biplane. Say, maybe that's the new clue Mr. Whitford wired me about. We must get ready for action! Andy in a new airship means business, and from the whiteness of the canvas planes, I should say that craft was on its first trip."

WARNED AWAY

"Tom, are you sure it's Andy?"

"Take a look yourself," replied the young inventor, passing his chum the binoculars.

"Bless my bottle of ink!" cried Mr. Damon. "Is it possible?"

"Quick, Ned, or you'll miss him!" cried Tom.

The young bank clerk focused the glasses on the rapidly moving airship, and, a moment later, exclaimed:

"Yes, that's Andy all right, but I don't know who the men are with him."

"I couldn't recognize them, either," announced Tom. "But say, Ned, Andy's got a good deal better airship than he had before."

"Yes. This isn't his old one fixed over. I don't believe he ever intended to repair the old one. That hiring of Mr. Dillon to do that, was only to throw him, and us, too, off the track."

Ned passed the glasses to Mr. Damon, who was just in time to get a glimpse of the three occupants of Andy's craft before it passed out of sight over the trees.

"I believe you're right," said Tom to his chum. "And did you notice that there's quite a body, or car, to that craft?"

"Yes. room enough to carry considerable goods," commented Ned. "I wonder where he's going in it?"

"To Logansville, most likely. I tell you what it is, Ned. I think one of us will have to go there, and see if Mr. Whitford has arrived. He may be looking for us. I'm not sure but what we ought not to have done this first. He may think we have not come, or have met with some accident,"

"I guess you're right, Tom. But how shall we go? It isn't going to be any fun to tramp through those woods," and Ned glanced at the wilderness that surrounded the little glade where they had been camping.

"No, and I've about concluded that we might as well risk it, and go in the airship. Mr. Whitford has had time enough to work up his clue, I guess, and Andy will be sure to find out, sooner or later, that we are in the neighborhood. I say let's start for Logansville."

Ned and Mr. Damon agreed with this and soon they were prepared to move.

"Where will you find Mr. Whitford?" asked Ned of his chum, as the Falcon arose in the air.

"At the post-office. That's where we arranged to meet. There is a sort of local custom house there, I believe."

Straight over the forest flew Tom Swift and his airship, with the great searchlight housed on top. They delayed their start until the other craft had had a chance to get well ahead, and they were well up in the air;

there was no sight of the biplane in which Andy had sailed over their heads a short time before.

"Where are you going to land?" asked Ned, as they came in view of the town.

"The best place I can pick out," answered Tom. "Just on the outskirts of the place, I think. I don't want to go down right in the centre, as there'll be such a crowd. Yet if Andy has been using his airship here the people must be more or less used to seeing them."

But if the populace of Logansville had been in the habit of having Andy Foger sail over their heads, still they were enough interested in a new craft to crowd around when Tom dropped into a field near some outlying houses. In a moment the airship was surrounded by a crowd of women and children, and there would probably been a lot of men, but for the fact that they were away at work. Tom had come down in a residential section.

"Say, that's a beauty!" cried one boy.

"Let's see if they'll let us go on!" proposed another.

"We're going to have our own troubles," said Tom to his chum. "I guess I'll go into town, and leave the rest of you on guard here. Keep everybody off, if you have to string mildly charged electrical wires about the rail."

But there was no need to take this precaution, for, just as the combined juvenile population of that part of Logansville was prepared to storm, and board the Falcon, Koku appeared on deck.

"Oh, look at the giant!"

"Say, this is a circus airship?"

"Wow! Ain't he big!"

"I'll bet he could lift a house!"

These and other expressions came from the boys and girls about the airship. The women looked on open-mouthed, and murmurs of surprise and admiration at Koku's size came from a number of men who had hastily run up.

Koku stepped from the airship to the ground, and at once every boy and girl made a bee-line for safety.

"That will do the trick!" exclaimed Tom with a laugh. "Koku, just pull up a few trees, and look as fierce as Bluebeard, and I guess we won't be troubled with curiosity seekers. You can guard the airship, Koku, better than electric wires."

"I fix 'em!" exclaimed the giant, and he tried to look fierce, but it was hard work, for he was very good natured. But he proved a greater attraction than the aircraft, and Tom was glad of it, for he did not like meddlers aboard.

"With Koku to help you, and Mr. Damon to bless things. I guess you can manage until I come back, Ned," said the young inventor, as he made ready to go in to town to see if Mr. Whitford had arrived.

"Oh, we'll get along all right," declared Ned. "Don't worry."

Tom found Mr. Whitford in one of the rooms over the post-office. The custom house official was restlessly pacing the floor.

"Well, Tom!" he exclaimed, shaking hands, "I'm glad to see you. I was afraid something had happened. I was delayed myself, but when I did arrive and found you hadn't been heard from, I didn't know what to think. I couldn't get you on the wireless. The plant here is out of repair."

Tom told of their trip, and the wait they had decided on, and asked:

"What about the new clue; the Fogers?"

"I'm sorry to say it didn't amount to anything. I ran it down, and came to nothing."

"You know Andy has a new airship?"

"Yes. I had men on the trail of it. They say Andy is agent for a firm that manufactures them, but I have my doubts. I haven't given up yet. But say, Tom, you've got to get busy. A big lot of goods was smuggled over last night."

"Where?"

"Well, quite a way from here. I got a telegram about it. Can you get on the job to-night, and do some patrol work along the border? You're only half a mile from it now. Over there is Canada," and he pointed to a town on a hill opposite Logansville.

"Yes, I can get right into action. What place is that?"

"Montford, Canada. I've got men planted there, and the Dominion customs officials are helping us. But I think the smugglers have changed the base of their operations for the time being. If I were you I'd head for the St. Lawrence to-night."

"I will. Don't you want to come along?"

"Why, yes. I believe I'm game. I'll join you later in the day," Mr. Whitford added, as Tom told him where the Falcon was anchored.

The young inventor got back to find a bigger crowd than ever around his airship. But Koku and the others had kept them at a distance.

With the government agent aboard Tom sent his craft into the air at dusk, the crowd cheering lustily. Then, with her nose pointed toward the St. Lawrence, the Falcon was on her way to do a night patrol, and, if possible, detect the smugglers.

It was monotonous work, and unprofitable, for, though Tom sent the airship back and forth for many miles along the wonderful river that formed the path from the Great Lakes to the sea, he had no glimpse of ghostly wings of other aircraft, nor did he hear the beat of propellers, nor the throb of motors, as his own noiseless airship cruised along.

It came on to rain after midnight, and a mist crept down from the clouds, so that even with the great searchlight flashing its powerful beams, it was difficult to see for any great distance.

"Better give it up, I guess," suggested Mr. Whitford toward morning, when they had covered many miles, and had turned back toward Logansville.

"All right," agreed Tom. "But we'll try it again to-morrow night."

He dropped his craft at the anchorage he had selected in the gray dawn of the morning. All on board were tired and sleepy. Ned, looking from a window of the cabin, as the Falcon came to a stop, saw something white on the ground.

"I wonder what that is?" he said as he hurried out to pick it up. It was a large white envelope, addressed to Tom Swift, and the name was in printed characters.

"Somebody who wants to disguise their writing," remarked Tom, as he tore it open. A look of surprise came over his face.

"Look here! Mr. Whitford," he cried. "This is the work of the smugglers all right!"

For, staring at Tom, in big printed letters, on a white sheet of paper, was this message:

"If you know what is good for you, Tom Swift, you had better clear out. If you don't your airship will burned, and you may get hurt. We'll burn you in mid-air. Beware and quit. You can't catch us."

"The Committee of Three."

"Ha! Warned away!" cried Tom. "Well, it will take more than this to make me give up!" and he crumpled the anonymous warning in his hand.

Koku Saves the Light

"Don't do that!" cried Mr. Whitford.

"What?" asked Tom, in some surprise.

"Don't destroy that letter. It may give us a clue. Let me have it. I'll put a man at work on that end of this game."

"Bless my checkerboard!" cried Mr. Damon. "This game has so many ends that you don't know where to begin to play it."

The government man smoothed out the crumpled piece of paper, and looked at it carefully, and also gazed at the envelope.

"It's pretty hard to identify plain print, done with a lead pencil," he murmured. "And this didn't came through the mail."

"I wonder how it got here?" mused Ned. "Maybe some of the crowd that was here when we started off dropped it for the smugglers. Maybe the smugglers were in that crowd!"

"Let's take a look outside," suggested Mr. Whitford. "We may be able to pick up a clue there."

Although our friends were tired and sleepy, and hungry as well, they forgot all this in the desire to learn more about the mysterious warning that had come to them during the night. They all went outside, and Ned pointed to where he had picked up the envelope.

"Look all around, and see if you can find anything more," directed the custom agent.

"Footprints won't count," said Tom. "There was a regular circus crowd out here yesterday."

"I'm not looking for footprints," replied Mr. Whitford, "I have an idea—"

"Here's something!" interrupted Mr. Damon. "It looks like a lead weight for a deep-sea fishing line. Bless my reel. No one could do fishing here."

"Let me see that!" exclaimed Mr. Whitford eagerly. Then, as he looked at it, he uttered a cry of delight. "I thought so," he said. "Look at this bit of cord tied to the weight."

"What does that signify?" asked Tom.

"And see this little hole in the envelope, or, rather a place that was a hole, but it's torn away now."

"I'm not much the wiser," confessed Ned, with a puzzled look.

"Why, it's as plain as print," declared the government agent. "This warning letter was dropped from an airship, Tom."

"From an airship?"

"Yes. They sailed right over this place, and let the letter fall, with this lead weight attached, to bring it to earth just where they wanted it to fall."

"Bless my postage stamp!" cried Mr. Damon. "I never heard of such a thing."

"I see it now!" exclaimed Tom. "While we were off over the river, watching for the smugglers, they were turning a trick here, and giving us a warning into the bargain. We should have stayed around here. I wonder if it was Andy's airship that was used?"

"We can easily find that out," said Mr. Whitford. "I have a detective stationed in a house not far from where the Fogers live. Andy came back from Shopton yesterday, just before you arrived here, and I can soon let you know whether he was out last night. I'll take this letter with me, and get right up to my office, though I'm afraid this won't be much of a clue after all. Print isn't like handwriting for evidence."

"And to think they sailed right over this place, and we weren't home," mourned Tom. "It makes me mad!"

But there was no use in regretting what had happened, and, after a hot breakfast in the airship, with Mr. Damon presiding at the electrical stove, they all felt more hopeful. Mr. Whitford left for his office, promising to send word to Tom as to whether or not Andy was abroad in the airship during the night.

"I wonder if that 'Committee of Three' is Andy and these two fellows with him in the airship?" asked Ned.

"Hard telling," responded his chum. "Now for a good sleep. Koku, keep the crowd away while we have a rest," for the giant had indulged in a good rest while the airship was on patrol during the night.

Not so much of a crowd came out as on the first day, and Koku had little trouble in keeping them far enough away so that Tom and the others could get some rest. Koku walked about, brandishing a big club, and looking as fierce as a giant in a fairy tale. It was afternoon when a message came from Mr. Whitford to the effect that Andy's airship was not out the previous night, and that so far no clues had developed from the letter, or from any other source.

"We'll just have to keep our eyes open," wrote Mr. Whitford. "I think perhaps we are altogether wrong about the Fogers, unless they are deeper than I give them credit for. It might he well to let the smugglers think you are frightened, and go away for a day or so, selecting a more secluded spot to remain in. That may cause them to get bolder, and we may catch them unawares."

"That's a good plan. I'll try it," decided Tom. "We'll move to-morrow to a new location."

"Why not to-night?" asked Ned.

"Because it's getting late, and I want to circle about in daylight and pick out a good place. Morning will do all right."

"Then you're not going out to-night?"

"No. Mr. Whitford writes that as goods were smuggled over last night it will hardly be likely that they will repeat the trick to-night. We'll have a little rest."

"Going to mount guard?" asked Ned.

"No, I don't think so. No one will disturb us."

Afterward the young inventor wished that he had kept a better watch that night, for it nearly proved disastrous for him.

It must have been about midnight that Tom was awakened by a movement in the airship.

"Who's that?" he asked suddenly.

"Koku," came the reassuring reply. "Too hot to sleep in my bank. I go out on deck."

"All right, Koku," and Tom dozed off again.

Suddenly he was awakened by the sound of a terrific scuffle on deck. Up he jumped, rushing toward the door that led from his sleeping cabin.

"What is it! What's the matter!" he cried.

There came the sound of a blow, a cry of pain, and then the report of a gun.

"Bless my cartridge belt!" cried Mr. Damon.

"What's the matter? Who is it? What happened?" yelled Ned, tumbling out of his bunk.

"Something wrong!" answered Tom, as he switched on the electric lights. He was just in time to see Koku wrench a gun from a man who stood near the pedestal, on which the great searchlight was poised. Tossing the weapon aside, Koku caught up his club, and aimed a blow at the man. But the latter nimbly dodged and, a moment later leaped over the rail, followed by the giant.

"Who is he? What did he do?" cried Tom after his big servant. "What happened?"

"Him try to shoot searchlight, but I stop him!" yelled back Koku, as he rushed on in pursuit. With a leap Tom sprang to the switch of his lantern, and sent a flood of light toward where Koku was racing after the intruder.

A False Clue

Full in the glare of the powerful beam from the light there was revealed the giant and the man he was pursuing. The latter neither Tom, nor any one on the airship, knew. All they could see was that he was racing away at top speed, with Koku vainly swinging his club at him.

"Bless my chicken soup!" cried Mr. Damon. "Is anything damaged, Tom?"

"No, Koku was too quick for him." yelled the youth, as he, too leaped over the rail and joined in the pursuit.

"Stop! Stop!" called Koku to the man who had sought to damage the great searchlight. But the fellow knew better than to halt, with an angry giant so close behind him. He ran on faster than ever.

Suddenly the stranger seemed to realize that by keeping in the path of the light he gave his pursuers a great advantage. He dodged to one side, off the path on which he had been running, and plunged into the bushes.

"Where him go?" called Koku, coming to a puzzled halt.

"Ned, play the light on both sides!" ordered Tom to his chum, who was now on the deck of the airship, near the wheels and levers that operated the big lantern. "Show him up!"

Obediently the young bank clerk swung the searchlight from side to side. The powerful combined electric current, hissing into the big carbons, and being reflected by the parabolic mirrors, made the growth of underbrush as brightly illuminated as in day time. Tom detected a movement.

"There he is, Koku!" he called to his giant servant. "Off there to the left. After him!"

Raising his club on high, Koku made a leap for the place where the fugitive was hiding. As the man saw the light, and sprang forward, he was, for a moment, in the full glare of the rays. Then, just as the giant was about to reach him, Koku stumbled over a tree root, and fell heavily.

"Never mind, I'll get him!" yelled Tom, but the next moment the man vanished suddenly, and was no longer to be seen in the finger of light from the lantern. He had probably dipped down into some hollow, lying there hidden, and as of course was out of the focus of the searchlight.

"Come on, Koku, we'll find him!" exclaimed Tom, and together they made a search, Mr. Damon joining them, while Ned worked the lantern. But it was of no avail, for they did not find the stranger.

"Well, we might as well go back," said Tom, at length. "We can't find him. He's probably far enough off by this time."

"Who was he?" panted Mr. Damon, as he walked beside Tom and Koku to the airship. Ned had switched off the big light on a signal from the young inventor.

"I don't know!" answered Tom.

"But what did he want? What was he doing? I don't quite understand."

"He wanted to put my searchlight out of commission," responded our hero. "From that I should argue that he was either one of the smugglers, or trying to aid them."

And this theory was borne out by Mr. Whitford, who, on calling the next morning, was told of the occurrence of the night. Koku related how he had found it uncomfortable in his bunk, and had gone out on deck for air. There, half dozing, he heard a stealthy step. At once he was on the alert. He saw a man with a gun creeping along, and at first thought the fellow had evil designs on some of those aboard the Falcon.

Then, when Koku saw the man aim at the big searchlight the giant sprang at him, and there was a scuffle. The gun went off, and the man escaped. An examination of the weapon he had left behind showed that it carried a highly explosive shell, which, had it hit the lantern, would have completely destroyed it, and might have damaged the airship.

"It was the smugglers, without a doubt," declared Mr. Whitford. "You can't get away from this place any too soon, Tom. Get a new hiding spot, and I will communicate with you there."

"But they are on the watch," objected Ned. "They'll see where we go, and follow us. The next time they may succeed in smashing the lantern."

"And if they do," spoke Tom, "it will be all up with trying to detect the smugglers, for it would take me quite a while to make another searchlight. But I have a plan."

"What is it?" asked the government agent.

"I'll make a flight today," went on the young inventor, "and sail over quite an area. I'll pick out a good place to land, and we'll make our camp there instead of here. Then I'll come back to this spot, and after dark I'll go up, without a light showing. There's no moon to-night, and they'll have pretty good eyes if they can follow me, unless they get a searchlight, and they won't do that for fear of giving themselves away.

We'll sail off in the darkness, go to the spot we have previously picked out, and drop down to it. There we can hide and I don't believe they can trace us."

"But how can you find in the darkness, the spot you pick out in daylight?" Mr. Whitford wanted to know.

"I'll arrange same electric lights, in a certain formation in trees around the landing place," said Tom. "I'll fix them with a clockwork switch, that will illuminate them at a certain hour, and they'll run by a storage battery. In that way I'll have my landing place all marked out, and, as it can only be seen from above, if any of the smugglers are on the ground, they won't notice the incandescents."

"But if they are in their airship they will," said Mr. Damon.

"Of course that's possible," admitted Tom, "but, even if they see the lights I don't believe they will know what they mean. And, another thing,

I don't imagine they'll come around here in their airship when they know that we're in the neighborhood, and when the spy who endeavored to damage my lantern reports that he didn't succeed. They'll know that we are likely to be after them any minute."

"That's so," agreed Ned. "I guess that's a good plan."

It was one they adopted, and, soon after Mr. Whitford's visit the airship arose, with him on board, and Tom sent her about in great circles and sweeps, now on high and again, barely skimming over the treetops. During this time a lookout was kept for any other aircraft, but none was seen.

"If they are spying on us, which is probably the case," said Tom, "they will wonder what we're up to. I'll keep 'em guessing. I think I'll fly low over Mr. Foger's house, and see if Andy has his airship there. We'll give him a salute."

Before doing this, however, Tom had picked out a good landing place in a clearing in the woods, and had arranged some incandescent lights on high branches of trees. The lights enclosed a square, in the centre of which the Falcon was to drop down.

Of course it was necessary to descend to do this, to arrange the storage battery and the clock switch. Then, so as to throw their enemies off their track, they made landings in several other places, though they did nothing, merely staying there as a sort of "bluff" as Ned called it.

"They'll have their own troubles if they investigate every place we stopped at," remarked Tom, "and, even if they do hit on the one we have selected for our camp they won't see the lights in the trees, for they're well hidden."

This work done, they flew back toward Logansville, and sailed over Andy's house.

"There he is, on the roof, working at his airship!" exclaimed Ned, as they came within viewing distance, and, surely enough, there was the bully, tinkering away at his craft. Tom flew low enough down to speak to him, and, as the Falcon produced no noise, it was not difficult to make their voices heard.

"Hello, Andy!" called Tom, as he swept slowly overhead.

Andy looked up, but only scowled.

"Nice day; isn't it?" put in Ned.

"You get on away from here!" burst out the bully. "You are trespassing, by flying over my house, and I could have you arrested for it. Keep away."

"All right," agreed Tom with a laugh. "Don't trespass by flying over our ship, Andy. We also might have a gun to shoot searchlights with," he added.

Andy started, but did not reply, though Tom, who was watching him closely, thought he saw an expression of fear come over the bully's face.

"Do you think it was Andy who did the shooting?" asked Ned.

"No, he hasn't the nerve," replied Tom. "I don't know what to think about that affair last night."

"Excepting that the smugglers are getting afraid of you, and want to get you out of the way," put in the custom official.

That night, when it was very dark, the Falcon noiselessly made her way upward and sailed along until she was over the square in the forest, marked out by the four lights. Then Tom sent her safely down.

"Now let 'em find us if they can!" the young inventor exclaimed, as he made the craft fast. "We'll turn in now, and see what happens to-morrow night."

"I'll send you word, just as soon as I get any myself," promised Mr. Whitford, when he left the next morning.

Tom and Ned spent the day in going over the airship, making some minor repairs to it, and polishing and oiling the mechanism of the searchlight, to have it in the best possible condition.

It was about dusk when the wireless outfit, with which the Falcon was fitted, began snapping and cracking.

"Here comes a message!" cried Tom, as he clapped the receiver over his head, and began to translate the dots and dashes.

"It's from Mr. Whitford!" he exclaimed, when he had written it down, and had sent back an answer, "He says: 'Have a tip that smugglers will try to get goods over the border at some point near Niagara Falls to-morrow night. Can you go there, and cruise about? Better keep toward Lake Ontario also. I will be with you. Answer.'"

"What answer did you send?" asked Ned.

"I told him we'd be on the job. It's quite a little run to make, and we can't start until after dark, or otherwise some of the smugglers around here may see us, and tip off their confederates. But I guess we can make the distance all right."

Mr. Whitford arrived at the airship the next afternoon, stating that he had news from one of the government spies to the effect that a bold attempt would be made that night.

"They're going to try and smuggle some diamonds over on this trip," said the custom agent.

"Well, we'll try to nab them!" exclaimed Tom.

As soon as it was dark enough to conceal her movements, the Falcon was sent aloft, not a light showing, and, when on high, Tom started the motor at full speed. The great propellers noiselessly beat the air, and the powerful craft was headed for Lake Ontario.

"They're pretty good, if they attempted to cross the lake to-night," observed the young inventor, as he looked at the barometer.

"Why so?" asked Ned.

"Because there's a bad storm coming up. I shouldn't want to risk it. We'll keep near shore. We can nab them there as good as over the lake."

This plan was adopted, and as soon as they reached the great body of water—the last in the chain of the Great Lakes—Tom cruised about, he and Ned watching through powerful night glasses for a glimpse of another airship.

Far into the night they sailed about, covering many miles, for Tom ran at almost top speed. They sailed over Niagara Falls, and then well along the southern shore of Ontario, working their way north-east and back again. But not a sign of the smugglers did they see.

Meanwhile the wind had arisen until it was a gale, and it began to rain. Gently at first the drops came down, until at length there was a torrent of water descending from the overhead clouds. But those in the Falcon were in no discomfort.

"It's a bad storm all right!" exclaimed Tom, as he looked at the barometer, and noted that the mercury was still falling.

"Yes, and we have had our trouble for our pains!" declared Mr. Whitford.

"What do you mean?"

"I mean I believe that we have been deceived by a false clue. The smugglers probably had no intention of getting goods across at this point to-night. They saw to it that my agent got false information, believing that we would follow it, and leave the vicinity of Logansville."

"So they could operate there?" asked Tom.

"That's it," replied the agent. "They drew us off the scent. There's no help for it. We must get back as soon as we can. My! This is a bad storm!" he added, as a blast careened the airship.

The Rescue on the Lake

For a time the Falcon shot onward through the storm and darkness, for Tom did not want to give up. With but a single shaded light in the pilot house, so that he could see to read the gauges and dials, telling of the condition of the machinery in the motor room, he pushed his stanch craft ahead. At times she would be forced downward toward the angry waters of Lake Ontario, over which she was sailing, but the speed of her propellers and the buoyancy of the gas bag, would soon lift her again.

"How much longer are you going to stay?" called Ned in his chum's ear—called loudly, not to be heard above the noise of the airship, but above the racket of the gale.

"Oh, I guess we may as well start back," spoke Tom, after a look at the clock on the wall. "We can just about make our camp by daylight, and they won't see us."

"It won't be light very early," observed Mr. Whitford, looking in the pilot house from the cabin, just aft of it. "But there is no use waiting around here any more, Tom. They gave us a false clue, all right."

"Bless my police badge!" cried Mr. Damon. "They must be getting desperate."

"I believe they are," went on the custom officer. "They are afraid of us, and that's a good sign. We'll keep right after 'em, too. If we don't get 'em this week, we will next. Better put back."

"I will," decided the young inventor.

"It certainly is a gale," declared Ned, as he made his way along a dim passage, as few lights had been set aglow, for fear of the smugglers seeing the craft outlined in the air. Now, however, when it was almost certain that they were on the wrong scent, Tom switched on the incandescents, making the interior of the Falcon more pleasant.

The giant came into the pilot house to help Tom, and the airship was turned about, and headed toward Logansville. The wind was now sweeping from the north across Lake Ontario, and it was all the powerful craft could do to make headway against it.

There came a terrific blast, which, in spite of all that Tom and Koku could do, forced the Falcon down, dangerously close to the dashing billows.

"Hard over, Koku!" called Tom to his giant.

As the airship began to respond to the power of her propellers, and the up-tilted rudder, Tom heard, from somewhere below him, a series of shrill blasts on a whistle.

"What's that?" he cried.

"Sounds like a boat below us," answered Mr. Whitford.

"I guess it is," agreed the young inventor. "There she goes again."

Once more came the frantic tooting of a whistle, and mingled with it could be heard voices shouting in fear, but it was only a confused murmur of sound. No words could be made out.

"That's a compressed air whistle!" decided Tom. "It must be some sort of a motor boat in distress. Quick, Mr. Whitford! Tell Ned to switch on the searchlight, and play it right down on the lake. If there's a boat in this storm it can't last long. Even an ocean liner would have trouble. Get the light on quick, and we'll see what we can do!"

It was the work of but an instant to convey the message to Ned. The latter called Mr. Damon to relieve him in the motor room, and, a few seconds later, Ned had switched on the electricity. By means of the lazy-tongs, and the toggle joints, the bank clerk lifted the lantern over until the powerful beam from it was projected straight down into the seething waters of the lake.

"Do you see anything?" asked Mr. Damon from the motor room, at one side of which Ned stood to operate the lantern.

"Nothing but white-caps," was the answer. "It's a fearful storm."

Once more came the series of shrill whistles, and the confused calling of voices. Ned opened a window, in order to hear more plainly. As the whistle tooted again he could locate the sound, and, by swinging the rays of the searchlight to and fro he finally picked up the craft.

"There she is!" he cried, peering down through the plate glass window in the floor of the motor room. "It's a small gasolene boat, and there are several men in her! She's having a hard time."

"Can we rescue them?" asked Mr. Damon.

"If anybody can, Tom Swift will," was Ned's reply. Then came a whistle from the speaking tube, that led to the pilot house.

"What is it?" asked Ned, putting the tube to his ear.

"Stand by for a rescue!" ordered Tom, who had also, through a window in the floor of the pilot house, seen the hapless motor boat. The men in it were frantically waving their hands to those on the airship. "I'm going down as close as I dare," went on Tom. "You watch, and when it's time, have Koku drop from the stern a long, knotted rope. That will he a sort of ladder, and they can make it fast to their boat and climb up, hand over hand. It's the only plan."

"Good!" cried Ned. "Send Koku to me. Can you manage alone in the pilot house?"

"Yes," came back the answer through the tube.

Koku came back on the run, and was soon tying knots in a strong rope. Meanwhile Ned kept the light on the tossing boat, while Tom, through a megaphone had called to the men to stand by to be rescued. The whistle frantically tooted their thanks.

Koku went out on the after deck, and, having made the knotted rope fast, dropped the end overboard. Then began a difficult feature of airship steering. Tom, looking down through the glass, watched the boat in the glare of the light. Now coming forward, now reversing against the rush of the wind; now going up, and now down, the young inventor so directed the course of his airship so that, finally, the rope dragged squarely across the tossing boat.

In a trice the men grabbed it, and made it fast. Then Tom had another difficult task—that of not allowing the rope to become taut, or the drag of the boat, and the uplift of the airship might have snapped it in twain. But he handled his delicate craft of the air as confidently as the captain of a big liner brings her skillfully to the deck against wind and tide.

"Climb up! Climb up!" yelled Tom, through the megaphone, and he saw, not a man, but a woman, ascending the knotted rope, hand over hand, toward the airship that hovered above her head.

KOKU'S PRISONER

"Bless my knitting needles!" cried Mr. Damon, as be looked down, and saw, in the glare of the great light, the figure of the woman clinging to the swaying rope. "Help her, someone! Tom! Ned! She'll fall!"

The eccentric man started to rush from the motor room, where he had been helping Ned. But the latter cried:

"Stay where you are, Mr. Damon. No one can reach her now without danger to himself and her. She can climb up, I think."

Past knot after knot the woman passed, mounting steadily upward, with a strength that seemed remarkable.

"Come on!" cried Tom to the others. "Don't wait until she gets up. There isn't time. Come on—the rope will hold you all! Climb up!"

The men in the tossing and bobbing motor boat heard, and at once began, one after the other, to clamber up the rope. There were five of them, as could be seen in the glare of the light, and Tom, as he watched, wondered what they were doing out in the terrific storm at that early hour of the morning, and with a lone woman.

"Stand by to help her, Koku!" called Ned to the giant.

"I help," was the giant's simple reply, and as the woman's head came above the rail, over which the rope ran, Koku, leaning forward, raised her in his powerful arms, and set her carefully on the deck.

"Come into the cabin, please," Ned called to her. "Come in out of the wet."

"Oh, it seems a miracle that we are saved!" the woman gasped, as, rain-drenched and wind-tossed, she staggered toward the door which Tom had opened by means of a lever in the pilot house. The young inventor had his hands full, manipulating the airship so as to keep it above the motor boat, and not bring too great a strain on the rope.

The woman passed into the cabin, which was between the motor room and the pilot house, and Ned saw her throw herself on her knees, and offer up a fervent prayer of thanksgiving. Then, springing to her feet, she cried:

"My husband? Is he safe? Can you save him? Oh, how wonderful that this airship came in answer to our appeals to Providence. Whose is it?"

Before Ned got a chance to answer her, as she came to the door of the motor room, a man's voice called:

"My wife! Is she safe?"

"Yes, here I am," replied the woman, and a moment later the two were in each other's arms.

"The others; are they safe?" gasped the woman, after a pause.

"Yes," replied the man. "They are coming up the rope. Oh, what a wonderful rescue! And that giant man who lifted us up on deck! Oh, do you recall in Africa how we were also rescued by airship—"

"Come on now, I got you!" interrupted the voice of Koku out on the after deck, and there was a series of thumps that told when he had lifted the men over the rail, and set them down.

"All saved!" cried the giant at last.

"Then cut the rope!" shouted Tom. "We've got to get out of this, for it's growing worse!"

There was the sound of a hatchet blow, and the airship shot upward. Into the cabin came the dripping figures of the other men, and Ned, as he stood by the great searchlight, felt a wave of wonder sweep over him as he listened to the voices of the first man and woman.

He knew he had heard them before, and, when he listened to the remark about a rescue by airship, in Africa, a flood of memory came to him.

"Can it be possible that these are the same missionaries whom Tom and I rescued from the red pygmies?" he murmured. "I must get a look at them."

"Our boat, it is gone I suppose," remarked one of the other men, coming into the motor room.

"I'm afraid so," answered Ned, as he played the light on the doomed craft. Even as he did so he saw a great wave engulf her, and, a moment later she sank. "She's gone," he said softly.

"Too bad!" exclaimed the man. "She was a fine little craft. But how in the world did you happen along to rescue us? Whose airship is this?"

"Tom Swift's," answered Ned, and, at the sound of the name the woman uttered a cry, as she rushed into the motor room.

"Tom Swift!" she exclaimed. "Where is he? Oh, can it be possible that it is the same Tom Swift that rescued us in Africa?"

"I think it is, Mrs. Illingway," spoke Ned quietly, for he now recognized the missionary, though he wondered what she and her husband were doing so far from the Dark Continent.

"Oh, I know you—you're Ned Newton—Tom's chum! Oh, I am so glad! Where is Tom?"

"In the pilot house. He'll be here in a moment."

Tom came in at that juncture, having set the automatic steering geer to take the ship on her homeward course.

"Are they all saved?" he asked, looking at the little group of persons who had climbed up from the motor boat. "Mr. Damon, you had better make some hot coffee. Koku, you help. I—"

"Tom Swift!" cried out Mr. and Mrs. Illingway together, as they made a rush for the young inventor. "Don't you know us?"

To say that Tom was surprised at this, would be putting it mildly. He had to lean up against the side of the cabin for support.

"Mrs. Illingway!" he gasped. "You here—were you in that boat?"

"Yes. it's all very simple. My husband and I are on a vacation for a year. We got fever and had to leave Africa. We are staying with friends at a resort on the lake shore. These are our friends," she went on, introducing the other gentlemen.

"We went out for a trip in the motor boat," the missionary continued, "but we went too far. Our motor broke down, we could get no help, and the storm came up. We thought we were doomed, until we saw your lights. I guessed it was a balloon, or some sort of an airship, and we whistled; and called for help. Then you rescued us! Oh, it is almost too wonderful to believe. It is a good thing I have practiced athletics or I never could have climbed that rope."

"It is like a story from a book!" added Mr. Illingway, as he graspsd Tom's hand. "You rescued us in Africa and again here." I may say here that the African rescue is told in detail in the volume entitled, "Tom Swift and His Electric Rifle."

. The shipwrecked persons were made as comfortable as possible. There was plenty of room for them, and soon they were sitting around warm electric heaters, drinking hot coffee, and telling their adventures over again. Mr. and Ms. Illingway said they soon expected to return to Africa.

Tom told how he happened to be sailing over the lake, on the lookout for smugglers, and how he had been disappointed.

"And it's a good thing you were—for our sakes," put in Mrs. Illingway, with a smile.

"Where do you want to be landed?" asked Tom. "I don't want to take you all the way back to Logansville."

"If you will land us anywhere near a city or town, we can arrange to be taken back to our cottage," said one of the men, and Tom sent the airship down until, in the gray dawn of the morning, they could pick out a large village on the lake shore. Then, in much better condition than when they had been saved, the rescued ones alighted, showering Tom and the others with thanks, and sought a hotel.

"And now for our camp, and a good rest!" cried the young inventor, as he sent the airship aloft again.

They reached their camp in the forest clearing without having been observed, as far as they could learn, and at once set about making things snug, for the storm was still raging.

"I don't believe any of the smugglers were abroad last night," remarked Mr. Whitford, as he prepared to go back into town, he having come out on horseback, leaving the animal over night in an improvised stable they had made in the woods of boughs and tree branches.

"I hope not," replied Tom. but the next day, when the government agent called again, his face wore a look of despair.

"They put a big one over on us the night of the rescue." he said. "They flew right across the border near Logansville, and got away with a lot of goods. They fooled us all right."

"Can you find out who gave the wrong tip?" asked Tom.

"Yes, I know the man. He pretended to be friendly to one of my agents, but he was only deceiving him. But we'll get the smugglers yet!"

"That's what we will!" cried Tom, determinedly.

Several days passed, and during the night time Tom, in his airship, and with the great searchlight aglow, flew back and forth across the border, seeking the elusive airships, but did not see them. In the meanwhile he heard from Mr. and Mrs. Illingway, who sent him a letter of thanks, and asked him to come and see them, but, much as Tom would liked to have gone, he did not have the time.

It was about a week after the sensational rescue, when one evening, as Tom was about to get ready for a night flight, he happened to be in the pilot house making adjustments to some of the apparatus.

Mr. Damon and Ned had gone out for a walk in the woods, and Mr. Whitford had not yet arrived. As for Mr. Koku, Tom did not know where his giant servant was.

Suddenly there was a commotion outside. A trampling in the bushes, and the breaking of sticks under feet.

"I got you now!" cried the voice of the giant.

Tom sprang to the window of the pilot house. He saw Koku tightly holding a man who was squinting about, and doing his best to break away. But it was useless. When Koku got hold of any one, that person had to stay.

"What is it, Koku!" cried Tom.

"I got him!" cried the giant. "He sneaking up on airship, but I come behind and grab him," and Koku fairly lifted his prisoner off his feet and started with him toward the Falcon.

WHAT THE INDIAN SAW

"Hello!" cried Tom. "What's up, Koku?"

"Him up!" replied the giant with a laugh, as he looked at his squirming prisoner, whose feet he had lifted from the ground.

"No, I mean what was he doing?" went on Tom, with a smile at the literal way in which the giant had answered his question.

"I wasn't doing anything!" broke in the man. "I'd like to know if I haven't a right to walk through these woods, without being grabbed up by a man as big as a mountain? There'll be something up that you won't like, if you don't let me go, too!" and he struggled fiercely, but he was no match for giant Koku.

"What was he doing?" asked Tom of his big servant, ignoring the man. Tom looked closely at him, however, but could not remember to have seen him before.

"I walking along in woods, listen to birds sing," said Koku simply, taking a firmer hold on his victim. "I see this fellow come along, and crawl through grass like so a snake wiggle. I to myself think that funny, and I watch. This man he wiggle more. He wiggle more still, and then he watch. I watch too. I see him have knife in hand, but I am no afraid. I begin to go like snake also, but I bigger snake than he."

"I guess so," laughed Tom, as he watched the man trying in vain to get out of Koku's grip.

"Then I see man look up at balloon bag, so as if he like to cut it with knife. I say to myself, 'Koku, it is time for you to go into business for yourself.' You stand under me?"

"I understand!" exclaimed Tom. "You thought it was time for you to get busy."

"Sure," replied Koku. "Well, I get business, I give one jump, and I am so unlucky as to jump with one foot on him, but I did not mean it. I go as gentle as I can."

"Gentle? You nearly knocked the wind out of me!" snarled the prisoner. "Gentle! Huh!"

"I guess he was the unlucky one, instead of you," put in Tom. "Well, what happened next?"

"I grab him, and—he is still here," said Koku simply. "He throw knife away though."

"I see," spoke Tom. "Now will you give an account of yourself, or shall I hand you over to the police?" he asked sternly of the man. "What were you sneaking up on us in that fashion for?"

"Well, I guess this isn't your property!" blustered the man. "I have as good a right here as you have, and you can't have me arrested for that."

"Perhaps not," admitted Tom. "You may have a right on this land, but if you are honest, and had no bad intentions, why were you sneaking up, trying to keep out of sight? And why did you have a big knife?"

"That's my business, young man."

"All right, then I'll make it MY business, too," went on the young inventor. "Hold him, Koku, until I can find Mr. Damon, or Ned, and I'll see what's best to be done. I wish Mr. Whitford was here."

"Aren't you going to let me go?" demanded the man.

"I certainly am not!" declared Tom firmly. "I'm going to find out more about you. I haven't any objections to any one coming to look at my airship, out of curiosity, but when they come up like a snake in the grass and with a big knife, then I get suspicious, and I want to know more about them."

"Well, you won't know anything more about me!" snarled the fellow. "And it will be the worse for you, if you don't let me go. You'd better!" he threatened.

"Don't pay any attention to him, Koku," said Tom. "Maybe you'd better tie him up. You'll find some rope in the motor room."

"Don't you dare tie me up!" blustered the prisoner.

"Go ahead and tie him," went on Tom. "You'll be free to guard the ship then. I'll go for Ned and Mr. Damon."

"Tie who up? What's the matter?" asked a voice, and a moment later the government agent came along the woodland path on his horse. "What's up, Tom? Have you captured a wild animal?"

"Not exactly a wild animal. Mr. Whitford. But a wild man. I'm glad you came along. Koku has a prisoner." And Tom proceeded to relate what had happened.

"Sneaking up on you with a knife; eh? I guess he meant business all right, and bad business, too," said Mr. Whitford. "Let me get a look at him, Tom," for Koku had taken his prisoner to the engine room, and there, amid a storm of protests and after a futile struggle on the part of the fellow, had tied him securely.

Tom and the custom officer went in to look at the man, just as Ned and Mr. Damon came back from their stroll in the woods. It was rapidly getting dusk, and was almost time for the start of the usual flight, to see if any trace could be had of the smugglers.

"There he is," said Tom, waving his hand toward the bound man who sat in a chair in one corner of the motor room. The young inventor switched on the light, and a moment later Mr. Whitford exclaimed:

"Great Scott! It's Ike Shafton!"

"Do you know him?" asked Tom eagerly.

"Know him? I should say I did! Why he's the man who pretended to give one of my men information about smugglers that drew us off on the false scent. He pretended to be for the government, and, all the while, he was in with the smugglers! Know him? I should say I did!"

A queer change had come over the prisoner at the sight of Mr. Whitford. No longer was Shafton surly and blustering. Instead he seemed to slink down in his chair, bound as he was, as if trying to get out of sight.

"Why did you play double?" demanded the government agent, striding over to him.

"I—I—don't hit me!" whined Shafton.

"Hit you! I'm not going to hit you!" exclaimed Mr. Whitford, "but I'm going to search you, and then I'm going to wire for one of my men to take you in custody."

"I—I didn't do anything!"

"You didn't; eh? Well, we'll see what the courts think of giving wrong information to Uncle Sam with the intent to aid criminals. Let's see what he's got in his pockets."

The spy did not have much, but at a sight of one piece of paper Mr. Whitford uttered a cry of surprise.

"Ha! This is worth something!" he exclaimed. "It may be stale news, and it may be something for the future, but it's worth trying. I wonder I didn't think of that before."

"What is it?" asked Tom.

For answer the custom officer held out a scrap of paper on which was written one word.

ST. REGIS.

"What does it mean," asked Ned, who, with Mr. Damon, had entered the motor room, and stood curiously regarding the scene.

"Bless my napkin ring!" said the odd man. "That's the name of a hotel. Do you suppose the smugglers are stopping there?"

"Hardly," replied Mr. Whitford with a smile. "But St. Regis is the name of an Indian reservation in the upper part of New York state, right on the border, and in the corner where the St. Lawrence and the imaginary dividing line between New York and Canada join. I begin to see things now. The smugglers have been flying over the Indian Reservation, and that's why they have escaped us so far. We never thought of that spot. Tom, I believe we're on the right track at last! Shafton was probably given this to inform him where the next trick would be turned, so he could get us as far away as possible, or, maybe prevent us leaving at all."

An involuntary start on the part of the prisoner seemed to confirm this, but he kept silent.

"Of course," went on Mr. Whitford, "they may have already flown over the St. Regis reservation, and this may be an old tip, but it's worth following up."

"Why don't you ask him?" Tom wanted to know, as he nodded toward Shafton.

"He wouldn't tell the truth. I'll put him where he can't get away to warn his confederates, and then we'll go to the reservation. And to think that my man trusted him!"

Mr. Whitford was soon in communication with his headquarters by means of the wireless apparatus on Tom's airship, and a little later two custom officers arrived, with an extra horse on which they were to take their prisoner back.

"And now we'll try our luck once more," said Mr. Whitford as his men left with Shafton securely bound. "Can you make the reservation in good time, Tom? It's quite a distance," and he pointed it out on the map.

"Oh, I'll do it," promised the young inventor, as he sent his powerful craft aloft in the darkness. Then, with her nose pointed in the right direction, the Falcon beat her way forward through the night, flying silently, with the great searchlight ready for instant use.

In comparatively short time, though it was rather late at night, they reached the St. Lawrence, and then it was an easy matter to drop down into the midst of the reservation grounds. Though the redmen, whom the state thus quartered by themselves, had all retired, they swarmed out of their cabins as the powerful light flashed back and forth.

"We want to question some of the head men of the tribe," said Mr. Whitford. "I know some of them, for on several occasions I've had to come here to look into rumors that tobacco and liquor and other contraband goods dear to the Indian heart were smuggled into the reservation against the law. I never caught any of them at it though."

With guttural exclamations, and many grunts of surprise, the redmen gathered around the big airship. It was too much even for their usual reserve, and they jabbered among themselves.

"How Big Foot!" greeted the custom officer, to one Indian who had an extremely large left foot. "How!"

"How!" responded the Indian, with a grunt.

"Plenty much fine air-bird; eh?" and the agent waved his hand toward the Falcon.

"Yep. Plenty much big."

"Big Foot never see bird like this; eh?"

"Oh sure. Big Foot see before many times. Huh!"

"What! Has he seen this before?" asked Tom.

"No. Wait a minute," cautioned Mr. Whitford. "I'm on the track of something. Big Foot see air-bird like this?" he questioned.

"Sure. Fly over Indians' land many times. Not same as him," and he nodded toward Tom's ship, "but plenty much like. Make heap noise. Come down once—break wheel mebby. Indians help fix. Indians get firewater. You got firewater in your air-bird?"

"No firewater, but maybe we've got some tobacco, if you tell us what we want to know, Big Foot. And so you've seen air-birds flying around here before?"

"Sure, Heap times. We all see," and he waved his hand to indicate the redmen gathered around him.

There came grunts of confirmation.

"We're getting there!" exclaimed Mr. Whitford to Tom. "We're on the right track now. Which way air-birds come, Big Foot?"

"Over there," and he pointed toward Canada.

"Which way go?"

"Over there," and he pointed toward the east, in the direction of Shopton, as much as anywhere.

"That's what we want to know. Tom, we'll just hang around here for a while, until one of the smugglers' airships pass over head. I believe one is due to-night, and that's why Shafton had that paper. It was sent to him to tip him off. He was sneaking up, trying to put your airship out of commission when Koku caught him. These Indians have used their eyes to good advantage. I think we're on the trail at last."

"Baccy for Big Foot?" asked the redman.

"Yes, plenty of it. Tom, give them some of Koku's, will you? I'll settle with you later," for the giant had formed a liking for the weed, and Tom did not have the heart to stop him smoking a pipe once in a while. With his usual prodigality, the giant had brought along a big supply, and some of this was soon distributed among the Indians, who grunted their thanks.

THE PURSUIT

"What plan have you in mind?" asked Tom of Mr. Whitford, when some of the Indians had gone back to their shanties, leaving a few staring curiously at the airship, as she rested on the ground, bathed in the glow of her electric lights.

"Well, I think the best thing we can do is just to stay right here, Tom; all night if need be. As Big Foot says, there have been airships passing overhead at frequent intervals. Of course that is not saying that they were the smugglers, but I don't see who else they could be. There's no meet going on, and no continental race. They must be the smugglers."

"I think so," put in Ned.

"Bless my diamond ring!" exclaimed Mr. Damon. "But what are you going to do when you see them overhead?"

"Take after them, of course!" exclaimed Tom. "That's what we're here for; isn't it Mr. Whitford?"

"Yes. Do you think you can rise from the ground, and take after them in time to stand a chance of overhauling them, Tom? You know they may go very fast."

"I know, but I don't believe they can beat the Falcon. I'd rather wait down here than hover in the air. It isn't as dark as it was the other night, and they might see us with their glasses. Then they would turn back, and we'd have our trouble for nothing. They've actually got to cross the border with smuggled goods before the law can touch them; haven't they?"

"Yes, I couldn't arrest them on Canadian territory, or over it. I've got to get them on this side of the border. So perhaps it will be as well to lie here. But do you suppose you can hear them or see them, as they fly over?"

"I'm pretty sure I can. The sound of their motor and the whizz of the propellers carries for some distance. And then, too, I'm going to set the searchlight to play a beam up in the air. If that gets focused on 'em, we'll spot 'em all right."

"But suppose they see it, and turn back?"

"I don't believe they will. The beam will come from the ground straight upward you know, and they won't connect it with my ship."

"But that fellow who was sneaking up when Koku caught him, may find some way to warn them that you have come here," suggested Ned.

"He won't get much chance to communicate with his friends, while my men have him," said Mr. Whitford significantly. "I guess we'll take a chance here, Tom."

So it was arranged. Everything on the airship was gotten ready for a quick flight, and then Tom set his great searchlight aglow once more. Its powerful beams cut upward to the clouds, making a wonderful illumination.

"Now all we have to do is to wait and watch," remarked Tom, as he came hack from a last inspection of the apparatus in the motor room.

"And that is sometimes the hardest kind of work," said Mr. Whitford. "Many a time I have been watching for smugglers for days and nights at a stretch, and it was very wearying. When I got through, and caught my man, I was more tired than if I had traveled hundreds of miles. Just sitting around, and waiting is tiresome work."

The others agreed with him, and then the custom officer told many stories of his experiences, of the odd places smugglers would hit upon to conceal the contrabrand goods, and of fights he had taken part in.

"Diamonds and jewels, from their smallness, and from the great value, and the high duty on them when brought into the United States, form the chief articles of the high class smugglers," he said. "In fact the ones we are after have been doing more in diamonds than anything else, though they have, of late, brought much valuable hand-made lace. That can be bought comparatively cheap abroad, and if they can evade paying Uncle Sam the duty on it, they can sell it in the United States at a large profit."

"But the government has received so many complaints from legitimate dealers, who can not stand this unfair competition, that we have been ordered to get the smugglers at any cost."

"They are sharp rascals," commented Mr. Damon. "They seem to be making more efforts since Tom Swift got on their trail."

"But, just the same, they are afraid of him, and his searchlight," declared Mr. Whitford. "I guess they fancied that when they took to airships to get goods across the border that they would not be disturbed. But two can play at that game."

The talk became general, with pauses now and then while Tom swept the sky with the great searchlight, the others straining their eyes for a sight of the smugglers' airships. But they saw nothing.

The young inventor had just paid a visit to the pilot house, to see that his wheels and guiding levers were all right, and was walking back toward the stern of the ship, when he heard a noise there, and the fall of a heavy body.

"Who's that?" he cried sharply. "Is that you, Koku?"

A grunt was the only answer, and, as Tom called the giant's name the big man came out.

"What you want, Mr. Tom?" he asked.

"I thought you were at the stern," spoke Tom. "Someone is there. Ned, throw the light on the stern!" he called sharply.

In a moment that part of the ship was in a bright glare and there, in the rays of the big lantern, was stretched out Big Foot, the Indian, comfortably sleeping.

"Here! What are you doing?" demanded Mr. Whitford, giving him a vigorous shake.

"Me sleep!" murmured Big Foot. "Lemme be! Me sleep, and take ride to Happy Hunting Grounds in air-bird. Go 'way!"

"You'll have to sleep somewhere else, Big Foot," spoke the agent with a laugh. "Koku, put him down under one of the trees over there. He can finish his nap in the open, it's warm."

The Indian only protested sleepily, as the giant carried him off the ship, and soon Big Foot was snoring under the trees.

"He's a queer chap," the custom officer said. "Sometimes I think he's a little off in his head. But he's good natured."

Once more they resumed their watching. It was growing more and more wearisome, and Tom was getting sleepy, in spite of himself.

Suddenly the silence of the night was broken by a distant humming and throbbing sound.

"Hark!" cried Ned.

They all listened intently.

"That's an airship, sure enough!" cried Tom.

He sprang to the lever that moved the lantern, which had been shut off temporarily. An instant later a beam of light cut the darkness. The throbbing sounded nearer.

"There they are!" cried Ned, pointing from a window toward the sky. A moment later, right into the glare of the light, there shot a powerful biplane.

"After 'em, Tom!" shouted Mr. Whitford.

Like a bird the Falcon shot upward in pursuit noiselessly and resistlessly, the beam of the great searchlight playing on the other craft, which dodged to one side in an endeavor to escape.

"On the trail at last!" cried Tom, as he shoved over the accelerator lever, sending his airship forward on an upward slant, right at the stern of the smugglers' biplane.

IN DIRE PERIL

Upward shot the Falcon. With every revolution of her big propellers she came nearer and nearer to the fleeing craft of the supposed smugglers who were using every endeavor to escape.

"Do you think you can catch them, Tom?" asked Mr. Whitford as he stood at the side of our hero in the pilot house, and looked upward and forward to where, bathed in the light of the great search-lantern, the rival craft was beating the air.

"I'm sure we can—unless something happens."

"Bless my overshoes! What can happen?" asked Mr. Damon, who, after finding that everything in the motor room was running smoothly, had come forward. Ned was attending to the searchlight. "What can happen, Tom?"

"Almost anything, from a broken shaft to a short-circuited motor. Only, I hope nothing does occur to prevent us from catching them."

"You don't mean to say that you're actually going to try to catch them, do you, Tom?" asked the custom officer, "I thought if we could trail them to the place where they have been delivering the goods, before they shipped them to Shopton we'd be doing well. But I never thought of catching them in mid-air."

"I'm going to try it," declared the young inventor. "I've got a grappling anchor on board," he went on, "attached to a meter and windlass. If I can catch that anchor in any part of their ship I can bring them to a stop, just as a fisherman lands a trout. Only I've got to get close enough to make a cast, and I want to be above them when I do it."

"Don't you think you can catch them, Tom?" asked Mr. Damon.

"Well, I'm pretty sure I can, and yet they seem to have a faster biplane than I gave them credit for. I guess I'll have to increase our speed a little," and he shifted a lever which made the Falcon shoot along at nearly doubled speed.

Still the other airship kept ahead, not far, but sufficiently so to prevent the grappling anchor from being tossed at her rail.

"I wonder if they are the smugglers?" questioned Mr. Damon. "It might be possible, Tom, that we're chasing the wrong craft."

"Possible, but not probable," put in Mr. Whitford. "After the clue we got, and what the Indians told us, and then to have a biplane come sailing over our heads at night, it's pretty sure to be the one we want. But, Tom, can't you close up on 'em?"

"I'm going to try. The machinery is warmed up now, and I'll send it to the limit."

Once more he adjusted the wheels and levers, and at his touch the Falcon seemed to gain new strength. She fairly soared through the air.

Eagerly those in the pilot house watched the craft they were pursuing. She could be seen, in the glare of the big searchlight, like some bird of gloom and evil omen, fluttering along ahead of them.

"They certainly have a fine motor!" cried Tom. "I was sure I could have caught up to them before this."

"How do you account for it?" asked Mr. Damon.

"Well, they're flying a good deal lighter than we are. They probably have no load to speak of, while we carry a heavy one, to say nothing of Koku."

"Diamonds aren't very heavy," put in Mr. Whitford grimly. "I think they are smuggling diamonds to-night. How I wish we could catch them, or trace them to where they have their headquarters."

"We'll do it!" declared Tom.

"Bless my stars! They've gone!" suddenly exclaimed Mr. Damon. "They've disappeared, Tom, I can't see them."

It was indeed true. Those in the pilot house peering ahead through the darkness, could not get a glimpse of the airship they were pursuing. The beam of the searchlight showed nothing but a black void.

All at once the beam shifted downward, and then it picked up the white-winged craft.

"They went down!" cried Tom. "They tried to drop out of sight."

"Can't you get them?" asked Mr. Whitford.

"Oh, yes, we can play that game too. I'll do a little volplaning myself," and the young inventor shut off the power and coasted earthward, while Ned, who had picked up the forward craft, kept the searchlight playing on her.

And now began a wonderful chase. The smugglers' craft, for such she proved later to be, did her best to dodge the Falcon. Those managing the mechanism of the fleeing airship must have been experts, to hold out as they did against Tom Swift, but they had this advantage, that their craft was much lighter, and more powerfully engined as regards her weight. Then, too, there were not so many on board, and Tom, having a combined balloon and aeroplane, had to carry much machinery.

It was like the flight of two big birds in the air. Now the smugglers' craft would be mounting upward, with the Falcon after her. Again she would shoot toward the earth, and Tom would follow, with a great downward swoop.

Ned kept the great lantern going, and, though occasionally the craft they were after slipped out of the focus of the beams, the young bank clerk would pick her up again.

To the right and left dodged the forward airship, vainly endeavoring to shake off Tom Swift, but he would not give up. He followed move for move, swoop for swoop.

"She's turning around!" suddenly cried Mr. Damon. "She's given up the flight, Tom, and is going back!"

"That's so!" agreed Mr. Whitford. "They're headed for Canada, Tom. We've got to catch 'em before they get over the Dominion line!"

"I'll do it!" cried Tom, between his clenched teeth.

He swung his airship around in a big circle, and took after the fleeing craft. The wind was against the smugglers now, and they could not make such good speed, while to Tom the wind mattered not, so powerful were the propellers of the Falcon.

"I think we're gaining on them," murmured Mr. Damon.

Suddenly, from the engine room, came a cry from Ned.

"Tom! Tom!" he shouted, "Something is wrong with the gas machine! She registers over five hundred pounds pressure, and that's too much. It's going up, and I haven't touched it!"

"Mr. Damon, take the wheel!" exclaimed the young inventor. "I've got to see what's wrong. Hold her right on their trail."

Tom sprang to the motor room, and one glance at the gas generating machine showed him that they were in dire peril. In some manner the pressure was going up enormously, and if it went up much more the big tank would blow to pieces.

"What is it?" cried Ned, from his position near the light.

"I don't know! Something wrong."

"Are you going to give up the chase?"

"I am not. Stick to the light. Koku, tell Mr. Damon to hold her on the course I set. I'll try to get this pressure down!" And Tom Swift began to work feverishly, while his ship rushed on through the night in danger, every moment, of being blown to atoms. Yet the young inventor would not give up, and descend to earth.

Suspicious Actions

The chase was kept up, and Tom, when he had a chance to look up at the speed register, as he labored frantically at the clogged gas machine, saw that they were rushing along as they never had before.

"Are we catching them, Ned?" he cried to his chum, who was not far away, playing the powerful light on the smugglers' craft.

"I think we're coming closer, but it's going to be a long chase. I don't see why we can't close up on 'em."

"Because they've got a very fast ship, Ned, and they are flying much lighter than we are. But we'll get 'em!"

"How are you making out with that gas machine?"

"Well, I'm doing all I can, but I can't seem to get the pressure down. I can't understand it. Some of the pipes must be clogged with a carbon deposit. I ought to have cleaned them out some time ago."

Ned gave a hasty glance at the gauge which showed the gas pressure. It registered six hundred pounds now, having risen a hundred in a short time.

"And she'll go up, sure, at eight hundred," murmured Ned, as he held the light steadily on the smugglers' aircraft. "Well, if Tom sticks to the chase, I will too, but I think it would be better to go down, open up everything, and let the gas escape. We could get the rascals later."

Tom, however, did not seem to think so, for he kept on with his task, working away at the pipes, trying to force the obstruction out, so that the gas from the generator would flow into the bag. At the same time he tried to shut off the generating apparatus, but that had become jammed in consequence of the pipe clogging, and the powerful vapor continued to manufacture itself automatically in spite of all that Tom could do.

The only safe way out of the danger, unless he could remove the obstruction, was to descend to earth, and, as Ned had said, open every outlet. But to have done that in mid-air would have been dangerous, as the large volume of gas, suddenly liberated, would have hung about the airship in a cloud, smothering all on board. If they were on the earth they could run away from it, and remain away until the vapor had blown off.

"Is Mr. Damon keeping her on the course, Ned?" asked Tom, pausing a moment to get his breath after a series of frantic efforts.

"Yes, and I think we're closing in on them a little."

"That's good. Are they still headed for the border?"

"Yes, I guess they're going to take no chances to-night. They're going right back to Canada where they came from."

"Well, we'll be hot after 'em. Whistle through the tube, and tell Koku to come here and give me a hand. He's with Mr. Damon in the pilot house."

Ned sent the message, and then gave his whole attention to the light. This was necessary, as the smugglers were resorting to dodging tactics, in an endeavor to escape. Now they would shoot upward, and again toward the earth, varying the performance by steering to the right or left. Ned had constantly to shift the light to keep them in focus, so that Mr. Damon could see where to steer, but, with all this handicap, the eccentric man did very well, and he was never far out in his judgment.

"By Jove!" suddenly murmured Tom, as he tried once more in vain to open a clogged valve. "I'm afraid we can't do it. Koku, lend a hand here!" he exclaimed as the giant entered. "See if you can twist this wrench around, but don't break off the handle, whatever you do."

"Me shove," replied the giant simply, as he grasped the big wrench.

Once more Ned glanced at the pressure gage. It showed seven hundred pounds now, and there was only a margin of safety of one hundred pounds more, ere a terrific explosion would occur. Still Tom had not given the order to descend to earth.

"Are you going to make it, Tom?" asked the government agent, anxiously, as he stood over the young inventor.

"I—I think so," panted Tom. "Are we near the Dominion line,"

"Pretty close," was the discouraging answer. "I'm afraid we can't get 'em before they cross. Can you use any more speed?"

"I don't know. Ned, see if you can get another notch out of her."

With one hand Ned reached for the accelerator lever on the wall near him, and pulled it to the last notch. The Falcon shot ahead with increased speed, but, at the same instant there came a gasp from Koku, and the sound of something breaking.

"There! He's done it!" cried Tom in despair. "I was afraid you'd be too strong for that wrench, Koku. You've broken off the handle. Now we'll never be able to loosen that valve."

Ned gave one more glance at the pressure gage. It showed seven hundred and fifty pounds, and the needle was slowly moving onward.

"Hadn't we better descend," asked Mr. Whitford in a low voice.

"I—I guess so," answered Tom, despairingly. "Where are we?"

Ned flashed the light downward for an instant.

"Just crossing over the St. Regis Indian reservation again," he replied. "We'll be in Canada in a few minutes more."

"Where are the smugglers?"

"Still ahead, and they're bearing off to the right."

"Going toward Montford," commented the government man. "We've lost 'em for to-night, anyhow, but they didn't get their goods landed, at any rate."

"Send her down, Ned!" exclaimed Tom, and it was high time, for the pressure was now within twenty-five pounds of the exploding point.

Down shot the Falcon, while her rival passed onward triumphantly in the darkness. Ned held the light on the smugglers as long as he dared, and then he flashed it to earth to enable Mr. Damon to pick out a good landing place.

In a few moments Tom's silent airship came to rest on a little clearing in the forest, and Tom, with Ned's help, at once opened every outlet of the gas machine, a thing they had not dared do while up in the air.

"Come on, now, run, everybody!" cried Tom. "Otherwise you'll he smothered!"

They leaped from the craft, about which gathered the fumes of the powerful gas, as it hissed from the pipes. Running a hundred yards away they were safe, and could return in a few minutes.

"We're in Canada," remarked Mr. Whitford, as they came to a halt, watching the airship.

"How do you know?" asked Ned.

"As we landed I saw one of the stone boundary posts," was the answer. "We're on English territory, and we can't touch the smugglers if we should see them now."

"Well, we'll soon be back in Uncle Sam's land," declared Tom. "We can go back on board the Falcon to sleep shortly. Jove! I wish I could have caught those fellows!"

"Never mind, we'll get 'em yet," counseled Mr. Whitford.

Waiting until he was sure all the vapor had disappeared, Tom led the way back to the Falcon. No great harm had been done, save to lose considerable gas, and this could be remedied. Tired and disappointed from the chase, they sought their bunks, and were soon asleep. In the morning Tom and Ned began work on the clogged pipes.

This work was nearly accomplished by noon, when Mr. Damon, coming back from a stroll, announced that they were but fifteen minutes walk from the St. Lawrence River, as he had seen the sparkling waters from a neighboring hill.

"Let's go over and have a look at it," proposed Ned. "We can easily finish this when we get back. Besides, Tom, we don't want to get to our regular camp until after dark, anyhow."

The young inventor was willing, and the two lads, with Mr. Whitford, strolled toward the historic stream. As they drew near the bank, they saw, anchored a little distance out, a small steamer. Approaching it, as if she had just left the shore at a point near where our friends stood, was a gasolene launch, containing several men, while on shore, in front of a small shanty, stood another man.

This latter individual, at the sight of Tom, Ned and Mr. Whitford, blew a shrill whistle. Those in the launch looked back. The man on shore waved a red flag in a peculiar way, almost as the soldiers in the army wig-wag signals.

In another moment the launch turned about, and put for shore, while the lone man hurried back into the hut.

"Hum!" remarked Tom. "Those are queer actions."

"Suspicious actions, I should say," said Mr. Whitford. "I'm going to see what this means."

MR. PERIOD ARRIVES

Greatly interested in what was about to take place, and not a little suspicious, our friends stood on the bank of the river and watched the motor boat returning. As it reached a little dock in front of the hut, the man who had waved the red flag of warning came out, and talked rapidly to those in the power craft. At the same time he pointed occasionally to Tom, Ned and the government agent.

"This is getting interesting," remarked Mr. Whitford. "We may have accidentally stumbled on something important Tom."

"See, they're signalling to the steamer now," spoke Ned, and, as he said this, his companions looked, and noted the man from the hut waving a white flag, in a peculiar manner. His signals were answered by those on the vessel anchored out in the stream, and, a little later, black smoke could be seen pouring from her funnel.

"Looks as if they were getting ready to leave," spoke Tom.

"Yes, we seem to have started things moving around here," observed Ned.

"Or else we have prevented from moving," remarked the custom agent.

"What do you mean?" Tom wanted to know.

"I mean that these men were evidently going to do something just as we arrived, and spoiled their plans. I would say they were going to land goods from that schooner. Now the are not."

"What kind of goods?" asked Ned.

"Well, of course I'm not sure, but I should say smuggled goods."

"The smugglers!" cried Tom. "Why, they can't be smugglers, for we are on Canadian territory. The river isn't the dividing line between the Dominion and the United States at this point. The St. Lawrence lies wholly in Canada here, and the men have a right to land any goods they want to, dutiable or not."

"That's just it." put in Mr. Whitford. "They have the right, but they are afraid to exercise it, and that's what makes me suspicious. If they were doing a straight business they wouldn't be afraid, no matter who saw them. They evidently recognize us, by description, if by no other means, and they know we are after smugglers. That's why they stopped the brining of goods from that vessel to shore. They want to wait until we are gone."

"But we couldn't stop them from landing goods, even if they know we are working for Uncle Sam," declared Tom.

"That's very true, but it is evidently their intention, not only to land goods here, which they have a perfect right to do, but to send them into the United States, which they have not a right to do without paying the duty."

"Then you really think they are the smugglers?" asked Ned.

"I'm pretty sure of it. I think we have stumbled on one of the places where the goods are landed, and where they are loaded into the airships. This is the best luck we could have, and it more than makes up for not catching the rascals last night. Now we know where to get on their trail."

"If they don't change the place," observed Tom.

"Oh, of course, we've got to take that chance."

"Here's one of them coming over to speak to us, I guess," remarked Tom in a low voice, as he observed the man, who had waved the flag approaching. There was no doubt of his intention for, as soon as he came within talking distance, the stranger called out:

"What are you fellows doing here?"

"Looking at the river," replied Mr. Whitford, calmly.

"Well, you'd better find some other place for a view. This is private property, and we don't like trespassers. Get a move on—get out!"

"Are we doing any harm?" asked the agent.

"I didn't say you were. This is our land, and we don't like strangers snooping around. That's all."

"Particularly when you are going to land some goods."

"What do you mean?" gasped the man.

"I guess you know well enough," was Mr. Whitford's reply.

The man suddenly turned, and gave a shrill whistle. Instantly, from the hut, came several men who had been in the motor boat. One or two of them had weapons.

"I guess you'd better go now," said the first man sharply. "You're not in the United States now, you know."

"It's easy to see that, by the *politeness* of the residents of this section," put in Tom.

"None of your back talk! Get away from here!" cried the man. "If you don't go peaceably—"

"Oh, we're going," interposed Mr. Whitford calmly. "But that isn't saying we won't come back. Come on, boys. We'll get over on Uncle Sam's territory."

The group of men stood silently watching them, as they filed back through the woods.

"What do you make of it?" asked Tom of the agent.

"I'm positive that I'm right, and that they're the smugglers. But I can't do anything on this side of the line. If ever I can catch them across the border, though, there'll be a different story to tell."

"What had we better do?" inquired Ned.

"Go back to our airship, and leave for Logansville. We don't need to land until night, though, but we can make a slow trip. Is the gas machine all right again, Tom?"

"Practically so. If that hadn't gone back on me we would have had those fellows captured by this time."

"Never mind. We did our best."

It did not take Tom and his chum long to complete the repairs, and soon they arose in the air.

"Let's take a flight over where those fellows are, just to show them what we can do," proposed Ned, and Tom and Mr. Whitford agreed to it. Soon they were circling over the hut. The launch was just starting out again, when a cry from the man who seemed to be a sort of guard, drew the attention of his confederates to the noiseless airship.

Once more the launch was turned about, and sent back to shore, while those in it shook their fists at Tom and his friends.

"We can play tag with 'em up here!" chuckled Ned.

"There's the small vessel that pulled up anchor a while ago," remarked Mr. Whitford, pointing to the vessel which had steamed around a wooded point. "They thought we had gone for good, and they were getting ready to land the stuff. Well, we'll know where to head for next time, when we watch for the smugglers at night."

Realizing that nothing more could be done, Tom sent his airship toward the camp, just outside of Loganville. But he did not land until after dark, when, making out the spot by means of the electric lights, which were set aglow automatically at dark, he descended.

"We won't try anything to-night," said Mr. Whitford. "I doubt if the smugglers will themselves, after their experience last night. I'll get into town, see some of my men, and come out here to-morrow night again."

Tom and Ned spent the following day in going carefully over the Falcon, making some slight repairs. The great searchlight was cleaned and adjusted, and then, as dusk came on once more Tom remarked:

"Well, we're ready for 'em any time Mr. Whitford is."

Hardly had he spoken than the tramp of horses' feet was heard coming along the bridle path through the woods, and a voice was heard to exclaim:

"There, now, I understand it perfectly! You don't need to say another word. I know it may be against the regulations, but I can fix that. I'm the busiest man in the world, but I just had to come up here and see Tom Swift. It's costing me a thousand dollars, but the money is well spent. Now don't interrupt me! I know what you're going to say! That you haven't time to bother with moving pictures. But you have! I must have some moving pictures of your chase after the smugglers. Now, don't speak to me, I know all about it. You can't tell me anything. I'll talk to Tom. Are we most there?"

"Yes, we're here," answered Mr. Whitford's voice, and Tom fancied the government agent was a bit puzzled by his strange companion.

"Bless my shoe string!" gasped Mr. Damon.

"Him picture man!" cried Koku.

"Mr. Period!" exclaimed Tom. "I wonder what he is doing here?" and the next moment the excitable little man, for whom Tom had run so many risks getting marvelous moving pictures, with the wizard camera, entered the clearing where the airship was anchored.

Hovering O'er the Border

"Well, Tom, you see I couldn't get along without you," exclaimed Mr. Period, as he rushed forward and grasped Tom's hand, having alighted in rather an undignified manner from the horse that he had ridden. "I'm after you again."

"So I see." remarked our hero. "But I'm afraid I can't—"

"Tut! Tut! Don't say that," interrupted the moving picture man. "I know what you're going to say. Don't do it! Don't go back on me, Tom! Have you the wonderful moving picture camera with you."

"I have, Mr. Period, but—"

"Now! Now! That'll do," broke in the excitable little man. "If you have it, that's enough. I want you to get me some films, showing you in chase of the smugglers. They'll be great to exhibit in our chain of theatres."

"How did you know I was here?" asked Tom. "Easily enough. I called at your house. Your father told me where you were. I came on. It cost me a thousand dollars—maybe more. I don't care! I've got to have those films! You'll get them for me; won't you?"

"Well, I—"

"That's enough! I know what you're going to say. Of course you will! Now how soon may I expect them. They ought to make a good run. Say in a week?"

"It all depends on the smugglers," said Mr. Whitford.

"Yes, yes! I understand, of course. I know! This friend of yours has been very kind to me, Tom. I looked him up as soon as I got to Logansville, and told him what I wanted. He offered to show me the way out here, and here I am. Let's have a look at the camera, to see if it's in good shape. Are you going to have a try for the smugglers to-night?"

"I think so," answered Tom. "As for the camera, really I've been so busy I haven't had time to look at it since we started. I guess it's all right. I don't know what made me bring it along, as I didn't expect to use it."

"But with your great searchlight it will be just the thing," suggested Ned.

"Yes, I think so," added Mr. Whitford, who had been told about the wizard instrument.

"Bless my detective badge!" cried Mr. Damon. "It may be just the thing, Tom. You can offer moving pictures of the smugglers in court, for evidence."

"Of course!" added Mr. Period. "Now, Tom, don't disappoint me."

"Well, I suppose I'll have to get the camera out, and set it up," conceded Tom with a laugh. "As you say, Mr. Damon, the pictures MAY come in valuable. Come, Ned, you get out the camera, and set it up, while Koku and I see to getting the ship in shape for a flight. You'll come along, Mr. Period?"

"I don't know. I was thinking of going back. I'm losing about a hundred dollars a minute by being away from my business."

"You'll have to go back alone," said Mr. Whitford, "as I have to be with Tom, in case of a capture."

"Ride back alone, through these woods? Never! The smugglers might catch me, and I'm too valuable a man to go that way! I'll take a chance in the airship."

Ned busied himself over the wizard camera, which had been stored away, and Mr. Period went with the young bank clerk to look after the apparatus. Meanwhile Tom and Koku saw to it that the Falcon was ready for a quick flight, Mr. Damon and Mr. Whitford lending whatever aid was necessary. The horses, which the agent and Mr. Period had ridden, were tethered in the clearing where they could get food and water.

"Did the smugglers rush anything over last night?" asked Tom.

"No, we evidently had them frightened. But I shouldn't be surprised but what they made the attempt to-night. We'll go back toward the St. Regis Indian reservation, where they were getting ready to unload that steamer, and hover around the border there. Something is sure to happen, sooner or later."

"I guess that's as good a plan as any," agreed Tom, and in a little while they started.

All that night they hovered over the border, sailing back and forth, flashing the great light at intervals to pick up the white wings of a smuggling airship. But they saw nothing.

Mr. Period was in despair, as he fully counted on a capture being made while he was present, so that he might see the moving pictures made. But it was not to be.

The wizard camera was all in readiness, but there was no need to start the automatic machinery. For, search as Tom and his friends did for a trace of the smugglers, they could see nothing. They put on full speed, and even went as far as the limits of the Indian reservation, but to no purpose. They heard no throbbing motor, no whizz of great propellers, and saw no white, canvas wings against the dark background of the sky, as Tom's craft made her way noiselessly along.

"I guess we've frightened them away," said Mr. Whitford dubiously, as it came near morning, and nothing suspicious had been seen or heard. "They're holding back their goods, Tom until they think they can take us unawares. Then they'll rush a big shipment over."

"Then's the time we must catch them," declared the young inventor. "We may as well go back now."

"And not a picture!" exclaimed Mr. Period tragically. "Well, be sure to get good ones when you do make a capture, Tom."

"I will," promised the young inventor. Then, with a last sweep along the border he turned the nose of his craft toward Logansville. He had almost reached the place, and was flying rather low over the country roads, when Ned called:

"Hark! I hear something!"

The unmistakable noise of a gasolene motor in operation could be distinguished.

"There they are!" cried Mr. Period.

"Bless my honeysuckle vine!" gasped Mr. Damon.

"The light, Ned, the light!" cried Tom.

His chum flashed the powerful beam all around the horizon, and toward the sky, but nothing was visible.

"Try down below," suggested Mr. Whitford.

Ned sent the beams earthward. And there, in the glare, they saw a youth speeding along on a motor-cycle. In an instant Tom grabbed up the binoculars and focussed them on the rider.

"It's Andy Foger!" he cried.

NED IS MISSING

There was a period of silence, following Tom's startling announcement. There were several plate glass windows in the floor of the airship, and through these they all gazed at the youth on the motor-cycle. Only Tom, however, by the aid of the glasses, was able to make out his features.

"Bless my spark plug! Andy Foger!" cried Mr. Damon. "Are you going to try to catch him?"

"Get him and break chug-chug machine!" suggested Koku.

"What do you suppose he's up to, Tom?" asked Ned.

"Andy Foger speeding along at this hour of the morning," remarked Mr. Whitford. "There must be something in the wind."

"Get a moving picture of him," urged Mr. Period. "I might be able to use that."

"I hardly think it would be worth while," decided Tom. "You see Andy hasn't done anything criminal, as far as we know. Of course I think he is capable of it, but that's a different thing. He may be out only on a pleasure jaunt, and he could stop us from showing the pictures, if we took them."

"That's so," agreed Mr. Period. "Don't run any risks of a lawsuit. It takes up too much of my time. Never mind the pictures."

"Just capture him, Tom, and see what he is doing," suggested Mr. Damon. "Bless my chewing gum! But he must be up to something."

"Well, he's aware of the fact that we're watching him, at all events!" exclaimed Mr. Whitford, for, at that moment, Andy, having seen the glare of the light, glanced up. They could see him looking at him, and, a second later, the Shopton bully steered his machine down a side road where the overhanging trees were so thick that he could not be made out, even by the powerful gleams of the great searchlight.

"He's gone!" gasped Ned.

"Afraid I guess," added Mr. Damon. "That shows he was up to something wrong. Well, what are we going to do?"

"Nothing, that I can see," spoke Mr. Whitford. "We can only go back to our camping place, and make another try. This Andy Foger may, or may not, be in with the smugglers. That's something we have yet to prove. However, we can't do anything now."

In vain did Ned try to get the bully within range of the light. They could hear the sounds of the motor cycle growing more and more faint, and then, as it was rapidly getting light, and as they did not want to be seen dropping into their camping place, they made all haste toward it, before dawn should break.

"Well, I can't spend any more time here," declared Mr. Period, when a hasty breakfast had been served.

"Will you ride back with me?" asked Mr. Whitford of the moving picture man.

"Will I? Well, I guess I will! You can't lose me! I'm not going to be captured by those smugglers. I'd be a valuable man for them to have as a hostage. They'd probably ask a million dollars ransom for me," and Mr. Period carefully straightened his brilliant red necktie.

Soon he and Mr. Whitford were riding back to town, taking a roundabout way, as the agent always did, to throw any possible spies off the track.

Everyone, even including the giant Koku was tired enough to take a sleep after dinner. It was about three o'clock when Ned awoke, and he found Tom already up, and at the wireless instrument, which was clicking and buzzing.

"Message coming?" asked the young bank clerk.

Tom nodded, and clasped the receiver over his ear. A moment later he began jotting down a message.

"Mr. Whitford says he has a tip that something is going to take place to-night," read the young inventor a few minutes later. "The smugglers have accumulated a big store of goods, and they are anxious to get them over the border. There are silks, laces, diamonds, and other things on which there is a high duty, or tax for bringing into the United States. He will be here early, and we must be ready for a start at once."

"All right. I guess we are ready now. Say, I'm going over to that little brook, and see if I can catch a few trout for supper."

"All right. Good idea. Don't be gone too long."

"I won't. Say, where is my coat, anyhow? I never can seem to keep track of that, or my cap either."

"Never mind. Wear mine, and you won't be delayed looking for them," so Ned donned Tom's garment and headpiece, and set out.

Three hours passed, and Mr. Damon prepared to get supper.

"I wonder why Ned doesn't come back with the fish?" he said. "It's time, if we're going to cook them to-night."

"That's right, he ought to be here," agreed Tom. "Koku take a walk over to the trout brook, and tell Mr. Ned to come here, whether he has any fish or not."

"Sure, me go, Mr. Tom!"

Koku was gone perhaps five minutes, and when he came back he was much excited.

"Mr. Ned he no there!" the giant cried. "But fish pole all broken, and ground all full of holes. Look like fight."

Tom started for the place where he knew Ned usually went to fish. Koku and Mr. Damon followed. On reaching it our hero saw indeed that the ground was "full of holes," as the giant described the indentations made by the heels of boots and shoes.

"There's been a fight here!" cried Tom.

"Yes, and Ned is missing," added Mr. Damon.

THE NIGHT RACE

The three looked at each other. For a moment they could not understand, and then, as they stood there, the meaning came to them.

"The smugglers!" whispered Tom.

"Of course!" agreed Mr. Damon. "And they must have taken him for you, Tom, for he had on your coat and cap. What can they have done with him?"

"Taken him away, that's evident," spoke Tom. "Let's look around, and see if we can find him."

They looked, but to no purpose. Ned had disappeared. There were the signs of a struggle, the fish rod was broken in several places, as if Ned had used it as a club, and the ground was torn up.

"Bless my tin whistle!" cried Mr. Damon. "What shall we do?"

For a moment no one knew what to say, then, as they looked at each other in silence, a voice called:

"I say! What's up? What's the matter? Where are you all? Hey, Tom Swift!"

"It's Mr. Whitford!" cried Tom. "He's just in time." Then he called in louder tones:

"Here we are! In the woods by the trout brook! Come on over! Ned is gone!"

There was a commotion in the bushes, the trampling of a horse, and a moment later the government agent had joined the others.

"What's this?" he cried. "Ned gone? What do you mean?"

"He's missing. The smugglers have him, I'm afraid," explained Tom, and then he gave the details.

"It certainly looks so," agreed Mr. Whitford. "His wearing of your coat and cap fooled them. They must have spied out this camping place, and they were in hiding. When they saw Ned coming to fish they took him for you. Having failed in their attempt to damage the airship, they decided to get her captain. Probably they thought that if they did the Falcon could not be run, and they would be safe. But they got the wrong man."

"Then we must get Ned back at once!" cried Tom. "Come on, we'll start right away! Where do you think we can nab them, Mr. Whitford?"

"Wait a minute," suggested the government agent. He seemed in deep thought, and paced up and down. It was clear that a great question was confronting him.

"Well!" exclaimed Tom impatiently, "if we're going to get Ned we must start at once."

"Perhaps it would be best not to try to rescue Ned at once," said the custom house man after a pause.

"What!" cried Tom. "Not rescue Ned, my best chum?"

"Not at once," repeated Mr. Whitford. "Look here, Tom. I know it seems a hard thing to say, but perhaps if we proceed on our original plan, to hover over the border, and get on the trail of the smugglers, chasing them to where they land the goods in the United States, it will be best."

"And not rescue Ned?"

"We can best rescue him by catching the smugglers."

"Then you think—"

"That they have him with them—on board one of their airships very likely. If we get *Them* we'll have *ned*."

"Then we'll get 'em!" cried Tom with energy. "Come on back to the Falcon. We'll get ready for a big flight!"

"Yes, I think they'll make a desperate effort to-night," went on the agent. "They have a lot of goods ready to rush over the border, and the fact that they tried to capture you, shows that they are ready to pull off a big trick. I think if we can catch them to-night, it will put an end to their operations, and, at the same time, bring Ned back to us."

"Where do you think they will start to cross the line?" asked Tom.

"Near the place where we saw the man waving the flags. I have information to the effect that they have a store of valuable goods there. They imagine that they have the master of the airship, and the owner of the great searchlight in their power, and that they can not be molested, so they will be bold."

"But they'll soon find out that Ned isn't Tom," said Mr. Damon.

"No they won't! Not if it depends on Ned!" cried Tom. "Ned is game. He'll soon get wise to the fact that they have taken him for me, and he'll carry on the deception. None of the smugglers know me intimately."

"Unless Andy Foger should be with them," suggested Mr. Damon.

"Oh, Ned can fool Andy any day. Come on, Mr. Whitford. We'll get the smugglers to-night, spoil their game, and rescue Ned. Somehow, I feel that we're going to succeed."

"Bless my tin dishpan!" cried Mr. Damon. "I hope we do."

Slowly, and with no very cheerful hearts, they filed away from the scene of Ned's capture. In spite of the fact that they did not think he would be harshly treated, they worried about him, Tom especially.

A hasty supper was eaten, and then, Tom, having seen that everything aboard the ship was in good order, sent her aloft on what he hoped would be the last chase after the smugglers. He decided to have Mr. Damon steer the craft, as this was comparatively easy, once she was started on her course, while the young inventor would manage the searchlight, and start the automatic wizard camera, in case there was anything to photograph.

Up and up went the Falcon, and soon she was making her way toward the St. Regis Indian reservation, near which it was expected the smugglers would start. Tom put out every light, as he wanted to remain in darkness, until he could see a moving glow in the sky that would tell him of a rival airship on the wing.

It did not take them long to reach the desired spot, and they hovered in the air over it, every one with tense nerves, waiting for what would happen next.

Tom did not want to show his searchlight just yet, as he feared the gleam of it might stop the operations of the smugglers. So he waited in dark-ness, approaching close to the earth in his noiseless ship several times, and endeavoring to see something through the powerful night glasses.

Suddenly, from below them, came a subdued throb and hum of a motor.

"There they are!" exclaimed Mr. Damon.

"I think so," agreed Tom. He looked below. He saw two flickering lights, rather far apart. Mr. Whitford observed them at the same moment.

"There are *two* of them!" exclaimed the agent, "*two* airships, Tom!"

"So I see. Koku, get out my electric rifle. We can't chase two, if they separate, so I may have to stop one. It's best to be prepared. I'm going to follow them in the dark, until they get over the border, and then I'll turn on the light and the camera. Then it will be a race to the finish."

The twin lights came nearer. Tom stood with his mouth to the signal tube that communicated with Mr. Damon in the pilot house. From a side window he watched the smugglers' airships. They shot upward and then came on straight ahead, to pass to one side of him. Now they were past. Tom started the wizard camera.

"Half speed ahead!" the young inventor signalled, and the Falcon shot forward. The night race was on.

THE CAPTURE—CONCLUSION

"Do you think they know we are here, Tom?" asked Mr. Whitford, as he stood at the side of the young inventor in the motor room.

"I don't believe so, as yet. They can't hear us, and, unless they have pretty powerful glasses, they can't pick us up. We can soon tell however, if they are aware that we are following them."

"Have you made any plan about capturing them?"

"No, I'm going to wait and see what turns up. I can't certainly chase two of them, if they separate, and that's why I'm going to cripple one if I have to."

"But won't that be dangerous? I don't want to see any of them killed, or even hurt, though they are smugglers."

"And I don't want to hurt them, either. If worst comes to worst I'm going to put a few holes in the wing planes of the smaller craft. That will cause her to lose headway, and she can't keep up. They'll have to volplane to earth, but, if they know anything at all about airships, they can do that easily, and not get a bit hurt. That will put them out of the race, and I can keep on after the big ship. I fancy that carries the more valuable cargo."

"I presume so. Well, don't bring the one to earth until you get over Uncle Sam's territory, and then maybe there will be a chance to capture them, and the goods too."

"I will," promised Tom. They were still over Canadian territory, but were rapidly approaching the border.

"I think I will send a wireless to my men in Logansville, to start out and try to pick up the crippled airship after you disable her," decided Mr. Whitford, and as Tom agreed that this was a good plan, the wireless was soon cracking away, the government agent being an adept in its use.

"I've told them we'd give another signal to tell them, as nearly as possible where we made them take to earth," he said to Tom, and the young inventor nodded in agreement.

"Ned in them ship?" asked Koku, as he came back from the pilot house to report that Mr. Damon was all right, and needed no help.

"Yes, I think Ned is in one of them," said Tom. "The big one most likely. Poor Ned a prisoner! Well, I'll soon have him away from them—if nothing happens," and Tom looked about the motor room, to make sure that every piece of apparatus was working perfectly.

The two airships of the smugglers were hanging close together, and it was evident that the larger one had to make her pace slow, so as not to get ahead of the small craft. Tom followed on relentlessly, not using half his speed, but creeping on silently in the darkness.

"We're over the United States now," said Mr. Whitford, after a glance earthward through the binoculars. "Let 'em get a little farther over the line before you pop 'em with your electric rifle, Tom."

Our hero nodded, and looked out of a side window to note the progress of the smugglers. For several miles the chase was thus kept up, and then, suddenly the smaller craft was seen to swerve to one side.

"They are separating!" cried Mr. Whitford, at the same time Mr. Damon called through the tube from the pilot house:

"Which one shall I follow, Tom?"

"The big one," the youth answered. "I'll take care of the other!" With a quick motion he flashed the current into the great searchlight, and, calling to Mr. Whitford to hold it so that the beams played on the small aeroplane, Tom leveled his wonderful electric rifle at the big stretch of canvas. He pressed the lever, a streak of blue flame shot out through an opened port, and, an instant later, the small craft of the smugglers was seen to stagger about, dipping to one side.

"There they come!" cried Mr. Whitford. "They're done for!"

"One shot more," said Tom grimly. "It won't hurt 'em!"

Again the deadly electric rifle sent out its wireless charge, and the airship slowly fluttered toward the earth.

"They're volplaning down!" cried Tom. "That's the end of them. Now to catch the other!"

"Take the lantern!" cried Mr. Whitford. "I'm going to send a wireless to my men to get after this disabled craft."

Tom swung the beam of the searchlight forward and a moment later had picked up the big aeroplane. It was some distance in advance, and going like the wind. He heard the automatic camera clicking away.

"They speeded her up as soon as they saw what was on!" cried Tom. "But we haven't begun to go yet!"

He signalled to Mr. Damon, who pulled over the accelerating lever and instantly the Falcon responded. Now indeed the race was on in earnest. The smugglers must have understood this, for they tried all their tactics to throw the pursuing airship off the track. They dodged and twisted, now going up, and now going down, and even trying to turn back, but Tom headed them off. Ever the great beam of light shone relentlessly on them, like some avenging eye. They could not escape.

"Are we gaining?" cried Mr. Whitford.

"A little, and slowly," answered Tom. "They have a bigger load on than when we chased them before, but still they have a speed almost equal to ours. They must have a magnificent motor."

Faster and faster sped on the Falcon. The other craft kept ahead of her, however, though Tom could see that, inch by inch, he was overhauling her.

"Where do they seem to be heading for?" asked the government agent.

"Shopton, as near as I can make out," replied the youth. "They probably want to get there ahead of us, and hide the goods. I must prevent that. Mr. Damon is steering better than he ever did before."

Tom shifted the light to keep track of the smugglers, who had dipped downward on a steep slant. Then they shot upward, but the Falcon was after them.

The hours of the night passed. The chase was kept up. Try as the smugglers did, they could not shake Tom off. Nearer and nearer he crept. There was the gray dawn of morning in the sky, and Tom knew, from the great speed they had traveled that they must be near Shopton.

"They're slowing up, Tom!" suddenly cried Mr. Whitford who was watching them through an open port.

"Yes, I guess they must have heated some of their bearings. Well, here's where I capture them, if it's ever to be. Koku, let down the grappling anchor."

"Are you really going to capture them, Tom?" asked the custom officer.

"I'm going to try," was the answer, as Koku came back to say that the anchor was dragging over the stern by a long rope.

"You work the light, Mr. Whitford," cried Tom. "I'm going to relieve Mr. Damon in the pilot house. He can help you here. It will be all over in another minute."

In the pilot house Tom grasped the steering levers. Then in a final burst of speed he sent his craft above, and past that of the smugglers.

Suddenly he felt a shock. It was the grappling anchor catching in the rail of the other air craft. A shout of dismay arose from the smugglers.

"You've got 'em! You've got 'em, Tom!" yelled Mr. Whitford.

"Bless my hasty pudding! So he has!" gasped Mr. Damon.

Changing the course of his craft Tom sent the Falcon toward the earth, pulling the other aeroplane with him. Down and down he went, and the frantic efforts of the smugglers to release themselves were useless. They were pulled along by the powerful airship of our hero.

A few minutes later Tom picked out a good landing place in the dim light of the breaking dawn, and went to earth. Jamming on the brakes he leaped from the pilot house to the stern of his own craft, catching up his electric rifle. The other airship, caught by the grappling anchor at the end of a long rope, was just settling down, those in her having the good sense to shut off their power, and volplane when they found that they could not escape.

As the smugglers' craft touched the earth, several figures leaped from her, and started to run away.

"Hold on!" cried Tom. "I've got you all covered with the electric rifle! Don't move! Koku, you, and Mr. Whitford and Mr. Damon take care of them. Tie 'em up."

"Bless my hat band!" cried the eccentric man. "What a great capture! Where are we?"

"Not far from Shopton," answered Tom. "But look after the prisoners."

There was a cry of astonishment from Mr. Whitford as he reached the sullen occupants of the smugglers' craft.

"Here are the Fogers—father and son!" the agent called to Tom. "They were in it after all. Great Scott! What a surprise. And here are a lot of men whom I've been after for some time! Oh, Tom Swift, this IS a capture."

"What right have you to use these high-handed methods on us?" demanded Mr. Foger pompously.

"Yes, dad make 'em let us go; we haven't done anything!" snarled Andy.

"I guess you won't go yet a while," said the agent. "I'll have a look inside this craft. Keep 'em covered, Tom."

"I will. I guess Andy knows what this rifle can do. See if Ned is a prisoner."

There was a few moments of waiting during which Koku and Mr. Damon securely bound the prisoners. Then Mr. Whitford reappeared. He was accompanied by some one.

"Hello, Tom!" called the latter. "I'm all right. Much obliged for the rescue."

"Are you all right, Ned?" asked Tom, of his chum.

"Yes, except that they kept me gagged. The men who captured me took me for you, and, after the Fogers found out the mistake, they decided to keep me anyhow. Say, you've made a great haul."

And so it proved, for in the airship was a quantity of valuable silks and laces, while on the persons of the smugglers, including Mr. Foger, were several packets of diamonds. These were taken possession of by Mr. Whitford, who also confiscated the bales and packages.

Ned was soon aboard the Falcon, while the prisoners, securely tied were laid in the cabin of their own craft with Koku to stand guard over them. Mr. Damon went to Shopton, which was the nearest town, for police aid, and soon the smugglers were safe in jail, though Mr. Foger protested vigorously against going.

Ned explained how he had been pounced upon by two men when he was fishing, and told how without a chance to warn his friends, he had been gagged and bound and taken to the headquarters of the smugglers in Canada, just over the border. They went by carriages. Then the Fogers, who, it seemed, were hand in glove with the law violators, saw him, and identified him. The smugglers had thought they were capturing Tom.

"It was your coat and hat that did it, Tom," explained Ned. "I fought against being taken away, but when I happened to think if they took me for you it might be a trick against them. And it was. The Fogers didn't discover the mistake until just before we started."

"They planned for a big shipment of goods last night and used two airships. I don't know what became of the other."

"We've got her, and the men, too," interposed Mr. Whitford, as this conversation was taking place several hours later in the Swift home. "I just had a wire from my deputy. They got right after the damaged airship, and reached her just as the men were hiding the goods, and preparing to dismantle the craft. We have them all, thanks to you, Tom!"

"And to think that the Fogers were in it all the while!" remarked Tom. "They certainly fooled us."

"I'm not done with them yet," said Mr. Whitford. "I'm going to have another look at their house, and the gardener's home."

"The Fogers were in dire straits, that's why they went in with the smugglers," explained Ned. "Though they gagged me, they didn't stop up my ears, and when they hid me in a little room on the airship, I could hear them talking together. It seems that the smugglers put up the money to buy the airships, and just happened to stumble on Andy to run the machinery for them. His father helped, too. They shared in the proceeds, and they must have made considerable, for the smuggling has been going on for some time."

"Well, they'll lose all they made," declared the agent. Later he, Tom and Ned made another inspection of the Foger premises. Down in the cellar of the gardener's house they found, behind a cunningly concealed door, a tunnel leading into the old mansion. Later it was learned that the smugglers had been in the habit of bringing goods across the border in airships, landing them in a lonely stretch of woods outside of Shopton, and later bringing them by wagon to the mansion.

Inside there, in some secret rooms that had been constructed off of the main apartments, the goods would be unpacked, put in different boxes, carried through the tunnel to the gardener's house, and thence shipped as "old furniture" to various unscrupulous agents who disposed of them.

The hiring of Mr. Dillon had been only a blind. Later the smugglers, in the guise of carpenters, made the desired changes. So cunningly had the opening of the tunnel in the cellar of the gardener's house been concealed, that it was only discovered after a most careful search.

There is little more to tell. With the capture of the two airships, an end was put to the smuggling operations, especially since nearly all the gang was captured. A few, those who brought the goods up the St. Lawrence, from the ocean steamers, managed to escape, but they had to go into hiding.

The goods captured proved very valuable, and partly made up to Uncle Sam's treasury the losses sustained. Tom was offered a big reward, but would not take it, accepting only money for his expenses, and requesting that the reward be divided among the agents of Mr. Whitford's staff, who needed it more than Tom did.

There was no difficulty about convicting the prisoners, including the Fogers, for Tom's wizard camera had taken pictures of the chase and capture, and the men were easily identified. Mr. Period was quite delighted with the roll of films that Tom gave him. Some of the smugglers were sent to prison for long terms, and others, including Andy and his father, had to pay heavy fines.

"Well, Tom Swift, I can't thank you enough," said Mr. Whitford, one day as he called to pay the young inventor a visit. "I'm ordered to the Pacific coast and I may have to send for you with your airship, and great searchlight."

"I don't believe I'll come," laughed the lad. "I'm going to take a long rest and settle down."

"He's going to get married!" exclaimed Ned, taking care to get behind a chair.

"If Mr. Tom marry, he keep Koku for servant?" asked the giant anxiously.

"Oh, I'm not going to get married, just yet, Koku!" exclaimed Tom, who was blushing furiously. "I'm going to invent something new."

"Bless my fountain pen!" cried Mr. Damon.

"Oh, Tom, it seems good to have you home again," said aged Mr. Swift softly.

"Dat's what it do!" added Eradicate. "Boomerang hab been monstrous lonely sence yo'-all been gone, Massa Tom."

"Well, I'm going to stay home—for a while," said Tom. And thus, surrounded as he is by his friends and relatives, we will take leave of Tom Swift.

Printed in Great Britain
by Amazon